Nightfall

A Novel

Andrew Wolter

Copyright © 2008 by Andrew Wolter

All rights reserved. No part of this publication may be reproduced, transmitted in any form or by any means, electronic or mechanical, including photocopy, recording, or any information storage and retrieval system, without permission in writing from the publisher. This is a work of fiction. Names, characters, places, and incidents are products of the author's imagination or are used ficticiously.

ISBN-13 : 978-0-6152-4369-6

Limited Hardcover Edition August 2008

Cover Art Desgin by Suzanne Ziemer © 2007

Published by:

Shadow City Press
16211 N. Scottsdale Road
Scottsdale, AZ 85254

Manufactured in the United States of America

Acknowledgements

My sincerest appreciation goes out to the many loved ones (both close and afar) who have helped shape me, along with this novel, as they patiently waited for these chaotic thoughts to make it to print. This has truly been a long and amazing journey!

To Mom, we have seen many dark times and we always triumph to enjoy the happiness that anxiously awaits us.

Gregory, you were there, through thick and thin, to guide and inspire me during the first drafts of Nightfall. I truly miss you!

Melissa and Sabrina, you are muses all your own; you are my mythical Sirens who make it all worth it!

My family—Dawn, Dacota, Niki, Chuy, Chad, Darrell, Olga, Rudy (RuRu), Deandra, Nicole, Joseph, and Alex—I love you all. Especially to my godson, Anthony Michael Joaquin, I'm sure you will enjoy this when you're older.

Stacy, I'm certain you recall the "old times." Thank you for never giving up on me.

A special thanks to Suzanne Ziemer, whose friendship and stimulating artwork has allowed the limited edition version of this novel to reach the masses.

To Steven, I extend the love in my heart and deepest admiration for being patient with me through the final production of this. Because of you, I am complete.

Also by Andrew Wolter

The Rules of Temptation

For Jessica, Mark, and Scott

I'll always remember the Goblin Dance

Nightfall

PROLOGUE

-1-

The young man shivered as a gust of air entered the mausoleum. Though he huddled in the corner of the stone crypt, arms hugged around legs that he kept pulled to his chest, he could not escape the icy draft of the wind. The cement emanated a cold sensation that seeped through his jeans and numbed his buttocks. The slab of stone that constructed the wall he sat against chilled his back through the thin flannel shirt he wore. The tomb echoed the sounds of his chattering teeth and the clanking of the wrought iron gate at the mausoleum's entrance.

The realization hit him that, perhaps, he'd made a mistake. He had not anticipated running out of money so quickly. After all, he had only spent a week at the motel. Being young, he hadn't a concept of finances. He hadn't a clue that the money he'd taken provided him with nothing more than a week's worth of housing and food. The original plan was to find a job as soon as he got to the city. The young man didn't think it would be that difficult, but he had been proven wrong. Another thing he had taken for granted was the gelid weather of a northern winter. Nonetheless, his innocent ignorance left him homeless, without money or food for the past three days, and residing in a cemetery tomb.

He hesitantly moved his hand down to the mausoleum floor, where he felt for the furry lump that had been the center of his contemplation for the last hour. The rat had scared the hell out of him when it had moved across his legs a short time ago. He had practically jumped out of his skin and hit the back of his head upon the stone wall. Both frightened and frustrated, the adolescent grabbed for the rodent with a fierce grip. The rat squirmed within his clasp and began squealing when the young man tightened his clutch. He could feel the small bones easily crush in his grip. The crackling sound of the rat's skeleton reminded him of the Rice Krispies he once ate when he use to live with his family.

The young man's stomach churned. The dead rodent was still warm. What would it taste like? *No*, he told himself. He couldn't do that! The thought of the wiry hair of the rat in his mouth made it less appetizing. Then again, he reflected, he could pull the hairy exterior off the flesh as he chewed it. It would be no different than pulling off the skin of fried chicken, which he disliked.

With that thought rationalizing the situation, he put the corpse of the rat to his lips. The hair was smooth. *I can do this*, he encouraged himself. He tilted his head to the side, mouth wide open, like the way he ate jumbo hot dogs back home. He was awfully hungry.

-2-

Through unorthodox sight, they watched him. Like a band of gypsies with crystalline vision, the adolescent gave prudence to their arrival. Their eyes feasted upon him with the same inhuman hunger he had developed for the rat. Yet, as much as they desired the teenager, they were ruled by a cosmic commandment preventing them from going to him.

He must come to them.

They had no doubt that he would.

-3-

When the young man first dug his teeth into the belly of the rat, he almost gagged. It took him three times, along with the constant rumbling of his stomach, before he was finally able to rip a chunk from the rodent. The warmth of blood spit at his cheek and visceral juices exploded in his mouth as he forced himself to chew on the tender meat. With inexperienced uncertainty, the teen used his teeth to divide the skin from the flesh and used his thumb and index finger to pull the hairy exterior from his mouth.

His taste buds were accosted by the salty taste of the rodent's bodily juices. Although the flesh itself was rather bland, the meat was warm and temporarily halted the shivering of his body. He repeatedly chewed on the soft tissue of his first bite until it was nothing but ground meat. When he was about to swallow, he had half the mind to spit the rat meat out. However, he willed himself to gather the courage that, ultimately, would alleviate his fear. Once the mangled meat of the rat traveled down his gullet and into his stomach, his appetite kicked into gear.

He took a second bite, and a third. He began chewing the meat less and swallowing larger pieces. He had instantly developed a precise routine for separating the skin from the flesh of the rat with his fingers and teeth. Occasionally, the prick of a soft bone against his inside cheek would create an obstacle. Yet, he quickly learned to casually extract the bone from his mouth as if it a tendril found while eating a turkey leg.

A subtle glow upon the cement floor of the mausoleum diverted the young man's attention from his prey. Instinctively, he threw the rat to the other side of the crypt and wiped the dripping juices from the soft hairs upon his chin with the sleeve of his flannel.

He hadn't realized how much energy he had gained from eating the rat, until he noticed the vigor he had to stand to his feet and investigate the mysterious glow. The faint color of orange, or maybe red, was cast upon the gray flooring. Surely, he thought to himself, it must be coming from outside. He cautiously crept toward the wrought iron gate of the mausoleum and peered into the darkness.

A fierce wind chilled his face as he winced across a sea of tombstones to discover the source of the mysterious glowing. Less than a hundred yards away, the youth spotted a black imprint stamped against the deep purple night. It was difficult to recognize, and his mind was too frazzled to understand it. It appeared as a flat piece of black air somehow misplaced in the atmosphere. It was bordered by edges that emitted a red-tinted blaze, like an angry fire.

Fire, he thought. *Warmth.* With that, he unhinged the gate to the mausoleum and pushed it outward. The screaming creak of the gate had him observant of his immediate surroundings. The paranoia of being caught by the police made his heart race. He was sure his parents had filed a runaway report on him. He'd be damned if he went back to their house and had to follow their stringent rules.

The gelid mouth of a midnight winter consumed the youth as he furthered himself from the still coldness of the mausoleum. He weaved in and out of the maze of graveyard headstones; back hunched and legs bent at the knees, as he approached the fire with the agility of a cat. The wind pushed against him several times from all directions, raising goosebumps upon his covered flesh. Surely, it would snow tonight. The chilled atmosphere only gave the adolescent more motivation to reach the warmth of the fire.

Midway through his stride toward the fire, the he came to a halt. Amidst the low howling of the wind, he thought he heard whispering. But it wasn't the type of murmur like that of a single person; the resonance upon the chilly wind announced multiple whispers, both low and high-pitched. The lower undertones were altogether muffled and hoarse, nevertheless scary. Then came a sound like paper being crumpled or torn in two. He sought out the darkness in all directions around him, acting the prey to an unknown animal lurking in the surrounding night. He clutched at his chest as he felt it tighten. His heart began to race and his stomach felt as if it were being tickled from the inside out. As his heartbeat quickened, his mind sped through the limitless possibilities of what the sound could be. A wolf? *No, couldn't be*, he told himself, wolves howl and he hardly found the city to be the setting for such an animal. Yes, perhaps a wild animal of some sort. *But animals don't whisper*, he quickly deduced. The tearing sound, he brought to mind, ignited images of his mouth tearing into the rat. Suddenly, the youth was awestruck in childhood terror.

He recalled a documentary he had once seen, perhaps five years ago when he was twelve. The program depicted the myths of monsters—from ghosts to vampires to…ghouls. Yes, he remembered, the segment about ghouls scared him the most. He recollected the prickling sensations of fear that had enveloped his body on many nights as he lay in bed. Sometimes, he imaged the hand of the horrid creature creeping up to grab him from under his bed. Or, worse yet, the shadowy image of the gangly monster as it emerged from his closet door. In the youth's fragile mind, he would envision the ghastly being slowly moving towards him, with hands that freakishly hung below its knees and sported rigid claws for nails.

To alleviate this nightmare becoming, he would always remind himself that, just as portrayed in the documentary, ghouls did not lurk in closets or beneath beds. No, instead they haunted cemeteries, hiding in the shadows of tombstones and feasting on the newly buried bodies of the dead.

The murmurs, along with the wind, hushed. The young man could hear his strongly beating heart in his ears. *What if it was true? What if ghouls did exist?* And, here he was, in the middle of their hunting grounds, late in the nighttime midst of the witching hour. His imagination began to get the best of him. *Ghouls! Oh god, they're going to eat me!* With that hindering thought keeping him stock still, he turned his attention back to the would-be fire and made a mad dash.

The young man refused to look behind as he raced through the necropolis. Though he felt something was chasing him, he rejected the idea of turning around and facing it. To either side of him, his peripheral vision gave way to a fast blur; he maintained his visual target of the radiance he was eagerly approaching.

Once the youth was in proximity of the glowing, it became discouragingly apparent that it wasn't a fire at all. It appeared a large, vertical rectangle of blackness against the night. Still, its borders emitted a fiery red. This piqued his attention. He had to get warm!

The young man raced to the radiance and stretched his hands toward the pulsing light.

-4-

The constant resonance of a static buzz escaped behind the young man. It was like that of a television channel gone off programming for the evening. The noise was off in a distance, perhaps in another room. *Yes*, the youngster dreamily reckoned, *Dad must have fallen asleep in front of the TV again.* He realized that he must've been in his own bedroom, between the conscious and subconscious realm of half-sleep. *In bed?*

If so, then he'd had the most vivid dream! He had runaway from home; he'd spent three nights living in a cemetery, in a crypt. It was so cold, and he ate a rat! The salty taste of the rodent's insides still annihilated the boy's taste buds. *No*, he battled with his mind; *I did run away, and I am in a cemetery.* Yet, the chilling wind no longer accosted him. Instead, he felt pleasing warmth.

With the inviting atmosphere easing his mind, the youth's eyes slowly fluttered open. What, at first, was only a blemished blur, revealed an impossible visual mystery. The young man, flabbergasted by his surroundings, hesitantly stood to his feet.

The burning orange of a whole new world had eclipsed the inky darkness of night. The young man stood, mouth agape, in awe of everything in sight. The landscape stretched out before him, a veritable orange-colored desert floor of cracked earth. In the distance, a sea of fire bubbled and swelled like an ocean of lava. Plumes of flames exhaled hither and thither from beneath the molten liquid, as if some fire-breathing creature gave off life beneath the smoldering fluid. He anxiously sought out the sky, but no matter how high he searched toward the heavens, he could only find a series of unending granite walls that peaked higher than any mountain range. The rocky mass reflected the orange glow of the fiery sea, as did the hard earth of petrified dirt. The youth could only compare his setting to that of a volcanic cavern.

Where the hell was he and, what's more, how did he get here?

The familiar guttural whispering he had heard while still in the cemetery interrupted his puzzling query. However, the raucous murmurs began to grow louder, perhaps closer. The young man stood frozen, unable to move in this unfamiliar world. From behind, the resonance of hoarse moaning became more evident.

No, he thought. *Can't turn around.*

The youth felt the heat of a fetid breath touch the nape of his neck and travel around to accost his nostrils.

Oh my god, oh my god! Don't want to see it! His posture grew stiff; his heart heavily pounded within his chest.

On either side of his shoulders, he horrifically observed two hands make their way from behind him and down to his chest. They appeared as human hands until the terrified lad noticed the monstrous, brown and tangled nails.

He trembled. It was as if the epicenter of an earthquake had emitted from his stomach, sending all of his limbs into an uncontrollable quaver.

He knew he had to turn around. But, before he could summon enough will to face the thing behind him—and, oh god, he knew what it was—the inhuman hands tightly gripped at his flesh and spun him around in a swift force.

The youth caught glimpses of what followed, as he fell to the ground, feverishly flailing his arms and legs about the hardened dirt and screaming with all his will.

A scraggly haired, almost bald subhuman was atop of him. Three more emerged from nowhere. Claws scratched deeply into his neck, legs and chest. Black eyes. Four monsters had mounted him. Four *ghouls*. His shirt had been shredded. His adolescent flesh had been torn by brown-black claws. Sunken jaws, like skeletal faces. Teeth. Jagged teeth!

He wanted to go home.

The young man's mind was launched into an ultimate frenzy of terror as he felt the multiple teeth of the creatures burrow into his stomach. The hot blood of his viscera pooled upon his chest as the gnawing pain of his flesh shot paralyzing sensations throughout his body. Soon, the life of the youth faded, as the gnashing of his flesh and slurping sounds of his fluids became a nightmarish lullaby that would put him to a sleep from which he would never naturally awaken.

He wished he could tell the rat he was sorry.

PART I

Welcoming the Night

"As nightfall does not come at once, neither does oppression. In both instances, there's a twilight where everything remains seemingly unchanged, and it is in such twilight that we must be aware of change in the air, however slight, lest we become unwitting victims of the darkness."—William O. Douglas

CHAPTER I

-1-

He often dreamed of demons these days.

Whether amidst the subconscious world of a deep, nighttime slumber or upon the inspiration of an unending daydream, the subject of demons endlessly fueled Stefan Powell's mind.

Stefan's imagination conjured demon types of both mythical and Hollywood likeness; his monsters were that of both beauty and beast. Some of Stefan's monsters donned tough, scaly exteriors and jagged, uneven teeth; while others resembled a charming, almost Victorian human facade, displaying long hair brushed against pale skin and distinguishing eyes filled with the black of night from pupil to sclera.

Stefan's mind was reluctant in discriminating against the various images of demons with which it visually summoned. After all, the demon imagery was nothing more than Stefan's own copings with life. When Stefan felt loneliness, as he sat in the confines of his apartment and wishing he had a love interest to share life with, his mind created demons of lust—creatures more human than monstrous, with smooth and flawless almond flesh, yet red eyes of determination. In times of anger, after dealing with a particularly belligerent customer at the record store, Stefan imagined demons of grotesque nature—monstrous to the extreme with craggy, maroon exteriors, tails adorned with rutted scales, teeth gnashing bloody flesh of an innocent being, and eyes dark as night.

His shameless beasts usually reflected each mood that he exhibited while careening through the optimistic existence feint by that of a dreamer. For though Stefan dreamed of demons, it was the concept of his evil conjuring that opened the door to his dream of writing poetry.

Stefan Powell had always had the gift of the written word. When he was seven-years-old, he wrote his mother a birthday poem that touched her so deeply, she had broken down into ridiculous tears. In junior high school, Stefan had written a piece for the school's annual poetry contest. The winner's poem was to be displayed in a published anthology available in all public school libraries. It came as no surprise to Stefan's mother, when her son was named the winner of the contest.

Deirdre Powell had always been willing victim to her son's poetic words—Stefan's poetry was full of fluidity, of words that magnified the heart, the soul, and all the good born of the world. On the day of her death, Deidre Powell grasped at the poem Stefan had written on that special birthday that had remained on her nightstand for so many years.

Perhaps his mother's death brought on the demons in Stefan's mind. For it would be those demons that would ultimately shift his poetry toward a darker genre of writing.

-2-

Stefan frantically played with the short, deep-brown locks of hair upon his head. He had rinsed his hair clean twice, and used forming cream, gel, and mousse to give it a wild shape. However, it came to no avail; Stefan was having a bad hair day.

"Fuck!" Stefan yelled in frustration. He was due at work in 10 minutes and it would take fifteen just to get to Laine's Music.

Normally, he wouldn't have cared how his hair looked. Stefan normally styled it simply, giving it a bit of volume with some mousse. However, working at the town's only music store, he felt obligated to present an edgy type of look to the consumers. It came with the environment.

Stefan rubbed the forming cream between his thumb and index finger, and then began to grab small locks of his hair to pull them in different directions. The overall hairstyle was to portray wispy spikes. As Stefan studied each created spike of hair in the mirror, it reminded him of the horns of some ferocious demon. Stefan scowled at the thought. Now was not the time to be inspired.

Spacing his fingers apart to form a loose comb, Stefan ran his hand from the back of his scalp, through the chocolate wisps upon his head, and pulled his bangs upward as it approached his forehead. He hadn't the time to mess with his hair any longer. Surely, this was always the beginning sign of a bad day for Stefan Powell.

Stefan grabbed his black tote bag and slung it over his shoulder as he crossed toward the exit of his apartment. "Another fucking day in Paradise," Stefan said aloud as he closed the door behind him.

-3-

Though his father had mysteriously abandoned the family when his son was nearly eight-years-old, Stefan Powell made the most of his childhood with his mother, Deirdre.

As a child, Stefan was more interested in reading than playing video games. While the handful of his friends played the latest game challenges in technological advances in front of their televisions, Stefan was reading R.L. Stine's *Fear Street* series of young adult-oriented horror books. The short novels about zombies, ghosts, and vampires fascinated Stefan. In fact, there were many nights that his mother would awaken for a glass of water and find Stefan asleep on the couch, sitting upright with a book to his side.

However, Stefan's draw toward the supernatural and uncanny wasn't limited to books. And, perhaps, one could easily assess that his passion for things that went bump in the night was the influence of his mother's own fondness of the unknown. Still, there was a communication between the two that conveyed an exciting playfulness to it all, a transference of emotion to which only a mother and son could feel and connect. It showed when a preview of the latest horror movie coming to theatres aired during a television commercial—Stefan and his mother's eyes would lock, and they automatically suggested to one another that they simply couldn't wait until the feature made its way to video. And one could easily bet on the fact that both Stefan and his mother would be at the local Hollywood Video rental store on the day the of the movie's release.

It happened often in those days—days when Deirdre worked a double shift at any number of the nursing homes in the Phoenix area and Stefan went to school and prepared dinner for the two—surely, nothing could beat their times together when they sat and watched horror movies in the living room. From movies about zombies to the B-horror movies celebrating the most recent scream queens in the horror industry—this was family time for Stefan and Deirdre Powell. Truly, nothing could stop the movies that incessantly engaged the two. A knock announcing a UPS delivery was easily ignored. The electronic chirps of a ringing telephone were altogether silenced by the screams of fictitious victims emitting from the television screen.

Oftentimes, mother and son prepared popcorn in the air popper, always making sure to add the extra butter that was quickly melting in a heated saucepan upon the stovetop. Another treat would be the plain vanilla ice cream with Smuckers caramel topping. Ah, how they cherished their desserts and horror movies! To Stefan and Deirdre, there was no better way to spend the time with each other.

During their movie time, they jumped in unison as the villain on the screen appeared from out of the shadows, they laughed at the acting skills of the amateur actresses in the low-budget productions, and they competed with one another by trying to figure out the ending of the movie midway through. Even more exciting were their late night discussions, into the wee morning hours, of the movies they had watched.

Deirdre and Stefan continued their tradition of watching scary movies for many years.

As an adolescent Stefan's edification for literature veered him from stories by young-adult horror authors and toward the literary classics. At fifteen, Stefan became acquainted with the works of Edgar Allen Poe. Poe's *The Tell-Tale Heart* was Stefan's first journey into the chilling works of classic literature. Every Monday, after school let out for the afternoon, Stefan eagerly made his way to one of the many branches of the Phoenix Public Library system to pick up another volume of Poe's homage to the written word of the dark and fantastic. Stefan would read deep into the night, refusing to fall prey to sleep until he had finished at least three tales. Stefan was all but obsessed with Poe's work—the way in which the antagonists often prevailed, the flow of the poems that played like the dreary sonata of a funeral procession and, most importantly, the voice that cast a somber and bleak tone that would haunt Stefan's mind long after the tale was over.

More frequently than not, Stefan would find himself slowly peering over his shoulder, such was the fright that Poe's works bestowed upon him. However, this confirmed to him that the author had succeeded in his task. The written word had formed pictures in Stefan's mind and those pictures presented a realistic vision that he could not doubt. Being scared authenticated the talent of the creator.

When Deirdre Powell arrived at home in the wee hours of the morning, Stefan would be just waking up and eager to discuss the latest revelations presented to him by Edgar Allen Poe. His mother would sit at the kitchen table with him, though she had worked a double on the graveyard shift, and reminisce some of the stories that Stefan had vividly explained to her. After all, she had explained to Stefan, she remembered Poe's work from the American Literature class she had taken in college.

Perhaps it was Deirdre Powell's knack for writing that her son had inherited. There was a time in which Deirdre wanted to write full time. In fact, in her college years, a number of her essays were highly acknowledged by her professors. They had pointed out Deirdre's "salable potential." Stefan was still an infant at the time, but it didn't stop Deirdre from working at a twenty-four hour, greasy spoon restaurant (mainly catering to derelicts who sat for three hours drinking coffee and leaving a measly quarter tip), maintaining her full-time college curriculum, and stay up late at night preparing query letters that would often come back "rejected" by numerous magazines. Still, Deirdre had the dream of writing for a living.

However, the dream was killed when Frank left. Deirdre often imagined her husband had left for another woman. But the fact of the matter was that Frank could not cope with Deirdre's incessantly busy lifestyle—between work, college, and writing. Not to mention, Frank often played Mr. Mom to their son as Deirdre appeared to have worked around the clock. But what Frank didn't know (in his day-to-day life of work, bills, family and, ultimately, retirement) was that, more often than not, that was the way of a dreamer. For a dreamer to have a passion to what he or she wants is one thing. On the other hand, to act out that passion, to make that goal a reality, it could easily mean working a full time job to pay the bills, maintain a social life, and make the dream a part-time job in itself. That is, if one is to expect to make something of his or her goals.

That is why Deirdre Powell never discounted Stefan when he asked her if he could be a "rhyming writer." Though Stefan meant he wanted to be a poet, Deirdre immediately knew that her son wanted to write. Yet, Deirdre was always realistic in explaining to Stefan that, although he wanted to write for a living, he should always find something else to make money with to pay the bills as he pursued his goal. Yes, Deirdre had told Stefan that through the years. From the time when he was seven, and wrote her a poem filled with imagery and love for his mother, to the time he had been published in his Junior High School's poetry anthology as a first place winner. Perhaps, Deirdre would have the opportunity to live the goal she had given up on through the success of her son. And, to that, she found no shame. After all, it was in the blood. Because of that, she could do nothing more than be proud of her son.

Through the years that followed, Stefan had shared every piece of work he had written with his mother. Stefan's infatuation for Poe had transpired into the works of H.P. Lovecraft. His poetry remained uplifting, yet a mysterious tone made its way in and out of his prose. Stefan's verses were jaded, but altogether loving (Deirdre felt this as an underlying dislike toward Stefan's father). Still, the two found no better time than discussing Stefan's latest poem as they pointed out the metaphors and similes. Deirdre couldn't have been more proud of her son and his dedication to his writing.

Ulitmately, and perhaps for the first time, Deirdre Powell found herself disappointed by Stefan after he'd graduated high school. Though his grade point average could have easily placed him in any number of highly sought after colleges, providing stellar creative writing curriculums, Stefan chose to opt for a full-time job working at a video rental store as he continued writing his poetry. What's more, Deirdre was veritably heart-broken when her son moved out of their home at the age of nineteen. Stefan decided that he needed his independence, having the need to explore the world with his poetry and sexuality. Stefan came out that he was gay a year previous, though it had no affect on Deirdre Powell. After all, she had always told him to be proud of whom he was, whatever the cost. Stefan also explained that he felt being a part of a classroom full of 150 students to one professor (and that professor's style of writing) would make him nothing save for a clone of the other students. Stefan wanted to retain his voice. It was *his* voice that would make him stand out amongst others!

Thankfully, amidst the sudden changes, that didn't stop their time together.

Stefan had his mother's work schedule down to a science. On Wednesday nights, he would visit with her and read her the new poems he had written. Deirdre observed the gleam in Stefan's sapphire eyes as he read his poems aloud and noticed the sharp angles that accentuated his high cheekbones as he told her of some of the magazines and e-zines he had submitted the poems to and from which he was eagerly awaiting a promising reply. Oh, how Deirdre remembered those days!

And she couldn't forget their scary movie nights either! Stefan came over every Saturday evening, usually with two or three horror movie rentals in hand. Just as they did when Stefan was a child, mother and son would feast on buttery popcorn and vanilla ice cream covered with Smuckers caramel topping.

One month after Stefan had turned twenty-four, his entire world had changed. Happiness led way to depression and any enlightenment (which could easily be found in a number of Stefan's poems) had been eclipsed by an overpowering darkness.

It was the middle of August, and the sun smothered Phoenix with its fiery beams. As Stefan grabbed the rented DVD's from the passenger seat of his truck, he'd noticed that the glossy exteriors of the cases were soft and hot. *The temperature easily reached 110-degrees today,* he had thought.

Stefan had waltzed up the entryway to his mother's home, opened the screen door, and gave a brisk knock at the door before opening it. He had always told her to keep her front door locked, especially living in a city the size of Phoenix. However, Stefan's mother always waved a hand at him. Secretly, Stefan knew that his mother could take care of herself had an intruder break into her home. She was rather strong like that—mentally, as well as physically. Deirdre Powell had been independent for so long, that she knew how to take care of herself.

Stefan immediately sensed that something was wrong as he entered the house. It was extremely warm inside the home, and Stefan knew that his mother wasn't a fan of the Arizona summers. In fact, one could always expect the temperature in Deirdre Powell's house to be chilly when she was home. She would always turn the dial of the thermostat to the line-marker indicating sixty-six degrees when she came home from work or a day of running errands.

"Mom?" Stefan had called out.

There was no response.

Stefan had made a second attempt. "Mother?" Stefan had always used the proper 'mother' when he was being serious. It had been a display of his sincerity and genuine concern. *Mother, I love you. Mother, I am gay.*

Stefan briskly walked toward the hall and past the living room, where the television remained silent of sound and picture. Into the hallway, he rushed. Stefan came to an abrupt halt as he reached the threshold of his mother's bedroom. The door was wide-open, but his mother had still been asleep in her pink, satin nightgown.

"Mom," he had loudly called.

And again. The second time, his voice was accentuated with a resounding timbre that echoed throughout the home.

With utter caution slowing each step, Stefan Powell advanced toward his mother's sleeping body upon her bed. He had been perplexed by her slumbering state. Her eyes had appeared half-open; her right hand had a paper clutched in it.

"Mother," Stefan had called again.

He had been directly over his mother, when he pushed at her side and had called out again. Stefan had noticed the whites of his mother's eyes—no sign of her beautiful, hazel pupils—and then a tear had escaped his own eye. Stefan had poked at her arm. There had been no response as he called for his mother again with an oncoming tremor to his voice. "Muuuuuthhhhherrrr."

Stefan had immediately grabbed the cordless phone and dialed 911.

As he had waited for the medics to arrive, Stefan grasped the paper that had been crushed in his mother's clutches. A quick glance at the page revealed the poem that Stefan had written for his mother on her birthday. At the time, he had been only seven.

The Maricopa County paramedics deemed Deirdre Powell dead on arrival. According to the coroner's autopsy, she had died of a stroke, in her sleep. There was no pain involved, as it was rather sudden.

Stefan hadn't believed a word of it. His mother had to have been conscious for a minute! At least, long enough to grab the poem he had written for her. No, there had to be something more to it, Stefan had repeatedly told himself on the days following his mother's death. His mother had always been healthy and rarely sick. It just didn't make sense!

However, there are many times in life where logic is thrown to the wayside as the unknown emerges. An afternoon drive can easily turn into a horrific collision; an innocent walk can lay way to a brutal abduction; and, yes, mothers who are seemingly healthy can die without warning. Yet, Stefan had remained in denial of his mother's death for the months that had followed.

Soon, Stefan had decided it better to leave Phoenix altogether. He had found it difficult to shake his mother's abrupt death from his thoughts. He had established it impossible to *not* spend time with her. It was then, that Stefan had begun to dream of demons. For he had known, deep within the most pure of hearts, that darkness could strike at any time.

-4-

Stefan's drive to work, from his apartment, was a short one.

He maneuvered his Nissan Pathfinder from the entrance to the Shadowood Apartments and onto Century Avenue. Century Avenue had recently been developed (along with the newly built Shadowood Apartments); therefore, it consisted of an eighth of a mile stretch that turned into Firehouse Road. Once on Firehouse Road, Stefan easily sped to sixty-five (although the speed limit posted was forty-five). Firehouse Road was absent of any visual stimuli, save for the desert. There were certainly no skyscrapers lining the road; not like in Phoenix.

Stefan blared his car stereo to the latest industrial crazed rock anthem, as he remained cognizant of any patrolling police cars idly camouflaged within the desert setting. Stefan slowed the SUV, so that he could listen to the rest of the song. After all, Laine's Music sat on the corner of Firehouse Road and Main Street. Yet, he was aware that he was probably late already.

Stefan was sure Laine, the owner of the music store, wouldn't be there today. His boss had a tendency of showing up late or not showing up at all, depending on the hour of the evening in which he lit his last joint.

In no time, Stefan was parking his vehicle a few hundred feet from the door of the building boasting his workplace. *Same ol', same ol'*, he thought before exiting the truck.

-5-

Seven months after his mother's death, Stefan had left Phoenix. Not only did the departure of his beloved mother play upon his mind like a haunting piano concerto, but also the city itself had begun to annoy him.

Stefan had become increasingly tired of the blaring horns, the incessant reports of crimes on the local news stations, and the buildings that towered all around his physical existence. It had all closed in on him, like some preying specter, and had caused him to begin experiencing the feelings of paranoia and claustrophobia. Perhaps, this was normal during the grieving process. But for Stefan Powell, it was bordering the lines of the insane, and he simply couldn't take it. Not to mention, Stefan had felt no inspiration for his poetry.

Stefan hadn't written a poem since the time of Deirdre Powell's death. There was one time, a month after her passing, Stefan had considered a funeral lament. However, it seemed too dishonest, too forced. He had known that his mother had always wished the best for him and his poetry. For these reasons, Stefan Powell quit his job at the video store, packed up his truck, and headed south for a sign.

He hadn't an idea where he was going, nor did he care. He had simply driven. For all he knew, he could've ended up in Mexico. The fact of the matter was that Stefan hadn't a care where he ended up. After all, there was nothing binding him to Phoenix any longer.

Eighty miles south of Phoenix, lay the town of Spook Valley. When Stefan had passed into the town limits and reached the town center, he had instantly felt at home. It wasn't so much as the idea of a small town setting as it was the tone that Spook Valley emitted. A shiver had crawled up Stefan's spine as he had glanced at the bronze sculpture of the town's founder, Jamison Spook. It wasn't a shiver from which one might recoil. Instead, it was the tingle upon the spine representing that this place had been right.

The town had been surrounded by desert and, as small as it may have appeared, it was up to date. After all, Spook Valley had been less than five decades old. Therefore, the buildings represented the modern architecture of glass and stucco, absent of the surrounding skyscrapers. And, still, there had been the nature of the desert outlining the entire town. It had been perfect inspiration for Stefan's writing.

The very day Stefan had arrived in Spook Valley, he secured an apartment at the Shadowood Apartment complex. The next day, Stefan had gotten a job at Laine's Music (Spook Valley's only music store). The following day, Stefan had met a practicing witch named Catrina Taylor. And a week after arriving in Spook Valley, Stefan had been inspired to start his first poetry anthology entitled *Dark Hearts*.

-6-

The jangling of brass bells announced Stefan's arrival, as he opened the door to Laine's Music.

The first thing that jumped out at Stefan was the orange and red signage along the front of the cashier counter. It read: *Hellfire's Third Album Available Tomorrow!* Stefan smirked. Why didn't Laine make the sign three weeks earlier? Stefan, along with the only other employee, Ricky, were sick of having customers ask about the new release of Hellfire's latest CD. *Well, better late than never*, Stefan thought.

Stefan passed a mid-aged woman who was heading toward the exit, then looked over to Ricky who stood behind the counter pointing down at the sign. "Like the sign says...tomorrow!" he snottily remarked to the exiting patron who, hopefully, didn't hear him. And if she did, thinking Ricky was being rude (the way Ricky was often rude to customers), where else would she take her business? Eighty miles away in Phoenix? That was one major advantage Laine Young's music store had—it was the only music store in Spook Valley. Perhaps, that key factor alone allowed the business to stay afloat, even turn a sizable profit during the holiday season.

"Now, now...be nice to the customers," Stefan voiced as he continued walking toward the employee back room.

Ricky glanced over, noticing Stefan, and announced, "You're late."

"Two minutes. As if you've never been late before," Stefan called back without pause.

"Whatever," Ricky languidly replied, as if he were already stoned.

Stefan walked into the back room, which consisted of a couple of lockers, a manual punch time clock, and a small table surrounded by folding chairs. A variety of rock posters lined the walls. They mainly consisted of local talent from Phoenix that had come to Laine's Music for autograph sessions. Some of the posters were signed, but the montage was like that of misplaced wallpaper. It reminded Stefan of the posters in a child's room which, through the years, grew tattered and were eventually replaced with more mature decoration.

Stefan grabbed his timecard and punched in. After throwing his backpack into one of the empty lockers, he made his way back to the front counter where Ricky remained daydreaming.

"How are sales today?" Stefan queried.

"Are you kidding me? What sales? These last two hours, I've had nothing but people asking about the new Hellfire CD! You'd think that Laine would place that sign in a more strategic place."

Stefan chuckled. "Nice use of the 50-cent words this morning."

"What?"

"'Strategic.' I've never heard you use such vocabulary, Ricky."

"Fuck you," Ricky joked. "We all can't be writers like you."

"Yeah, well." Stefan's mind wandered toward the north shelving with CD's sloppily strewn as if they'd been thrown onto the shelves. "I guess I'll straighten those shelves," Stefan told Ricky, hoping he'd get a hint and help.

"Cool," his co-worker replied.

Stefan mentally scolded Ricky for his laziness, as he walked toward the north shelving units of the store and began straightening CDs. So many of the CDs were out of alphabetical order that Stefan wondered if Ricky had even bothered to organize the shelves during closing shift the previous night.

The north shelves of Laine's Music cased all the new releases. With the release of the latest Hellfire CD hitting the store tomorrow, Stefan began making a large gap in a couple of the shelves as to create room for the many copies that would be arriving later in the day.

Stefan gazed back at the front counter, where Ricky simply leaned forward, dumbly studying Stefan. It was as if Ricky had never seen a person clean or organize. Then again, Ricky was only nineteen, and a high-school dropout. Ricky's idea of organization was limited to making sure roaches from his joints weren't mixed into the same overfilled ashtrays as his cigarette butts. Stefan had always wondered how Ricky got a job at Laine's Music. Then, after a few weeks of working the job with his fellow employee, and the many occasions when Ricky' eyes were obviously bloodshot, Stefan derived a conclusion. Ricky shared the same fervor for marijuana that Laine, the store's owner, had. Stefan often wondered if Laine and Ricky had ever gotten together, outside of work, to get high. Such thoughts had prompted other curiosities within Stefan's mind. Had Laine ever seduced Ricky into sexual acts while getting stoned together?

Stefan was sure Ricky was straight. It showed in his stoner image—the long, dirty blonde hair, concert t-shirts and torn jeans, and the lanky body of a junkie who saluted the rock star life. Ricky would often mention the groupies he would have if he were ever to become a superstar. He'd say that he would be on a tour bus, heading toward the next city, with two women on either side of him and one below. The two would be lapping at his chest and lips with their anxious tongues, while the one on her knees would be sucking his "rock cock." To such imagery, Stefan would always inform Ricky that he had given him too much information. "That's right," Ricky would nonchalantly announce, "you're into guys."

Laine Young, on the other hand, liked women. Though he harbored an affinity toward guys as well. In fact, he adored younger men Ricky's age. And, although Laine was a passive, laid-back type of guy who was nothing more than a hippie looking to make a living off his passion for music, Stefan found him to be very persuasive with the younger guys. It was in Laine's casual demeanor and the way with which he soothed those with his soft voice. It was almost charming, had Laine not been in his forties.

And, although Stefan had frequently observed Laine's attempt to win over the rocker girls by having them come over and get high with him, Laine's bisexuality emerged when such vixens donned in leather clothing were nonexistent.

Stefan had witnessed Laine checking out Ricky on at least a dozen occasions—always eyeing the kid's ass as he bent over or walked away from Laine. And Stefan couldn't help but wonder if he had ever put the moves on Ricky. Or, perhaps, Laine had lured the young man home with him to smoke some weed. From there, who knew where the night would lead? There was always a type of tension between Ricky and Laine, as they worked together. Stefan couldn't pinpoint it. Yet, he couldn't help but think that he was reading too much into it. Once again, the writer in him reared its ugly head.

"Having fun," Ricky called across the store.

"Yeah right," Stefan replied. "I'm making room for the new Hellfire CD."

Ricky remarked with sarcasm. "Joy. I can't wait."

Stefan chuckled.

"Oh, by the way, Catrina called earlier."

I wonder why she didn't call me at home, Stefan thought. "What did she say?"

"Nothing. I told her you weren't in yet, and she said she'd get back at you later."

Stefan hadn't spoken to Catrina in a couple of days. It was so unlike him. Usually, they found themselves calling one another on a daily basis, simply touching base and seeing how each other's day had gone. He had been so busy putting the final changes on his poetry anthology, *Dark Hearts*, that it was usually too late in the evening by the time he was finished. Not to mention, more often than not, Stefan would be mentally exhausted from the creative process. Still, Catrina being his best friend, he made it a note to call her later that evening. *I hope she doesn't cast a hate spell on me.* Stefan laughed on the inside.

*****

From the Journal of Stefan Powell

On lunch break.

I'm so sick of this place! There has to be something more!!! I mean, every day it's the same old fuckin' routine. It has to change some time, doesn't it? I mean, I certainly don't see myself, decades down the road, still residing in Spook Valley and working for Laine. And, if I still am (God help me), I hope that all the members of Hellfire have died off from drug overdoses! If I get one more customer asking about their new CD, I think I'm going to burn down the fuckin' display! Besides, didn't hair bands disappear in the early nineties?

Ricky doesn't seem to mind. Not that he likes the band. He simply doesn't give a shit. He has a way of smiling like a madman every time we get a customer that asks about the band's new CD.

Laine hasn't been around today. He's probably still getting over last night's pot-hangover. What a hippie! But, hey, he has this store and he has two great guys running it. He's the boss. I suppose he can do whatever the hell he wants. At least he is free from the rat race of Life.

I haven't spoken to Catrina in a couple of days. I've been working so hard on getting my random thoughts together for "Dark Hearts." Once this book of poetry is finished, I hope I can find a publisher for it! I desperately need this. This is my calling—Stefan Powell, Poet!

I'm going to call Catrina this evening and see what she's up to.

I think I'll hit the outskirts of town after work. To the desert for more peace and inspiration. My best writing happens in the desert. Not sure why. At least Spook Valley offers something to me.

Gotta go! Ricky says I have a call from Catrina. Speak of the devil...errr....witch!

******

Stefan placed his journal back into his locker and raced out of the employee break room to the front counter of Laine's Music. He picked up the phone receiver to greet his best friend. "Hey there."

"Hey stranger." Catrina's voice was gentle and melodic, like a harp being strummed.

Stefan immediately felt guilty for not calling her in the past two days. Suddenly, he wondered if something was wrong with his friend. After all, she had been persistent in getting a hold of him today. Prompted by that thought, Stefan asked, "Is everything all right?"

"Everything is fine," Catrina reassured. "I missed hearing your voice."

"I know. I've felt so pressured to get *Dark Hearts* done—"

"How's it coming along?"

"Slowly. I was thinking about getting some final inspiration for the book this evening."

"Another date with the desert?"

"You got it." Stefan laughed.

"I thought you'd found some hot guy and took off on a beeline to Vermont."

"I wish," he sighed.

"What's wrong?"

"Oh, nothing. Just the rat race blues again. I'm so sick of the same routine of working and getting nothing accomplished. I mean, this morning when I came to work, I was somewhat excited about this stupid Hellfire CD. It's bringing in a lot of people, and you know how slow this place can get without some major promotion. Now, I'm so disgusted every time somebody asks about the damn thing."

"Don't stress yourself out."

That was all Stefan needed. Catrina's voice solacing him. Perhaps that was what he had been missing the past couple of days. "I know. It will get better."

"There you go," Catrina confirmed.

"You know, part of being my best friend is having to deal with this slump I get in from time to time."

Catrina hysterically laughed. "Time to time? All the time, sweetie. That's all right, I still love you."

"Love you too. How's life on your end?"

"Oh, let's see...I did a reading for myself last night. The cards indicated that I had a major life change coming."

"Oh shit! Don't tell me you're going to become a fucking lesbian." Stefan couldn't contain himself.

Catrina all but choked as she burst into hilarity. "No, hopefully not *that* life-changing. Anyway, we should get together soon. Maybe dinner at your place."

"You got it, girl."

"I have to get ready for my shift at the Tavern."

"Ugh. You're pulling a late-nighter?"

"It pays the bills," Catrina said, matter of factly.

"All right, then. I'll catch up with you tomorrow."

"Sounds good. Take care, sweetie. Love you."

"Love you too. Talk to you tomorrow." With that, Stefan hung up the phone receiver.

Stefan glanced at the clock and hoped the rest of the day would go by fast. He simply couldn't wait to leave today. He was itching to reach the stimulating sanctuary of the desert on the outskirts of Spook Valley. The deserts called to him the way they never had before. In that calling, Stefan sensed something fantastic would occur. It tickled his stomach, just thinking about the idea. In his sudden anticipation, Stefan felt the oncoming of completion.

CHAPTER II

-1-

Catrina Taylor hesitantly walked into the Violin Street Tavern. She wasn't ready for another night of drunken men grabbing her ass or commenting on her tits as she served drinks to the local ruffians of Spook Valley. The latter was one of the reasons she was wearing a larger shirt branding the bar's name. She had grabbed it from Valerie before leaving her shift the night previous.

The Violin Street Tavern was nothing more than a neighborhood dive bar. The pub housed two pool tables (in dire need of being fixed) and a dozen round tables that barely accommodated four barstools each. Oftentimes, the men who congregated at the Tavern would pull three or four tables together to form one large cheering section for the football game that would be playing on the television above the bar. Catrina hated Monday Night Football! What's more, she despised how the middle-aged men (with wives anxiously waiting for them at home) yelled catcalls at her and made obscene advances toward her.

Catrina made her way behind the bar. "How's it going?" she sighed to Valerie.

Her co-worker, Valerie Saunders, was counting her tips and didn't bother looking up. "Lively crowd tonight. I'm glad you're closing."

"Lovely," Catrina commented.

"That's alright. I have to close on Wednesday. I can hardly wait." Valerie's voice was etched with sarcasm. She pushed the multiple dollar bills deep into the front pocket of her jeans.

"Andy around?" Catrina hoped the owner of the Violin Street Tavern wasn't still lurking in the shadows of the establishment's dingy corners.

"He's in the backroom," Valerie muttered.

"No. Actually, I'm right behind you stupid bitches," a throaty voice announced from behind.

Andy Sullivan was the owner of the Violin Street Tavern, and had been since the early eighties. He had gained the respect of the patrons who revisited with his sincere love of sports and his reputation for screwing his all-female staff. Not to mention, he offered half-price drinks during the sports playoff seasons. To the customers of the Violin Street Tavern, Andy Sullivan was well regarded—he had the cutest, young girls in Spook Valley, and he had a business that catered to the typical redneck.

Valerie stood silent, almost afraid as if she a crooked employee with her hand in the cash register till.

"Excuse me," Catrina voiced as she turned around.

"Don't try to get snide with me missy," Andy warned. "I do believe you need a job."

"I'm out of here," Valerie pronounced as she made her way around the bar.

"Bye, Val." Catrina called.

Valerie Saunders didn't reply.

Catrina stood, staring deep into the eyes of her employer. "The only reason you don't fire me is because you know, as well as I do, that no local girl is going to give this place the time of day."

"You're skating on thin ice, Catrina."

Catrina could hear the tremble in Andy's voice and observed the twitch of Andy's forehead. Both of which were telltale signs of his nervousness. She had never known Andy Sullivan to exhibit such signs of anxiety with any other bartender. The reason being that none of the other girls ever stood up to him.

"Are you finished?" Catrina asked, an ear-to-ear smile permeating her porcelain face.

"No. As a matter of fact, I'm not." Andy rebutted as he tugged the bagginess of her t-shirt. He moved in close to Catrina, and she could smell the scotch on his breath. "What's this shit?"

"All my other shirts were dirty," she lied.

"I have extras in *your* size," Andy stated. "Grab one from my office and change it to it. A *small* size.

A chagrin replaced her once cynical smile, as she walked past the owner of the Violin Street Tavern to change.

Andy yelled after her. "What do you think this place is, a goddamn rest home?"

Her employer's voice caused Catrina to tremble within herself. She could feel her stress mount as her shoulders tensed. *Have another one and fall over you stupid prick,* she mentally admonished.

As she grabbed the shirt from Andy's office, Catrina heard the sound of glass smashing to the floor and a heavy thud. She raced back from the back of the establishment and covered her mouth with one hand as she turned the corner. To her astonishment, Andy Sullivan was flat on his back, behind the bar. Next to him, a bottle of Johnny Walker Red had, evidently, tumbled to the floor and broken into numerous shards.

Somewhat in a daze as to what had just happened, Andy looked up at the numerous patrons who peered at him from the other side of the bar. "I can't move my arm. I think it's broken."

Catrina didn't know whether to laugh or appear shocked.

Andy turned his attention to her. "What the hell are you looking at? Call the paramedics and clean this shit up!"

Catrina picked up the receiver of the phone and dialed 911. As she did so, she felt a rush of guilt invade her body. She promised herself to think carefully before wishing bad things on other people. Still, the warming rush of accomplishment flooded Catrina's body as she thought of the incident. With Andy Sullivan on his way to the Spook Valley Medical Center, she knew she wouldn't have to wear that undersized t-shirt after all.

-2-

Stefan's day appeared to have inched by during his shift at Laine's Music. He hadn't made more than a dozen transactions the entire day. Just as Ricky's morning had begun, Stefan experienced the same brand of customer—those who were anxious to find out when the new *Hellfire* CD would be released. It slowly pulled on the strings of Stefan's temper. He simply couldn't fathom the mentality of those who would inquire about the band's recent release when, all the while, it appeared as a large poster board announcement affixed to the front counter at which they stood during their inquiry. Sure, he wanted to yell, wanted to scream at the top of his lungs, *don't you see the fucking sign on the counter!* But that was Stefan's inner voice, his voice that came out in his prose. The true expression that escaped his throat was, "The new *Hellfire* CD debuts tomorrow." And the ear-to-ear grin of the questioning customer was worth seeing by Stefan relaying the information in a kind and even tone.

That was customer service. His pleasant voice was the reason Laine had hired him. It all lay in the soft-spoken niceties Stefan possessed—the way with which he could remain calm in dealing with the eclectic clientele. Stefan recalled a time when Laine had made a mention to him that, when he was fully trained, Laine would be firing Ricky. As Laine had explained it, he had never cared for Ricky's crude remarks and callous attitude for the store in which he worked. Nonetheless, years later, Ricky was still an employee of Laine's Music. Stefan could never quite understand what power Ricky held over Laine. Then, he watched, for the first time, as Laine checked out Ricky and convinced him to start closing the store with Laine. Was Ricky performing sexual favors for Laine, to keep his job?

There was a part of Stefan that was turned on by the idea—Ricky blowing Laine during a late night, when the store was closed, the lights were extinguished, and the sensuous voice of Jim Morrison howled throughout the store's speakers as Laine was on the brink of orgasm. Then again, Stefan wasn't that hopeless. He was desperate enough to give a blowjob to the owner of Laine's Music, nor was he into the physicality of Ricky—lanky structure with a hardcore rock star exterior, still only a frightened child on the inside. No, thoughts like that killed the idea of perfect lovemaking with another man.

Deep within his heart, Stefan knew and expected his lover to be better than that. There would be candlelight and soft kisses upon each other's trembling flesh. Foreplay would commence; foreplay revealed by the teasing of tongues on nipples and the lapping of stomachs. It was the substance of romance novels, the true meaning of making love. And when Stefan would find such a man, if ever, he would recognize him as his soul mate.

It was six o'clock when the jangling bells announced another customer to Laine's Music. Stefan turned toward the CD player, as he replaced the industrial sounds of Nine Inch Nails with the love torn beats of Erasure. Laine had always instructed the guys to change the music to accommodate all patrons of the store. '*Oh lamour*,' the lyrics proclaimed, '*broke my heart and now I'm waiting for you.*'

"The new *Hellfire* CD comes out tomorrow," Stefan called back.

"I hope so. I certainly ordered enough copies."

Stefan immediately recognized the voice and turned to find Laine Young entering his music store.

Laine appeared tired. Dark circles drew attention to the aging lines beneath the hippie's eyes. Uneven wisps of dirty blond hair accentuated his middle-aged face, though he made his best attempt of using a rubber band to pull his shoulder length hair into a ponytail. Of course, his eyes were bloodshot. However, that was obviously the result of the joint he'd smoked along the way.

Stefan acknowledged his boss. "I emptied some bins for the new CD over there." He pointed toward the north wall of the store.

"Awesome," Laine commented. I'll fill them tonight when I close so that they'll be ready first thing in the morning."

Laine scanned the perimeter of the store. "Ricky around?"

"Nah. He left a couple hours ago."

A slight frown adorned Laine's face, then a smile. "You want to hang around a bit, Stefan. Close up and go back to my place to celebrate *Hellfire*'s latest craze?"

Stefan couldn't believe that his boss was actually trying to hit on him. Who did Laine think he was, Ricky? "Sorry," Stefan innocently apologized. "I have to get some writing done."

"Oh...yeah...right." Laine's eyes looked toward the ceiling as if he in deep contemplation. It suddenly hit him. "Your poetry, right?"

"Yes," Stefan smiled. The fact that Laine remembered that he wrote was a miracle in itself, what with all the pot he smoked.

"*Dark Love*, right?"

"*Dark Hearts*," Stefan corrected. In an instant, Stefan lost respect for his employer. If there was one thing that irked Stefan, it was those with whom he confided the title to his book only to find that they couldn't remember it.

"*Dark Hearts*," Laine repeated. "And your poems are about—"

"Demons," Stefan finished.

"Wow, man, that's pretty heavy."

"How's that? We all have our demons, don't we Laine?" Stefan stared down Laine, with mischievous eyes that looked up at him.

"What's that supposed to mean?"

"Nothing," Stefan replied as he grabbed his bag. "The till zeroed out and I'm leaving."

As Stefan began walking toward the exit of Laine's Music, he heard Laine anxiously mumble, "Gotta give Ricky a call."

-3-

Although she had lived most of her teenage life in Phoenix, Catrina ran off to Spook Valley to escape her stringent parents. She was sick of their constant nagging and, on top of that, she had almost killed her mother.

Rob and Angie Taylor thought Catrina didn't have enough friends and hung out with the wrong crowd. She was always "listening to that sinful music, watching those movies that would corrupt her mind, and dabbling into Satan's world." *Hell*, she thought, *my parents belong in Spook Valley more than I do.*

And it was true.

Spook Valley was the type of town that harbored families whose Sunday outings included church service in the morning and a picnic in the park afterward. Very few people such as Catrina Taylor resided in Spook Valley—few men that sported the long hair of a rocker type of lifestyle, only a couple of women donning the dark clothing and black lipstick found in that of the once-popular Goth culture, and, as far as Catrina Taylor knew, only one practicing witch.

Catrina's fascination with witchcraft, or Wicca (as its religious belief was deemed) began shortly after her brother, Lysander Taylor, ran away from home. She had been only twelve years of age when Lysander disappeared on that winter's night ten years previous. She had not known where her brother had gone, but Catrina surely knew that the cause of his running away was a result of their parents' strict upbringing. Catrina recalled the many weekend nights that her brother (who went by the shortened name of Zander by everybody save for Mother and Father) had been accosted in Christian tongues by their parents for coming home late, or smelling of beer after being out with his friends. And she couldn't help but remember the evening when Zander yelled at their father how much he hated him and Father said Zander was going to Hell if he didn't live the life of a responsible Christian boy.

Catrina had enjoyed the evenings that she and Zander had secretly spent together as their parents slept soundly. They would both pretend to go to sleep, in their respective bedrooms, then Zander would creep into Catrina's room where they would engage in playing board games and watch scary movies. Monopoly was always Zander's favorite game, and Catrina couldn't stand how he always had a way of purchasing Park Place and Boardwalk within the first twenty minutes of game play. Subsequently, upon the next trek around the square board, Catrina's metal horse token would land on the blue-framed properties adorned with red, plastic hotel pieces. She easily lost the game to her older brother each time, and Zander would smile with a defeat exhibiting both good sportsmanship and love.

Beyond the games and frightful movies, there were the talks shared between brother and sister. Catrina was always interested in what Zander did with his guy friends from school. From the parties that had consisted of ritualistic drinking games to the teenage trash talk spoken between adolescent girls who were secretly kissing all the guys in school, Catrina had always listened to her brother's tales with perked ears and widened eyes. On many occasions, she had found herself chuckling at Zander's stories, and her brother would *shhhh* her for fear of waking Father and Mother. After all, had Rob and Angie Taylor found their children up during the witching hours of the evening, they would punish them with groundings for Catrina and belt lashes for Zander.

Still, despite the threat of their strict parents, Zander would risk anything to converse with his sister in the late evening and learn about her life beyond a quiet dinner table. It had always been quite mutual, their conversations. Though Zander was seventeen and Catrina merely twelve, they'd talked as two grown adults, as two best friends that had confided their secrets to one another that dare never reach the ears of their parents. Catrina would excitedly tell Zander of the cute boys in her sixth grade classroom. Zander would joke with her about kissing them and, as usual, comment about her having the ugliest pigtails that no boy could ever learn to like.

Both Catrina and Lysander Taylor lived in two worlds as they grew up. There was the world of Christianity and the church, of Father and Mother's rigorous upbringing which included grace at the dinner table and prayers as they kneeled by the side of their beds (promptly at 8:30pm). Then there was the time when their parents inevitably slept. It was the only time that the two could share the true bond that mended the love of a brother and sister. It was a moment when prayers went unanswered, for the two gave not to sleep. Instead, they confided in one another and spoke with tongues that dare not speak such words in the presence of Father and Mother. At least, not without punishment.

But it would all come to an end. It was simply a matter of time.

Time—how slowly it could pass in the presence of hate and depression. Yet, how quickly it flew by as one found freedom away from the oppression of authority.

A week before Christmas, a young Catrina Taylor awoke and stretched her arms beneath her feathery pillow to hear the sounds of a rustle. She scrambled to all fours as she arose and retrieved the piece of paper from beneath her pillow. A tear escaped her eye as if prophesying what was to come. She had known.

The paper revealed to be a short letter written in a sloppy, quick script. *Catrina, you know I can't be here any longer. You know why. It is for the best. I want to find a better place, because I need to be the man that I am becoming. I will always remember our talks. And, someday, I will see you. I love you, sister! Zander.*

The tears had flooded Catrina's eyes and streamed down her swollen cheeks. She didn't want to believe it. Her brother, gone?

Catrina jumped from out of her bed and feverishly ran into Zander's bedroom, heart caught in her throat in hesitation of the irrefutable truth. It had to be a dream! Yes, it must have been a nightmare; surely, she would awaken at any time. However, as Catrina Taylor opened the door to her brother's bedroom, her fears had been confirmed as she was welcomed by the empty room and a bed not slept in.

"Where is your brother?" the voice of her mother had demanded.

Catrina had turned and ran past her mother, back to her bedroom, without a reply. Moments later, Angie Taylor had stormed into Catrina's bedroom. Beside her bawling daughter, she had fixed her sight upon the crumpled letter with which Zander had left for Catrina. Angie Taylor had quickly snatched the letter as Catrina turned and yelled for her to give it back. Her mother had read what was written. "It's mine," Catrina shrieked at her mother. "He wrote it for me and you can't take it!"

Angie Taylor had taken an open hand and slapped her daughter across her right cheek. "Stop screeching like a devil child," she had commanded.

Catrina had gone silent. *I hate you*, she had wanted to yell. Instead, she had turned facedown onto the mattress of her bed and silently sobbed. She had heard the footsteps upon the wooden floor as her mother exited the room. From beyond her bedroom, Catrina had listened to her mother tell her father of Zander's letter and of his running away. "Our son is dead to us," Father had proclaimed.

Catrina had already missed Zander. How could she survive in such a household without the one person whom she had to open her heart? Catrina had recalled reading somewhere how, in the old days, families would light a candle to burn brightly in the window for the return of a loved one. As much as she had wanted to light a candle for her brother's homecoming, she'd known that it would be impossible to do such. After all, Father and Mother said that candles were objects of the Devil.

-4-

Stefan slowed his SUV and made a right off Firehouse Road. He hadn't been more than a mile and a half from the music store before he decided to veer off the asphalt and upon the desert landscape, such was his anticipation to write. The crunching of dried brush and the popping of rocks emitted from beneath the vehicle's tires as Stefan cautiously maneuvered his vehicle deep enough into the desert surrounding Spook Valley so that nearby traffic was out of audio range.

Sunsets were the inspiration for Stefan's writing. They were the quintessential gleaming of a sparkling eye before darkness fell, perhaps like that of a tear before the oncoming of a crucial loss to emptiness. At least, that was the metaphor Stefan used to inspire his book of poems. The sunset—it was the last ray of hope before nothing was left. And once darkness pervaded, the demons of the human mind ensued. Within such insanity, anything was possible. It was at that time that the human mind became subhuman. It was in that instant that the feelings of rage transformed humans into demonic creatures that hatefully clutched with razor-sharp nails for vengeance of a jaded lover, gnarled at the night skies with bloodied and jagged teeth for death upon their rival, and fucked like crazed animals in super-speed fashion. The human heart—void of love—would become nothing more than a dark heart.

Stefan brought his Pathfinder to a halt near a small, barren area surrounded by stumpy century plants and high-reaching saguaros. This was to be the place tonight; it would provide a different angle of the sunset and was far enough toward the heart of the desert that he would not be disturbed by passing motorists.

After shutting off the engine to the vehicle, Stefan grabbed his journal from his satchel and opened the truck door to exit. The dirt floor of the desert warmed his feet through the soles of his Nike sneakers. The shrill sounds of the surrounding cicadas welcomed Stefan as he moved toward the front end of the SUV.

Stefan leaned against the bumper of the vehicle and opened his journal to begin writing. Before doing so, he gazed into the resplendent sunset as it was in its final minutes of being eclipsed by the clouds that would quickly bring darkness.

-5-

As she had grown through her adolescent years, Catrina Taylor refused to forget about Zander. She had constantly reminded herself of his youthful face of almond flesh accentuated by his growing of a goatee. Every night, before she had gone to bed, she had whispered her love to him and prayed for him to come home. She hadn't a clue as to if he was safe and healthy or struggling somewhere in the streets of Phoenix. Sometimes, when Mother had taken her grocery shopping, Catrina would peer at the transients roaming the downtown area. She'd searched for his face in hopes of seeing him. However, her fantasies never materialized. The one thing Catrina Taylor did put her faith in was that she would see Zander one day, just as he had promised in his letter to her that fateful morning.

Although, Father and Mother hadn't made it easy by pretending that they no longer had a son. In church, they would introduce their "only child" Catrina to new members of the congregation. There was never the mention of their son's name. In fact, Father had made sure to warn Catrina that he would take a belt to her if she were to mention his name in public. Zander's running away had been a sin to Father and Mother. He was part of Satan's army. Rob and Angie Taylor would have refused to welcome him with open arms had he ever returned home.

The memory of her brother consumed Catrina through her high school years. She had befriended very few and had been considered by her classmates as a loner. Some of the ruffian students had deemed her *Carrie*, referring to Stephen King's character in the Brian De Palma film. Although, unlike Carrie White, Catrina Taylor was a beautiful girl with porcelain flesh and auburn curls that spilled down her back.

It was in high school, that Catrina Taylor became interested in the study of Wicca. In her senior year, her history class studied the Salem Witch Trials of the seventeenth century. Catrina's mother had a field day upon discovering the classroom study and had written a threatening letter to the school superintendent for teaching students such "devil worship" material. Nonetheless, Angie Taylor's letter was of no great concern. After all, the Salem Witch Trials were mentioned in most history books and that, in turn, classified it as criteria that could be learned in History class.

Catrina Taylor had been enthralled by the thought of witchcraft and magic. It was, at that time, that Catrina's focus had slowly shifted from thoughts of her brother to the practicing of Wicca. In spite of her hopes of seeing Zander, as time past, Catrina's faith in such had slowly diminished and had been replaced with her newfound belief.

Catrina was fascinated by the thought of the worship of nature that Wicca offered. The idea of Earth as a *mother* and of the God and Goddess as complimentary polarities that balanced nature allowed Catrina to identify with a belief that didn't seem so out of reach. Surely, she walked upon the Earth every day of her life and was always surrounded by the elemental brothers and sisters of earth, air, fire, and water. Yes, this was something she could believe in and from which she could draw power! Mother Earth had become her true *mother.* Wicca, altogether, had become Catrina's confidant that had replaced the memory of Zander.

Although she had wanted to delve into the spellcasting aspect of Wicca, there was no way that she could get away with it under the roof of Rob and Angie Taylor. Mother would surely freak at the sight of a pentacle! She would've ranted and raved about how the five-pointed star was the pentagram of the devil. And the idea of candles would've been indisputably out of the question. Still, Catrina could chant as she gazed at the new moon from her bedroom window. Father and Mother would never know.

And so it was that Catrina Taylor had chanted on many nights. Her chanting had been kept to a low whisper so that Father and Mother would not hear. She had intoned for love in her life in the form of a best friend. And she had whispered, upon the nights of a thumbnail moon, for peace and joy that would overcome the oppression of her home life.

There were times when it had seemed that her wishes for something that she'd chanted for would come true. It had seemed to quiet down at the Taylor residence. Mother and Father had stopped demanding her to go to church. On another occasion, she had wished for new clothing and Mother had, on a whim, decided to take her out to the mall to get an outfit (although Father hadn't approved). It had appeared that Catrina's parents were communicating less and leading lives that were more independent. Though she'd never aspired for such, perhaps that was a part of the *true mother* allowing peace to come into her life.

On her twentieth birthday, Catrina's mother presented her with a card that contained a one hundred dollar bill. "I want you to spend this on something you really want," Angie Taylor had informed her daughter who had, for the first moment in a long time, donned a smile. "I'll drive wherever you would like to go to spend it. Then I'm going to take you out for dinner. My treat."

Catrina had been overwhelmed by her mother's kindness. Birthdays in the Taylor house were celebrated with a simple 'Happy Birthday' and nothing more—no cake, no festive streamers, and certainly no neatly wrapped gifts. "What about Father?" Catrina had questioned her mother regarding Rob Taylor's attendance.

"Your father is extremely exhausted from work."

The truth was that Rob Taylor would not condone such gifts with which his wife had given to their daughter in observance of her birthday. He had preached about birthday presents being nothing more than love exchanged through greed for the material world with which the Devil often tempted mankind.

"Any idea where you would like to spend it?" Mother had changed the subject and gestured toward the currency gripped tightly within Catrina's hand.

It had taken Catrina but a moment to know exactly where she wanted to take her birthday cash. "There's a bookstore...downtown."

Angie Taylor had slowed the family sedan alongside the curb as Catrina directed her. The black awning boasted letters in the script of calligraphy, and Mrs. Taylor had made out the first word on the awning—Janson's.

"I'll just be a minute, Mother," Catrina informed. "I know what I want, so you can wait in the car." Catrina had grabbed the handle of the passenger side door.

Janson's, Mrs. Taylor had thought in her mind. It must have been a used bookstore. For a moment, Catrina's mother had felt proud to know that her daughter recognized the value of a dollar. However, as the remaining words that announced the establishment became deciphered, Angie Taylor had begun to feel the brimming of dread roil in her stomach. Janson's Occult Shoppe.

Catrina had been halfway out of the vehicle before her mother yelled for her. "Catrina Louise Taylor! Get in the car now!" She had frozen, knowing that Mother had seen the name of the business. *Shit*! She had eased her body back into the vehicle and shut the passenger side door. Catrina had turned toward her mother who invited her glance with a slap across the face. "What in God's name do you think you're doing?"

"Mother, they have a couple of books I would like to read," Catrina had attempted to remain calm, although a tear had fled her eye.

"Your father was right. I was wrong in thinking that I could change so that I wouldn't lose you too."

"Mother, there is nothing wrong with buying a couple of books. You said I could spend it on what I want."

"Oh," Angie Taylor had crazily guffawed in sarcasm as if she the victim of a joke to which everybody found funny but her. "I see. So you choose to spend it on books written by the Devil himself! He's touched you hasn't he? Satan's touched you, my child."

Catrina was unable to control herself. She had taken the abuse repeatedly. The preaching—how it made her want to scream. The constant persecution—how it had writhed within her like a seed of hate awaiting sustenance to blossom into a tree of rage. "Yes," she snidely remarked. "Satan has touched me, Mother. He does it every night when he fucks me with his enormous cock."

Angie Taylor had become instantly infuriated by her daughter's sarcasm. She had taken her hand, drew it far behind, and laid the hardest slap upon Catrina's face that she had ever done in her life. "Damn you!"

Catrina had felt her left cheek go instantly numb. Her hatred for her mother had grown into pure fume. Before her mother had a chance to shift the vehicle into drive, Catrina Taylor had quickly ejected herself from the passenger side and onto the sidewalk. Lowering her head into the vehicle, she had glared at her mother. Their eyes met as if in the ultimate showdown. "I hate you," Catrina seethed. "I hope you die."

Angie Taylor had driven away to leave her daughter on the downtown streets of Phoenix. Two miles north, on McDowell Road, Angie Taylor would meet her daughter's wrath in the form of another driver who would run a red light and t-bone her vehicle. She would live, if only due to her daughter's partial guilt of what she had said. However, Angie Taylor would live the life of a devout Christian. She had promised her husband to never stray from God again. From that point, Angie Taylor would remind herself that money truly was the root of all evil.

Two years had passed since the last time Catrina Taylor had seen her mother. For that day had been the day that the Taylor family had renounced Catrina as their only child. If anybody were to ask Rob and Angie Taylor now, they would say that they have no children.

Since then, Catrina had made a leap of independence by moving to a small town far enough from Phoenix, her family and the haunting memories of Zander altogether. Shortly after she arrived in Spook Valley, she secured a job at the Violin Street Tavern, a local bar in which she had proven her falsified barmaid skills to the bar owner, Andy Sullivan. Then again, it didn't make a difference what she filled out on the employment application, for she knew that Andy was just interested in looking at her ass half the time. Not long after she learned that her beauty and mystique could be put to good at Violin Street Tavern and earn her great tips, she signed a year's lease for her first apartment in her twenty-two years of life. And, very shortly, she befriended a man that had become her first and best friend, a man with whom she had learned to love. His name was Stefan Powell.

-6-

From the Journal of Stefan Powell

Sunsets are so beautiful, yet so mysterious. The skies grow a nuclear orange that segues into a brilliant, almost neon, purple as the sun rests on this side of the world. Twilight is welcomed; yet, who knows what lurks in the inky blackness of the night. Surely, in this desert, snakes. And I don't plan to be around when they show with their rattles, creating a native song of hypnotic wonder. They say snakes can see in the nighttime. I believe it.

Ahhh, here we go...

My image of night
Is a throng of naked torsos falling to the floor,
A frustration of minds that cannot unlock the door to my room,
And a reveling in the power with which you cursed me.
My love, so free now—
During your midnight glamour and unrequited kisses.

I lost it.

Another inspiring moment lost to the unwanted sounds of nature.

Something is weird. The crickets and cicadas have stopped altogether. All that is left is a sound like that of static. Fucking weird! The more I keep listening, I think I can almost hear the sound of my own heart beating—but it is amplified. Or, maybe, it is the sound of another's heart!

OK, I managed to scare myself again! I'm out of here! Late.

As much as Stefan anticipated in the very act of gripping the handle to the driver's side door of his Pathfinder, the booming thuds grew louder with each rushed breath he took. He grabbed for his chest to feel at his pulse. It began racing. Although his heavy heartbeats choked his throat, Stefan deduced that the rhythmic sounds, like that of finely tuned tympanis, did not emit from his body.

Stefan turned and observed the desert beyond the area with which he had parked. The deep purple of dusk displayed a landscape both enchanting and haunting, as the beginning of night drew its inky blanket over the region. The thunderous beating was coming from beyond the sagebrush, and Stefan was beside himself in his decision to investigate the foreign sound. Surely, he was scaring himself out of his wits. It was probably nothing more than a jackrabbit thumping away upon the hardened dirt of the desert floor. Yet, it seemed more than that. The resonance was constant, and there was something about it that called to Stefan.

With utter caution, Stefan advanced toward the open desert, in the direction of the sagebrush that surrounded his vehicle. His heart quickened and he instantly came to a halt. For a moment, he thought he saw two crimson beads against the welcoming night. A demon, like in his poetry? *No*, he told himself. *My demons would protect me, then make love to me, and* then *try to haunt me.* Stefan produced a half-smirk at the grandiose idea.

An instant crackle infiltrated the night, like that of a fiery log or a whip of fire searing against the blackened atmosphere. Stefan was eager to turn back to the vehicle and leave. However, a static resonance joined the constant thuds and lured Stefan like a hypnotist controlling his subject. Stefan fearlessly walked into the inviting unknown the desert held for him. As he past the sagebrush and continued toward the mystery that held his curiosity captive, Stefan noticed a ruby red glare within proximity.

Like a moth to a flame, Stefan languidly strode toward the strange glowing cast by the seeming impossible red tint. In his reverie, he began telling himself that this experience was nothing more than a dream. And that was exactly what Stefan convinced himself of as he drew close to the red glowing in the center of the desert. For it was, that no phenomena such as this had a reasoning that could be located in the annals of any text which provided credence to scientific explanation.

Stefan's jaw dropped as he observed the mysterious site before him.

A jet-black canvas appeared against the twilight atmosphere of the evening, as if some impossible darkness lay flat against the night. The shadowy magnificence stretched from the floor of the desert, high above Stefan's head. It was as if the unearthly spectacle loomed over Stefan by fifteen feet and reached to either side of him by another eight, such was its colossal size. Glowing, ruby embers that appeared to seep down all sides of the impractical figure, as if the nighttime horizon had been sliced and bled upon the borders of the shape, highlighted the vertical rectangle.

Stefan hastily took a step backward. His lower lip trembled as the air rushed inward during a deep breath. His heart pounded with the thuds of the timbre before him. His pulse was practically in harmony with the rhythm of the vibrating that emitted from all around him. *One...two...three...four*—Stefan could count the loud beats of his heart. *One...two...three...four*—such was the pulsing from the bloody outline of the inky rectangle in front of him. *Thud-thump...thud-thump...thud-thump...thud-thump*—his heartbeats were in tune with the fantastic pulsation of the edges that bordered the possible hallucination.

A dream! Yes, a nightmare! Surely, that was the answer to this mysterious apparition. Stefan made a mental grasp for any type of clarification that could explain the foreign display of darkness that welcomed him. And the throbbing outline that beamed in red brilliance—how was that even possible? *How did this thing get here? What enigmas lay in the outlying deserts of Spook Valley?* What in God's name had he stumbled upon?

A shot of adrenalin burst through his veins as a gelid chill ran along the nape of Stefan's neck. He instantly turned away from the spectacle that loomed over him, only to find that the night surrounded him. He was instantly blinded to the darkness that greeted. Staring at the radiant border of that monolithic spectacle made it unable for his eyes to focus on the sagebrush and century plants nearby. With his back turned to the hopeful illusion, butterflies tearing through his stomach accosted Stefan. The tickling sensation sent shivers up his spine and to the base of his skull.

He had to get out of here! The ordeal made such an impact on Stefan's heart, that he began feeling pains in his chest. No, he couldn't handle this any longer.

The pulsing thud continued to permeate Stefan's surroundings so that rational thinking was veritably impossible. However, Stefan willed himself to start walking away from the horrific marvel taking place behind him. It didn't make a difference if he was blinded to the path with which he had trod.

Stefan covered his ears as he pushed to take one, two and then three steps. The hammering instantly ceased.

Stefan halted in his tracks, slowly pulling his hands from his ears. The night exhaled a dead silence and, for a moment, Stefan thought he had gone mute. "Fuck," he yelled into the darkness. He took a steady breath after his fears were subsided by the sound of his voice.

A breeze rushed from behind, pushing up the back of Stefan's shirt and cooling the clammy flesh upon his back. *Where did that come from?* He immediately panicked. *Keep walking*, Stefan told himself. However, the young man became frozen with terror from the sounds that emitted from behind him.

"*Hellllllllp meeeeeeee*," the voice hollered, accentuated by the vibrato of bloodcurdling horror. It was almost a screech upon the hush of the accompanying night, had it not been for vocal chords that prevented such. For it was that the grieving cries belonged to that of a man. Once again, the cries infused the unusual stillness.

Immediately, Stefan commanded himself to run. Yet, at the same time, his rampant curiosity took the helm of his vivid imagination. After all, this had to be nothing more than a fantastic experience brought on by bogeymen lurking in the dark recesses of his dreams. Surely, he would wake up at any time! Yes, he was frightened. Yes, his heart rapidly fluttered. But Stefan knew that once he awoke, it would all fade into a memory with which he would relive, one day, upon creation of another piece of haunting prose.

Turn around, he told himself.

The *thud-thump* resonance began, as if it a metronome measuring each pivot Stefan made. He would face the dreamlike phantasm once again. He turned with utter caution. Rivulets of sweat trailed down to his narrow chin and formed beads that fell and moistened the dirt of the desert floor.

The pulsating continued along with the ungodly screams for help. It was as if a symphony of horror had been playing within an amphitheater mysteriously built upon the surrounding desert of Spook Valley.

Thud-thump. Helllllllp meeeeeeeee!

Stefan turned his body so that it was fully facing the fantastic sight. His eyes swelled from the uncanny scene unfolding before him. His jaw fell, leaving his mouth agape as he forced himself to breathe.

A pale arm protruded from out of the inky darkness that tore through the atmosphere of night. The bloody border of the rectangular apparition pulsed without interruption, and a rosy tint reflected from the limb that reached outward. The definition of the arm was made apparent by a slightly rounded bicep and angle of a forearm that tapered and connected to a hand with fingers clenching at the night. The fingers of the hand tightly folded down against themselves in obvious struggle to grapple at anything. The fingers grasped for Stefan.

Stefan took an involuntary step back from the arm that reached out toward him. The maddened butterflies tore through his stomach and infiltrated his entire body as he trembled uncontrollably. "My god," Stefan exclaimed. However, he could not hear his own voice against the chaotic resonance pronounced by the manifested poundings and screams for aid.

Stefan had no doubt that the cries for help most certainly emitted from whatever was attached to the arm stretching toward him. Yes, *whatever*! What monster lurked beyond this enigmatic doorway? What's more, what was on the other side of the blackness that divided the night before him?

Stefan wanted to cry for the horror playing out before him, but fear trumped many of the emotions that stormed his mind. He wanted to scream, but was in awe of the terror displayed before him. Most of all, Stefan wanted to run, but a rush of courage took over. Suddenly, Stefan Powell would become a savior.

Everything happened so quickly.

The shouting of the alien voice incessantly collaborated with the vibrant pulsations of the object that towered Stefan. His heart and mind were in a furious frenzy, unable to admit all that was occurring. The fight or flight of adrenaline raced through his body and pricked at his flesh from the insides, as if it would burst from his veins and spurt from his pores at any time.

Stefan took his right hand and grasped at the arm reaching from the dark unknown. The arm was freezing cold. Stefan's entire body jolted from the chill. He immediately cupped his left hand over the hand belonging to the unidentified victim of the eclipsing enigma that held him captive. Stefan positioned himself so that his knees were slightly bent, and leaned forward. Then, with all his might, Stefan thrust his body back, pulling at the arm. Before Stefan's back met with the ground, he witnessed eyes that were as jet-black as the image from which the arm emerged. Along with the eyes, he saw elongated teeth, like the fangs of some wild monster. A wild roar burst into the night, shaking the ground all around him.

The vibrations were the last phenomena Stefan experienced before his sight was obscured by complete darkness.

-7-

A bottle of Budweiser launched into the air and made a hollow clatter as it smashed to the floor.

"Heya," a patron with a sour face slurred. "You alth righth?"

Catrina Taylor jerked from her reverie. "No," she stated, refusing to glance at the wrinkled face of the older customer.

Something was amiss. Catrina closed her eyes for a brief moment, silencing all drunken laughter within the Violin Street Tavern. The instinct hit her in the gut the way in which a women's intuition is commonly unexplained but proves true. That impulse, in some way, related to Stefan.

Catrina rushed to the back room and picked up the phone. She anxiously dialed Stefan's home phone number. After four rings, there was no answer.

'Hey, you reached Stefan. Leave me your rant and I'll send you back a holler.'

A lengthy beep followed the message played by his voicemail greeting.

"Stefan, it's Catrina. Call me as soon as you get this. I hope you're all right. Love you."

Catrina Taylor had never fallen prey to a sensation such as the one with which she had just encountered. Sure, she'd had strong instincts before, but this was something completely different. This left her empty inside. It reminded her of a similar sentiment that had troubled her years ago, when Zander had left their family home.

She had to get a hold of Stefan.

CHAPTER III

-1-

Stefan Powell awoke from bad dreams. The upper half of his body bolted upright as he detested the thought of falling into another sleep plagued with dreaded images. Beads of sweat streamed down his smooth, naked chest. The sweat of fear reached beneath his flesh and consumed his fragile mind, propelling his memory to recall the images that haunted his sleep the previous evening.

His frightened mind recollected pieces of the dream sequence the way a psychic envisions a victim's killer through the method of psychometrics—brisk flashes of events and objects all blurry around the edges. *The desert*, he thought, *the desert outside of town.* A black doorway—a monolith of futuristic stature—and blood oozed and hesitantly dripped around its sharp border. It appeared as a black opal eating away at a delicate ruby. The sounds of a thunderous drum—a blaring thump, thump like that of a god's heartbeat. It had been a hypnotic loudness, the way it pulsed in a steady, luring rhythm, and it drew Stefan closer to the black opening. *A black doorway in the desert?* It didn't make sense. It was a dark rip upon the shadowy air—a tear in the atmosphere. And, as Stefan approached the phenomenon, the baritone cries of a young man permeated the world around him. A young man screaming in terror undefined, as a lithe forearm jutted from the gigantic, black rectangle.

But there was something driving Stefan to save the man. It was as if he were possessed by an ultimate courage; normally, he would have run from such a horrid and enigmatic sight. When Stefan had a strong grasp of the frigid hand that appeared from out of nowhere, a terrifying apparition emerged. Monstrous was the only word in Stefan's shock-induced mind that could describe it.

Then he awoke.

Stefan pondered the nightmare. Yes—*a nightmare*—he could call it that now. No ghastly screams to be heard or monsters lurking in the closet or gangly creatures grotesquely squeezed beneath the bed—they were in the desert; they were in his dreams. He was safe now, protected in his compact apartment. He was secure in his bed and away from the dry, barren terrain of the desert. However, the desert encompassed Spook Valley, taking the town into its dry arms. And Stefan knew he would eventually return there, for it was either the desert or Phoenix that were his only refuges from the thirsty life of this town. Stefan preferred the peaceful sounds of nature versus the blaring horns of major city traffic. The naturally shaped cacti were more appealing than the towering skyscrapers of glass and steel that grazed the overpopulated capital of Arizona.

The blinding rays of the morning sun spilled through the half open blinds and bathed Stefan's naked body in comforting warmth. The sun shone upon him as it did every morning, as if it could use its bright, flaring light to speak in simple words. Praising him or warning him, Stefan would never know. Yet, this morning, something significant about the fiery star howled at him.

Spring. Yes, the first day of spring and the sweet green smell of the oleanders would permeate the air and, more than likely, agitate Stefan's sinuses. But still, it was spring. The semi-cold Arizona winter was over. No more overcast days of gloom and doom, and walls of dust attacking Spook Valley from all sides. Spring—and the temperatures would easily remain in the ninety-degree range. Stefan would eagerly switch the central air thermostat in the apartment to seventy-six degrees. That also meant a larger bill from the electric company and that, in turn, meant that he had to sell a few more poems or get the anthology out which he had put together over the course of two years.

Stefan cupped his hands over his nose and thin lips. He could feel the warmth of his dampened forehead. His eyelids remained closed as he took in a deep, relaxing breath, freeing him of his dreamt evil. He let out a sigh of exasperation. *The worst part is over*, he told himself. *Time to get on with your day.*

Rising from the bed, the sight of his Nike sneakers paralyzed Stefan. They were near the foot of his bed. But their white color was caked with the brown of dirt and dust. *Desert dirt.* He remained frozen, attempting to figure out the previous night and what *had* actually taken place. As much as he willed his mind to return to the remembrance of the previous night, no matter how much he jarred his memory, the only image that came to his mind's eye was that of the black doorway eerily present in the darkness of the desert.

The aromatic smell of fresh-brewed coffee wafted into the room. "What the hell," Stefan remarked as he forcefully lunged from his bed, abandoning the pondering of possible events that may have taken place the night before. *There's somebody here!* He violently swung open his bedroom door and sprinted through the brief, narrow hall that led to the remainder of his apartment. As he turned to the gurgling sounds of the coffee maker, he became instantly spellbound.

A comely figure stood in his kitchen, donning an androgyny Stefan had viewed only in history books. The young man's creation was an undying passion of the gods, as if they created perfection in this exquisite piece of animate art. They molded the young man from the whitest of ivories, working their steady hands with meticulousness and sinful lust. The young man's arms and legs were sculpted thin, yet bared definition and tone. His chest was chiseled into bulging orbs with the finest accuracy. The young man's face was finished with a narrow Roman nose and full, voluptuous lips. His cheekbones were highlighted with hands of patient precision. And for eyes, they gave him emeralds. His blazing, dark hair encircled the oval likeness of his face, clashing with the paleness of his complexion. A faded, opal-colored shirt hung open, exposing the young man's ashen chest.

"Who-are-you?" Stefan asked, pausing between each word. He was bemused by this fine young man and felt an extreme comfort run through his adrenaline-induced body. At this point in time, Stefan's thoughts wouldn't allow danger, only desire. The thought of a stranger such as the man before him, breaking into his apartment, did not jolt him.

"My name is Breckin," the beautiful man responded in a smooth, deep voice. He began opening cupboards, obviously in search of coffee mugs, but kept his sight upon Stefan. His searing, green eyes were full of admiration as they targeted Stefan. "Thank you."

"What did I do?" Stefan questioned, his mind bombarded with mass confusion. He positioned himself so the wall beside him supported his body. Stefan didn't know why, but the sight of Breckin obviously making coffee did not shock him. This stranger in his house; why wasn't he on the phone to the police?

"You saved me last night, Stefan."

How does he know my name? His mind raced for answers, for some rational response. "I don't understand."

And than it hit him.

"You mean the dream," he laughed. "It *was* a dream," Stefan said, reassuring his self.

Breckin gazed deeply into Stefan's eyes; emeralds meeting sapphires that could hypnotize anybody. "It was no dream, Stefan. You *were* there. You saved me from that awful place."

"Place? What place," he queried once again. *The black doorway in the desert? In the dream?* But, according to Breckin, the nightmare wasn't a bad dream at all. It had actually happened.

Suddenly his mind reminisced the previous evening. It was coming to him now. He was viewing the sunset, gathering inspiration for *Dark Hearts*, his poetry anthology. When the sun fell is when it all happened. It was no dream, he realized; it was a loathsome reality.

"What year is it?" Breckin curiously asked.

Stefan wanted to storm into laughter until he noticed the genuine look of concern etched upon Breckin's face. Feeling awkward by supplying an answer to such a question, Stefan responded to Breckin. He pointed to the *Men of Latin America* calendar that boasted the current month and year above a scantily clad male model that lay sprawled upon the sands of an exotic beach.

"Three years," Breckin spoke aloud as his sad face fell. Coming out of his reverie of amazement, Breckin spoke in anticipation. "I have a lot to tell you and we must be prepared by nightfall."

"I still don't underst—"

Breckin interrupted. "I'll explain everything but, first, you should shower and get dressed." He moved his eyes to Stefan's black silk boxer shorts and produced a slight smirk. It was the first time he had smiled in three years, the first time since he was taken into the darkness, that black emptiness where evil and mayhem stormed the parallel land, thriving on the human consciousness and preying on believers to set it free. "Coffee will be on the table when you return."

"You want me to leave you alone? I don't even know you." Stefan nonchalantly chuckled.

"I've been here all night, Stefan. I'm not going to hurt you." Breckin turned from Stefan and began rummaging through the overhanging cabinets for coffee mugs.

Stefan couldn't help but think of how the man's innocent gestures brought on an odd comfort. Perhaps it was the way in which Breckin innocuously shuffled through the cabinets, attempting to guess at which cabinet housed the coffee cups. Maybe it was the authentic gaze of Breckin's eyes when he'd inquired about the present year. Needless to say, Stefan's intuition instructed that he could trust the man who stood before him. With that, he exited the kitchen and made his way toward the bathroom.

Stefan quickly showered, slapping the cold shampoo into his hair and rubbing bar soap over his naked limbs. He wasted no time, for he wanted to see Breckin again. He couldn't explain his eager mindset of seeing the stranger who had greeted him that morning. Nor could he understand his sudden, undying longing to be near the young man. Still, Stefan wanted to be part of his newfound friend's world and, most importantly, he wanted an explanation.

Stefan opened the glass door of the shower and stepped out into the chilly air that pierced his body. He swiftly toweled off, pulled a black t-shirt over his head, and buttoned up a pair of old, Guess jeans.

Wiping the foggy condensation from the medicine cabinet mirror, Stefan abruptly cringed against the wall behind him. He gripped his fingers into the plaster of the wall as a monstrous apparition unexpectedly greeted him.

The mirror cast the reflection of a hideous beast. It donned a chiseled armor of flesh that appeared maroon and tightly wrinkled, as if it a detailed molding that had been set afire in the kiln of an accomplished sculptor. Stefan drew in a deep breath and paused from exhaling. For unlike the stillness of such a statuesque creation, the creature's oversized mouth—stretching from the lower corners of its beady, ruby eyes—slowly opened and exposed hundreds of jagged, inhuman teeth that protruded in various directions. Stefan's throat tightened as the oozing saliva that surfaced from beneath the beast's upper lip hypnotized him. The slime was like that of inky syrup that slowly trickled down all sides of its mouth and over the red-stained, thick fangs.

Consumed by a reverie that arrested all thoughts from his mind, the world around Stefan Powell slowed to a crawl. Beaded sweat traveled along either of his short sideburns at a snail's pace. His heartbeat, though heavily throbbing from the haunting fear that paralyzed his breathing, thudded in a lingering cadence that echoed the intensity of every beat deep inside Stefan's eardrums. The ooze from the creature's mouth seemed to take minutes to seep a quarter inch. Then, with the suave precision of a magician who can casually walk though walls, the beast projected its robust arm from beyond the silvery glass. The mirror gave no physical indication that established such a scene of madness. The glass did not bend outward or ripple as if it a silver pond from which something emerged. Instead, it remained intact as the inhuman arm reached further toward Stefan.

Stefan gawked at the rigid, brown nails as he dug his own fingernails deeper into the wall behind him. He was so focused on the creature that his mind didn't register the wince of pain that came as a result of the tips of his fingernails separating from his fingers. Yet, the numbing sensation afterward reflected the paralysis that engulfed his body. Stefan wanted to scream more than anything. To holler for help would get Breckin's attention and surely bring the stranger to his rescue. Yet, the outsized lump in his throat restricted Stefan's voice box. Closer came the grotesque nails that protruded at least three inches from the fingers of the creature, and Stefan's eyes met with the beast's demonic irises. The eyes of the sinister apparition pierced into Stefan's soul with their ominous blood color. Stefan experienced the tingling sensation of his brain being invisibly molested by the unknown force before him. His entire body trembled. The creature's jaw hung low, its triple-spiked tongue anxiously wiggling as if it hungry. Stefan could veritably detect the odor of rotted flesh beneath the nails of the beast—perhaps that of a previously victim—such was the proximity of the creature's hand.

Stefan used all his will power to exert inner pressure on his lungs in an attempt to force a scream from his throat. Just as two of the tips of the beast's twisted nails grazed the tender flesh of his lips, Stefan produced an awkward yelp that was that of part scream and part cry. The pace of the world around him returned to normal as Stefan's back went flat to the wall and he twisted downward toward the linoleum floor. Stefan briskly moved on all fours and clambered to his feet. From the corner of his eye, he caught a fleeting glimpse of an overpowering swipe from the creature's arm. It was a final effort for the monster to capture his elusive prey; yet, Stefan successfully exited and avoided the sinister grasp altogether. The walls of the hallway violently shook around Stefan as a thunderous roar emitted from behind.

Stefan gasped for air, and he was practically out of breath by the time he reached the end of the short hallway and bolted into the kitchen. Breckin casually sat at the oval cherry-wood dining table, and greeted Stefan with a cup of coffee that steamed before an empty seat.

"You have to tell me what the hell is going on! There's something in the bathroom. It came from the mirror and tried to grab me," Stefan prattled. "What was that thing?"

Breckin remained calm and collected. "Sit down, Stefan," his voice overpowering. "Don't worry; they can't hurt you during the daylight. They can only terrorize you, subjecting your mind to the evil hold they have on you. And believe me Stefan, they have you in their sights."

Breckin could feel Stefan's inquisitive stare hold him. He imagined Stefan demanded answers. Surely, he beckoned for an explanation. It showed in the timbre of Stefan's voice when he emerged from the bathroom, escaping the grasp of the beast's reflection in the mirror. It was apparent in the way he gawked at Breckin, eyes wide open and mouth agape as if he were still recovering from the terror he had witnessed thus far and wanted nothing more than the whole story of what was happening.

This was Breckin's time. It was his moment when he could finally explain to somebody what horror had trapped and held him prisoner for the last three years. This was his first day back into the world. Breckin was like a new baby delivered into the world by Mother. *Three years*, Breckin continuously pondered in his mind. *For three years, I've been gone from this Earth.* It all felt so hazy and unreal, like a dream, just as Stefan recalled having when he saved Breckin from the desert and pulled him to safety. Why couldn't it all be one terrible nightmare? Why couldn't the fogs of trepidation lift and leave his life for good? And that place—that other place was so cold; yet flames burned everywhere. And the evil—everywhere was nothing but evil—monsters, torture, cacophonous screams permeating the atmosphere, and the promise. The pact. Breckin could easily call it Hell, but the minions who stormed the land deemed it the *Nightworld.*

Stefan sat at the dining room table, ignoring the coffee that had been prepared for him. He was too shaken by the baffling incident in the bathroom.

"You're not touching your coffee," Breckin casually pointed out.

"I'm wide awake, thank you. I want you to tell me everything. Tell me what's going on," Stefan insisted.

Breckin sat straight in his chair and took in a deep breath. "They call it the *Nightworld*," he began.

"Great," Stefan sighed. "Who are 'they' and what is this '*Nightworld*?'

Breckin didn't know how to begin. Stefan wanted an explanation, but Breckin held doubt that Stefan would be able to cope with the truth. At least, the entire truth. So it was that Breckin continued his story. But in his guilty heart, he was limited to telling Stefan only so much. The remainder would have to wait and the truth discovered by unweaving this web of horror one strand at a time, probably throughout the course of days. For now though, to give enough information to save their lives was explanation enough.

Breckin ignored Stefan's inquisition and continued. "You kept an open mind when you allowed it to manifest, so I'm expecting you to keep an open mind during what I'm going to tell you.

"Last night, in the desert, *they* saw you before appearing. They read your mind and were certain that you were a believer. They wanted you for their next victim, their next abductee.

"I need to make one thing clear to you," Breckin emphasized as he moved closer to Stefan. "What you did, Stefan, was not wrong. If you had not opened the doorway, somebody else would have. It happened to me three years ago. All by myself, subconsciously allowing my dark thoughts to cause its appearance," Breckin paused and a tear came to his eye.

"Who are 'they' and what did I do?" Stefan asked.

Breckin wiped the falling tear. "It's evil, Stefan. It is pure evil. You've heard of Pandora's Box, haven't you?"

Stefan nodded, vaguely recalling the myth.

"This is similar. This is a different world, another land that doesn't exist here on Earth. A doorway gaps this realm and the dimension of another called the *Nightworld.* The only way the doorway can be opened is from the mind of a believer in this world.

"It is a place filled with chaos, Stefan. It has always existed; the evil has always been around. They observe the happenings in this world and they prey on humans for whatever reason they choose. Whether it is for the thrill of the hunt, or to torture in eternal damnation, or as a sacrifice to their God. Vampires, demons, specters, werewolves—you believe they exist don't you?"

Stefan was in awe of Breckin's words. Was the man sitting before him actually listening to the words that came from his mouth? It took a minute for Stefan to realize he was on the spot for an answer. "Well, yeah, I mean, I've read books on occultism. Hell, what curious mind doesn't?"

"The books were just a catalyst. They stored doubt of this world in your mind. Somehow, you wanted this."

I wanted this? Stefan thought and then he began to correlate anything in his life that could be connected with such fantasy. Something went off in his head like the answer to an age-old enigma. "*Dark Hearts!*"

"What?" Breckin was quickly lost.

"I've been working night and day on my poetry anthology *Dark Hearts.* The poetry revolves around…well…darkness. Namely demonology." Another light went on in his mind. "Wait...the bathroom. It was a demon I saw in the mirror."

"It's possible," Breckin stated as he sighed for Stefan to understand all he was trying to convey. "But it's not just demons. You have to understand that, until they capture you, they'll come in many forms and they'll get you anyway that they can."

"Why didn't they take me last night, in the desert?"

"You put them off guard, Stefan. You saved me. I had been looking for a way to escape. Coincidentally, you were there for me. They didn't expect that to happen."

No, Stefan thought, *you saved me.* He instantly felt indebted to Breckin. Those creatures could have taken him last night, but Breckin was there. It was Fate. There was no question about it.

"When will the doorway close?" Stefan pondered.

Breckin's face went rigid. A chill crawled up his spine. "You opened the doorway. It will not close until they get you. It can take them a day, a month, or a year. They will stop at nothing. And now, more than ever, they want you for taking me from them."

Stefan's heart still pounded in his throat. He picked up the mug of coffee and sipped and the hot liquid. "How did they get you?" he asked Breckin.

Breckin instantly averted his emerald eyes from Stefan.

Stefan knew he had hit a nerve.

Breckin returned his gaze to Stefan. "Let's just say that I got too close to my research." Breckin sighed. He refused to relive that day that incessantly played in his mind for the past three years. "It's not important."

"Not important?" The young man's answer instantly frustrated Stefan. "Reality check…I pulled you from some cosmic 'doorway' in the middle of the desert, I was almost attacked by a demon that came from the mirror in my bathroom, and you don't even know what year it is! To top it all off, you're trying to tell me that there's another world where monsters exist who prey on people such as myself because of our 'open minds.' C'mon, Breckin; I deserve more than 'it's not important.'" Stefan instantly felt a wave of guilt rush over him. He wanted to quickly apologize for his snappish meltdown. On the other hand, Breckin's explanation scared him.

"I don't like to talk about it, Stefan. I've replayed it over and over for the years I was held captive in the Nightworld.

Suddenly, Stefan felt sorry for Breckin. He remained quiet as Breckin continued.

"All I can tell you is that it occurred so quickly. A black doorway appeared and, before I knew what was happening, I was pulled into their world. I was grasped from behind and I was taken into a world of utter darkness and chaos." Breckin stopped. Tears unexpectedly escaped his emerald eyes the way he had escaped from that terrible world.

Stefan reached out his hand and placed it on Breckin's smooth cheek. He wanted to solace the man before him, the man that had been a stranger until the intimate horrors of his life were revealed.

"I'll be all right. But," Breckin hesitated, "there's one other thing that you should know."

Stefan almost laughed. *There's always something else*, he thought. "OK."

"There is a promise they keep, a sort of pact. I don't know many of the details because only the Order speaks of it in closed conversation."

"You mean The Order of Perennial Darkness."

Breckin nodded.

"What is this 'pact'?" In all reality, Stefan had heard enough and didn't want to know. Then again, he had no choice but to know everything about this new world that was about to eclipse his life. He must know for his safety. Not to mention, for Breckin's well-being.

"They speak of a day when the doorway will remain open forever. A day when they will no longer need a believer to make it happen. They want to rule the Earth with their evil. It has something to do with thirteen of them coming into this world and a sacrifice. I don't know much more than that."

"So what do we do now?" Stefan quizzed.

"I don't know." Breckin viewed the face of the grandfather clock in the living room. It revealed the beginning of the first afternoon hour. "We have about seven hours before the evening arrives. We must prepare. I'm thinking, since these creatures will be entering this realm, that the legends of warding off certain evils will apply. We need some supplies and I need some clothes."

"I know just the place to go," Stefan remarked. "You can wear some of my clothes until then."

Stefan was much calmer now that he knew the worst of it, now that he had heard Breckin's claim. Yet, his guilt wouldn't let him forget what he released into this world. It didn't matter if he did it by mistake or not. It was he who was responsible. What he had allowed to manifest was a gateway for evil to pass, an evil that was much of madness and more of sin.

-2-

Night fell.

A tall, shadowy figure stepped through the gateway with intent to kill the one who escaped and take the other who had opened the doorway. That young man was bound to suffer the worst of agonies. That man had taken one of their own, and he was to be theirs for eternity. But now, the man named Stefan would have to take Breckin's place.

The figure stood tall, clad in a cloaked wardrobe. He held a large, leather satchel to his side.

Scanning the vacant desert, he turned back to face the shaded portal. Another form emerged from the shadow on night. The sound that comes with the passing through the portal is that of static intensified. And when silence filled the night again was when the creature knew it had crossed into this new world.

The newcomer donned a crimson ascot that glowed blood red against the inky night. His cape gently lifted and ballooned behind him from the slight breeze that welcomed him. He lifted his arm into the air to observe the reattached molecules of his flesh. The passing into this world was a success. The ominous creature peered with hungry eyes to his colleague and smiled, sporting elongated fangs.

Chaos was on its way to Spook Valley.

-3-

Stefan covered the bathroom mirror with a white cloth and recalled how great the day had been, regardless of the most horrid discoveries he had come to known. The time he spent with Breckin was pleasurable and it almost made him forget that, tonight, they would be protecting themselves from the wrath of evil.

Today was one of the most enjoyable days Stefan had experienced in months. He found himself growing closer to Breckin as the hours before dementia passed. They chatted like old, best friends reuniting for the first time in years. They managed to laugh together and savored the moments they spent in the needed daylight as they sought the provisions that would assist in their battle against the *Nightworld.* They were like two lost souls discovering a found mate, relishing the love they secretly kindled for one another.

At one point during the day, when they had visited Anna's Crafts, Stefan had grabbed for Breckin's hand. When Breckin responded to Stefan's gesture by interlacing their fingers, the confirmation of Breckin's affection toward Stefan had been made clear. Stefan was tickled by the butterflies in his stomach. He'd produced the first genuine smile possible since Breckin's tale of the Nightworld and its apprehensive mission. Stefan unexpectedly realized that it was possible for affection to grow in the midst of the forewarning of impending destruction. Yes, love could flourish in a world that had been instantly shifted into a realm of monsters and mayhem. He couldn't let that feeling go, no! For it was that he longed for such a love to come his way. Stefan needed this the way a human requires oxygen to live. Love was his oxygen. No need for vengeful hearts and luring demons. Breckin hung the moon and pushed away any dark thoughts that could have inspired much poetry in the once-despondent mind of Stefan Powell. Their time together was one too golden to pass.

But it had passed.

The daylight had been consumed by the appetite of the night. Stefan wished that none of this were happening, that it was all nothing save for a terrible nightmare—the stalking evil, the monsters, the pact, the *Nightworld*—everything except Breckin.

How he loved to love Breckin. The stimulation of having somebody for him to wrap his arms around and hold in comfort as well as share his deep, intimate thoughts with boosted his self-esteem as a poet and a ripening man. Stefan respected Breckin's entire image, especially the way he presented himself in public with his reserved manner. After searching for what seemed to be lifetimes, Stefan would hold on to this lovable man. It was all he had left and Breckin inspired him more than anything in the world did.

However, with everything there comes a price. With Breckin, came malevolence. Stefan would have to contend with it and there was no denying that.

"All done," Stefan informed Breckin as he strolled into the living room. Breckin was sitting on the plush carpet, closing a dispenser of salt. How serene he appeared to Stefan, another factor he admired about him.

"You got all the mirrors?" Breckin asked.

"Yes, every one."

"Good. Then we've done everything we can for tonight."

"What's the salt for again?"

"Placing salt along the thresholds of a home prevents warlocks and witches from passing."

"This all seems so childish," Stefan remarked and gave a small chuckle.

"Maybe," Breckin agreed, "but if it will save our lives, I'm completely for the idea."

"Agreed," Stefan said. "I'm getting tired. I'm going to let you have my bed and I'll crash out here on the couch."

Breckin flinched. "Can you sleep in the bed with me? I want you by my side tonight, Stefan."

Stefan was amazed by Breckin's request and, at the same time, flattered. Secretly, he too wanted Breckin's presence close by.

The lights went out in the apartment. All light was extinguished save for a candle in the bedroom. Stefan and Breckin crawled into the bed and lay next to each other. Winds blew their rage against the curtained window, making howling sounds into the night.

"Hold me, please," Breckin pleaded tenderly.

Stefan placed his arms around Breckin and cradled him slowly as the light from the candle projected the shadows of a sacred love.

-4-

Two figures stealthily approached the front door to Stefan Powell's apartment.

One pulled an oak stake and a sledgehammer from his bag of accessories. He raised it above the closed door with intent to plummet the weapon into the person who would greet them. The other, the vampire, pounded hard on the door as they stood waiting.

-5-

Stefan caressed Breckin's naked back as Breckin positioned his hands on Stefan's smooth chest. Their mouths locked in a deep, lustful kiss that could transform seconds into heavenly centuries.

The candle flickered.

Breckin withdrew from Stefan's tasteful lips, pecking at his chest. Stefan returned the foreplay by kissing Breckin's ivory shoulders and neck, taking in each heart-racing breath as he retracted.

The luminescence of two pale bodies moved with ecstatic sync in the semi-lighted bedroom.

Breckin placed his mouth firmly onto Stefan's, tasting the essence they both craved and desired. He moved his mouth along Stefan's handsome face, down toward his neck, leaving a moistened path of silky kisses. Breckin recoiled from Stefan's neck as the *other* lust filled his being and he arched his body back.

There was a loud rapping at the door. Stefan heard it but was engrossed by Breckin.

Breckin opened his mouth wide so that the fangs that shot through his gums had room to push through. The bloodlust was too much to contend with and he no longer had the will power to fight it. Breckin struck hard at Stefan's neck, pushing his fangs into the tender flesh and experiencing the substance of his soul mate.

CHAPTER IV

-1-

Catrina Taylor sat upon the gray plush of her living room carpet, her supple legs stretched outward in V-formation with a deck of Tarot cards sprawled between them. She had only purchased the deck from Janson's Occult Shoppe, in Phoenix, last week. A slight chuckle grazed her lips as she mocked the fact that Spook Valley was such a traditional town—the mere idea of occult was considered a black cat that crossed one's path.

The residents of Spook Valley doubted the slightest squint of an eye and shared the common thread of basing trustworthiness on one's outward appearance. When Catrina Taylor had first moved to Spook Valley, she'd instantly thought that she'd relocated to the bible belt of the Southwest. Though she had attempted to kindly greet the townspeople as she shopped at B & K Grocery or as she perused the various antique and trade shops that lined Main Street, she'd discovered that the residents of Spook Valley turned their cheeks to her. Instantly, Catrina had thought the town was nothing more than the growth of a village built on religious fundamentals. However, after taking a trip to the Spook Valley Public Library, the discovery of the town's history proved otherwise.

The perfectly squared, red-bricked library appeared one of the tallest buildings in town. It boasted three floors and weakly loomed above the streetlights that illuminated the corner of Main and Century Streets. Its structure was third in height, just falling short of the police department and the six-story clock tower that reached above the second floor of the town's courthouse. Although the library contained three levels, the public used only two. Whatever information was housed on the third floor was both an urban legend amongst the town's children and a mystery to others. Only those who worked in the library were privy to that part of the town's mysteries.

Within a few weeks of her arrival to Spook Valley, Catrina Taylor had scoured the library for answers to the town's history. She had secretly prayed to her God and Goddess that she had not run away from the religious fanaticism of her parents and into a community possessing similar beliefs. Thankfully, Catrina had discovered an abundance of small publications that depicted Spook Valley's brief history. A man named Jamison Spook founded the town in 1971. Jamison was a future entrepreneur who thrived on building small communities that would eventually boom into treasured real estate markets. Catrina had no interest in learning more about Jamison or his short life, for she had her answers. The town was less than a half-century-old; it was somewhat modern. There hadn't been time enough for generations to carry on religious values. The residents of Spook Valley comprised a melting pot of religion and beliefs. Catrina realized that the townspeople simply didn't care for outsiders or those who bore no recognition in their easy day-in to day-out lives they had relocated here to enjoy. It came as no surprise. After all, those who moved to Spook Valley did so to escape the chaos of the city. The residents of Spook Valley were simply suspicious.

Catrina Taylor had recently become suspicious as well, but for a different reason. Catrina hadn't heard from Stefan since yesterday afternoon. She was aware that Stefan had planned to visit the desert alongside Firehouse Road after his shift at Laine's Music. This was a tradition he repeated since he'd begun writing his book of poetry. How she wished he had called her last night! She wanted so much to explain what had happened with Andy Sullivan, the owner of the Violin Street Tavern. She wanted to share in the reveling of sweet justice that was deserved by Andy since the first day she'd started working in that filthy place. Not to mention, the uneasy feeling that gripped at her stomach made it a priority to speak to Stefan last night. Surely, he got her voice message. Still, he didn't call her the entire day. She couldn't help but feel that something wasn't right.

Catrina pulled her long, auburn hair behind her shoulders, allowing the brown red strands to fall down the length of her back and just barely touching the carpet. It was getting late and she didn't have a shift at the tavern tonight, so she decided to do one more Tarot reading. This one, for Stefan.

After mixing the cards around, as if they were within an imaginary cauldron, Catrina shuffled the deck and focused her mind on Stefan and his comely face. She laid all the cards in a Celtic cross formation in front of her and began reading the images. The Lovers as his "immediate possibilities." Catrina smirked; *that could be me*, she fantasized. But as much as Catrina wished that Stefan's sexuality leaned toward the female persuasion, she was well aware that he preferred the company of men. She instantly realized that the rest of the cards in the spread referenced a disturbing atmosphere and could not understand why. After all, Stefan's readings were usually better than her own were. There was the *Tower* card—a blazing explosion ignited through the cracks of a cylindrical building—and that could be derived as chaos. Then there was the *Death* card that donned a skeletal reaper standing over an army of decayed bodies plagued by destruction. That card was in the place of the formation that signified what was before Stefan. Finally, the outcome, the last card. When Catrina turned the card over revealing *The Devil*, she knew that something was amiss. There was a churning in her stomach, a gut instinct made physical, as she destroyed the formation of the layout and began shuffling them again.

-2-

Stefan's body quivered as he felt the warmth of Breckin's fanged kiss draw blood from his neck. He knew not what was happening; he only lay in his bed and listened to the slurping sounds of his seducer as the pace of his heart felt as if it was slowing. Breckin's sensual game of foreplay gave Stefan a rush he had never discovered in all his life and he prayed that he could fulfill Breckin's pleasures and pains as well.

Breckin sucked from Stefan's neck and Stefan became dizzy and disoriented. His eyelids closed as his body melted into a state of bliss.

Beyond the sounds of his own heavy breathing, beyond the suckling sounds that caused his stomach to flutter with uncharted experiences, Stefan was alerted to the loud banging that emerged from the other room. "Wait," his raspy voice broke to Breckin. "I hear something. I think it's the door."

Breckin retreated from Stefan's neck and the illumination of the slow burning candle allowed Stefan to view the ruby stain of blood on Breckin's lips. Along with this observation, he gawked at the two abnormally long fangs that surpassed Breckin's lower lip. Stefan was forced to shut his eyes. He was like a frightened boy who had finally seen the monster from the closet emerge, and the monster sat atop of him, had caressed him, and seduced him in such a way he had never expected. Stefan's heart was compelled to speed up its frightened rate, but it couldn't do so as it pumped hard against the wall of his chest that shivered in goose bumps.

Struggling to remain calm, Stefan opened his eyes and chocked the ghastly image of Breckin as a figment of his imagination. After all, between last night and tonight, he had seen so many crazy things—the dimensional doorway in the desert, a demon in his bathroom mirror, and a man who was as real as he was and shared a love that had never been ignited in Stefan before. To Stefan's wish, Breckin's appearance was no different from the way Stefan remembered him—utterly mesmerizing to the naked eye. There were no fangs that protruded from Breckin's mouth, nor did the redness of blood decorate Breckin's lips the way Stefan grotesquely recalled.

"Stefan," Breckin spoke, breaking the silence of their first night together, "do not answer the door."

"Why?" Stefan questioned with a queer expression on his face. "Who's out there and what can he do to us?"

"I have a bad feeling about this, Stefan."

"I'm going out there," Stefan boldly remarked as he got up from the bed and pulled his shorts on. "You know, I do have *some* friends in Spook Valley."

Stefan exited the bedroom and halted as he got to the door.

THUD-THUD-THUD, the beating on his door continued. He placed his hand on the doorknob and began to unlock it when the next set of hollow thuds forced him to stop. He stared at the door and a sudden uneasiness plagued his stomach in tremors. Stefan became startled and nearly jumped out of his own body when Breckin came from behind and placed his icy hand upon Stefan's sweaty, naked shoulder.

"Please, don't open the door," Breckin implored him.

"Nobody can hurt us, Breckin; no one can enter, remember? That's what you said," Stefan affirmed.

Breckin eyes fell to the ground in despair, knowing that this wasn't completely true. He certainly knew what was out there; after all, he could veritably feel its presence. Once tainted by the Nightworld, one knew of the uncanny giddiness that swarmed about the head when another was around. Breckin knew that they had come here to recapture him and abduct Stefan. The minions would kill the two of them, subjecting them with agonizing stages of sheer pain while he and Stefan would slowly rot away in the darkness of their world, their energy diminishing bit by bit and molecule by molecule.

Stefan firmly grasped the lock between his thumb and index finger and as he turned it to the left, he looked back at Breckin who was avoiding his glance. Stefan turned the doorknob and forcefully pulled the door open. He stood stock-still in shock when he observed the two men looming over him.

The cloaked man spoke and Stefan witnessed fangs that erupted from the tall man's gum line. "Now the pain will begin," he calmly spoke with a British accent to his hoarse tone. Stefan was paralyzed with fear as he peered to the other man who held a stake high in the air, ready to plummet it into Stefan.

"NOOOO," Breckin projected his that were like a wolf's howls that ripped through the nighttime skies. "Stefan, hurry, shut the door!"

It was too late.

The stranger with the sharpened oak stake grabbed Stefan by his hair and forcefully pulled him across the threshold of the apartment. Stefan fell to the cold, cemented ground and watched in great panic as the man entered his home. *Breckin*, Stefan's mind raced, *he's going after Breckin.* Stefan quickly got to his feet.

The other one, the vampire, prevented Stefan from going to save his newfound lover. The creature roared in chaos and through the veil of unending hair, Stefan was exposed to the creature's green eyes that glowed with unnerving hunger.

The blood on Stefan's neck enticed the vampire as it grabbed hold of Stefan and dynamically drove its fangs deep into his jugular vein. The blood-lusting monster drilled deeper than Breckin, its fangs experiencing the pulsing rhythm of the vein. With Breckin, it was gentle and that was nothing compared to this. This was the most extreme pain Stefan had ever felt. The muscles in his neck hardened, attempting to keep the night creature from digging any deeper with his ivory-like weapons. *Breckin*, his dying mind called. Then he heard Breckin, that wonderful but seemingly long-missed voice that seemed to be fading in the distance.

"Get away from him," Breckin hollered with all his determined will.

Stefan felt a tremendous force knock him and his assassin down to the ground. Stefan's body felt lithe. He could not move and his vision began to blur. Yet, there was enough sight left in his eyes, enough light in his soul to observe Breckin heroically taking the oak stake that the other once held. The weapon was caked in blood and dripping gore and Breckin attempted to drive it into the creature that had attacked Stefan.

The vampire suavely escaped as he drew up his cloak, creating a black wall of material between him and Breckin, and blocking Breckin's effort. Breckin pierced the cloak with the stake. When he pulled it from the hole that had been formed, the cloak gently floated to the cement.

Breckin threw the bloodstained stake into the apartment and fell to Stefan's side. He picked Stefan up from the ground and carried him across the threshold and back into the apartment. Breckin wept, a tear slightly escaping his duct, as he knew all along that he had killed the other one. The other man sent to destroy the two of them was dead.

He focused on Stefan's lovely face, kissed Stefan's forehead, and shut the door behind them both. Breckin knew his lover's energy was diminishing and there was only one thing he could do. And that one thing would change Stefan's life forever.

-3-

Catrina left her apartment in haste when she couldn't get a hold of Stefan by means of telephone. Something was wrong; there had to be. It said so in the Tarot, and this was confirmed when Stefan didn't answer his phone. Her stomach folded in anxiety, shooting a tickling fear throughout her body.

She sped down Firehouse Road in her used Acura. Firehouse Road was dark and desolate—no streetlights to calm the fear of the inky world that enveloped her. No, there was nothing this way save for the desert that consumed the asphalt from either side of the road. Yet, this was the fastest way to Stefan's place.

Faster she drove and then, without warning, the image flooded her head. Seconds later, she slammed on the brakes as the image came before her in the beams of the headlights. The Acura screeched to a halt, and the car's mechanical screams infused the night.

At first, Catrina thought it a dog or a coyote. However, with a closer look of the vivid flash before her, she recognized it as a man. It was a man or maybe a sideshow freak because dark hair covered his body. Along his chest and his face and down his back, nothing but a body of short fur. And those eyes, those insidious eyes that blazed like molten lava.

She practically shrieked at the hideous sight, and then all at once it was gone, vanished from before her as quickly as it had appeared.

Was it all in her head or was it really there? Were the deserts of Spook Valley home to monsters? No, she rationalized; *it was something more than that. It was some type of vision.*

Catrina Taylor floored the gas pedal and raced down Firehouse Road. The entire time, her mind focused on Stefan and the feeling that he may be in danger.

-4-

Static.

It sounds like electrical scratches in the hollow night air. Lightning—charges of protons and electrons making love and creating a hue of indigo that has never been witnessed by the naked eye. Flesh forming, pouring upon the limbs as if the skin itself is melting and developing into hardening wax upon the bones and muscle. It hurts sometimes, when one crosses from the Nightworld and into the realms of Earth. Sometimes it feels like a million needles pricking all over the body. At first it begins as a slight itching and, within seconds that can only be measured in the Earth realm, the itching briskly leads to a horrible burning sensation as if one's viscera and soul are on fire in the pits of Hell.

He emitted from the portal, content with the success of crossing worlds. He felt good; his body felt free and uninhibited. The cold air of the desert brought out his animal instinct, made him want to make love to another creature. His flawless body kissed with the night in a tongue that was a mixture of both man and creature. Yes, make love to this all and feel an orgasm in the way he'd never experienced in the *Nightworld.*

He had his orders though, and this he knew. He had his target and had to carry out this horror. But with this horror, emerged a sense of freedom.

CHAPTER V

-1-

The man stood naked, hiding in the desert shrubbery that surrounded the Shadowood Apartments. He gazed down at his nudity, organ partially erect, as if he were taking an inventory of all his limbs. Yes, he had successfully come through the portal from the Nightworld into this realm and, yes, every toe and finger was intact and undamaged. His body had survived the transition and he was the man once remembered. Sadly, however, he realized that he was only half a man. The other half of him was something horrific and wild.

The whole man he had once been, the young man with an affinity for music, died back during the Summer of Love. He had no idea how long ago that had been or what year it was now. He had heard stories of the others crossing over into the Earth realm, had heard their returning tales of an age of technology where the cities were overgrown with towers of steel and glass, but this had been his first experience outside of the Nightworld since he was first abducted and became one of them. In the Nightworld, one must gain rank to cross realms and one must prove himself to his brethren. One must make it a point that he will not attempt escape if given access to the portal. The Order would slit such a being from end to end and torture one in the emerald fires should they try to escape them. And not only would he have to answer to the Order of Perennial Darkness, he would also have to answer to their god…his god…*Damia.*

All the souls of the Nightworld were connected to *Damia.* Sometimes, when the anticipating thoughts of escape became a mental image, the roaring voice of *Damia* forewarned him of utter damnation. The voice was like a bell being struck, as it vibrated the fragile inhabitants of the Nightworld and controlled attempting such flight. All of them heard *Damia*'s voice and he was their horror, their absolution, and the only reason for their existence.

"We exist to serve him," the man whispered, trying to assure himself of his obedience to the Nightworld before *Damia*'s bellowing voice declared it. *Damia knows all; he sees everything; he is beyond beast.* The man mentally spoke the words of trepidation that were his only defense against thoughts of escape and longings to fall in love.

The comforting breeze massaged his flesh, and he wondered how long it would be before the beast in him emerged. With his mission in mind, he studied, through the shrubbery, at the second floor apartment window where a lighted room played host to his targets.

-2-

Breckin cradled Stefan in his arms, rocking him gently like a newborn and examining the deep purple that edged around the puncture wounds on his neck. Breckin had washed the gashes with a warm cloth so that the dried blood would be less a temptation to Breckin's own bloodlust. With rest, Stefan would regain his energy. Breckin assured himself of that.

The two of them lay upon the plush carpet of the living room floor, waiting for one of their only weapons—the sun. Stefan made contact with Breckin's eyes.

"He's out there, you know," Stefan languidly spoke. "He's waiting."

"Shhhhh," Breckin calmly mouthed.

"Where did the other guy go?" Stefan asked, realizing the last time he had seen the partner to the vampire was before Breckin rescued him from the vampire's bloody kiss.

"He's gone; I killed him."

"Where's the body?" Stefan curiously inquired.

"Vanished. Gone. They are not part of this world, Stefan. Their bodies break down into nothing but a quick wisp of smoke and their souls go back to the Nightworld. They return to *him.*"

"Who?"

"Relax, Stefan. Please." Breckin shut his eyes. He mentally damned himself for being rescued from the Nightworld by Stefan. Yes, and it was his fault that Stefan was subject to this world of horror. He would never be able to right his sins, not even for an eternity in Hell.

Stefan's words attacked Breckin with angry inflection. "I thought you said we would be safe," he cried. "I thought that we had kept them from entering the apartment!"

Breckin couldn't begin to explain, but he knew that he would have to. Guilt fell upon him as he revealed a new chapter in this terror-filled, dissolute dream. "The other man, the one who came after me and I killed. He was human. He was a hunter for the Nightworld. You cannot stop a human from entering your home no matter how much evil runs through their veins. The thing that attacked you and wanted your blood, he as well, could have easily entered the apartment."

"What the hell is he? A vampire? Are you telling me that thing is a true vampire?"

Breckin took in a deep breath. "Yes. He is a vampire and we did nothing from keeping vampires from entering."

"Why not?"

"Because, I would have not been able to enter the apartment either."

Stefan witnessed fangs instantly shoot downward from Breckin's upper gums and press into his lower lip. "Oh, God, it's true," Stefan exclaimed. He tried wiggling away from Breckin with the only strength he had left, but Breckin held him with a power unmeasured to a human.

"Calm down! Please, Stefan. Listen to me. I'm not here to hurt you." Breckin sighed. "I cannot change what I have become. In the beginning, I wanted it so badly. This ultimate fantasy played in my head on a daily basis. But afterward, I realized it was too complex to comprehend. What I *did* understand was that evil existed within the survival. I learned that I needed blood to stay alive and I could only do so by hurting others, perhaps even killing them. It was this that I could never fathom in my once rational mind. But I am this way, Stefan. It cannot be changed."

Stefan was at a loss for words, yet he let Breckin hold him. Though he remained weary of Breckin's intentions, he had no other choice but to trust this man he was growing to love. He would simply have to be cautious around Breckin, watch his every move, and keep himself prepared should such an attack on his body be at the heart of Breckin's motive. "What about the other one, the vampire that escaped us? I know he's right outside. He's waiting and probably listening to every word we're saying."

"He's in the Earth realm now," Breckin offered. "We'll wait for sunlight."

"But you were out in the daylight and it didn't affect you," Stefan counterattacked.

"Some are immune and some are not."

"What if he is?"

Breckin gazed into Stefan's frightened eyes with a determination he had never felt before. For, now, Breckin had something to live for, somebody to love. "Then we'll have to kill him. We'll drive a stake deep into his heart. I have already done it once tonight. I will not hesitate to do it again."

Stefan eased his eyelids down, forcing the world in front of him to fade to black, and let out an exasperated sigh. Why couldn't it all be as it used to? Viewing the late night movies in black and white, writing poetry well into the early morning hours, and enjoying the freedom of being on his own—those luxuries once taken for granted were now detained by evil. Even the man Stefan so much loved was part of this dark adventure that his mind had opened. What possible hope was there left? Stefan couldn't answer his own questions and couldn't imagine when this nightmare would end. When could he get on with his normal, boring life in Spook Valley?

A light rapping on the door broke Stefan from his meditation. He bolted from his comfortable lying position and made an eager glance over to Breckin who already had the oak stake.

Together they stood and cautiously approached the front door. It felt like déjà vu to Stefan. It created a panic in his stomach, this broken record playing for the second time this evening. Would there be a third time? Could he change it this time?

The knocking persisted.

"When I nod my head," Breckin slyly planned, "pull the door open wide and stand beside it. I'll drive the stake into its heart before it has a chance to attack."

"OK," Stefan whispered. His heart pounded so hard he felt he didn't have enough breath to go any further.

On the other side of the door, Catrina Taylor continued to knock at her best friend's apartment. She knew he had to be there because she saw the light on in the front room. If there was anything she knew about Stefan Powell, it was the fact that he was a stickler for turning off all the lights should he leave anywhere.

Stefan grasped the door handle, his hands sliding on the brass due to the sweat that formed all over his palms. Breckin raised the oak stake high so that he had a clear shot at their adversary's heart. Turning the knob, Breckin gave the official nod to open the door.

Right before the lock clicked, a voice called from the other side. "Stefan? Are you home?" The knocking continued.

To his surprise and delight, Stefan slouched from the stiffening of suspense. "It's all right, Breckin. It's Catrina." And Stefan smiled in a way Breckin had never seen the man smile before.

"Catrina?"

"Yeah, she's my best friend."

Stefan opened the door and Catrina stood in the doorway, ginger hair spilling all about her shoulders. She exploded into playful laughter and embraced Stefan. "Why did it take you so long to answer the door?"

He apologized and gestured to Breckin.

"How have you been, woman?"

Catrina made a quick glance to Breckin. "Fine. Well, you know." She beamed with excitement. "I guess I was…well…gosh, I was just overreacting," Catrina explained, trying not to sound too overwrought.

"Oh, another one of those 'feelings'," Stefan said matter-of-factly and managed a fake smirk.

"I didn't know you had company," Catrina announced as she motioned to Breckin.

"Oh, where are my manners? Catrina, this is Breckin. Breckin, meet the only practicing witch in Spook Valley."

The three of them laughed. It was the first sounds of joy that emblazoned the night thus far. Catrina gripped Breckin's hand in a friendly shake.

Cold, so cold. Static, humming, and the sound of a hundred demons hushing her mind. That sound, it reminded her of the television blaring the after hours snow when she was a child. So loud and so insidious. And then, the vision from before—the man-beast with fur upon his entire body and those gleaming, evil eyes. More detail this time—snarled teeth and a roar that may have emitted from the furthest reaches of an undiscovered animal kingdom; a powerful howl into the night.

Catrina recoiled from Breckin's grip. She briskly forced her stare to the carpet. "I just wanted to make sure you were doing fine. I haven't seen you in a while," she tried lying.

"I'm fine," Stefan lied as well. He couldn't tell her. No, not her. He knew he wasn't all right, but Catrina worried too much at times and he didn't want to burden her with the night's events either. Still, he could tell the change of tone in her voice after meeting Breckin. Perhaps she was just a bit jealous of his gaiety. Perhaps.

"Well, I should get going," Catrina declared. "It's so late and all. Maybe I'll be by in the morning and I'll cook you breakfast."

She began making her way out of the apartment.

"That would be great," Stefan thanked. "I have to be to work by eleven though."

"It's not like the music store busy that early?"

Breckin's eyes shot up from his silence. This was the first time he'd known where Stefan worked. The thought excited him—to know that Stefan was as real as he was, and this was no nightmare that they lived. This was reality.

"Well, with the new Hellfire release," Stefan explained.

"Gosh, I wish that band would give it up already," she joked.

Stefan and Catrina chuckled, reveling in their true friendship. Before Stefan closed the door, she gave one final stare to Breckin. Breckin remained straight-faced and unscathed by the seriousness of Catrina's powerful gaze. In her mind, Catrina knew there was something ominous about that man.

Stefan locked the door behind Catrina and against the night. He and Breckin exchanged no words as Stefan retired to the bedroom in hopes of sleep.

-3-

Stefan lay in bed as he peered over to the digital clock on the cherry wood nightstand that read 4:43. *This is preposterous*, he thought. There was no need for Breckin to remain awake in the living room, keeping guard. Stefan felt that the creature he'd contended with would not return. Not tonight anyway. The sun would be rising soon. Besides, he couldn't get to sleep and he felt unsafe without Breckin by his side. That thought gave him ambition to get up and tell Breckin it was time to get some sleep through this whole nightmarish ordeal.

Stefan left the bedroom and, as he sleepily wandered into the living room, his eyes shot open and his heart raced to an uprising speed, almost breaking through the weakened mold of his body.

The vampire had returned! The creature stood away from him, pinning Breckin to the floor.

Stefan thought fast and scanned his immediate surrounding until he spotted the oak stake that Breckin had used earlier. His limbs were so drained that he could barely move; yet he used all the vigor left in his body to retrieve the stake. Breckin's immortal life depended on it.

Weapon in hand, Stefan tried running up behind the vampire. He wasn't surprised to find that his body wouldn't allow it. Between fright and battle, his body was beyond worn. With the last fuel of his adrenaline, Stefan had to mentally drive his sluggish frame toward the creature.

Breckin and the vampire struggled as every stride that Stefan made felt like three. The slowness of Stefan's heroism was for the better, as the vampire had no idea that he was approaching from behind. The creature tilted its head back, bearing fangs that were so atrociously long and foreboding that Stefan practically halted in his steps. Before the creature of the Nightworld had time to take the blood of his own, Stefan used his dead weight of his weakened body to fall with the stake. The blunt end of the stake knocked the wind out of Stefan as it was plummeted into the vampire's back. The monster jerked and buckled, making a cry to hell as Stefan was bucked into the air and roughly thrown off to the side.

Blood spewed in all directions from the vampire's ivory corpse. Thin sprays of crimson redecorated the apartment's beige-colored walls with a gory remembrance that immediately haunted Stefan. The creature's undead body floated into the air, levitating in agony as it wailed with deafening screams. In an instant, the carcass dissipated, leaving wisps of black smoke that thinned into the air.

Breckin jolted to Stefan's side, hauling him from the floor.

"Is he dead?" Stefan asked, out of breath.

"Yes. You saved my life."

"I love you, Breckin," Stefan abruptly spoke, his lower lip quivering in a becoming cry. It donned on him that he had just professed his love for a man he'd known less than forty-eight hours. But it felt right.

"I love you too," Breckin reassured him.

They held each other in the blood-bathed room. Stefan was appalled by the pungent odor of death; yet, there was a feeling of victory that eclipsed all of his senses. It was he who had slain the vampire! It was he, Stefan Powell, who had saved his newfound lover's life.

The fangs, the stake through the heart—those grisly sights brought concern to Stefan's mind. One day, would Breckin go through the same agony? Would his screams ring as helplessly as he decayed in front of the eyes of his own slayer? Stefan didn't want to imagine Breckin dead. On the other hand, Breckin would outlive him if he were cautious.

"Breckin?"

"Yes."

"Is it true that you'll live forever?"

"Yes, Stefan, it is true," Breckin answered, exhausted from the events of the night.

"I want you to turn me into what you are," Stefan blatantly said.

"What?" Breckin was instantly caught off guard. It was apparent that Stefan didn't know what horror also came with the gift of immortality. If it could be called a gift. "Are you out of your mind?"

"Breckin," Stefan proclaimed, "I want to be with you always. I don't want you to watch as I grow old and die. I need you, Breckin." He meant this.

As strange as it may have sounded, he did need Breckin. Breckin was the companion he had searched all his life. And now that Stefan had him, he did not let this mysterious man go.

Breckin understood where Stefan was coming from; for he loved Stefan just as much and wanted nothing to happen to him. Not to mention, if Stefan were to become a creature of the night, it would make him more powerful for future battles. It was a given that they had many battles ahead. After all, the Nightworld would stop at nothing.

"First, you must feed," Breckin tutored Stefan as he took his index fingernail and made a small tear into his own neck. Breckin firmly placed his lips upon Stefan's and gently pulled back, giving Stefan his last kiss of mortality.

"Take me away from this chaos," Stefan begged. He opened his mouth, accepting the metallic taste of Breckin's forever blood that spilled in generous drops of glistening ruby.

-4-

Catrina made it home safely, though her nerves were so tense that she wouldn't have been surprised had she been involved in a wreck. Along the way, she meditated to the God and Goddess, wanting answers of this Breckin character. Why hadn't Stefan mentioned him before and what exactly was it about him that made her tremble and feel cold?

Unlocking her apartment door, Catrina sauntered in and turned on the light. As she closed the door behind her, a gasp spilled over her lips. Upon the door, written in blood with a shaky, sharp script was one word. BEWARE. Next to the word, were four long scrapes upon the door that tore through the wood paneling. Scrapes or possibly claw marks made by some animal. Yet, still, there was one other thing, one revelation upon the door that sent chills throughout her body and formed gooseflesh upon her arms. One of the cards from her Tarot deck was pasted on the door. Catrina shuddered as she pulled it from the bloody stickiness that affixed it there. It was the card of *The Moon.*

Little did she know that, on the other side of the town, eternal love was being born in Spook Valley.

CHAPTER VI

-1-

The fiery rays of a morning sun peered over the dirt hills and illuminated the town of Spook Valley. The time was just after dawn. It was the time of the day when the barren lands of desert that encroached the town cast a brilliant orange of reflective heat from the hard dirt. The spring green silhouettes of cacti and yucca were like cardboard props that stood in their cutout forms against a possible setting of a vintage western film.

With the warmth of the sun came a serenity that fell upon the dehydrated land. The ginger and purple hues of daybreak extinguished the shadowy doorway to the Nightworld. Nowhere in sight was the monolithic, rectangular inkiness that hovered above the desert floor. Nowhere to be seen was the dark doorway that transcended time, dimensions, and bridged two worlds opposite in nature. Although the doorway was not visible to the naked eye, it remained in the same place Stefan had discovered it. It simply camouflaged, made invisible by the dazzling light of a dawning sun. The portal remained in place, for it would not close until the pact was executed. If *Damia,* the Order of Perennial Darkness, and the minions of the Nightworld had their way, the doorway would never close.

Three hours after dawn, Spook Valley was coming to life. Rolled up copies of the Spook Valley Daily were already delivered to the town's residents, lazily thrown toward the cement carports but landing in the dewy wetness of morning lawns. It was another weekday in Spook Valley and things were normal beyond the lives of Stefan Powell and Catrina Taylor. Traditional family men gave pecks on the cheeks of their wives, goodbye kisses, as most of them made their morning commute to other towns between the eighty-mile span to Phoenix. Jobs were scarce in Spook Valley. Unless one worked for the local government or was young and single, the town didn't hold enough job security to support a family. Spook Valley consisted mainly of locally owned businesses—two craft stores, one music store, a movie theatre consisting of two separate screens, a coffee shop, and a plethora of bars. The local restaurants that had opened and closed throughout the years couldn't compete with the professional service and franchise power of dining establishments in the neighboring towns. There was no economy in Spook Valley, no monies to be made. Thus, some of the richer family men of the town supported their families by making the lengthy drive to Phoenix, to their corporate, suit-and-tie workplaces. This was the law of the land. Spook Valley was a getaway from the growing crowds of the city; however, residents would always have to return to Phoenix for their needs. Independence was longed for but not conventional.

The wives of this traditional town packed their kids' lunches and sent their children off to the neighborhood bus stops where they would be transported to Edison Elementary School. The elementary school was centrally located near the town square where Main and Saguaro Streets crossed each other and marked the courthouse, police station, and a white-latticed gazebo. Within the gazebo, the bronze statue of the town's founder, Jamison Spook, held a frozen hand to its brow in a gesture of determined search to find the perfect site safe from the busy life of the city.

Jamison Spook had discovered the desolate land and developed the community of Spook Valley in 1971. Before expanding the area into what would be a new town eighty miles from the state capital, Jamison was an entrepreneur who resided in Phoenix. He made his money from the architectural designs he created for the hungry corporations of downtown Phoenix. Although the population of the city could view his abstract designs of unparallel angles, Jamison could not cope with his veritable overnight success and popularity. His name graced the city's papers and was well known in the surrounding suburbs. Jamison's ultimate dream had always been to create his own town, his own housing developments designed by his nonfigurative eye. After the development of Spook Valley, and after residing all alone in his ideal town for six years, Jamison Spook died of unknown causes. Although there were many more innovative ideas and blueprints to be introduced to society, Jamison passed on too early but was preserved as a legend.

Now, Spook Valley thrived in its isolation like an unborn in its mother's womb. The town was the focus of what would, one day, become another legend talked about, but never believed in the town records. For within the town's perimeter, another world thrived in its own dimension of darkness.

-2-

Stefan Powell awoke from his slumber, half-dazed and experiencing a hunger beyond what he comprehended. He lay awake in his bed, staring to the ceiling that was immersed in the yellow colors of daylight that peered through the Venetian blinds. Stefan felt lost, as if the past days of his existence were nothing real, as if they a blurry dream filled with images of love and monsters. Still, the residue of everything that had happened, nibbled at his thoughts—discovering the doorway (the Nightworld), the terrifying visit from two creatures hellbent on destroying him, and the embrace and love of Breckin.

Stefan turned his head to find Breckin peacefully asleep beside him, face precious with its sharp angles and ivory carved texture. Had the threatening thoughts of the past days not been present, Stefan would've been in harmonious content. True, Stefan was falling deeply in love with Breckin, but he also came to the realization that ever since he had saved Breckin from the threshold of the Nightworld, he had become the target to something unnatural. Something supernatural.

Straining to rise from bed, Stefan cringed from the bruised pain upon his neck. He exited the bedroom, leaving Breckin to his world of mysterious dreams, and entered the bathroom where he examined his neck in the mirror. On the right side of Stefan's neck, near the base, were two miniscule punctures in his flesh. Recalling Breckin's claim of being a vampire and of the night before, Stefan placed his hand over the wounds, covering it in disbelief. What did it mean? Was he now a creature like Breckin? And that craving, that awesome hunger for something more than a meal in his rumbling stomach. What was it that could alleviate that craving? Only blood?

Breaking his reverie of inquiries, Stefan was alerted by the wavy motion of the mirror. It was like an ocean of silver undulating in a vertical movement. Only another sign, another remembrance of his new life. Just a tease, yes, a way for the Nightworld to let Stefan know that it was still there, waiting and watching. Reminding him of the demonlike creature he had once seen in the same mirror, Stefan turned from the reflective sea of glass. He remained calm and stepped from the bathroom. When would all of this end? His mind would not cease pondering the many questions.

Stefan jolted from Breckin's presence awaiting him in the hallway.

"Good morning," Breckin greeted.

"Yeah," Stefan replied. "Morning. I have to get to work soon."

"Oh, yes, of course." Breckin paused as he recollected Catrina's words the night previous. "The music store, right?"

"Yeah." Stefan fell silent. He couldn't find the words, any iota of conversation to exchange with Breckin. And how odd it was—the ability to not engage in discussion with the one he loved.

"I know what you're feeling," Breckin broke the tense calm. "You have that craving, don't you?"

Stefan didn't speak. He nodded his head.

As if answering Stefan's mental questions, Breckin said, "You need to feed; you need blood."

Blood, Stefan thought. *I am inhuman, an animal. I am creature and no better than those monsters that tried taking my life.*

"You wanted this. You wanted me to give you this, remember?" Breckin asked. Stefan noticed how Breckin seemed to be reading his thoughts, how every response from Breckin was a question or concern from his mind that Breckin answered.

"Maybe…I didn't realize…"

"Don't worry, Stefan. You will not have to kill anybody. You can feed from me."

Breckin approached Stefan, brushing his naked body against his lover, and bit deeply into his wrist. A fount of crimson gushed from his wound and Breckin brought his wrist to Stefan's mouth.

Stefan hesitated at first, tasting the blood of his lover with a cautious tongue, then he placed his mouth over the gash, suckling the red fluids of life. The taste was salty, almost metallic at first, but then the flavor of Breckin's blood was like that of a bittersweet merlot. Stefan savored every drop he could as the hunger within him subsided.

Breckin was elated with his new forever partner. Now, somebody that he loved and that loved him and that would live in a world of eternal pleasures—boundless adoration. Without warning, a thunderous voice pervaded his vampiric mind. It was a voice that he knew just as he knew his own self. *Damia*—the voice of the god whom he could not escape, not even with his rescue from the Nightworld. That voice! That haunting and boisterous voice. *You belong to me! You cannot escape. When you are captured and brought back to the Nightworld, you will answer to me. I will rip your soul apart.*

Breckin shivered as a tear ran down his porcelain face.

-3-

Catrina fluttered her eyelids open. Her eyes burned and felt sticky from the lack of sleep the night before. She glanced over to the tarot card she still held in her hand, still tacky from the blood that pasted it to the door. *The Moon.* She was awake until the wee hours of the morning, pondering the warning on her front door scrawled in blood: BEWARE. What did it mean? What did *any* of it mean? The warning with the Tarot card, the vision of the hideous man covered in fur and, not to mention, this Breckin character whom she had just met last night. Something wasn't right. There was a disturbance in the universe somewhere, possibly a break in Spook Valley's quaint life.

She arose from her bed, her lengthy hair disheveled and tangled all about her small shoulders. *It has to do with Stefan*, she rationalized. But what was it about the *Moon* card? What did it mean and where in this new web of mystery did the card and the warning on her door play in? From her bedside nightstand, she pulled open a drawer and consulted her *Witches Almanac.* After perusing through the pages of the calendar in the booklet, Catrina discovered that the full moon was only a night away.

She needed answers today. She had to know what was going on. Not only for Stefan's sake, but also for her own. Somehow, she was now implemented in a horrifying enigma that she did not invite. It knew *her* though. It knew Catrina Taylor, the practicing witch, and had entered her home, leaving a bloodied word of caution as a calling card. Was she an obstacle of some terrible plot? She did not know. What she did realize was that all of this started the night that she had that gut instinct regarding her best friend, Stefan Powell. And that, she knew, was the key to all of this. It was Stefan that she must visit, away from his newfound friend, and get answers.

Catrina quickly dressed with the intent to discuss this with her friend. He would be working alone at the music store today. And, if anything, that was a start.

-4-

Laine Young, a forty-something hippie that moved to Spook Valley ten years ago to make his dream a reality, owned Laine's Music. Laine had always wanted to own his own music store ever since he could remember. At one time, before he discovered Spook Valley's absence of such a business, he had spent two years developing a business plan and pitching it to many of the financial institutions in Phoenix. It appeared, however, that with the powerful franchises in the city, Laine didn't stand a chance with his own business. As one loan officer bluntly denied, "There is nothing you can offer to consumers that they can't get cheaper at one of the 'big boys.' There is no room for profit." With that, Laine discovered Spook Valley. Once he moved to the small town, his music store was opened within months. Since then, Laine had made enough money to support him and even hire two other employees. One of those employees was Stefan Powell.

Stefan was perusing some of the same alternative-style titles Laine adored when he met the young man. Laine learned that Stefan was like him: Stefan had a dream and determination with his own poetry that Laine had with his goal of opening a music store. Laine instantly liked Stefan, was attracted to him, and when Stefan mentioned that he was looking for work, Laine instantly hired him. In the three years that Stefan worked for him, Laine knew he could come to depend on the young man. He entrusted him with opening and closing the store and he confided in Stefan's handling of the monies of Laine's Music.

Laine relaxed in his home, as he had nothing to fear with Stefan opening the store this morning. Maybe he would give Stefan a call later this afternoon and check how the sales were.

Stefan was making room in the bins for the shipment of Hellfire's newest compact disc. Through all the complicated and apprehensive situations of the past couple days, he still had a job to do. And Laine had told him to make sure there was plenty of space for Hellfire's latest release. It would sell out in no time—that is what Laine had insisted to Stefan.

Stefan felt charged, full of energy, and he attributed this to the blood he had tasted from Breckin's body. In just under two hours, between assisting customers and answering the phone, Stefan had cleared a sizable area for the new Hellfire release.

The jingling of a copper bell alerted Stefan of a customer entering. Save for himself and the person who had just entered Laine's Music, the place was empty. Stefan observed the young man who had entered the store and was instantly magnetized to him. The young man had jet black, short-cropped hair, broad shoulders crowning his physique, and a smooth, cinnamon face that emitted a pleasant, virgin smile.

"Can I help you?" Stefan offered.

The young man spoke. But it was more than his smooth, harmonic voice that entranced Stefan. Stefan had never seen the young man before, given that he had known many of Spook Valley's residents who'd regularly visited Laine's Music. "Yes," the singsong voice requested, "Credence, The Doors, or maybe some Strawberry Alarm Clock."

"Oh, a classic rock enthusiast," Stefan pinpointed.

"Classic?" the young man questioned. "Oh, yes, I do indeed have a weakness for 'classic' rock n' roll."

"I've never seen you here before. Are you new to Spook Valley?"

"Yes," the young man answered. "I just moved here from Los Angeles."

Stefan admired this man. The inflection of his voice was like an undiscovered rhythm and the young man's lips appeared soft and tantalizing. "Why not Phoenix?"

"What?"

"Why didn't you move to Phoenix? I mean, considering it is a city comparable to L.A."

"Oh, I wanted to get away from the city actually. You see, I'm a songwriter."

Stefan perked up. *Another writer of poetry*. "I'm a writer," Stefan mentioned matter-of-factly. "I write poetry."

"Really?" the man questioned with genuine amazement.

"Yeah, I'm working on a collection titled 'Dark Hearts.'"

"Sounds intriguing."

Stefan felt quickened by the man's compliment of his anthology's title and then introduced himself. "I'm Stefan. Stefan Powell. Resident of Spook Valley for, let's see, three years now."

"Hello Stefan. My name is Aaron Dabney. Resident of Spook Valley for a day."

The two of them laughed. There was more than a connection of friendship; there was a physical and spiritual connection. Stefan was as instantly attracted to the man named Aaron Dabney as he had been to Breckin. In the past days, it seemed that all of the beautiful people poured forth, and it was a longing revelation to his desire.

The door to Laine's Music announced another customer as the jangling of the bell joined the laughter of the two men. When Stefan glanced over to the entrance of the music store, he recognized Catrina. "Hey, Catrina."

She moved toward Stefan in a heated pace as if she were angry with him. "We have to talk," she whispered.

"Just a moment," he told her and directed his attention back to Aaron. "The classic rock is at the end of this aisle," he gestured with a pointing finger. "Do you want me to show you?"

"No," Aaron replied, "I'll find it on my own. It was nice meeting you Stefan. Perhaps we can get together soon."

"That'd be great," Stefan announced. "Let me know if you need any help finding anything else."

"I will." The newcomer to Spook Valley disappeared down an aisle of compact discs.

"What's up?"

Catrina didn't know how to ease her way into what was on her mind, so she spilled it forth. "What's going on?"

"What do you mean?"

"Who's Breckin? I've never seen him in town before. When did you guys meet and when did you decide to move him in?"

Stefan was caught off guard and didn't know how to explain it to Catrina. Although her mind was very open, he couldn't find the words to explain everything that had happened over the past two days. "Gosh, Catrina. I have so much to tell you."

Catrina Taylor stood attentive and, at the same time, her eyes shot a glance to the customer in the store whose gaze made its way to the conversation she was having with Stefan.

-5-

Breckin couldn't stand it anymore. Damn that voice! The voice of *Damia* continued to molest him and fill his world with a driving timpani beat. *Damia*'s voice informed Breckin that he would pay for his escape from the Nightworld, that there was no escaping him, and that he should give up. In addition, he should assist the Nightworld with the capture of Stefan. The time was coming, the time of the pact come to pass, and Stefan would take a major role in its execution.

"NO!" Breckin shouted. He would not give in. *Damia* could invade Breckin's thoughts all he wanted. Still, Breckin refused to surrender. No, not now, not any longer. He had given a portion of his life to the Nightworld and was determined to give no more. They would have to kill him first, yes, desecrate his body among the fiery landscape of the Nightworld. And Breckin would put up a fight to the very end. Of that, he was sure.

There is no escaping me, Damia's voice bolstered. *I will give you one more chance to change it all before I decide to devour you.*

Although Breckin eagerly covered his ears with his hands, he couldn't help but wonder if *Damia*'s bargain may save him from doubtable errors he had made.

-6-

Darkness permeated the immeasurable lands of the Nightworld. Two of the six from the Order of Perennial Darkness—Saint Trace and Saint Collin—knelt before a stone altar. They donned brown robes with hoods concealing their true faces. The small flames that encircled them in their ritualistic setting swayed eagerly in a dance of the forbidden. Their hands were placed flat upon the altar as they communicated with *Damia.*

The time has come, Damia roared. *The doorway between our worlds must remain open.*

Saint Trace confirmed first. "God *Damia*, this will come to pass."

The two that entered on the last eve have been destroyed, and I have my concerns for our once-brethren called Breckin.

The second voice, the voice of Saint Collin, cackled in a gurgled hoarseness. "Breckin is no match for us, God *Damia*. If he will not comply with your word, he will be destroyed."

And the other we have sent. I have my doubts about him as well.

"Aaron will not fail us," Saint Trace confirmed.

Damia roared with an inflection unable to be measured by that of any storm of the Earth realm. Surely, in his godliness, he was resolute in taking over the Earth realm. There was nothing more standing in his way/ *Damia* would stop at nothing in any dimension to make sure that chaos had a new land to prevail.

CHAPTER VII

-1-

Chance. He said he would give me one more chance to change it all. To change it, yes! But at what cost? Breckin's breath was heavy as he tried to will the thunderous voice of *Damia* from his mind. Sweat beaded and dripped from his forehead, from his smooth, hairless chest, and infused his palms that he clasped over his ears. It didn't matter how much Breckin wanted the voice to disappear and return to its own realm of molten fires and endless night. For it was that he, like the other minions of the Nightworld, was mentally connected to *Damia.* All of them, every last creature and abductee turned monster, seemed to have an invisible thread tied from their souls to *Damia*'s own soulless existence.

Surrender to me, Breckin, and I will make your torture less agonizing. Your pain will be nothing compared to what it could be once I come through the doorway and take over your precious Earth. There is no escaping me, Breckin, the boisterous voice of *Damia* cautioned.

True, Breckin realized, there had never been a successful escape from the Nightworld. The violators had always been caught, always punished and tortured in the most horrific ways, as the clans of the Nightworld bore witness and were forced to watch. This is what happened when one attempted to escape and didn't serve God *Damia.* Indeed, these were to be the carnival of horrors he would face. And, when and if Breckin was captured, what would his agony be like? What terrible ending would his soul have to endure? Would his body be flung into the oceans of liquid fire that illuminated the crimson black world? Or would his body be tormented by means of being stretched to ripping point in four separate directions by the skeletal horses that gaited through the realm with their empty sockets and clacking bones? Still yet, would his physical body be slowly shredded with the precision of a death artist as each layer of skin, muscle, and viscera were stripped away in painful awe? All these thoughts plagued Breckin's mind, along with the bellowing roar of *Damia*'s voice. He could do nothing but tremble. Cry and tremble.

I'm demanding you to take my hand back into the Nightworld, Breckin. Is that such a horrible thing to ask? Is it that awful for you to take back the hand of the God who has ruled over you, who has given you sustenance when your body hungers, who has graced you with powers unimaginable? And all I ask in return is that you give Stefan Powell to us. He opened our doorway; he is to be the sacrifice for the clashing of the Nightworld and the Earth realm. You know this as well as I. Damia's voice was softer in its inflection, yet still authoritative and overbearing.

Breckin couldn't endure the mental demands of *Damia.* In his heart and immortal soul, he knew he had to. He could not surrender, no! And he would not give Stefan to the Nightworld! He did not want the Nightworld back in his life and he was repulsed of the hell on Earth that would transpire should the door between the realms remain open forever.

But that voice! That thunderous rhythm of a timpani solo that rumbled on and on; it seemed he could not escape it.

"Would Stefan know that it was I who betrayed him?" Breckin yelled to the atmosphere of Stefan's apartment, already feeling alleviation from the bellowing voice of *Damia* and, at the same time, a pang of guilt invaded his stomach.

-2-

Catrina could not believe what she was hearing from her best friend as they stood conversing in Laine's Music.

Stefan had explained the whole ordeal of the days past. From the demon he saw in the mirror, Breckin's vague tale of capture three years previous, the Nightworld and what he knew of the "pact", his attack from the vampire the night previous, to the confession of what Breckin had turned him into.

It wasn't that Catrina was skeptical. After all, she was a practicing witch. However, everything that Stefan had told her was too much to take in all at once. It was like a system overload of the indiscriminate synapses in her brain. In the same instance, it made perfect sense of her vision and the warning scribed on her door in a monstrous script. All of it, this whole mystery was unraveled to her and Catrina felt she could learn from it, understand it, and possibly help Stefan and his new friend, Breckin. Yet, she could not comprehend the last thing Stefan had told her, about his being a creature of the night. *Nosferatu, drinker of blood, you are not permitted to cross the threshold of my home,* she couldn't help to think. But she could not distance herself from the only person she had befriended in Spook Valley. No, not Stefan. Catrina couldn't simply forget of Stefan's claim and abandon him. She was already involved somehow, and that was obvious from the cautioning word that she found bloodied on her apartment door. All that Catrina could do was begin to understand, crack the riddle like a sleuth of the supernatural, and put an end to all this madness. And it was madness. It was a horrifying dream unable to be awakened from and a heart-racing reality turned sour.

"So you're telling me that you are a vampire?" Catrina asked, feeling stupid and naïve for attempting to understand.

"Yes," Stefan replied. "I suppose I am."

"And you will live forever? Do you fear the Cross? How is it that you are able to exist in the sunlight?" The questions began pouring from her rational mind.

Stefan explained it to her the way in which Breckin had explained it to him. All vampires were different, of different bloodlines and distant generations. What may kill one vampire, may not affect another. He needed her to understand and he wanted nothing more than the continued friendship they had always shared and cherished.

Catrina glanced over to the only customer in the store, the same man that had left Stefan in suspended conversation when she had entered Laine's Music. The young man's eyes were fixed upon her and a chill raced up Catrina's spine, causing her to involuntarily spasm.

"What's wrong?" Stefan questioned.

Catrina casually gestured to the man with her eyes. "Who is that guy?"

"His name is Aaron, umm, Dabney I think. He just moved into town from L.A. He's a songwriter," Stefan anxiously added.

Something about the man disturbed Catrina. Perhaps it was the way he kept an eye on the two of them as they conversed. Or maybe it was the way his eyes stared her down, as if she were a threat to some possible relationship between him and Stefan. Even still, it may have been the way his ears perked up during certain portions of Stefan's explanation of events as he told them to her. There was a similar uncanny feeling she felt the night before when she met Stefan's friend, Breckin. This led her to her next inquiring thought.

"What about Breckin?"

"What about him?" Stefan queried with a subtle hint of defensiveness to his tone.

"There's something about him I don't like. I felt it last night when I shook his hand."

"You probably just picked up on what you didn't know last night. Now that you know what he is and about the Nightworld, I'm sure that uneasy feeling will subside."

"I don't know," Catrina attempted to agree. "Maybe your right." However, in her mind, she knew that Breckin could not be trusted. Stefan may have fallen for Breckin's charm and good looks, but Catrina made a mental note to be cautious around the young man.

"OK," Catrina continued to decipher the mystery of the warning that continuously haunted her mind like a stalker's threatening, poison-pen letter. "What does the moon…or…the *full* moon have to do with any of this?" At that same moment, she shot a glance to the customer, Aaron, as the sound of compact discs hit the linoleum floor.

"The *full* moon? I can't help you out there. We can ask Breckin. He may have a better idea than I do."

From out of nowhere, Catrina spoke the words that she felt ashamed to ask of her friend. "Do you love him?"

Stefan was caught off guard and practically gasped from his best friend's words. "I think I do. That's why I decided to have him change me into what he is. I do not want to lose him, Catrina."

"How do we stop all of this?"

"I'm not sure," Stefan responded.

A wave of nervousness swallowed Catrina's body. What the hell was happening in Spook Valley and, furthermore, was there any way to stop this "pact" that Stefan had mentioned. Was there such a way from keeping the alleged doorway between two worlds from remaining open for all time? *Action had to be taken*, she rationalized in her thoughts. And, still, there was the moon. What was about the moon and the warning on the door? Perhaps that was the most important piece of the puzzle thus far. It was the one thing that called to her more than a potential hell on Earth. The enigma drove deeper into Catrina's mind, until the rest of Stefan's story became nothing but secondary priority. The moon. It was an inevitable calling to her, a mission to be executed by her graceful moves and her materialistic, Wiccan mind.

"I'll be over tomorrow night for dinner," Catrina announced.

"Dinner?" Stefan quickly recalled the plans he had previously made with her. "That's great. I'll cook dinner for us all."

With that, Catrina hugged her friend, experiencing a slight tremble as she felt the iciness of Stefan's neck brush against her chin, and exited Laine's Music.

Before the door closed behind her, she gave one final glimpse at the newest resident of Spook Valley. She could have sworn that his eyes reflected a fierce ruby color. She thought this—possibly imagined this—but wasn't sure. Just like the last two nights of her life.

-3-

Stefan began replenishing the "New Releases" bin that contained the latest compact disc release from Hellfire. Stefan studied the cover of the band's third release, taking special notice of the *doorway* at the top of the stairs that led from the artist's depiction of Hell. *If only they knew.*

He had forgotten about Aaron, who must have been perusing the classic rock aisles of the store for over two hours. Stefan all but jumped when Aaron placed his hand upon his shoulder.

"I didn't mean to frighten you," Aaron cordially apologized.

"No…I mean…you didn't. I'm just on edge lately."

"No problem, man. As I said earlier, I would like to see you again. Perhaps…while you're not working."

Stefan was enamored by Aaron's request. Aaron, with those luscious, varnish-colored eyes and a drop-dead gorgeous smile framed with bee-sting lips. Stefan felt an animalistic urge within himself, a tingling that inundated his entire body and his stomach like some junkie-rush from the tip of a fervent needle at the end of a chamber full of heroin. He could practically imagine taking Aaron home with him, stripping Aaron's muscular frame of its clothing, and making rough love to him. Yes indeed, to touch that inviting neck with an impassioned tongue and eager teeth—just a taste of Aaron's tempting flesh. That flesh could only taste sweet, sweet as the man who stood before Stefan. No. Stefan had Breckin at the apartment. Breckin who had given Stefan the treasure of eternal life and, with that, undying love.

"Stefan?" Aaron asked, breaking Stefan from his daydream fantasy of lust.

"Yes, we will get together soon. I'm working tomorrow. Same time," Stefan offered.

"Then I'll be by tomorrow," Aaron announced, slight smile on his lips.

That boyish face. Those beautiful lips. Just to kiss them, thought Stefan. "Alright, I'll see you tomorrow. Oh, did you find anything you wanted?" Stefan observed that Aaron's hands were empty of any purchase.

"Nah, I'll come back by tomorrow. I was too busy paying attention to you."

Stefan was flattered by Aaron's remark, and that was the comment with which Aaron left him in suspense.

"By the way," Aaron curiously spoke upon exiting. "That girl, the one you were speaking to."

"Catrina?"

"Yes. Catrina. You're lucky to have such a beautiful friend."

"Thanks." Stefan viewed Aaron's departure from Laine's Music, all the time imagining what it would be like to embrace Aaron in the heated moment of lovemaking.

The remainder of Stefan's day, after Aaron left, went by too quickly to measure. Customers began to trickle into Laine's Music for Hellfire's newest CD. The owner, Laine Young, called around three o'clock to inquire about the sales. Laine had told him that Hellfire's latest release would be a hot seller and he was right. Stefan had to fill the bin twice within a three-hour period. Laine hit the nail on the head, once again, and Stefan was glad that Laine had ordered as many copies of the disc that he had. After all, Stefan didn't want to hear people bitching how they couldn't get a copy of the CD and then have to put up with the comments of customers having to travel to Phoenix and give their business elsewhere.

Before he knew it, it was ten minutes until five o'clock and Ricky, Stefan's relief shift, had entered Laine's Music.

"Keep this bin full," Stefan instructed as he pointed to the "New Releases"

section. "Hellfire is selling like crazy."

"Figures," Ricky snorted as he ambled through the double doors that led to the employee room. "Pussy band." Ricky obviously didn't think too much of Hellfire or their latest release.

Stefan counted down his register drawer, zeroed out on his paperwork, and impatiently left the music store in anticipation to get to the apartment and see Breckin. Stefan needed to make love to Breckin, to cure the burning in his organ that had been aroused by Aaron. But, even through the short drive home, south on Firehouse Road and making a left onto Century Avenue, where the Shadowood Apartments stood in all their stucco and glass glory, Stefan could not keep his mind off the face that he had been enraptured by in the music store today. Aaron's face—the face of angel cast from the City of Angels. That face called to him, invited him to pleasure yet to be discovered, and would become an image that superseded all others in his life. Temptation—how magical and addicting it was.

-5-

Night fell and the deep purple, once again, consumed the daytime skies with midnight colors.

In the Nightworld, Saint Trace lowered the hood of his cloak and revealed a sardonic smile to Lillian. His features were skeletal, almost feline, with parched, yellow flesh that clung to his bones as if a tight layer of masking tape held it in place. Saint Trace's eyes were sunken into his head and created a hollow ring of purple above his high cheeks and below his forehead. He was hideous and exquisite all the same. He was the treasure of an abstract artist's desire, a beauty to be fucked and, yet, never to be seen after the fornication.

Lillian stood by her horse, her beast of pet pleasures, consisting of fleshless, yellowed bones and an insidious, big-toothed grin. How she loved the bony texture of its back between her legs, its rigid surface teasing her clitoris and exciting her with each fleeting gait. The sinful delights of the Nightworld, how she longed for every one of them and revered in them as a child discovering the cries that would bring its mother in with a bottle of milk. She tapped the flank of the undead creature and observed as it ran off between the ultraviolet lakes of molten juices. Its bones giving a dull sheen of orange on off-white. Lillian stared at the already distant creature with her dead, black eyes. Lillian was an eternal minion of the Nightworld; known as Lillian the succubus, the demonic seducer of human men.

"You have your orders, Lillian," Saint Trace affirmed.

"Yes," she replied in a smooth sexual voice of tenor saxophone bliss. "Capture the one called Stefan and stop the other, the girl, from interfering with God *Damia*'s vision."

"She is very intuitive, this one called Catrina," Saint Trace cautioned.

"Her soul is ours," Lillian remarked. "If she will not bow to God *Damia*, then she will be destroyed." An appetizing yet subtle grin permeated Lillian's bold features and then she stepped into the inky blackness of the doorway. The world in which she had visited before summoned her like an inviting lover ready to please with an organ of enormous size and thrusts of stamina.

Static.

Molecules disintegrating, fissuring, and reforming.

Successful entrance into the Earth realm.

-6-

Breckin closed his eyes as his tongue burrowed into Stefan's mouth. It was like nothing he had ever experienced before from Stefan; it was like the virgin kiss of a one-night-stand. Breckin imagined a world with only Stefan and he—another planet, a distant realm, full of butterfly kisses and serpent licks. The voice of *Damia* didn't find its way into his thoughts and Breckin endeavored not to think of the possible bargain between him and his once-god of the Nightworld.

"I missed you," Breckin said in a heated, untamed breath.

"I want you," Stefan retorted. He placed his hands on the cold skin of Breckin's chest, feeling the curves that he had grown accustomed to and playing with erect nipples that he had teasingly bitten during hardened foreplay. A gripping between thumb and index finger; a pinch, oh how it filled Stefan's body with the invigorating juices of aching, sexual adrenaline. A lick with his tongue to Breckin's neck, brisk nibbles with his upper and lower canine teeth, and a savoring of porcelain flesh in his mouth. Stefan's hand moved downward, over a flat, hairless stomach and onto Breckin's semi-erect organ that felt warm to his touch and like the texture of crushed velvet. Rub with an anxious hand, making it harder, and kiss deeper so that the tongue can graze the throat. A true kiss. A lover's kiss.

Breckin responded with roving hands that found their way beneath Stefan's t-shirt. He anxiously pulled the cotton fabric over Stefan's head and began kissing about Stefan's sculpted chest and neck. *God Damia and the Nightworld do not exist here; it is only he and I. It is only a world of uncharted possibilities and neverending love.* Breckin's lapping tongue made its way to Stefan's jeans as he avidly unbuttoned and pulled the pants down so that he could taste Stefan's organ with his lusting kisses. To his liking, Stefan became instantly firm and inhumanly bulged within Breckin's mouth. Yes, amazing and without boundaries, an Italian tower reaching toward the heavens in absolute tribute. Breckin bobbed his mouth up and down Stefan's rigid cock and could feel the soft presses of growing veins abrade his lips.

Stefan's head fell back in ecstatic gesture and he moaned in sexual content. All the while, he imagined Aaron's face and Aaron's voluptuous mouth upon his organ. At the same time, he imagined Breckin. It was as if the two comely men in his life competed in the flesh and in his mind as well.

Stefan and Breckin would eventually move from their positions. They would relocate to Stefan's bedroom where the two of them would make love all through the peaceful night, each with his own secret thoughts eating away at the desires of the fantastic. For now, however, they were two bodies beneath a sky full of guiding starlight. They were in a world all their own, in a world of sex undiscovered. A world without vengeful monsters.

-7-

Valerie Saunders waited outside Violin Street Tavern until 2:45am. The stars of the early morning lit up Violin Street and all the two-story buildings of Towne Central in their bright shimmer. Her shift had ended almost an hour ago and Rodney, her boyfriend, was late for the third time this week. He had to be screwing some bimbo. Either that, or he was too stoned to notice the time. Regardless, she wasn't going to wait for another hour to pass. Surely, she could walk back to her apartment. It was only a half hour walk at the most. Straight down Violin Street, until she got to Century Avenue—the Desert Dawn Apartments weren't that far from the Tavern after all.

The one thing that did trouble Valerie, however, was the fact that there were no streetlights between here and Century Avenue. Violin Street was desolate of anything between here and the apartments. It was simply a two-lane road with nothing but desert surrounding it. Darkness. It reminded her of a time when she was ten years old and her stepfather would lock her in the hallway closet for being bad. Damn him! Son-of-a-bitch! Valerie was just a child and in the uncomfortable blackness of the confided closet. Hangers reached down from the overhanging darkness like some bogeyman tangling its horrible fingers through her hair. Bastard! How dare he put her through such trauma!

Valerie was sick of waiting and cared not of the darkness she'd instantly built her courage to walk through. She grabbed her blonde strands of shoulder-length hair with both hands and wrapped a rubber band around them, pulling them into a tight ponytail. Valerie slung her purse over her right shoulder and began walking.

The journey had been silent and her mind had been flooded with mental projections of her stepfather's punishments. Darkness coiled itself around her, enveloping Valerie in its blue-black hues and forcing her heart to skip beats each time she heard the sound of a snake's rattle. To be safe, she strode down middle of Violin Street, the middle of the road of which she barely made out the dashed center line.

Almost there, Valerie anxiously thought as she could view the lights of the Desert Dawn Apartments in the distance. She tried looking at the watch on her wrist but could not make out the time.

A sudden breeze fanned the wisps of her flaxen bangs and brought numbness to her earlobes. Valerie came to a halt and heard the sound of footfall nearby. The steps were even and made the sound of dirt beneath them. The desert around her! She began walking faster, heart beginning to pound in her throat. She realized that the sound of the footsteps matched the pace of her own. Once again, she stopped in her tracks, looking all about Violin Street and the surrounding area. From beyond the reaches of Violin Street, Valerie heard a growling that could only be described like that of a coyote or a mad dog. As her heart raced faster, the pit of her stomach contracted in nervous convulsions.

Valerie searched the darkness of Violin Street for a hopeful coyote. She anticipated in circles and dizzied herself from the constant revolving. A crackle of dry shrub made itself present as Valerie attempted to mark the source of the noise. She saw nothing.

Suddenly, from behind the frightened girl, *it* emerged with no remorse. Its elongated, hideous claws slashed chunks of flesh from her neck as her bloodcurdling scream was replaced with a choking gurgle. Valerie fell to the street and grasped for her neck as it became harder for her to breathe. The creature lunged atop of her, tearing with its lengthy nails at her arms and legs. Valerie experienced the creature's blistering, acidulous claws cleave through her supple breasts and slice downward, puncturing her lungs and filling them with her own bloody liquids. The pain was unbearable; it hurt so badly and her wounds felt as if they were being chewed. The mauled girl pulled back her hands and observed the blood running that warmed her arms. As she dropped her limbs to her side, before everything went black, Valerie was saved from her suffering by the gruesome face of her assailant. Once she saw it, her heart burst into an unexpected halt.

The glimmering asphalt of Violin Street became colored in ruby.

The beast let off a howl toward the waxing moon and the resonance of its inhuman cry echoed throughout the deserts of Spook Valley. Tomorrow was the full moon, a destined moment of full transformation. The beast howled again, the lamentation of its life expressed through a boorish whimper, and a small percentage of Spook Valley's residents flicked on their porch lights.

The howling was something new to Spook Valley. The only person who'd witnessed its bellows of defeat became nothing more than a shredded corpse that lay in the middle of Violin Street.

CHAPTER VIII

-1-

Catrina Taylor dreamed of monsters and moons, of savage beasts roaming the streets of Spook Valley and globular pearls that illuminated the night. One monster, in particular, called to her dreamy mind, like a haunting addiction—a creature that appeared as a man covered in dark, coarse fur and bore jagged teeth stained with the pink residue of blood.

In the dream, she was in her apartment and heard the wood-splitting sound of vicious scratches at her front door. Catrina's subconscious would not answer the door and would not leave the bed upon which she sat. Fearful tears streamed down her renaissance features as she clasped her hands over her ears and burrowed her face into her lap. No matter how hard she'd tried to escape the vehement scratches, rhythmically scraping at the front like a deadly metronome, Catrina knew she had no other choice but to face it. Face the creature, for there was no escaping it. There was nowhere to run from its animalistic grips. Those horrible scratches upon her door...they would not cease! They taunted her mind, plunged her into a game of cat and mouse. Memories of childhood bogeymen awaited beyond the door.

The nightmare continued as Catrina finally arose from her bed and cautiously exited from her room into the hallway. Once there, her gaze shot down the short length of the narrow walls to find the creature inside her own apartment. The monstrous animal was turned away from her and Catrina watched in awe-striking silence as the creature scrawled a bloodied word of caution upon her door. BEWARE. Afterward, the furry beast placed its elongated claws upon the surface of the door and grated the wood with the tips of its nails. The wood of the door split and curled beneath the monster's right hand of evil. It came to an abrupt halt. The creature paused, holding stock-still. Catrina's heart skipped a beat as the beast slowly turned toward her. She gasped for air and would have screamed had her lungs held such breath. However, all sounds were muted—nothing in that world of damned silence, save for a low growl from the creature that now came face to face with her. Saliva dribbled from its sharp teeth and the eyes of the beast were somehow familiar to Catrina, though she knew not from where. It lunged forth and as Catrina used all her might to produce a scream, a dreadfully hollow and powerful howl emitted from the beast's mouth. The howling encapsulated her world, its timbre imploding unto a center into which Catrina was surrounded. Only then, at the point of a potentially violent attack on her body, did Catrina jolt from the dream with her heart practically begging to explode from her heaving chest

Awake now. Catrina's body was flooded with the warming sunlight that spilt through the half-open blinds and fell upon her ivory flesh. A profusion of sweat traveled along her feminine curves, from the crevices behind her knees and beneath her arms. Pulling her lengthy hair from her face, Catrina noticed the dampness of the ginger locks that weighed them down. *A nightmare. Yes, only a bad dream.* However, Catrina knew there was more to the frightful event than a simple wayward plunge into the dark caverns of her subconscious. The dream had meaning; perhaps it was another vision. And the howling, she recalled. Didn't she hear a similar howling late into the night previous? That could have been the catalyst that provoked it, surely. What's more, the eyes. She recollected the eyes of the nightmare creature and was absolute that she had identified those same eyes recently. But where? Those fierce ruby-colored eyes—how they consumed her waking moments.

She arose from her bed, slid into a velvet robe of burgundy hue, and made an exit from the bedroom.

Instantly, she recalled the same gesticulation in comparison to the dream. Carefully she stared down the narrow length of the hallway, at the front door where the inhuman marks still branded it, and was set at ease when she found that there was no beastly man that awaited her.

As she advanced to the living room, Catrina Taylor lurched from the scene before her. Upon the mirror, in the same hurried and bloodied script that she had discovered on the back of her entry door, was a message. It was a sentence of caution that sent her insides into a panicked frenzy. Although the blood appeared dried, rivulets of the substance that poured down the reflective glass while each letter had been formed with a sharp finger, made the mirror look as if it were shattered in red. The admonition read: *I warned you. You must leave town before it is too late.*

When was too late? Then, suddenly, it struck Catrina. Tonight. The full moon.

-2-

Stefan awoke before Breckin. He could still feel the salts of their cold flesh intermingling and making scientific love to each pore. Away from the grasp of his vampiric lover, Stefan escaped the tangle of sheets that molded their bodies together and headed for the kitchen in his proud nudity. It was as comfortable as before, to prance around the apartment in the nude, just as comforting as he found it to be with Breckin. Their lovemaking the night before was like a wild fantasy, a new realm undiscovered by Stefan's tongue and genitals. Only in an erotic novel, could Stefan find such sexual bliss and sensual movements.

The aroma of coffee filled Stefan's nostrils with hunger. The coffee pot's timer had gone off a half hour earlier and was ready to be poured. Stefan retrieved a cup from the cupboard, poured himself a small amount of the liquefied caffeine, and stirred in two teaspoons of sugar. He pulled open a drawer from the breakfast bar, opposite of the coffee pot, and recovered a spiral notebook and pen with which he took to his seat upon the glass surface of the dining room table.

Sipping the coffee once, Stefan took no time in turning the green cover of the notebook as he began to write.

From the Journal of Stefan Powell

This journal is now acting as a tool to keep record of the latest oddities in my life. I hope it to assure my sanity when this entire, unusual ordeal has passed.

I never knew of madness until I met it on a desolate, desert landscape that surrounds this town. Only minutes separate the point of my inspiring land of escape and this small town that is beginning to live up to its name: Spook Valley. It was in that desert that I collected revelations for my morbid poetry. It was in that desert that I could leave the boredom of this thirst-for-life town. It was a place where I could gather thoughts absent from clatter created by small town gossip. And it was in that same desert that I subconsciously opened a doorway to another world. It is a world where chaos rules the dreaming lands and its foreboding inhabitants define their perfect victims in this reality as being believers in the "unknown."

That evening changed my life. The sunlight became my anticipated friend and the dark, twilight hours became a recurring nightmare from which I continuously pray to awaken. In that same night, I rescued a young man named Breckin from the evil clutch that had held him for nearly three years. He has become my lover, my portal to sanity, and soon to be my mentor.

What is human? Every man, woman and child on this Earth is human (save for the monstrous minds that inhabit the heads of serial killers). Most humans have families, dream at night, and have a certain life expectancy. As odd as it may sound, I cannot claim to be human anymore, although the emotions are still there. I will witness friends die around me (even the youngest in age); I do not dream, for dreams are a part of my everyday life; and I will never die (not a natural death anyway). My humanity left when Breckin turned me into what he is: a vampire.

I cannot blame Breckin for what he has done to me, for I wanted this fantasy when I found it to be true about him. I longed to be with him always, never seeing a day death might separate us. But now, regret storms my fearing mind. I'm not sure what it is I'm supposed to do in this new life I have received. The act of drinking blood repulses me and I know nothing about the vampiric race. I can only depend on what Breckin tells me and teaches me in the three years that he has lived this immortal life.

Furthermore, I feel I may have fallen in love with Breckin too quickly. I came to this conclusion when I met a young man named Aaron Dabney at the music store yesterday. The moment I saw him, I was instantly attracted to him. He, too, is a writer of words—a songwriter—and he moved to Spook Valley from Los Angeles to pursue the serenity of a small town for his writing.

Aaron reminds me of myself, or the way I was before I begged Breckin to change me. Aaron is trying to make a name for himself and pursue his dreams, just as I had so long ago wanted. I'm hoping that I have truly made a good friend, somebody not from this town and a person that may, one day, understand me.

If I see him at the music store today, I was considering inviting him to dinner. Catrina also mentioned that she might come by the apartment tonight for dinner. On the other hand, I don't know if it would be too obvious—my infatuation with Aaron, as he sits across the dining room table from me.

On an entirely different note, my life was absent of disruption from the Nightworld last night. Breckin says that is what the other "dimension" is called by its minions. I'm still very confused about what this "Nightworld" actually is. Was it always around and in what way can it be stopped to prevent the doorway between the two worlds from being open forever? Sometimes, I think of going out to the desert where I discovered it. Just to see it again; just to assure that I am not crazy. But then, the monsters that the evil world contains petrify another part of me. I feel that the way Breckin and I conquered those creatures that tried to kill us the other night may prove that we are stronger than the Nightworld. Breckin disagrees, saying that they are patiently waiting to catch us off guard. He told me that the Nightworld knows what scares us and each night that we subdue its attempted grasp, it will only strike more powerfully until it breaks down our resistance.

As I've stated before, I have never known such madness.

Stefan dropped his pen as Breckin languidly entered the room. Breckin's skin was flushed with a pasty luminescence Stefan had never witnessed before. Breckin veritably glowed.

"Are you all right?" Stefan immediately asked.

"I'm fine—a little weak from not feeding since the night I fed from you." Breckin sighed as he pulled a chair to the dining room table next to Stefan and noticed the closed notebook. "Are you working on your poetry?"

"Uhhh," Stefan hesitated, "no. I'm just starting a new journal. You know…ideas and stuff like that." He suddenly felt a wave of shame pass over him for not telling Breckin the truth. But Stefan knew that it would break Breckin's heart if he were to read what he had actually written. Especially, the paragraph of regret for what Breckin had turned him into.

Stefan's curiosities raced back to what Breckin had mentioned earlier, about needing to feed. What Breckin meant was "drink blood." After all, he was creature of the night, a vampire who, like any other such species, needed to fulfill that craving, that awesome hunger. Automatically, this set off Stefan's mind into wondering how *exactly* Breckin would accomplish this. What's more, who would be the unknowing person grazed by Breckin's fanged kiss? Stefan feared asking Breckin these questions but, most of all, he feared that he too was just like his undead lover.

"I have to be to work in an hour. I'm having Catrina over for dinner tonight. Oh, and I may invite someone else."

Breckin's eyes shifted in wonder at Stefan's cryptic announcement. "Someone else?"

For the first time, Stefan could sense a tinge of jealousy in Breckin's words; Breckin's inflection was different, more serious, and filled with a slight despair.

"Yeah, Aaron Dabney. Some guy I met at the store yesterday. I think you'll like him. He's from Los Angeles and writes songs. He's a really nice guy," Stefan affirmed.

Breckin ran a hand over his forehead as if to wipe the sweat of worry away. "So, then, is there anything I can do to prepare for the feast tonight?"

"Just be your wonderful self," Stefan said as he smiled, arose from the chair, and planted a tender kiss on Breckin's lips.

-3-

The headaches persisted every time Aaron thought of Stefan. The sharp spears drove into his forehead like exquisite knives of eternal pain.

Aaron had grown to like Stefan. Stefan was a gentle young man, a beautiful man with almond skin and boyish curves. Aaron wanted Stefan in the way he had never wanted a man before. He imagined making love to Stefan—their mouths melting into each other's, their bodies moving in rhythms untainted by the most brilliant of sonatas, and their organs swelling and pulsing and driving into each other throughout a night of magic swirling about them.

Aaron was finding it difficult to hurt Stefan, capturing him for God *Damia* and the rest of the minions of the Nightworld. If escape from the Nightworld were possible, Aaron would have ejected himself from the dark plain of everlasting shadows long ago. No, he could not find it in himself, not even in all his beastly form, to threaten Stefan with dangerous motives. On the other hand, what other choice was there?

The throbbing. Aaron's head pulsed in shear agony as his imagination created the simulations of him and Stefan. Another throbbing, but this filled his ears with an audible sound, like that of knocking. And then, the headaches subsided, God *Damia*'s weaponry took a break as Aaron continued to hear the knocking on the motel door. Who knew he was here? Surely, Stefan wouldn't have gone through the trouble to track him down, would he? With a minute's shred of elation and, after the door was opened, a despairing pang of loss in his stomach, Aaron greeted his visitor. It was Lillian.

Lillian's hair was long and curly, jet black in its color, and spilt down her back and over her shoulders in a wave of volume despised in this present time. *This present day*, Aaron thought, and the only images of the Earth realm that came to mind were that of rock bands, getting high, and cult leaders. Lillian was bone thin, petite, yet had the power of a warrior, this Aaron knew from knowing her in the Nightworld. She was powerful, she was a force all her own, and she had no conscious. Emotions would not scathe her, would not weaken her from killing any man and then playfully squirming in his blood and viscera afterwards. Lillian was truly a monster and, as far as Aaron had known in his four fretful decades in the Nightworld, she was the oldest of the minions next to the Order of Perennial Darkness and God *Damia* himself.

"May I come in?" Lillian's voice was sensual and soothing, like a musician's tenor that romantically flowed from his saxophone.

"Of course." Soon, all images of making love to Stefan vanished from Aaron's mind. "What are you doing here?"

Lillian took a seat on one of the motel room's recliners, brushing the wisps of black bangs that hung in her eyes. "Saint Trace sent me. It appears that God *Damia* may have doubts about your carrying out the orders to capture this man, Stefan. I guess they didn't want to take any chances given that he and Breckin destroyed the other two. We're wondering, or I suppose I should say *I'm* wondering, why you are biding your time, Aaron."

Aaron couldn't look Lillian in her eyes, those deep, obsidian eyes that intimidated him with their entire monstrosity. "Biding my time?" Aaron asked with a tone of defensiveness. "I don't understand. I only crossed over two nights ago."

"And you have already had one encounter with Stefan. That was the perfect opportunity to take him, Aaron!"

"It was daylight and at his workplace," Aaron attempted to rationalize.

Lillian insanely cackled at his response. That was the one thing she despised about the "children" of the Nightworld, the ones who had not grasped and comprehended the power and awesome wonders of the Nightworld. The new ones. "Aaron, I don't think you understand." She sat up in straight posture from the recliner and stared deep into Aaron's soul.

"You, I, God *Damia*, the Order, and all the rest of the Nightworld have a chance to rule over the Earth realm. We have an opportunity to take over a planet so vast and diverse. Do you feel we should let anything get in our way, especially something as petty as abducting the one who will allow it all to happen during his shift at work, during the daylight hours? Aaron, the human race has no control over us; we overpower them in every possible fashion. They are weak; they cannot fight back because we are the unknowns; and their weakness is that they love. They love and that gives them a sense of guilt to anything harmful they do. We must capture Stefan. We must get Breckin as well, or kill him should he not come to us willingly. There is a woman. Her name is Catrina. Have you seen this woman, Aaron?"

Aaron's psyche was in awe from the strength of Lillian's words. "Yes, I have seen her. Yesterday, at Stefan's place of work. She appears intelligent and strong."

"She will be no match for us, Aaron. The two of us, Aaron; we will make a devastating dream into reality. Together, there will be no stopping us. Cast away your doubts. You will bring me close to Stefan and to this Catrina woman. You will introduce me as a friend from out of town…or a sister; yes, a sister. We must act quickly so that the Order can cross over and we can perform the ritual."

Nodding his head, Aaron began thinking of kissing Stefan again. *A kiss before dying.* All of a sudden, stabs of pain penetrated Aaron's lower back, his stomach, and his jaw line. Stretch. His anatomy would stretch and twist into something monstrous before the end of the next morning. Tonight. And the moon would be shining at its fullest.

-4-

At 3:29pm, Breckin fell to the linoleum of the kitchen, his vision blurring and a massive pricking of pain travelling through his already dead veins. Sweat poured from his forehead as he attempted to get back on his feet. He mentally cursed himself for ignoring the bloodlust for this long. As a vampire, Breckin simply couldn't win the struggle of this hunger consuming him.

The spell had passed and it felt as if there was room to breathe once again. But for how long?

Stefan was at work and would be home within a couple of hours. Home...and he would be having guests over this evening. Still, Breckin knew he must make the time to satiate his hunger. That time must be tonight! There could be no more procrastinating, no more pretending to be human.

An unsuspecting someone on the lonely streets of Spook Valley would become a target.

CHAPTER IX

-1-

Night was coming for Spook Valley.

The final gazes of daylight peaked over the mountains in the distance, spilling hues of purple and orange over the town as if to capture the land in all its glory. The moon was on the horizon, grand and overpowering in its full cycle. So close to the Earth was the globular monstrosity that it appeared the two worlds could collide at any time. The day bowed out to the encroaching night and, soon, the fiery breath of the sun would be diminished, leaving only a brilliant luminescence that could be witnessed one night of each month—the full moon.

However, tonight's full moon would be different for select lives of Spook Valley. Catrina knew this as surely as she knew the bloody writing on the door to her apartment and, this morning, upon her mirror. Warnings. Both cryptic messages implied that she remain at a distance from Stefan. And the cards, the Tarot, warned of the full moon. In her gut, Catrina knew that she must be with Stefan tonight. She had to accompany him throughout tonight. For the safety of her best friend, yes. Not to mention, to understand his latest claim of being a vampire. How much could she believe? Was Stefan *truly* a vampire, a creature whose sustenance depended solely on the blood of others? Or had he been sucked into some lie, some brainwashing and manipulation, from his live-in lover Breckin? Catrina would get to the bottom of this. Tonight, dinner with Stefan and Breckin. This was her chance to confront Breckin and find out what the hell was going on.

Catrina Taylor slipped into some old Guess jeans and pulled a cotton Burgundy shirt over her head. The shirt was one of her favorites as it was adorned with a silkscreen picture upon the front of The High Priestess tarot card from the Rider/Waite deck. Catrina observed her small hands for stains of blood. Clean, yes! The blood from the mirror had been scrubbed off and her hands were no longer dyed in pink. Who was trying to warn her anyway? And, why, with messages scrawled in blood? To scare her? True, Catrina had been shocked by the bloodied script. Then again, she had her own beliefs in Wicca, her own convictions to the God and Goddess that she felt would protect and guide her.

Catrina's apartment became flooded in darkness as the day was coming to a close. She walked across the living room, flicked on the switch to the floor lamp, and searched for her keys. She would be leaving for Stefan's soon.

It was already 6:30pm and Ricky had still not shown up for his shift at Laine's Music. Stefan double-checked the penciled-in schedule that was a waste of time for the owner, Laine, to fill out. After all, with only two employees, Stefan and Ricky knew the hours they worked by heart and they never altered them. The schedule confirmed that Ricky was supposed to show at 5:30. He was an hour late. This was typical of Ricky, as of late; the pattern of his tardiness only grew with each passing day. First, it began with Ricky being five minutes late, then twenty minutes, soon a half hour and, now, here he was an hour late. Sure, Ricky was young, Stefan rationalized, but what was the sense of having a job if he couldn't show up for his damn shift?

The day at the music store had been quiet for the most part. There were some latecomers for Hellfire's latest compact disc. There had been an older couple from San Diego, passing through on their way to Phoenix, who stopped by to find a gift for their daughter who they were anxious to visit. The couple had told Stefan that their daughter was into "light, new age" music. Stefan offered them the new disc by Enya. Then, of course, Aaron had come by the store. Aaron, a beautiful descendant of Adonis, surely. Aaron appeared different today; he seemed more on edge or hurried. Although, Aaron seemed rushed and Stefan didn't have much time to speak to him, Stefan still managed to give him an invitation to dinner tonight at his place. Aaron gratefully accepted.

And what would transpire from the dinner tonight? Tonight, Stefan and Breckin and Aaron and Catrina—a gathering in the making, a feast that Stefan somewhat feared only because he was in love with Breckin and falling for Aaron. Would it be noticeable, his affection for Aaron? Stefan had a good idea that he wouldn't be able to keep his feelings for Aaron from Breckin. However, there was no use in worrying about that now. Right now, Stefan's concern was whether or not Ricky was going to show up for work. God forbid if Catrina and Aaron showed up at the apartment before him. For some reason unknown to Stefan, Breckin had not made a good impression upon Catrina. Stefan only hoped that the dinner tonight would serve as an icebreaker to everybody's doubts and uneasiness.

At a quarter to seven, the brass bells over the entrance to Laine's Music jingled. When Stefan looked to the door, he found Ricky rushing in and heading to the back of the store.

"Sorry I'm late man," Ricky loudly called.

"It's your paycheck," Stefan responded nonchalantly.

Ricky emerged from the back room and was attaching his name badge to his shirt. "I was up all night last night. I didn't get to bed until noon today." Ricky laughed. "Has it been busy?"

"Not too bad," Stefan said as he began counting down his cash drawer.

"Any more hype over that stupid Hellfire CD?"

"Nah. A couple of people came in for it this morning." Stefan was inserting the profits of the day into a pouch and began filling out paperwork in a hurry.

"You in a rush?"

Stefan didn't answer as he was briskly punching numbers on the 10-key and finished the paperwork. "The drawer's at a hundred, I zeroed out for the day, it's all yours. Oh, yeah, I'm late for dinner."

Stefan marched out of the store as Ricky yelled, "Later."

The night air was warm and inviting as it lightly breathed upon Stefan's neck. Suddenly, his stomach cramped. It wasn't a sharp cramp, the type of pain that would double one over; however, it was strong enough to force him to halt in his tracks. He turned to look into the window of Laine's Music. Past the cardboard signage and toward the back of the counter, he viewed Ricky. Stefan's gaze studied Ricky's disheveled, dirty blonde hair, the kid's tiny forearms and lanky form, and his thin lips that Stefan would never dream of kissing. The taste of hunger produced a rivulet of drool that spilt over Stefan's lips as his focus on Ricky made its way to the boy's neck where a vein in the shape of a wishbone pulsed uncontrollably through the flesh. The cramp and hunger soon subsided. Stefan tightly closed and reopened his eyelids. What was he thinking?

He made his walk along the sidewalk of Firehouse Road, turning up Main Street where his truck remained parked alongside Laine's Music. As he unlocked the truck door and slid into the driver's seat, Stefan felt as if he were being watched. He glanced about the area quickly and, soon, dismissed this feeling too.

-3-

Breckin had just finished preparing salad when he realized that Stefan was late. *He should have been here an hour ago*, Breckin thought. Dinner was almost ready, probably another fifteen to twenty minutes. The water was rolling to a boil and all there was left to do was cook the pasta. He had also set up four places at the dining room table. Two for him and Stefan, one for Catrina, and another one for the mysterious man Stefan had mentioned he would possibly be inviting to dinner. Who was the young man and, what's more, why did Stefan immediately invite him over after just meeting him?

The thirst for blood roiled Breckin's insides, invited him to leave the apartment and go on a hunt for the substance. The sanguinary craving had tantalized Breckin all through the daytime hours and he had thought of leaving earlier. But the daylight was no time to find an innocent from which to draw blood. No, he would wait until later this evening. After the dinner, after the guests had left, and, more than likely, as Stefan slumbered in their bed. Breckin couldn't do such a thing in front of Stefan and have Stefan witness his attack for blood. Yet, he knew, eventually, that Stefan would soon need to satiate his own hunger. Until then, Stefan could get by on Breckin's blood. Soon, though, that wouldn't be enough. The thirst for blood in a vampire only gets stronger with each passing feeding, and for one to neglect that yearning would be for one to take a stake to his own heart.

A knocking on the door broke Breckin from his deliberations. He instantly panicked, for Stefan had a key to the front door and he knew not which of the guests had arrived before Stefan. Mentally, he prayed that it was Catrina, for he had already met her. As for the other, Aaron, Breckin would feel uncomfortable around him, as he had not yet been introduced to the man.

Opening the door, Breckin saw Catrina standing, almost in shock, to be greeted by him instead of her best friend. She barged in without saying a word, carrying a bottle of wine, and looked about the living room.

"Where's Stefan?" she asked.

"He hasn't got back from work yet."

"Oh, I see." Catrina relaxed upon the sofa and handed over the bottle of Merlot she had purchased for the evening. "This is for dinner."

"Thank you," Breckin said as he took the bottle and gently placed it on the kitchen counter. "And thanks for coming as well."

Catrina gazed at the walls and ceiling of the apartment. Although she had been here many times before, she studied the architecture of the home as if it were her first time in the place. Catrina's eyes inadvertently met up with Breckin's. "I came because Stefan invited me."

Suddenly, she realized how cruel she was acting to Breckin. "I'm sorry. It's just that I don't know you that well." And this was true. God was this true. She dare not finish the rest of what was on her mind—how she felt a cold feeling, a shiver of uncertainty that caused the flesh over her spine to be raised in goose bumps. Perhaps Stefan was telling the truth about Breckin turning him into a vampire. Perhaps Breckin indeed was a "creature of the night." Perhaps. And how would she broach this with Breckin, how could she get up the courage to discuss the plethora of ideas that were invading her mind and causing her daylight hours to be filled with nightmarish visions?

A silence fell between them, a silence of not knowing people who have entered the life of your best friend.

Breckin broke the muted atmosphere of the apartment. "Actually, to be honest with you Catrina, I was glad it was you and not the other guest."

Other guest? Catrina thought. "Oh, someone else will be joining us tonight?"

"Yeah," Breckin said as he sat down in the recliner, feeling a bit more comfortable that the two of them could engage in some type of conversation. "I think Stefan said his name was Adam…wait, no…Aaron. That's it."

"Aaron?"

"Stefan said it was some guy he just met at the music store."

Instantly, Catrina felt uncomfortable. She repositioned herself upon the couch and appeared upset by Breckin's announcement. Aaron? Yes, Aaron, the man in the music store yesterday. Aaron, the one with the inquisitive eyes. Those ruby eyes, she recalled. The color she may have imagined before exiting the store yesterday. Ruby! Like the eye color of the creature in her dreams. Or, Catrina pondered, were they visions? That's where she had seen those sinister eyes before!

Now, Catrina was in a bind. She certainly didn't get a good impression from this "Aaron" character, but she didn't know how much she could trust Breckin either. Could she entrust that Breckin would hear her out, hear the story of her latest visions and the enigmatic and gory warnings that she had recently encountered? Should she mention and share her feelings of uneasiness regarding Aaron with Breckin? Were the warnings meant for her, cautions of Breckin or Aaron? Who was the beauty? Who the beast?

And here it was—the moment of truth. Catrina mentally prayed to the God and Goddess that she was doing the right thing. With that she said, "Stefan told me about the two of you."

Breckin didn't flinch whatsoever. "I'm sure he did." And he gave off a small chuckle.

"I mean, about your being a vampire. About you turning him into one. About the Nightworld and how he saved you."

Breckin froze. The cat was out of the bag, the cards were on the table, and the truth had entered the room in a game of cutthroat. There were no more mysterious glances, no secrets left unsaid. Catrina knew who he was, who he *truly* was, and there was no more denying or hiding behind an erroneous mask.

"Did he tell you everything?"

"Everything that he knows. But I have questions of my own."

Breckin and Catrina were immersed in conversation and talked to each other as friends reunited for the first time in years. The discussion was unlike a discussion anybody would ever have. It consisted of mayhem and monsters, of enigmas and the supernatural and, most of all, of discovering the true nature of who Breckin was to Catrina and vice versa. Halfway through the chat, Catrina began to empathize with Breckin and how he had come to be the monster that he was. She began to understand Breckin, understand that the extrasensory sensations she developed while being near him were not necessarily bad at all. They were plain and simply, intuitions of something otherworldly and alien to the realms in which she existed. And, although the conversation revealed much to Catrina about the Nightworld and all their intentions, there was still the question of the "pact," the promise to bridge the Nightworld and the Earth realm together for all time to come. How were they to get answers and conquer this evil if Breckin didn't even know of the conditions revolving the "pact?" Needless to say, Catrina found herself growing fonder of Breckin with each passing sentence. Still, there was a threatening sentiment there that she could not refute. Perhaps it had nothing more to do with his routine to exist. But when Breckin had told Catrina about his recent mental encounter with God *Damia*, she was convinced that this was the source of that threatening sensation. *Breckin must remain strong,* she thought. For, she knew, that he could easily turn traitor against Stefan. And it was all in the hopes of saving himself from eternal damnation. For this, Catrina could hardly blame Breckin. Yet, on the other hand, she would not see her friend betrayed by anybody.

-4-

In the midst of Breckin and Catrina's discussion, Stefan walked through the door of the apartment. He was elated to see the two of them sitting together and talking as if they had been acquainted for some time. This was a good thing. That meant that Catrina did indeed approve of Stefan's relations with Breckin.

"Sorry I'm late," Stefan announced, walking into the living room. "Ricky didn't get in until an hour after his shift."

"That's all right," Breckin replied, "Catrina and I were just talking."

"Hey Stefan," Catrina said, rising from the couch and giving her friend a firm hug.

From there, Stefan made his way to Breckin and planted a small kiss upon his lips. Catrina, feeling somewhat embarrassed by the affection, shot her eyes to the ground as the two men hugged.

"Is dinner done?" asked Stefan. "Aaron hasn't shown yet?" And with that question, Catrina and Breckin both bridged a brisk gaze to each other. "Are you two all right?"

"Yeah," Catrina perked up.

"I was going to go ahead and began serving dinner," Breckin relayed to Stefan and Catrina. "Do you think your friend Aaron will show soon?"

"He said he'd be here."

The three made their way to the dining table as Breckin began to serve the salads and Catrina uncorked the wine and began pouring the blood red Merlot into their glasses.

The chime of the doorbell sounded in the apartment and all three of them knew it could only be the long-awaited Aaron. Sure enough, as Stefan opened the door and invited the unseen stranger in, Aaron emerged into the apartment.

Catrina slightly cringed, grabbing her glass of wine and taking a large gulp. All the while, she made the attempt not to look so obvious as she eyed Aaron. Catrina looked into his eyes for a split second but could not view the possibly imagined ruby irises that she could have seeing the day before.

Breckin glared up and immediately came to an abrupt stillness. This was Aaron; this was the mysterious man, in the flesh, that Stefan had said Breckin would like so much. Of course, he was attractive—blonde wisps framing the sharp contours of his androgynous face, pectorals and biceps that stretched the cotton fabric of his shirt, and alluring eyes that could captivate a sinful population. Aaron appeared familiar to Breckin, as if the man were from his barely remembered life in New Orleans, long before Breckin's own abduction.

Stefan introduced Aaron to Catrina by saying, "You've already met Catrina."
Catrina nodded to Aaron and Aaron commented. "Yes, the ravishing best friend."

"This is Breckin."

The psychic feeling crawled over both Aaron and Breckin as the flesh of their hands met and shook. It was that revelation that announced another from the Nightworld. Surely, Aaron had felt it, for he knew all about Breckin—about his escape from the Nightworld and his relationship with Stefan. But, Breckin could not pinpoint how he knew Aaron. Had he known him long ago, before his abduction by the Nightworld, when he was a regular man, a man without supernatural impulses?

"Have we met before?" Breckin asked, his brow moving in curious wonder.

"I'm sorry, I don't believe we have."

Regardless of Aaron's answer, Breckin knew that he had seen him before somewhere. And that feeling, that sensation of others from the Nightworld, why had it consumed his body? Was Breckin experiencing this feeling because of Aaron, or did it mean that there was another nearby, ready to strike.

"Pull a seat up to the table," Stefan offered to Aaron. "We were just beginning to eat."

They proceeded from the salad to the main course and, all the while, a hush of sorts pervaded the dinner. Instead, the dinner conversation was not made with speech, but with eyes. Catrina kept eyeing Aaron, trying to get some unnatural message from the God and Goddess about him, some warning or a sign of assurance. Breckin's eyes observed the lust and tension between Stefan and Aaron, trying to deny that any such sexual desire could exist between them. Stefan's gaze went between Breckin and Aaron, the two men he had grown attached to, and, every now and again, he smiled at Catrina in that friendly smirk he was prone to give her. Complete silence, save for the high-pitched squeaks of the fork tines scraping plates. Soon, the doorbell rang again. Everybody's dinner appetite came to a standstill.

"Oh, gosh," Aaron said, breaking the symphony of hungry mouths and sipping lips. "I'm so sorry, Stefan. I forgot to mention that my cousin was to arrive in town tonight. I gave her your address and invited her over for dinner."

Stefan was caught off guard. He hadn't even known about any of Aaron's relatives, let alone a cousin. Wouldn't he have mentioned earlier during there meeting at the music store, during Stefan's invitation to Aaron for dinner? Then again, Aaron seemed in frenzy and they hadn't the time to say much at all. "Ummm, well, go ahead and answer the door Aaron."

Catrina blasted a curious glance to Breckin and he returned her inquisitive look with one of his own.

They all stood from the dining table as Aaron attended to the door. The woman came into view, standing in the doorway, with black strands of hair that spilt all about her shoulders and bosom. The woman attempted to cross the threshold of the apartment, and then swiftly pulled back her leg. *They have protected the house*, she thought. She could not enter unless invited by Stefan. Warlocks were banned from this house, and so were demons. The woman gave a scornful look to Aaron, as if he should've immediately read her mind. And if Aaron could've read her mind, it would say: *Have Stefan invite me in! Finish this!*

Catrina, Stefan, and Breckin approached the front door to meet Aaron's guest.

Aaron began introducing the woman to the three. "This is my cousin—"

Breckin instantly interjected the introduction. "Lillian!" Breckin quickly recalled the existence of the woman that stood just outside the apartment. Lillian, from the Nightworld. The one who rides skeletal horses and is the oldest known soul in the Nightworld, next to the Order and God *Damia* himself. Lillian, a powerful succubus spawned of evil that had caused Breckin to tremble in all the eternal nights he had spent in that dreaded place. And, now, a new revelation…Aaron! Yes, he could remember where he had met Aaron before. Aaron had been abducted years before him. Aaron, too, was part of the Nightworld! Aaron was a monster! Aaron was a….

Catrina was interrupted by Breckin's severe announcement and didn't catch much sight of the woman. Stefan turned back to Breckin. "What?"

"Stefan!" Breckin screamed. "She's from the Nightworld! Close the door! Close the fucking door!"

Catrina jumped to the door, caught a dominant gaze from the woman called Lillian, and slammed it shut, not forgetting to lock both the handle and the deadbolt.

Aaron was shocked. He was in between the urge to bring the Nightworld's revelation to pass and, at the same time, save Stefan from this chaos.

A cacophonous wail filled the night, like a million babies crying in deep voices, gurgled and with hoarse tones. It was monstrous, simply monstrous, and there could be no other sound in the world that pulverized everybody in the apartment and caused their adrenaline to race through their veins with such speed.

Breckin's heart pounded. How could he be this blind? Between the fear and the hunger for blood, his body could not withstand such a battle. Breckin ran to Stefan's side in attempt to pull him from Aaron. "Stefan," he gasped, "he's in on it too." He gestured toward Aaron. Catrina took a step back from the entire ordeal.

"I don't know what you're talking about," Aaron counterattacked. And then, before Aaron could say another word, he viewed the full moon through the open blinds. He grunted in instant pain and fell to his knees. Aaron's breathing became erratic and hoarse.

"What the hell's going on, Breckin?" Catrina hollered.

"Get him out of the apartment!" Breckin yelled back.

"I have to go," Aaron informed Stefan. It was obvious that he was in pain. Aaron's shoulders began contracting in a spasm all their own. Catrina, full of amazement, caught a brisk glance of Aaron irises turning ruby-colored.

Stefan was confused beyond all reality. "Aaron, are you all right?"

"Get away from him!" Breckin possessively pulled Stefan with a strong hand that practically ripped Stefan's shirt.

"What the hell are you doing?" Stefan raged back to Breckin.

Catrina's mouth fell into a state of shock as she watched Aaron on all fours contract and exhale in an agony unknown to the world of reality. She found herself turning to Breckin who was holding Stefan from aiding Aaron. "The man in my dreams," she said. "He's real, isn't he?"

There was no confirmation from Breckin whose entire attention was directed at keeping Stefan from going to Aaron. Aaron's body jolted upward, hands thrown into the sky as if he were some insidious creature about to pounce upon an innocent victim. Catrina saw that Aaron's lower set of teeth had gone jagged and jutted over his upper lip. Aaron grasped at both locks and threw the door open, quickly exiting the apartment. There was no "cousin Lillian" in view. Catrina thought of Breckin, the vampire who she had been able to sympathize and come to terms with, and realized that maybe she could do the same with Aaron. After all, if Aaron wanted to hurt Stefan, or any of them for that matter, he could have done so. Once Aaron bolted from the apartment, Catrina made the decision to follow him.

"What's going on?" Stefan questioned Breckin. "What happened to Aaron? Where did Catrina go?"

Breckin wanted to explain, but knew that he didn't have much time before he himself would have to escape the apartment to fulfill his own bloodlust. Breckin took Stefan into the bedroom, laid him down on the comforting mattress, and prayed for Stefan to fall to a quick sleep. Instead, Stefan continued asking questions, his mind racing with all that had just happened. With no other recourse, Breckin's fangs protruded from his gums as he viciously, and resentfully, attacked Stefan's neck with a tearing kiss. Breckin drove his teeth deep into Stefan's neck, sucking and reveling in the bloodshed until Stefan lay limp in his arms. Breckin had drawn enough blood to induce unconsciousness in Stefan. Still, with all that blood traveling through Breckin's veins, it wasn't enough. He needed blood not of his own kind. He required the virgin blood of the innocent.

-5-

Catrina ran across the asphalt of Firehouse Road, through a darkness that was only illuminated by the light of a full moon. She knew she could come to terms with Aaron, could talk him into resisting the Nightworld. It made perfect sense. He could have taken them all, killed them all for that matter. But, no, he didn't. He ran instead, leaving behind the possibility of murder and abduction. And Lillian, where was she during all of this?

Catrina, running out of breath, pushed through the sagebrush and tumbleweeds of the desert. Suddenly, she heard the growling as surely as she had heard it the night before in her dreams. At first, it seemed to emit from an area before her. Then, the menacing snarl seemed to be coming from all around her. Catrina turned in circles. She was alone, in the surrounding desert of Spook Valley. If Stefan and Breckin's stories were true, somewhere around here was a doorway. And somewhere around here was Aaron, or, the beast that Aaron had become. This thought appalled Catrina; yet she had faith that she could help Aaron overcome all of this. And, maybe, he had answers about the "pact;" maybe he could help them all destroy the Nightworld.

Catrina's courage dropped into her stomach where butterflies screamed in horror. And then, before she knew it, a beast emerged from the shadows of the night. It was like the creature in her dreams, the beast in her visions. The body was covered in coarse fur, black and brown enveloping all of Aaron's flesh. It stood on two legs and had claws protruding from its hands and feet. The mouth of the creature narrowly erected from its face and its teeth were jagged. Thick saliva oozed from the tips of their whiteness. The eyes glowered at Catrina in their ruby color, evil and altogether sinister. The beast growled, looking and relishing Catrina in its eyes. This was Aaron. This is what Aaron had become. He was a werewolf and there was no denying that.

Catrina endeavored to remain calm and stood still like the victim of a rattlesnake. She did not move, only watched. The creature angrily growled with its impending eyes locked on its prey.

"Aaron," Catrina called. "Aaron, I know it is you. You can fight this Aaron."

The werewolf came closer, taking each step in assured attack.

"Aaron, I know it was you who tried to warn me. I know you can fight this Aaron."

Still closer came the beast and Catrina began to make a slight step backward. Her heart wanted to tear through her chest and she couldn't believe that she had come this far. She was face to face with a facet of the Nightworld. This evil was beyond anything her mother or father had warned her of by practicing her craft. No, this was true evil. This was horror.

"For Stefan, Aaron," she said. "Please. Do this for Stefan."

The creature paused and, in the moment, in that one shred of hope, Catrina stood her ground. "Yes, Aaron, for Stefan. I know how much you care for him." And this much was so very true. Catrina knew the glances that the two men had shared, the sacred and secret gazes of lust that had filled the dining room tonight and had also been made present in the music store the day before.

The beast came to a complete stop. If Catrina could see better in the darkness, perhaps she would have witnessed a tear escape the werewolf's eye. The creature arched its neck back and howled at the moon. The terror enveloped Catrina, that sound that had visited her dreams since the first vision. The howling haunted her, its ear splitting sound filled with both terror and pain.

The werewolf turned and got on all fours as it bolted away from Catrina and strode in a rhythm that measured in gracefulness to any of Nature's animals. Catrina's shoulders fell and relaxed in a victory of sorts.

-6-

Breckin left Stefan unconscious at the apartment as he prowled the streets of Spook Valley. He searched for a victim, though he knew that one would not be this far from the center of town. He ran down Firehouse Road. Ravenous hunger enveloped every muscle and vein in his being.

Soon, Breckin was near Main and Violin Streets, where small crowds were roaming in and out of the Violin Street Tavern. *Too many people*, he rationalized to himself. He made his way back in the direction from which he came. Soon, Breckin found himself near the crossings of Main Street and Firehouse Road. It was there that Breckin recognized the sign of Laine's Music. *Ricky*, he thought. Yes, and Ricky was working all alone.

Breckin got on his haunches and pushed open the door to Laine's Music. The jingling of brass bells permeated the stores silence.

Ricky called out to the open door in which nobody could be seen. "Hello?"

"*Ricky*" The voice that called the name sounded desperate and lusting at the same time.

Ricky strolled from the counter to the front door that was now closed. He opened the door and looked around. He saw nobody.

Ricky.

"Is this some kind of joke?" the young man loudly asked.

Breckin briskly emerged from behind the door. In one fleeting motion, he grabbed Ricky by both shoulders and drove his fangs deep into the boy's neck. The blood was like syrup relished in the Garden of Eden and Breckin sucked away at the porcelain neck that nourished him. There was no taste like this in the world, no desire satiated such as the blood of a young man flowing over his mouth, onto his tongue, and down his throat. This was heaven; this was like coming into the mouth of a stranger.

The young man named Ricky fell limp into his arms and Breckin eased him down onto the gray sidewalk that would be his final resting place.

-7-

Catrina Taylor stood in the darkness of the desert. She was victorious of her rationalizations with Aaron, with the animal that Aaron had become. She knew not where the beast ran off to and only pleaded that he transform into the human he was earlier.

From behind, Catrina heard the rustling of brush. Before she had time to turn around, Lillian emerged in all her monstrous form. She was a demon, a succubus whose power was unmatched. Lillian moved in her brown, leathery-textured armor, sporting elongated blue-black nails. With a single swipe, the creature from the Nightworld clawed into the flesh of Catrina Taylor.

The agony was like acid on her back. Catrina fell to the desert floor as she felt the intense burning sensation crawl all over her body.

The moon, she thought.

Stefan.

Breckin.

Aaron.

Help me.

Oh my god, help me!

The caustic feeling enveloped her body. Burning—yes it burned! Creeping, it did, all over her back and her buttocks, over her thighs and over her arms. Scraping and crawling like an army of unstoppable maggots. Where was there salvation?

Darkness.

Catrina closed her eyes and feared the darkness.

CHAPTER X

-1-

Breckin sauntered the dark stretch of Firehouse Road en route to the apartment. He felt alive. Yes, alive once again! The feeling of anticipated breathing and the unbridled yearning for blood had subsided. Breckin was at his fullest strength once again, at the peak of his supernatural senses, and this was something he had not felt since his existence in the Nightworld. This he could attribute to the reaping of blood from the young man Ricky. Poor Ricky. Ricky who had been working the last shift at Laine's Music and had been the only possible victim for Breckin's bloodlust.

Although Breckin harbored feelings of regret for killing the young man, he had no other choice. He must be strong for the battle brimming in Spook Valley, and the battle had truly begun. The realization of this hit Breckin when he witnessed the familiar face of Lillian attempt to enter Stefan's apartment. Surely, she was an unexpected guest, a guest of horrific denomination. And she ran! Lillian ran from the scene, off into the streets of Spook Valley or the surrounding desert, nobody knew for certain. But she was here, in this place and at this time, lingering in the shadows with the precision of a wild animal, as only a creature from the Nightworld could master.

Lillian was certainly no stranger to Breckin. When the Nightworld had first abducted him, three years previous, it was Lillian who had scared him from attempting to escape. The woman's sinister, obsidian eyes could veritably see through him, into his mind, and know what he was thinking at any given time. Lillian's graceful and hypnotic moves were like an undulating current of sexual desire—the way her hips swaggered like a metronome conducting a symphony of destruction, her sensual and controlled voice that brushed past her bee-sting lips, and the way she rode upon Breckin, gliding up and down his aroused sex, when she had seduced and had her way with him.

Lillian had her way with every creature of the Nightworld. She was the Devil's whore, a demon whose existence and strength was dependant, if not limited to, the seduction of men. *Oh, hellish woman, how is it that you were not borne of Satan's cock itself?* Still, beneath the mask of her comely, Victorian beauty, Lillian was a horrid monster. Breckin had seen her in full transformation before, tracking those who had escaped through the doorway. A hairless creature she would become, wrinkled skin the texture of leather, the color of glistening brown, and claws in their rigid, gnarled state that were synonymous with a hungry mouth of teeth. It would take a strong creature or, possibly, the combined strength of such, to destroy an adversary like Lillian. Then again, there were still the Saints and God *Damia* himself to contend with. But if the doorway could be closed, if it could be sealed before they had a chance to get through and perform the initiation of their ritualistic pact, perhaps they would all be saved. Perhaps, Breckin could have a new lease on life. If so, would he remain a vampire or would he live this nightmare for the rest of his life? What's more, Breckin realized, the only way the doorway could be closed right now would be for the Nightworld to obtain Stefan.

There were no definite answers in the midst of this trepidation.

-2-

Sizzling.

Catrina could hear the faint sound of the flesh on her back sizzle and her only nightmarish vision was that of her skin deteriorating, of it being eaten away by the acrid tearing feeling. She knew not what had attacked her, knew not if was Aaron whom she had witnessed run off into the night in his animal form. Where was Stefan? And Breckin, how she trusted Breckin now that she knew his story.

Help me, she tried sputtering over her lips. Catrina's body was disabled by the pain, that awful agony that crawled all over her, covering her body in acidic tinges and pinpricks of anguish. Why couldn't she pass out now? Hadn't people in immense pain passed out from their wounds, from the body's ultimate discomforts? Calling out to her friends with her voice was useless, for she could barely find the peace of mind to form the words, let alone scream them over her shivering lips. Catrina would use her mind. Surely, Stefan would hear her as surely as her instinct led her to him in the first place. The bond between best friends always carries with it an unknown, supernatural link of sorts. Call it intuition; call it a psychic bridge, but just call. *Just call out to him! Stefan! Stefan! Help me! Save me, Stefan!*

Catrina heard the coarse voice of a woman come from behind her.

"White witch!" it hissed.

Catrina attempted to look up from the hard, desert floor. She slithered to her side as if she a snake that inhabited the land. In her sights, Lillian emerged.

Lillian was no longer the creature that had attacked Catrina. She now stood, in all her feminine form, naked and with her raven hair spilling over concealed breasts. "Yes. White witch. Try with all your might as the strength leaves your body. Call to your man! Call to Stefan and bring him here! You humans are such easy prey." Lillian screeched uncontrollably into the night.

This woman, this creature that sent horror through Catrina's being just as it could captivate a mind filled with lust, was reading her thoughts. Catrina needed protection from this horrific woman.

"And *they* said you were a powerful one," Lillian laughed in sarcasm.

God and Goddess, Catrina directed her inner voice, *save me from this evil.*

Lillian knelt before Catrina and cupped Catrina's chin in her hand. "Dear Catrina, there is only one God and his name is *Damia.* It is to him with which you will bow before. It is he that, should you call to him right now, will grant you forgiveness and give you the strength to rise. Such a weak one, you are."

I WILL destroy you.

Lillian's guffaws shot into the night. The mixture of hatred and comic relief was filled with so many calamities that it could only be described as a resonance of insanity. Instead of replying to her with her serpent tongue, Lillian responded to Catrina with her own mind.

Catrina...I AM destruction.

Catrina could not shiver, though she wanted to. She could not tremble from Lillian's revelation, could not back away from those fearing words. The creeping pain deferred all of her thoughts.

Static. A whistling tear that fills the desert. To some it may be nothing more than the sound of sagebrush rustling against sagebrush from an overpowering wind. To others, it may have been a trick of the mind—a low, monotonous hum present, but denied. To the few believers of Spook Valley, however, it was a sign of the doorway opening between the Nightworld and the Earth realm. Surely, Lillian knew the resonance of dark worlds interfacing. And Stefan and Breckin were acquainted with the dreaded electrical impulses that framed the monolithic doorway. Surely, Aaron knew. He had entered through the doorway...

And now it all made sense! Now, Catrina understood the dismaying timbre of the electromagnetic sound. Between Stefan and Breckin's stories, Catrina realized that she lay within yards, if not feet, from the doorway to the Nightworld.

Lillian's focus fell from Catrina to the buzzing that called to her. Her black irises followed the sound of the whine that scurried through the cacti and desert plant life. Lillian stood in all her dark, magical wonder.

Catrina knew not what it all meant. The doorway was opening, she gathered that much. But why? Recalling the information that Stefan and Breckin had both entrusted her with, Catrina grasped that either somebody was entering the Earth realm or leaving it behind. More than likely, somebody was coming *from* the Nightworld. Catrina's mind raced in awe. Vampires, werewolves, and creatures of evil—what new terror would Spook Valley come face to face with next? What possible new abomination could be born from the Nightworld? The Nightworld…that horrid place that spawned monsters of unimaginable measure like the Devil's Bride giving birth to a deadly army of zombies. Worse yet, Catrina couldn't help but be frightened by the concept of her own capture. What if the doorway was opening, not for one to cross *from* the Nightworld, but for those detestable creatures to abduct her and take her from this Earth? As much as she panicked, she could not find it in herself to escape or even attempt to move for that matter.

Lillian spoke as if speaking to the presence of the night. "Yes. I'm coming, God *Damia.*" And then Lillian went on bended knee, back to Catrina. "Stay here, witch. I'll be back for you."

Pass out, yes! Please, take me away from all of this, this nightmare come true, this impossible agenda of hell on Earth. Comprehending that if she called out to Stefan, he would eventually come, she chose another name. For Catrina understood that she had become the bait of an insidious trap. If Stefan came, the Nightworld would get what it wanted.

Breckin. Breckin. She prayed with all her might, every ounce of conviction to the God and Goddess, that he would hear her.

-3-

Stefan awoke from bed, and the inky gloom of night engulfed him. At first, he had not known if he'd been dreaming. Could it all be just one inescapable nightmare? A long nightmare that one incessantly continues to awaken from but to no avail? And now, was it all over? Did the dream come to an end? Did Breckin exist? Did the Nightworld exist? Was any of this real?

To his dreaded comprehension, he came to terms with the events of the night. It did happen—the guests, the dinner (his mouth was dry from the taste of the Merlot), and the confusion. What exactly happened? *Aaron*, he thought. Aaron ran from the apartment when Breckin accused him of being a part of the whole horrible scenario. But wasn't he? After all, Aaron was the one who endeavored to bring that Lillian creature into the apartment. However, why didn't Aaron try to hurt any of them? Perhaps Aaron was from the Nightworld but, if that were the case, Aaron is trying to escape the minions of that place in the same fashion with which Breckin had.

Stefan tried to piece all the events of the night as he lay in bed. How he had gotten to the bed, he did not know. Something was wrong with Aaron though. Stefan recalled how Aaron had fallen to the ground and became instantly ill. And Catrina, Catrina ran after Aaron. Then…yes! Then Breckin suddenly attacked Stefan! Stefan brought his shaky fingers to his neck where Breckin had left his mark—two puncture wounds that were still fresh and sticky with Stefan's blood. He could not find any rationalization in his waking mind as to why Breckin would do such a thing to him. What *exactly* was happening? Furthermore, Stefan played around with the idea of if Breckin was the *good* guy in all of this. After all, had it not been for Breckin, Stefan would've never been sucked into this awful game of monsters and death. Yes, it was he who had saved Breckin. It was he, Stefan Powell, who knew nothing of the Nightworld until its revelation consisted of Breckin's hand grasping for safety into the desert night. From the womb of darkness, Breckin wanted to escape. But what was his ulterior motive?

Stefan groggily rose from the bed. The lights in the apartment were completely out. No sign of Breckin. No sign of Catrina. Nothing. Where did they all go?

Weak from Breckin's surprising attack, Stefan languidly strolled into the living room. First, he switched on a light and, then, he turned the television on. The news was on and Stefan was about to switch the television off when he saw the news reporter standing in front of Laine's Music. The Channel Ten insignia flashed in it brilliant red performance as the report of "breaking news" had begun:

"I'm standing just outside of Laine's Music in Spook Valley, eighty miles from Phoenix, where an apparent coyote attack has claimed another victim in only two nights. Tonight's victim was nineteen-year-old Richard Boren. From what we gather at the crime scene, Richard's body was found just outside of the music store where he worked. Sources are unsure as to why the young man left the store; however, the grisly result ended in death. Richard's body was said to be attacked by a wild dog…or…a coyote; his body was horribly mauled and rushed to Spook Valley Medical Center where the young man was pronounced dead only minutes ago. Right now, officers and the chief of the local Animal Control are combing the area for the vicious animal. This is the second night that this quiet town has been struck with horror. As you may recall, last night, resident Valerie Saunders was attacked within a mile of this area and suffered similar wounds. Local authorities are urging anybody who may come in contact with such an animal to call Police or Animal Control immediately. They've asked that you please do not approach the animal yourself. Channel Ten News will keep you updated with any further information. Once again, nineteen-year-old, Richard Boren has died from a violent animal attack…"

Stefan's hand was clasped over his mouth; he was shocked by the broadcast. He had only left Laine's Music hours before. *Violent animal attack?* Then, it had struck him like a haunting sonata: Breckin! Yes, Breckin needed to feed. Oh God, how could he have done this? And it could be confirmed, as Breckin was nowhere to be found right now. Stefan's heart jumped into his throat.

-4-

BrrrrECKin…BrrrrECKin…

The faint tone sounded as if it were being called down a long, unending tunnel. The resonance bounced off the night skies and all around Breckin. The pitch was muffled, yet a high tone accentuated certain parts of his name. The 'B' at the beginning of his name was heavy with inflection and then quieted with the rolling of diminishing 'R's. And, then, the 'ECK' in his name, loud then trailing off into an echoing vibration.

Brrrr—ECKin!

Breckin could hear it from all sides as he made his way home upon Firehouse Road. It came from the surrounding desert; it came from within his mind in the same fashion that God *Damia* could mentally call to him. But this wasn't God *Damia*'s voice; this wasn't that awful roll of thunderous reverberation. This voice was softer, familiar. Catrina! Surely, it had to be Catrina's voice.

Something was wrong with Catrina! Breckin recalled how she had run after Aaron when Aaron had bolted from the apartment. *Before Aaron's transformation.* What fate had Catrina met up with? Breckin had no other choice but to find her, save her from whatever terror upon which she had stumbled.

Breckin picked up his pace, searching the encroaching desert on either side of him. He followed her voice, her psychic mind calling to him, as if it were a new prey he was attacking, as if his finding her depended upon his own survival.

Catrina's voice grew louder and faint at the same time. Her will power was amazing, yet her voice had a trembling quality blended into it.

Breckin scurried off Firehouse Road, into the desert, not too far from the apartment. Finally he found her and he harbored no doubts whatsoever that it was Catrina who called out to him as he discovered her practically lifeless upon the desert floor. Her back had been maimed by something monstrous and Breckin knew that monster's name had to be Aaron Dabney.

"Catrina!"

She had very little energy and could barely turn to see Breckin looming over her. Her body shivered in uninvited pain, her eyes frozen in shock. When she found what strength she had left to speak, one word sputtered over her lips: "Lillian."

That's when Breckin heard the doorway of the Nightworld opening. That static sound—how he longed to forget that horrid tone, how he remembered it during his escape as if it had only occurred a few minutes previous.

"I'm going to get you out of here, Catrina." Breckin lifted Catrina and she dangled in his arms like a victim from which he had just finished drawing blood. As he hauled her body and stepped onto Firehouse Road, Breckin saw the red and blue flashes of a police cruiser no more than a hundred yards down the road.

-5-

Aaron Dabney had fully transformed into a werewolf. He ran on all fours in the desert outside of Spook Valley. The creature weaved in and out of cacti and sagebrush, the sticky sweet aromas infusing and teasing his sense of smell. And, still, there was that other scent, the scent that smelled metallic and pungent, the scent of blood. How the werewolf craved and yearned for the taste of blood upon its lapping tongue, for the soft shredding and melting of flesh in its watering mouth. What conscience it did have, during its confrontation with Catrina, was now completely expunged from its animal mind.

It sprinted further, its paws softly beating the hard desert ground beneath it in a hypnotic gait, and the obscure figures of all the oversized plants that it dodged and raced passed became nothing more than shadows swiftly moving from the corner of its eye. Faster and further, and yearning for the bloodshed of a luminous, full moon night, the werewolf came to an abrupt halt. A trail of dust folded and billowed from beneath its hind legs. The beast inhaled the night air, sniffed for the smell of prey, and directed its sights near a century plant that unnaturally jostled as if something were hiding beneath it. From the edge of the plant, a plump jackrabbit began jumping toward a safe haven. The creature was quicker than the jackrabbit and lunged onto the small, furry animal before it had a chance to put its hind legs into motion. Clawing and biting into the animal, the werewolf pulled on the head and the bushy tail of the jackrabbit at the same time as it ripped into two wriggling, gory halves from which blood jutted. The beast Aaron had become burrowed its erected nose and mouth into each half, painting its face in the crimson carnage of its prey. Suckling the blood, viciously tearing through the quarry's flesh with razor-sharp teeth, and lapping at the tinny delights of the jackrabbit's viscera—the beast reveled in appetizing satisfaction. When the carcass of the animal plopped to the ground, the werewolf arched its back and neck high toward the full moon and let out the loudest howling it had ever known. The animalistic screech haunted the night.

-6-

"Where have you been?"

Breckin had just walked through the door to the apartment and expected Stefan to be asleep. Instead, Stefan had been sitting on the living room sofa, all lights still extinguished, a creature of the night using the shadows as its cover. Breckin remained silent, trying to muster the night's events into a comprehensive series of play-by-plays by which Stefan would be satisfied. And, still, he had to tell Stefan about Catrina.

"I asked where you have been." Stefan's voice was authoritative, demanding, and had gone down an octave in inflection.

"Stefan," Breckin spoke as he approached the man who was surely fueled with a becoming inquisition. "It's Catrina."

Stefan jumped to his feet. "What about her? What happened?" Stefan required answers now and this Breckin certainly knew.

"She was just taken to Spook Valley Medical. I found her in the desert."

"Is she all right?"

Again, silence.

"Is she all right, goddammit!?!?"

"She was hurt," Breckin explained. Before Stefan had a chance to explode with any further emotion, Breckin continued. "Not too bad. I think...I think Aaron did it to her."

"What?" Stefan was fuming with hate. "Oh, we're going to involve Aaron in this again, are we?"

"Stefan," Breckin rationalized, "I know him from the Nightworld. I KNOW HIM."

Stefan became infuriated, yet brought his voice to a laughter of sarcasm. "Let me ask you something, Breckin. Is it jealousy; is that it? Are you jealous of Aaron?"

"No! You're not thinking straight, Stefan. I can tell by your color that you need to feed. Let me feed you, Stefan." Breckin offered his wrist.

Stefan's knees folded beneath him and he gently fell upon the carpet with his head hanging down in despair. He may have been crying, but Breckin couldn't tell. Suddenly, the faint words of accusation formed over Stefan's quivering lips. "I know where you were tonight, Breckin. I know about Ricky. I know about the girl from last night too."

Girl from last night? Breckin's mind raced. "Stefan, what girl?"

"Don't talk to me, Breckin. Leave me alone," Stefan solemnly requested.

Breckin walked closer to Stefan. "Catrina will be fine, Stefan. You need to feed though. You cannot deny the hunger coursing through you."

"Get the Hell away from me," Stefan ordered. "You did this to me, Breckin. *You* did this!"

Breckin recoiled. "You wanted *this*."

"Leave!"

Breckin retreated to the bedroom and closed the door behind.

Stefan sat in the darkness of his apartment, mulling over everything from the rescue of Breckin, to what Breckin had turned him into, to the death of Ricky and the girl named Valerie. And now Catrina. Stefan firmly believed that it was Breckin who attacked Catrina and *not* Aaron. No, Aaron couldn't do a thing like that.

The hunger. That insatiable hunger fed from Stefan's mind of scurried emotions. Yes, perhaps he did need to feed. He didn't want to be this way. No. Why had he chosen this? Out of love for Breckin? Love blinded by the first nights with an unknown stranger? How he wished he could take it all back! And, Aaron. Where was Aaron?

Stefan thought of his name, of his boyish curves, and of tasting those lips.

Stefan basted in the sorrow for everything that had happened. He felt responsible for Ricky's death, he felt responsible for Catrina's wounds. At the heart of that liability, one name formed in his mind, one person who'd brought all of this upon him: Breckin. Stefan was sure of what he must do next—to stop the hunger, to take away the blame, to avenge those who were hurt, and to, quite possibly, give him a freedom that subsided the supernatural hunger that made an attempt to consume his body.

The plan was already forming and was making sense with each calculable thought…

…Stefan contemplated Breckin's vicious attacks for hours. It wasn't the fact that Breckin needed blood, but that he had taken lives. Stefan couldn't fathom the strength of the bloodlust within Breckin's nature. It was ungodly.

What could he do to stop Breckin? Certainly, Stefan felt love for Breckin. However, there were no other alternatives. Stefan needed to be free of this! Free of this curse that haunted his every thought now, free of the bloodshed, indeed! *Deliver me from this evil…deliver me from the hunger, the pangs…and give me a chance to start over.* He pondered Breckin's claim of Aaron being from the Nightworld. To this, Stefan didn't have a doubt. But he could learn from

Aaron, and Aaron didn't have the bloodlust that Breckin contained. Stefan would fight this battle. He would destroy the Nightworld, but first, it must begin at the source.

Stefan quietly rose and walked into the kitchen where he slyly opened the pantry door. He gazed down and studied the oak stake that they had kept after destroying the vampire that had threatened their lives in a time that already seemed eons ago. *If I were to destroy Breckin, as he once told me, all other vampiric creatures born of the vampire's blood would return to their human form…deliverance.*

Stefan retrieved the stake and silently sauntered into the bedroom where Breckin soundly slept. Breckin lay peacefully, in his comely, naked form, upon the bed. Stefan couldn't believe how murderous the mind of this man he had grown to love had become. But Breckin *had* done it! He wasn't in the apartment when Stefan had awakened. There was Ricky, Catrina, and what about what Breckin had done to Stefan himself?

A rolling tear came to Stefan's eye as he raised the stake high above his head. Stefan began to drive the stake downward, intending to plunge it through the heart of his undead lover.

-7-

Two lives would be changed.

Before the rays of the sun awoke the town of Spook Valley, just before dawn crept in and quenched the night, two newcomers would arrive in Spook Valley.

One would think—*freedom.*

The other—*havoc.*

Two men crossed the town limits of Spook Valley. One's crossing would be natural, a walk along a highway and into the cradling grasp of the town. However, the other's entrance into Spook Valley would be completely unnatural, and the sound of static would permeate his world upon entry.

Still, both men would be entering a town where there were no limitations to the boundaries of the natural world, a town of treacherous illusions and monstrous encounters.

Spook Valley was a town where the ultimate battle of good and evil would be fought to the very end.

CHAPTER XI

-1-

Uncomfortable warmth fell upon Breckin's cheek. It was the kind of heat sensation that told you the sun was rising and spilling its rays upon you through overlooked blinds that you should have closed the night before. It was the kind of warmth that sends an irritation through the rest of your body when you've stayed up at all hours of the night and cannot open your eyes to the uninvited day. And yet, at the same time, it was the type of experience that could go beyond explanation. After all, it could only be a sign of serenity, of Mother Nature's awakening—*how she shines her beacon upon you.* Face a new day and forget yesterday; you are alive and one could only dread the limitless possibilities should you not wake to sunlight cascading upon your naked body.

Through a cracked, sticky eyelid, Breckin's blinded vision could barely make out the shadowy figure hovering over his body. Breckin's limited sight made its way from the belly of the figure up to the torso, over the shoulders and to the two arms that were stretched outward with a long pointed object above him. It was a dream certainly, but Breckin didn't dream, hadn't had such possible images invade his sleeping mind since a time before he came in contact with the Nightworld. *The Nightworld.* All of a sudden, it made such horrible sense. Somebody was trying to kill him!

Breckin forced his eyelids open. The stinging from a night filled with unease and lack of sleep endeavored to make him squeeze his eyes shut. Instead, his eyes bulged in horror as he witnessed the sharpened point of an oak stake plummeting downward.

Breckin instantly threw both hands into the air, grabbing the assailant's grip on the weapon and stopping it right before it pierced his chest. His adversary continued to put heavy strain on the weapon and Breckin used his own strength to keep it from entering his heart. In a cautious and fleeting act, Breckin slid to the left, still holding his assassin's forceful hands, and leapt from the bed. To his shock, he made out the face of his lover, Stefan, and tore the stake from Stefan's grasp, powerfully heaving the weapon across the bedroom and against a wall.

"What the hell are you doing?" Breckin hollered. Out of survival, his canine teeth elongated and pierced his lower lip.

Stefan stood his ground and refused to recoil from the slight metamorphoses of Breckin's features. "I wanted you dead!"

"What? What is wrong with you?"

"You killed Ricky; you murdered that woman Valerie. You hurt Catrina; I know it was *you* who tried killing her!"

Breckin was repulsed by the fact that Stefan believed all of that. In Stefan eyes, Breckin was not a man that he'd spent nights making love to or to whom he revealed his innermost secrets and desires. Instead, Breckin was a horrible monster. Breckin couldn't believe that Stefan saw him in that perspective. "I told you already, Stefan. I'm guilty for Ricky's death and I cannot change that now. I cannot go back in time and alter what I did. If I could, after seeing all the confusion this has brought upon you, then I would do it in a second! But I didn't kill anybody else. You have to believe me, Stefan. And I would never hurt Catrina. Think about it, Catrina and I were getting along well last night before you arrived for dinner. As a matter of fact, I was the one who rescued her. I saved her and had her taken to the hospital. Why would I put her in danger?"

"Then who did?"

"It was Lillian," Breckin explained with an exasperating sigh.

"Lillian?"

"Yes, you remember don't you? The woman that Aaron invited over; that horrible lady that Aaron said was his 'cousin.'"

Stefan flailed his arms in the air out of frustration. "Here you go again with Aaron."

"I *know* Aaron from the Nightworld, Stefan. He is a part of this whole thing."

Stefan sat upon the edge of the bed, taking in a deep breath as he sorted all the facts in his confused mind. "I realize he's from the Nightworld. But did it ever occur to you that he escaped that place? Did you ever stop to think that, just maybe, he is not on *their* side? He could have killed us all last night, you must realize. If it was his directive to do so, then he wasn't making much of an effort to carry it out."

Breckin mulled over Stefan's logic regarding Aaron. "I know. I can't quite figure it out. But I wouldn't trust the man either."

Stefan became calmer and now the thought of taking Breckin's life seemed non-existent. Why had he attempted it in the first place? To save himself? To put an end to this horror that he ultimately felt had no resolution? "Is he like us?" Stefan asked. "I mean, is he a vampire?"

"I'm not sure what he is," Aaron lied. He knew Stefan was already a mental wreck. Telling him what he knew of Aaron would only make it worse. Not to mention, he had to worry about his own safety after witnessing Stefan's attempt at destroying him. No, what Aaron was had to be discovered by Stefan. "I only know that I have seen him in the Nightworld before. I don't know if he harnesses any *special* powers and I don't know how long he's been a captive of that place."

"What about the 'pact?' Does he know anything of this 'pact' that the Nightworld is trying to carry out?"

Breckin's eyebrows knitted in confusion.

"Remember, you told me about a pact. You told me the morning after I saved you that the Nightworld was trying to keep the doorway between that world and this one open for all time. I think you said it was something about thirteen creatures from the Nightworld entering through the doorway and a sacrifice. Does Aaron know anything about this? Does he know how to stop it?"

"I'm not sure. If he was held captive as I was, he would have probably only heard about the pact through conversations held by the Order."

"And this 'Order' as you call them. Who are they?"

Breckin took in a breath, wishing not to speak of them, wanting no memory of that place of darkness. "The Order of Perennial Darkness are the oldest of the Nightworld. They see over all the abductions and are the deciding factor of the Nightworld. I guess you could say that they are the driving force behind *Damia's* revelation. They are the ones who overlook the land for him and make sure that nothing goes wrong. There are six of them total, and they are powerful as a whole. Ultimately, they are the group that will bring the pact to reality. It is rumored that each one of them hold's his own information about the pact."

"What does that mean?" Stefan queried.

"I mean each one of the Order of Perennial Darkness is like a piece of a puzzle. Each of the Order holds a piece of information as to how the pact will be initiated and each is forbidden to release that information until the time of the pact. That way, if any of them is forced to tell somebody about the pact, he would not have *all* the information to disclose."

"That's very secretive," Stefan remarked. "Very scary. We need to find out who knows of this pact; we need to find out if Aaron has any information that can help keep this from happening. Wait a minute!" Stefan words came to a halt as he tried piecing together what he had known thus far of *Damia*'s vision. *Thirteen. Thirteen will come through the doorway.* "Remember when you told me that thirteen people…or…creatures would pass through the doorway?"

"Yeah." Breckin could already see where this was going.

"Well, there are four so far—the two that tried to take us that night, which we destroyed, Aaron, and Lillian."

"Actually, if you're taking count, there are five thus far."

"Five?"

"Yeah, remember? I came through the doorway too."

"You're right. That means that eight more will have to pass before the pact can be carried out." Stefan appeared triumphant in his logic.

"Stefan. There could be many more that have already come into this world that we don't know of yet."

Instantly, Stefan's victorious logic fell to a dismaying level. "Then we have to act fast. I have to speak to Aaron and find out all he knows. And I have to visit Catrina in the hospital and see if she's all right."

Stefan wanting to meet with Aaron irked Breckin and caused him to writhe with unease. "I wish you would stay away from Aaron."

"I can't," Stefan admitted.

"Why?"

"I'm beginning to feel close to him."

Those words hit Breckin and pulverized his stomach. Words like that, nobody wishes to hear. Especially when Breckin gave all the love for anything in this world to Stefan. He and Stefan were going through this whole nightmare together. They had shared *everything* together and now this. Breckin hadn't the words to reply to Stefan. And if he were to cry, if he were to fall to his knees and weep before the man he himself loved with all his being, what solace would Stefan offer? The battle had taken a new turn, a new twist as only an abstract nightmare could make. Breckin's battle not only consisted of fighting off the evil of the Nightworld from taking over the Earth realm, but now it had somehow become a battle of winning the love of the man he cared so much for.

Tense silence pervaded the room as both Breckin and Stefan gazed at each other's expressions. Their eyes were glossy with restrained tears. It was as if the two men were facing off in an emotional struggle—who would let his tears run first? Who had more love for the other? Stefan retreated from the confrontation and ambled out of the bedroom.

-2-

It was like floating and swimming in a sea of clouds, but it wasn't scary. After she got use to the idea that she would not fall to an unknown landing, Catrina Taylor felt safe and comforted by the feeling of zero gravity. She was now learning how to maneuver her body, how to grasp for the empty sky and shove the air to either side of her, just like when she would swim in her parent's pool under the blistering heat of summer. It was reminiscent of being underwater, everything a sapphire blue of liquid, and she could push the water behind her and kick her feet in tiny strokes to go even faster. *Underwater and not needing to come up for air*, she thought—a dolphin, a beautiful dolphin gliding through the aquatic world of a jeweled sea. Mother's womb, certainly this must be Mother Nature's womb and she was a pink fetus within it. Moving, kicking, and floating in the liquid world— Mother would not let her be harmed, for this was a place of solace; this was a place of serene pleasures. How she reveled in her floating, in her love for this atmosphere! And there! There was Stefan in his most handsome form, smiling with those pursed lips; an act that made his charming dimples show. And there was mother and father, Angie and Rob Taylor, whose smiles she had not been used to seeing. But they smiled at her now; they approved of their daughter. Look, over there, even Zander was here! *Where had you gone?* she wanted to ask. But it didn't matter. He was here now too. They were all here in this place and Catrina wept tears of joy.

In the distance, there was a repetitive beep interrupted by long pauses. Catrina's heartbeat was steady, but weak. She laid in the hospital bed—eyes closed, a small clear tube tapping her vein and feeding her intravenously, comatose to the rest of the world. Her body was still, as if it was being prepared for her funeral, but she was barely breathing. She was holding on. For some reason unknown to all but Catrina herself, she refused to pass on.

The man observing her took his hand and moved her rumpled hair from her face. He studied her features—the tiny nose that curved with perfection, the cinnamon strands that framed her face, and the small mouth with lips that were dry and chapped. He returned to the chair beside the hospital bed and couldn't believe that this was Catrina.

-3-

Laine Young had been at his store since the wee hours of the morning, since the local police called him and told him that one of his employees was found mauled in front of his business. At first, Laine thought it to be a prank. He couldn't conceive of such a thing happening. Maybe in Phoenix sure, with the drive-by shootings and the late night robberies, but never in Spook Valley. To make it worse, when Laine arrived to the scene of the crime, he was the one who identified the body. He was the person who bore witness to Ricky's lifeless corpse. Dear God, the boy appeared so horrible with his lips curled back and his eyes bulged in fright. Not to mention, the pale purple color of his skin. It was nauseating and it was horrifying, but it was real.

While the police were outside the store jotting their reports and the media was beginning to swarm the event, Laine counted the monies for the day and took a brisk inventory. Nothing was stolen; this was not part of a robbery gone badly. This ruled out foul play and led the police to believe that it was another coyote attack. Laine couldn't believe it. In his ten years in Spook Valley, there had never been such an attack from a coyote. Sure, a few years back, there was the little girl who had been lost in the desert after dark and met up with such an animal. But she was more frightened than wounded. A few scratches, a weak bite into her small leg, but never a death. Especially in the middle of town, practically the town square!

Laine had to take his mind off the fretful event. He had just unlocked the door of Laine's Music and was officially open for business. Laine would more than likely work until Stefan came on shift this afternoon. He was shocked by the fact that Stefan had not called him yet regarding the news. Laine only hoped that Stefan was aware of what had happened; he prayed that Stefan was not oblivious to the news and that he himself would not have to explain what had happened to Ricky when Stefan arrived for his shift.

The bells over the entrance to Laine's Music jangled, forewarning Laine that a customer had entered the store. Laine turned his attention to the young man approaching the counter. The boy's hair was jet black and wavy in the lengthy front that encased his visage. His eyes gleamed in brilliant emerald and his face was smooth and white like a porcelain doll, delectable.

"Can I help you, sir?" Laine called out to the young man.

The boy refused to speak until he reached the counter. He placed both of his hands upon the Formica and interlocked his fingers. "Yes. I was inquiring if you had any job openings to be filled."

That voice, thought Laine. The voice certainly didn't match the rest of the young man! It was silky with the nuance of a singer's voice; it was a harmonic voice, a voice that could soothe one to sleep if it sang a melodic lullaby.

Laine turned from the counter and reached behind to a shelf where a ream of generic applications was buried. Tearing a page from the ream, he faced the young man again and placed the paper on the counter. The kid was unrecognizable to Laine and, in a place like Spook Valley, practically everybody knew everyone or was aware of his or her existence. "You're not from here, are you son?"

"No sir," the young man spoke. "I'm from Tucson. I just moved to Spook Valley." The boy chuckled. "I kind of liked the name of it."

Once again, Laine was astounded by another feature and that was the boy's kindness and mannerisms. The young man appeared more like a Goth reject than a studious gentleman. Laine took notice of the silver hoop earrings that climbed the man's ears: four on the right and three on the left. "What's your name, son?"

"Oh, I'm sorry." The kid extended his hand. "I'm Lucien."

"Lucien?"

"Yeah, I know it's kind of odd. I have missionary parents."

Laine chortled. "Nothing wrong with that, kid."

Lucien returned the owner's smile with his own.

"I'm looking for somebody to cover a few morning shifts and a couple afternoon shifts. I'm very lenient to work for. As long as you respect me, I will respect you. You'll have to be flexible but, for the most part, the position is a steady one. Can you handle that, Lucien?"

"Yes sir."

"OK, go ahead and fill out this application. Right now, I have one other guy working for me so there will only be the two of you."

"That's no problem, sir. May I ask his name?"

Laine shot an inquisitive glance to the young man. Why would he want to know such a thing? "His name is Stefan. Why do you ask?"

"Oh," Lucian responded, "I just like to know the names of the people I work with so that I can greet them properly instead of having to ask their name myself."

"Alright then. Go ahead and have a seat over there and let me know when you're done filling out the application."

Laine watched as Lucien took the application and began filling it out. As much as he had liked Ricky and made several attempts to get him wasted so that he could take advantage of him, Laine had instantly forgotten him. The boy name Lucien allured him and took his mind off any possible mourning he could have mustered for Ricky—such was the remarkable charm of the newcomer to Spook Valley.

Laine was bemused by his luck to have such a person inquiring about a job so quickly after Ricky's untimely death. In fact, Laine was thankful that he wouldn't have to search for the HELP WANTED sign. It was amazing and, at the same time, unbelievable. However, it seemed, these days, Laine Young had to learn to expect the unexpected.

-4-

You failed me! The voice inside Aaron's head roared. The sound was so boisterous that it didn't give Aaron a chance to breathe.

How dare you fail me like that!

"No, God *Damia*," Aaron called out in his vacant motel room. "I was caught off guard. It was the girl…Catrina."

You went against my wishes and warned her. You will learn to never defy me, Aaron. But Catrina will be out of the way soon enough. I need you to assist Lillian with destroying Breckin. And I want you to hold Stefan captive!

"I don't know if he trusts me enough to—"

He trusts you, the thunderous voice affirmed. *You must contain him until the others arrive! Soon, our worlds will be as one. If you defy me this time Aaron, your curse will be nothing like what you have experienced thus far.*

The curse. Yes, that horrible curse causing his body to shift from man to beast. How he loathed it! Aaron wished he could go back and that was it. He mentally prayed that he could go back to the day before the Nightworld consumed his life. Right now, everything was too terrible to face—his transformation into a wolf, the bellowing of a powerful and fearing god, and the feelings he held for Stefan that he knew could never be carried out. To take Stefan and run off far to another city or even another place, that would be bliss. But where would they go? Where *could* they go that couldn't be reached by God *Damia* and the minions of the Nightworld? The only other alternative was if the Nightworld was destroyed, but that seemed an impossibility in itself. Aaron wanted to think of nothing else right now than to hold Stefan close to him

-5-

Stefan couldn't begin to wonder where to search for Aaron. Aaron had never mentioned to him where he had lived or where he was staying. In fact, the only contact Stefan ever had with Aaron was when Aaron came by Laine's Music while he was on shift.

Stefan drove past Laine's Music, turned north onto Main Street and made a right onto Saguaro Street where Edison Elementary was closed for the beginning of summer vacation. Stefan drove around the town square, past the monumental courthouse and police station and near the central park where kids ran amuck in the green grasses. Stefan didn't know where else to go, for Spook Valley was such a small town. Sure, he could go back and drive west on Violin Street, but the only thing out there was a small motel that bordered the town. Unless…it was possible that Aaron was staying at the motel. Then again, what was Stefan to do? It was unlikely that he would pound on every door at the motel until he found the party opening the door to be Aaron. He had to find

Aaron! As for Breckin, Stefan wasn't sure what to do with him yet. He still harbored feelings for Breckin, yet there was something about Aaron that enraptured him beyond what Breckin could offer.

Stefan had no direction and he realized he was doing nothing more than circling the center of town. Giving up his hopeless search for Aaron, Stefan maneuvered the car east and headed toward Jamison Lane, en route to the Spook Valley Medical Center. He had to be assured that Catrina was all right. Perhaps, she would have answers for him.

Spook Valley Medical Center was a ground level hospital that was equipped with basic medical needs. For anything of a nature too serious, such as a heart attack, victims would be transported by helicopter to St. Joseph's Hospital or one of the other major hospitals in Phoenix. For this, Stefan was grateful' for that meant that Catrina's wounds were not of an extremely pressing nature.

Stefan walked the long corridor to the nurse's station. The sweet smell of disinfectant filled his nostrils as he passed the many rooms of which he peered into to find his friend. When he reached the attending nurse and asked for Catrina Taylor's room, she directed him to the corridor known as the East Wing. Room 246 is what the nurse had told him after he explained that he was not a family member but a good friend to Catrina. She had informed him for future visits that visiting hours were between seven am and eight pm.

Stefan made his way down the East Wing, his shoes squeaking upon the shiny white floor with each anticipated step. Once he reached Room 246, he gently pushed the door open and viewed Catrina's motionless body upon the hospital bed. She appeared so innocent and defenseless. The beeping of the heart monitor declared that she had a pulse. Was she sleeping? Stefan had to see her.

Upon his entrance, Stefan noticed the man sitting in the chair beside Catrina. The man's skin was almond and outlined by curly, chocolate hair that matched his trim goatee. As handsome as the man was, Stefan put all lusting thoughts aside and instantly felt threatened. Before he had a chance to speak, the mysterious stranger stood to his feet and advanced toward Stefan. The man towered over Stefan; he must have been six-feet two inches in height, if not taller.

The man spoke. "They say her vitals are weak and she lapsed into a coma, but I think she'll pull through. Earlier, she smiled."

This looming, unfamiliar person perplexed Stefan. "Who are you?" Stefan snapped at the stranger.

"I go by Zander, but my name is Lysander."

What? Who? Stefan's mind raced with questions.

"I'm Lysander Taylor. Catrina's brother."

CHAPTER XII

-1-

The doorway to the Nightworld was shielded by the light of day that cascaded upon Spook Valley. If anybody who had witnessed the monolithic design had made a claim of its existence to a resident of the town, nothing in the heart of the encasing desert would be found. Ironically, daylight was a friend of the Nightworld, for it safeguarded the entrance and made it invisible to all who passed through the desert where which it stood in all its magnificent horror. Still, there were few who were indeed aware of the doorway's existence. To those who knew it existed, their own worlds and normal lives had been an unstoppable nightmare. On the other side, in the realms of darkness that molded and crawled throughout the Nightworld, a plan was being made to keep the doorway open for eternity.

Lillian stood before the Order of Perennial Darkness, in all her demonic pride. This was usually the custom for a creature of the Nightworld when in the presence of the Order or God *Damia.* When a creature stood before any of the hierarchy of the Nightworld, he or she usually donned his or her *true* form. It didn't matter how monstrous or appalling the monster standing before the Order was. In this place of trepidation, this place where creatures of all nightmares and wild imagination roamed the land, there were no secrets.

It wasn't until Lillian appeared before the Order, did she realize how much she missed the sultry climate of the Nightworld. Although, she had only been gone for a short span of time (time itself having no significance in the Nightworld), Lillian cringed at the thought of the heat she experienced in the Earth realm. The warmth there, in that desert town named Spook Valley, was artificial compared to the environment of the place she called home. No, that was false climate; that was heat filtered through ozone and toxins that permeated the polluted air. In the Nightworld, the searing temperature was natural, unbearable to the many strangers the Nightworld had abducted. The atmosphere was a product of the brilliant orange rivers of lava that twisted and crawled throughout the rigid terrain of red molten rock. In this place, shadows could catch fire. Lillian donned a placating grin as sweat dribbled in between the leathery orbs that were her breasts.

All six of the Order gathered around Lillian in horseshoe formation, confiding in her the information they shared with virtually no other minion of the Nightworld. However, Lillian was different from the other creatures that stormed this land. She was the oldest of the creatures and had existed longer than all besides God *Damia* and the Order themselves. She was one that could be trusted; she was the most vicious soul that resided in the Nightworld. Lillian had never failed her brethren.

Saint Trace began speaking, for he appeared the leader of the group, these Saints of darkness. Saint Trace usually appeared before Lillian without the hood that covered his grotesque features. Yes, she had witnessed his beautiful eyes of sunken gore and desiccated face many of times. However, when the Order met in a group, they all remained cloaked and donned brown hoods. "The Day is drawing near, when our world will merge with the realm of planet Earth."

Lillian's scaly snub of a tail slithered back in forth in accomplished excitement. "I, too, am looking forward to this coming day, my brethren."

Saint Collin remarked, his gurgling voice spilling words over his lips like bloodied pleas of a dying man. "But we must keep the one called Stefan from learning the secrets of the pact."

Next, Saint Dante spoke and he did so in a rushing, hoarse whisper. "I wouldn't mind crossing over and making him suffer myself if not—"

"For the pact," Saint Israel finished. Saint Israel was the youngest of all the Order and his voice was closer to normal than the rest of the group. His voice reflected that closest to human inflection.

Saint Cassius began fueling the conversation, as if each must speak, as if each man must finish the collective thought. For they were one collective consciousness, they were the six heads of a proverbial beast and their weaknesses lay in their dependence upon one another. "This is true; we cannot kill Stefan at this time. For it is written that he is the One. But we must keep him from contacting the others, from getting any information of us from them. It seems that there were ears listening at times when we were unaware."

"Yesssss," Saint Batiste hissed in high resound. "The two who have betrayed us, Breckin and Aaron."

"God *Damia* has assured me that Aaron will cooperate with us. In fact, he will be the one who lures Stefan into our grasp. And," Saint Trace added, "he will assist Lillian with Breckin's demise."

"Yes," Saint Israel affirmed. "Breckin will learn that nobody escapes us."

Lillian writhed in her rubbery and withered skin as if in discomfort. "And what of the witch called Catrina?"

Saint Collin sloshed the answer. "She is already dying. She is a vegetable to the world and can neither speak nor move."

"But I only wish her death were more painful," Lillian contested.

"You have your target, Lillian," Saint Trace informed her. "Now run off demon child and create the coming of a revelation."

Lillian pivoted on one webbed foot and casually strolled upon the jagged paths of the Nightworld. With each step, she came closer to the doorway leading to the Earth realm.

Beneath the cover of crackling fires and torturous screams, the Order of Perennial Darkness chanted in a rhythm of dark and harmonic chords as they bowed their heads at the feet of God *Damia.*

-2-

Stefan was in a state of shock as he managed to mumble a response to the tall man before him. "Catrina's brother?"

"Yes," the man named Lysander (or, Zander, as he liked to be called) asserted.

It took no time whatsoever for Stefan to figure this one out. Indeed, he knew he was face to face with a creature from the Nightworld. Stefan knew Catrina Taylor inside and out; he knew of her horrible family that consisted of a bitch of a mother and a bastard of a father and *never* a brother. So it was that Stefan prepared himself to contend with the unexpected creature before him. "Catrina doesn't have a brother."

"I assure you she does," Zander calmly spoke.

Stefan didn't buy it. Catrina was his best friend, they had shared years of close friendship and she never mentioned once ever having a sibling. Something clicked. Wheels of terror turned in Stefan's head as he realized that this man was here to keep Catrina restrained, kill her if he had to. "You won't get me you fucking beast," Stefan spoke. "And you won't get her."

"What are you talking about? I love my sister." And then the tables turned. Once Zander had enough crazy accusation from this young man, he decided to break out his own word weaponry. "Who the hell are you? What are *you* doing here?"

"I'm her best friend and she has never spoken a word about a brother named Zander."

Zander's eyes cast downward and his shoulders slouched. "Perhaps she still hates me." With that, he plopped down into the chair next to Catrina's hospital bed. He placed his face in his large hands and rested his elbows onto his knees.

Stefan held back his hostility. Perhaps he was wrong. Oh god, and what a terrible thing, what such terrible things to say to a brother grieving for his comatose sister. Stefan brought his own vocal tone down to level of compassion. "Why would she hate her own brother?"

Zander pulled his face from his hands, using both index and middle fingers to wipe the tears forming in his eyes. He addressed Stefan with a voice full of enrapturing smoothness. "Are you *really* her best friend?"

Stefan nodded.

"Does she like it here, in this place, in this small town away from our mother and father?

"Since I've known her for just over two years, I've only seen her cry once," Stefan commented. "She's a very wonderful woman." Stefan approached Catrina's still body. Her chest slowly heaved up and down from the respirator covering her mouth. He ran his fingers through the tangled strands of her auburn mane. Stefan wanted to kiss her, pretended in his mind that she was Sleeping Beauty and he was the long awaited prince that would awaken her from her forever sleep. And he did—he gently pressed his lips to her forehead and felt a bit dismayed when her eyes didn't flutter open.

Without warning, Zander cut in and distracted Stefan from his reverie of hope. "You see, I left her."

"How do you mean?" Stefan asked, his mind fully curious.

Zander continued and Stefan listened. Yes, his sympathetic ear was open to Zander now since Stefan harbored suspicion that this man was telling the truth. If he was, Stefan would be learning something new about his best friend, something that runs deeper than friendship. *Some secrets are worth keeping; some tales are better left untold so that the tears won't well. Keep the tears back, my star child; keep your face beautiful and your mouth turned upward in a smile. Sometimes, the past is worth forgetting.*

"When I was seventeen and Catrina only twelve, I left for New York. I actually didn't have it planned as to where I was heading. I just knew that I couldn't stay in that house any longer with our mother and father. She told you of our parents, didn't she?"

Stefan slowly nodded. Sure, he knew the stories of Rob and Angie Taylor and how they accused Catrina of being involved with Satanism just because she listened to certain music or put on too much eye shadow. Stefan recalled how Catrina had told him about her many days of locking the door to her room, not eating or sleeping or even using the bathroom, just so she could escape the sight of her parents. Her parents wanted to rule her life, choose Catrina's friends, clothes, and extracurricular activities. Well, she eventually got fed up with their strict rules and Christian ways and left. She up and went with no warning just as Stefan now knew that Zander apparently did when he was seventeen.

Zander talked on. "Well, I was the only thing that Catrina loved in that whole damn house. She and I used to stay up late, play games, listen to music, and talk all through the night. Of course, we remained quiet so that Mother and Father wouldn't bitch us out for not getting our 'forty winks.' She confided a lot in me and she always knew, at the times when she had to cry or get something off her mind, she could come to me. I would be there, comforting her, shielding her tears from the horror of Mother and Father. One day, I just couldn't take their strict rules any longer. I was sick of it all. I was seventeen and wanted my own life, not the life they wanted me to have. So, I up and left. I didn't say a word to anybody, but I did leave Catrina a note under her pillow before I slipped out of my bedroom window.

"Since then, I have had no contact with any of the family. I had a keen sense that Catrina hated me for doing that to her and I've felt guilty for a long time. Then it felt like a dream, like a nightmare I finally woke from, and my past fell away piece by piece until I forgot about even her." Zander gestured to his sister who lay unconscious.

"So how did you find her here?" Stefan curiously queried.

"Believe it or not, the Spook Valley Police contacted me when she was admitted. I had apparently been the person to contact in case of an emergency.

The strange thing is that I don't know how they got my number in New York. Catrina never knew how to contact me."

"You'd be amazed at how they can track people these days with only a name," Stefan shrugged off the weirdness of it all.

"When they called, I was in complete shock. My sister; I had a sister. I had to remember and I tried to picture the face of a twelve year old in my mind. I cried on the airplane and when I got to the hospital, I could not believe how she had grown into such a fine woman. I can't wait until she wakes up."

"Neither can I," Stefan added. After all, he was hoping that Catrina could supply him with answers of how she was injured. Was it Breckin? Aaron? Or was Breckin telling the truth when he explained that it was the powerful Lillian who'd attacked Catrina? Only one person knew…and she lay in a coma.

Zander briskly changed the subject, obviously not wanting to think of Catrina's condition. "Why did you call me a 'beast'?"

"Huh?"

"Earlier, before I gave you the exciting and short biography of my life from age seventeen to age twenty-seven, you yelled that I wouldn't get you or Catrina. You called me a 'beast.'"

"Oh, I didn't mean that," Stefan apologized. "It was nothing." He dare not tell Zander of this whole nightmarish ordeal, of the Nightworld and of the pact. No, there was no need to bring another into this mixture of carnage and dread.

"What *exactly* happened to her?"

"I don't know," Stefan lied as he stared into Zander's russet-colored eyes. How could he lie like this? How could he tell such a horrible fabrication to Catrina's long lost brother?

"I'm sorry," Zander expressed regret as if he a polite Englishman, "I didn't catch your name."

"Oh," Stefan extended his hand. "I'm Stefan Powell." Stefan observed a flinch in the wrist of Zander as he shook his hand, however slight. What did Zander know that he didn't? Did he have the same sense of extrasensory perception that his sister had?

Both men looked over Catrina Taylor and studied her every breath. They mentally prayed for her to awaken. Yet, both doubted, that there was such a god to answer their prayers…

-3-

…yet she floated…

Through the sea of billowing whiteness and among the electric blue of her surroundings, Catrina Taylor basted in her unnatural flight. She didn't have to see her reflection to know that she was smiling from ear to ear. Once again, there they all appeared, like specters in a dream—Stefan, her parents, Zander, and another. In the distance, she could have sworn she heard chanting like that of a clan of monks. And if she attempted to catch the below in the corner of her eye, like an unpleasing stalker that ruined her delight, she thought she saw flames. No. Instead, she looked straight ahead and all around her to the revisiting images of her friends and family. She practically laughed in mockery when she caught a glimpse of Stefan and Zander holding hands. Suddenly, from behind her, she felt a presence like when one knows that somebody is standing behind him but is too afraid to turn and face whatever it may be. Catrina used both of her arms to sway the air to the left of her soaring body. When she maneuvered her body to the image behind her, she caught a brief glimpse of blonde hair, flawless skin, and ruby eyes. Aaron! But Aaron's image slipped downward into that place of crimson and heat. She must go and save him. Catrina kicked her feet behind her, descending from her comforting altitude. She tried to yell his name, but no sound emitted from her vocal chords. Instead, she could only perceive her mouth moving in the shape of the hollowed word that formed over her lips.

Aaron…

-4-

…*Aaaaaronn.*

Aaaaaronn.

The voice called to Aaron within his head, but it didn't belong to God *Damia*. No, this voice was softer, gentler, and could only be that of an innocent. It sound as if he had heard that voice before. The only difference was that it was clearer at the time, not hollow as if it were being projected down an endless tunnel.

It didn't take Aaron Dabney long to recognize that voice. It was Catrina! Yes, it was the woman who he almost attacked the night previous and she consoled him in his beastly form, causing him to run away in a rage of embarrassment. Sure enough, it had to be her! But where were the soft tones of inflection coming from?

Aaron stood up from the recliner of the motel room and advanced toward the window where he peered outside, left and right, trying to locate Catrina. Was she in trouble?

Aaron! The calling was louder, crisper, more human than ghostly as it had sounded before.

He soon thought of Stefan. Aaron reminisced of the relationship between Catrina and Stefan. So was it Catrina who was in trouble or Stefan? His mind raced in confusion. Between this new disclosure and the words of God *Damia* that incessantly haunted him, his only concern was of the safety of Stefan. From the bowels of the Nightworld, God *Damia* instructed Aaron to hold Stefan captive, like a prisoner for the hungry pleasures the minions of that place had in store for him. Yet, on the other hand, Catrina called out to Aaron and he knew not if it was a warning or certainly a plea for help.

In the end, Aaron had to take it as some type of warning. Warning, yes. A warning just as he had done with Catrina when he scrawled a script of blood on her door and mirror and pasted the Tarot card of the Moon upon her door. That was his way of warning her about not getting involved and to beware of his own shapeshifting self, if not for her own protection. Instead, Catrina became more curious and, ultimately, ignored the words of caution he'd left for her. Instead, she attempted to crack the mystery of the cryptic messages and god knows what happened to her that previous night in the desert when he had run off on all fours.

Warnings become mysteries and the human race is beguiled by such mysteries with their curiosity. Aaron was no different. Although he projected from the Nightworld as a creature, he had once been a human. So it was that, with the last human feelings he had left, Aaron ventured from the motel room en route to Stefan's apartment. The calling of Catrina's voice informed him that something was terribly wrong. If God *Damia* didn't like it, well, then Aaron would just have to suffer the consequences later.

-5-

By five o'clock, Laine Young still had not heard from Stefan. He was due in for his shift at one o'clock and Laine was tired, wanted to sit in a comforting recliner, forget about the past fifteen hours, and pour a tall tumbler of Jim Beam to relax him. Laine never thought himself as an alcoholic before today; for he wanted, no he *needed* the sweet/sour taste of bourbon to comfort him. Or perhaps it was a reaction to all of the stress of having to arrive at the store in the wee hours of the morning, view the mangled body of Ricky, and train the new kid, Lucien.

Time had passed quickly as he trained Lucien. The kid, as eccentric as he appeared, was well mannered and a quick learner. In addition, the teens and twenty-something customers took to Lucien with his black hair, emerald eyes, and pale skin. Time was forgotten as Lucien asked question after question about bands and shipments of new arrivals. He impressed Laine with his integrity and willingness to learn.

It was late in the afternoon, and Laine had allowed Lucien on the register for the past two hours. Laine made careful observations from the corner of his eye to see if the kid was trying to pocket any money. Good, moralistic help, especially young help, was hard to come by these days if you expected to make a dollar for yourself. Still, it seemed that Lucien was honest and didn't hesitate once as he took the money from the customers, counted their change back properly, and instantly closed the till of the register.

Why hadn't Stefan called? It wasn't like him at all. The kid only missed two days in the years that he'd worked at Laine's Music. *Something was wrong*, Laine thought to himself, and then the phone rang.

"Laine's Music, this is Laine."

"Hey, it's Stefan," the voice from the other end answered his prayers.

"Where have you been?" Laine asked with a shock of concern in his voice.

"Catrina's in the hospital."

"Oh, I'm so sorry."

"I can't make it in today, Laine."

"Did you hear about Ricky?"

"Yeah," Stefan paused. "I did."

"Are you going to be all right?"

"Yeah, I'll be fine."

"Take all the time you need off, kid. I just hired a new guy to help."

"Good," Stefan said with a sigh of relief. "I didn't want you to have to run the place alone."

"Don't worry about it, kid," Laine assured him.

"OK. I'll call you tomorrow and let you know how things are going."

"You do that, Stefan. Please, get some rest."

"I will."

"Bye."

"Good bye."

There was a long pause between Stefan's closing and the click of the phone. *Poor guy,* Laine thought. He turned his attention to Lucien, hesitating with the offer that mulled in his head.

"How would you feel about working a double? I mean, closing the store up? Would you feel comfortable enough if I wasn't here?" Laine knew he was taking a risk.

"Sure," Lucien agreed in his singsong voice. "Isn't Stefan coming in?"

"No. He has some things he needs to deal with. I can give you my home number though, if there are any problems." Laine desperately wanted to go home and needed some rest.

"OK. I can do that," Lucien responded matter-of-factly.

"Good," Laine said. "This is your night to prove yourself, kid." Laine realized, however, that Lucien didn't have a key to lock up. Laine only had his key and old man Owens, the town locksmith, had just closed shop. Feeling desperate to get home, Laine made another big risk, considering that he had only known Lucien for a day. At this point, however, it didn't make a difference. Laine wanted to get home.

"I'll tell you want I'm going to do and I'm only doing this because I trust you, kid."

Lucian's ears perked up.

"I'm going to give you the keys to my truck and I want you to go to Stefan's place to get his key so you can lock up."

"OK," Lucien agreed, a smile on his face ignited by the instant trust that the storeowner of Laine's Music had in him.

"I'll tell you what though…," Laine endeavored to appear mean and stern. "…you put as much as a scratch in her, I'll take it from your paycheck."

"No problem," Lucien reassured. Exactly the words that Laine wanted to hear.

Laine began giving directions to the Shadowood Apartments, where Stefan resided. He told Lucien that he expected him back within forty-five minutes and no more. He instructed Lucien to retrieve the key to the store from Stefan and, if Stefan had a problem, to give him a call.

Lucien strode out the door of Laine's Music and got into the owner's truck, firing the engine quickly. Laine almost cringed, but he trusted the kid.

-6-

After hanging up the receiver of the phone, Breckin instantly began asking Stefan questions. There were no kisses hello, no embraces with the obligatory *where have you been all day?* Breckin wanted answers.

"Did you find him? Did you find *Aaron*?" Breckin forced a sarcastic emphasis on Aaron's name.

"Actually," Stefan replied, "I didn't. I did meet someone else though."

"Oh?" Breckin acknowledged in complete wonder.

"Yeah. Believe it or not, it was Catrina's *brother*." Stefan laughed for the first time Breckin had seen him laugh since they'd met.

Breckin remained calm. *As long as it wasn't Aaron.* "I didn't know Catrina had a brother. Then again, I haven't known Catrina as long as you have."

"That's the thing," Stefan admitted. "I didn't know she had a brother either."

Wait a minute. An alert went off in Breckin's head. "Stefan, I have to ask you this. I mean…ummm…are you sure he is her brother?"

"What do you mean?"

"You know damn well what I *mean*," Breckin snapped. "Isn't it funny how he suddenly appeared from out of nowhere?"

"Oh, I know what you're trying to say. Are you saying that, now, Catrina's brother is involved with the Nightworld?"

"Now that you mentioned it, what's his name?"

Stefan became instantly infuriated with Breckin. "Fuck off," he yelled. Just as quickly as he had said those words that stabbed Breckin in the heart, Stefan wanted to take them back. Surely, he didn't *really* mean that. Stefan gazed into Breckin's bright green eyes and remembered how he had come to love the man at who he now yelled. *I remember*, he thought. *This is the man I saved. This is the man I have grown to love, every inch of body and each nightmarish vision. And the bliss, there was a bliss of animal lovemaking, a synchronicity of lusted bodies that tore at each others flesh all through the nights that ended with a embrace that could last forever.* What was he doing? What the hell had gotten a hold of Stefan and turned his hatred toward this man who'd given him the gift of eternal life? Was it the passion for Aaron? The desire for flesh undiscovered?

"I'm sorry," Stefan expressed regret.

Breckin was in awe of Stefan's instantaneous change from revulsion to love. Still, with the Nightworld on the brink of making a major leap in initiating the pact, Breckin could not let the idea of Stefan's new acquaintance sift through his fingers and go without notice. "What's his name?" Surely, Breckin would know if it was one from the Nightworld, for he knew the names by memory, his life was nothing more than monsters and torture and names in that place.

"His name is Zander," Stefan gave in.

Breckin searched his mind for the name, making an attempt to recollect the evil that he'd come face to face with on a regular basis. "Zander?"

"Yeah, it's short for Lysander."

There was a knock at the apartment door and Stefan immediately went to answer it. *Please,* he imagined, *let it be Aaron. I so wish to see him! Let it be Aaron and let him come into my home and we will talk of this pact. I will show Breckin that he isn't as bad as Breckin thinks and maybe they will learn to appreciate one another. Perhaps we'll hold hands together and chant a prayer for Catrina to her God and Goddess. Perhaps we'll all cry for her. Perhaps we'll all hold each other together. Perhaps.*

To Stefan's disappointment, he saw a young man that appeared a colored opposite of Aaron. Instead of blonde hair, this guy donned black. Instead of tanned skin, this kid's flesh was pale. "Can I help you?"

"Are you Stefan?"

Upon hearing those words, out of immediate protection for his lover, Breckin ran to the door to view the guy standing at the threshold.

"Yes, I'm Stefan, why?"

"I'm Lucien," the young man said. "Laine hired me at the store and wanted me to come by for the key so I can close tonight."

Stefan didn't think twice about giving the kid the key off his key ring. After all, Laine had already mentioned that he'd hired a new guy. So this was he—sleek in his black clothing and clearly donning the façade of a Hollywood vampire.

"Wait a minute," Breckin spoke as he attempted to grab Lucien's arm. There was something wrong about this guy.

"I'm sorry; I have to go. Laine is expecting me back." With that, Lucien turned from the two men and started down the cement staircase.

Stefan glanced to Breckin. "What's wrong?"

"I don't know. Something just doesn't...I don't know." Breckin was at a loss for words and couldn't quite pinpoint the air of discomfort he experienced in the brief presence of Lucien.

"Aaron!" Stefan blurted his name as if he was Stefan's savior. He rushed out the doorway of the apartment.

Breckin targeted Aaron in the parking lot of the Shadowood apartments, just as Lucien was pulling out in a Nissan Frontier. Breckin studied Stefan clumsily rushing down the stairs toward Aaron. No, he couldn't let Stefan near that man! Standing in the wide space of the open doorway, Breckin stared at the two.

Stefan ran to Aaron and, as he came within proximity, he wrapped his arms around the man. Aaron was unsure as to how to take this, yet he didn't hesitate to place his own arms around Stefan's broad shoulders and hold him. *Just revel in this touch for the moment!* How graceful it was, how quaint and utterly relieving!

"You're all right," Aaron acknowledged.

"Of course I am," Stefan replied. "But I need to talk to you. I need to talk to both you and Breckin. Will you please come up to the apartment?"

Aaron gazed up to Breckin who stood in the entrance of the apartment. Their eyes locked for a brisk second before Aaron turned away from the cold stare. "I'm not sure that's a good idea."

"It's fine," Stefan gave surety. And then, "You're not out to harm us, are you?"

"No!"

"Then you're fine. Breckin's just a little on edge. To be honest with you, he doesn't trust you with me."

"Really? I just came because Catrin—"

"What about Catrina?" Stefan asked, cutting off Aaron's words.

"Nothing. Let's talk inside."

Stefan and Aaron climbed the stairs, side by side, and all the while Breckin glowered at the two. Approaching the apartment, Breckin maneuvered to the side of the doorway and let the two enter.

"Aaron," Breckin beamed. "What are you?"

"What?" Aaron asked, caught off guard.

Breckin turned his back to the outside, standing in the doorway with both hands pressing against the panes, in a wanton Jesus-Christ-pose, and staring at the two men who accompanied each other in the entryway. Breckin felt the tingles crawl all over his shoulder and lower back—the sensation that another of the Nightworld was close by…Aaron. He shrugged it off and stood his ground. "I asked, 'what are you?' What creature are you? I know I've seen you in the Nightworld before."

Aaron was dumbfounded. He couldn't just admit, right here and now, that he was cursed with the horror of being a werewolf. Not in front of Stefan, no!

There were so many faces and names for Breckin to take in. There were so many reasons to keep Stefan protected from the Nightworld, so many mysteries that Breckin had not realized—Aaron, Catrina's *brother* Zander (or *Lysander*), and Lucien. Which body was host to the evil that could destroy Stefan and lay the path for destruction upon the Earth realm?

"I'm not here to harm you," Aaron replied.

"Then why are you here?" Breckin rudely asked.

Stefan glared at Breckin with scorn. How dare him! Above Breckin's shoulders, beyond his frame that stood in the open doorway, Stefan viewed another figure. He hollered; Stefan screamed at the top of his lungs in disbelief. "BRECKIN!!!"

She had appeared behind Breckin, a vibrant and abrupt shadow against the dusk of another evening. Lillian lunged forth, an oak stake in her hands, and forcefully drove it into Breckin's back. There were two sounds: the exasperated cry of Lillian (her warrior breath of determination) and the horrid sound of the sharpened stake pummeling into Breckin's flesh, like the sound of a shovel pulverizing sand.

Neither Stefan nor Aaron could move; they both stood frozen in trauma.

Lillian roared in defeat, leaving the stake buried in between Breckin's shoulder blades. The resonance of her voice was like a low moan that incessantly repeated over and over. She gazed at both Stefan and Aaron, and then casually strolled away from the scene, knowing that she could not cross the threshold of the home.

Stefan reached out. "No," he viciously bellowed.

Aaron stood bemused by the untimely scene, amazed by the endless efforts of God *Damia*'s minions.

Breckin arched his back in an unending and hollow scream that ignited the room with craze. His heart had been pierced and he could feel the awful agony. The undying pain began in his chest and ruptured throughout his arms and legs. Breckin's feet began to rise from the ground until his entire body was floating horizontally in the air. His flesh began to break down—the skin of his pale arms and legs melted from his bones and, before dripping onto the carpet, it dissipated into the atmosphere. All the time, Breckin shrieked toward Stefan, attempting to turn his dissolving head toward the man he loved. Breckin's frame shivered and trembled in convulsing rhythms, shaking so hard that he could feel the grinding of bone against bone—that scratching sound that caused his stomach to regurgitate, that awful sound like paper being torn to shreds and it was happening to *his* body! He could not lose, no! He could not let Stefan fight this battle alone. *Oh God, if ever there is one, let this not happen! Please! Stop this from happening!* Yet the dripping of his pale flesh was consumed by air and an implosion of all Breckin's insides was sucked into some unknown wormhole of dark horrors. His skin went to gory liquid, the liquid to ash, and the ash to the air. *Hold you, yes! Would hold you if I had a body; would protect you with each molecule from that place.* And right before Stefan's amazed eyes, Breckin's body became nothing but dark wisps that curled into the atmosphere.

Stefan reached out with an ever-gripping hand. *No, this can't be happening*, he wanted to assure himself. But it was. Oh god in dear Heaven, it was! A tickling feeling engulfed Stefan as he wept.

Aaron stood as a statue, surely with granite limbs and frozen eyes.

Stefan extended both his arms, endeavoring to grab the smoke that Breckin had become, in an attempt to hold him one last time. But he knew he wouldn't. This was horrifically and impossibly the end. Stefan cried; oh, how he cried. This was all he had left; this was his only known positive link to the Nightworld. Now, it had been taken from him. This love. How he recanted every bad thing he had said to Breckin. How he had wished to hold back all those negative words. This was real and, yet, seemed like another dream. This was the death of somebody that he could never imagine dying. Stefan fell to his knees, tears anxiously running down his cheeks.

An invigorating sensation crawled through Stefan's insides. It squirmed through his viscera and tickled as it exited the pores of his flesh. Stefan immediately comprehended what it meant. It was the vampiric essence leaving his body. Stefan Powell was returning to human form. But he also realized that it meant that the vampire who'd turned him had been destroyed. Breckin was dead. It was the chilling truth that he could not deny.

CHAPTER XIII

-1-

Evil lurks in the shadows of your every move.

It has numerous faces, for you have been graced by the many visages of comely features and delectable curves. And, isn't that queer? Isn't it amazing, at the same time, how the faces of Evil are precious and no different from yours? Perhaps Satan was the most ravishing of angels within the bowels of Heaven. That reference wouldn't surprise you now, would it? Then again, the lusting features of Evil are only facades; they're simply a gift of temptation to you—the nice guy, the normal guy, the one whom Evil awaits with the patience of an ageless god. And you've seen the monsters behind the masks, you been terrified by their jagged teeth and scaly flesh. It makes you tremble, doesn't it? Have you ever trembled like that before? Surely as a child hiding beneath his sheets, fretting from an imaginary bogeyman, you've witnessed the shivers of dread. But have you ever trembled as a man before?

It waits.

It could be outside your front door right now, couldn't it? And you know you're not overreacting to the concept because you've seen it at the threshold of your home on more than one occasion. So where else can you go now? How can you escape something that lingers at every corner you turn like an overzealous stalker? But it's just a small town, Spook Valley, and that scares you even more. You wonder if that terrible place harbors enough evil to put the whole town at risk and then you immediately dismiss the revelation, for you already know the answer to that. Innocent residents of the town have already fallen, conquered like pawns in a bloody game of chess where a 'checkmate' may dictate a future of carnage and mayhem. Flesh of the bystander has been shredded and mauled, blood spilled upon the once peaceful streets of Spook Valley. Nowhere to go but to remain prisoner in your own home, and how much longer will that be a safe haven? Yes, you've seen Evil at your doorstep and wonder what it would be like if the threat was reversed. Perhaps you should stand at the threshold of Evil's doorway; but how would you ever keep your heart from bursting with the fear of what lies on the other side?

Evil has an insatiable appetite and its hunger grows with each passing day. You've been eyewitness to its yearn for the flesh. You've seen it consume the lives around you. You're best friend unconsciously rests in the hospital, the truest friend you've ever known. It frustrates you, the fact that you can hold her and pray for her and she does not motion toward your empathy. That same evil has stricken down your lover and you have never known such awe, never experienced such pain from the demise of a loved one. And you weep; you weep for those emerald eyes and oval face of a demi-god. It's all right, go ahead and cry, for you are only a man now. Allow the one beside you to console your body. Know this though—beware of all; for the one closest to you may be a vessel for Evil. The stranger roaming the streets may be a beast on the prowl. Even a best friend, may be tainted with the touch of Evil.

It waits and is slowly consuming you. What can you do to stop it now?

-2-

The inky shades of night returned to Spook Valley. It was deep into the waning hour of midnight as time proceeded from the cusp of the witching hour to the silence of the after meridian. The night skies were so clear and free of clouds that a million stars cast their brilliance downward and illuminated the small town where one fell to his death hours previous. *Wish on those stars, you most certainly would if you believed wishes could come true.*

Stefan writhed in his lonely bed, a bed he had grown accustomed to sharing with Breckin. He tossed and turned and every position in which he attempted to fall to sleep felt uncomfortable, empty. Though his body was exhausted with the pangs of emotional outpour, his mind raced with thoughts of Breckin and of his horrible death. Death? No, it was murder! That monstrous beast Lillian had destroyed Breckin and that could not be forgotten. Her beautiful face remained an unforgettable image of trepidation in Stefan's haunted mind.

Stefan threw his body to its other side and endeavored to close his eyes. Yes, wouldn't it be great if it was all a nightmare? *Remember those strong hands? Do you remember their touch upon your naked flesh—a soothing of his fingers along the small of your back and how they roved over your hips and firmly cupped your stomach? And what about his breath? Do you recall the rhythmic soothing of his breath against the nape of your neck as his arm wrapped around your chest and held you close? The lovemaking—could you ever experience something close to those heated thrusts and liquid motions? Strange how the person you thought you could do without disturbs your every thought. Funny how you don't know what you've got until it's gone.*

Stefan beamed out of his bed, unable to sleep with the unending images of Breckin that permeated his mind. He wiped at the moist flesh around his eyes and languidly strolled out of the bedroom, wondering if Aaron was still awake in the next room.

-3-

Laine could finally sleep. The realms of dreamland cradled and solaced Laine from his overexertion of a long day, possibly a longer and more trying day than he had been used to. As soon as Lucien had returned with Stefan's key to the store, along with Laine's truck (which remained absent of any dents or scratches), he gave Lucien a quick overview of store closing procedures. In a matter of minutes, Laine had left his music store in the hands of Lucien and headed home. Once there, it only took Laine ten minutes (after downing a bourbon and smoking a cigarette) to make his way into his bed and pull the covers over his body. He made sure the cordless telephone was right next to him, should Lucien have any problems or questions.

It seemed that Lucien closed Laine's Music with ease, because it was shortly after one in the morning that Laine continued his long uninterrupted sleep until he fluttered his eyes open and noticed the orange numbers on the digital clock that rested upon the nightstand. He reveled in his assurance that he was able to trust Lucien. He closed the store without a hitch. Another good employee whom he now had working for him.

A lithe shape moved in the corner of his bedroom and Laine immediately opened his eyes wider to make out the form. *Was there somebody there? Had a prowler entered his home?* Laine realized that it had to be a trick of light playing against the shape of his jean jacket that hung on the freestanding coat rack. Inanimate objects can appear as anything the human mind makes them out to be when there is no light to distinguish the borders and outlines of black on black. But then, to Laine's astonishment, the figure moved from out of the corner and approached the foot of his bed.

It was a woman. She was the most captivating and gorgeous female Laine had ever encountered. The stranger's face appeared delicate, sculpted from the unimagined soft clay of ivory, and her eyes glistened and gave off a light of their own. Her dark, wavy curls of hair spilt over her shoulders and in front of her breasts. Laine glanced down beyond the hair that concealed the woman's frontal nudity and made a visual trail down to her flat, supple stomach. She was completely naked as Laine made out a trim and contained patch of hair between the woman's thin legs. Laine's own sexual organ was growing excited and firm. Although he preferred younger men, Laine couldn't help but to feel aroused by the beauty looming over him.

"Who are you?" Laine called out and broke the tempestuous silence.

The woman placed an index finger to her lips. "Shhhhhhhh." The sound was so gentle and powerfully erotic.

Laine reached out his fingers to touch the woman's stomach; her flesh was icy yet smooth. The woman bent her knees and fell forward onto the bed. Both of her hands that broke her fall were on either side of Laine's head. She ripped away the sheet that came between Laine's body and her own. Now Laine could feel her naked body on his own, her cold flesh upon his warm body. His firmness anxiously pressed against her inner thighs and Laine experienced a tingling sensation that shot through his entire body.

The woman kissed about Laine's chest, her tongue lapping at his hairs and making a wet path down to his stomach. She brought her face up to his and touched his lips with her own full, wet lips. The woman licked the side of Laine's face and then his ear. "Join us," she whispered in a soothing voice.

"What?" Laine asked, getting more excited and about ready to orgasm. "What's your name, baby?"

"Lillian."

Lillian, Laine thought. *Like a lily. A fresh blossom in the summer; a beautiful flower. Summer breezes lifting her soft petals. Nothing could be more appropriate for this stunning woman.*

"Call Stefan over," Lillian whispered as she tongued the lobe of Laine's ear.

"Stefan? What?" *How had she known Stefan?* As much as it excited Laine, for he did find Stefan cute and had always imagined fucking the young man, the thought bewildered Laine in the heated moment.

"Shhhhhhhhh."

Lillian raised her hips in the air and brought her crotch down onto Laine's hard shaft, straddling it in the way she always did to the men she visited in their dreamy states of mind. She slid down the length and Laine moaned in an ecstasy he hadn't experienced in a very long time. Lillian placed her hands on Laine's shoulders, riding his organ up and down in a slow and slick motion.

Laine's eyes were closed as soon as Lillian consumed his cock. He felt her moving up and down, his mouth agape, lips drying from the pushes of breath that blew over them. A tickling began forming at the base of his cock and Laine grunted as he began pushing himself deeper into Lillian. When he opened his eyes, his body recoiled into the mattress as far as it could go. The comely stranger named Lillian no longer sat upon him. Instead, it was a monstrous beast, absent of any hair and with skin that was scorched and repulsive. A tongue of impossible length shot from the creature's mouth and lapped at his chest. Laine was repulsed and tried to push the beast off him, however it retaliated, gripping both of his wrists and forcing them back onto the bed.

Lillian rode Laine as she did her skeletal horses in the Nightworld; each stride and every push made her insides feel explosive.

As much as Laine endeavored to resist the creature, its crotch continued to bob up and down upon him. Oh, it felt so good and, at the same time, was horrifying. The bubbling sensation began to travel up his cock, toward the tip.

Lillian went faster, up and down, and held Laine's hands from resisting her. Faster and faster, and a sardonic grin grew upon her demonic face. "Join us!" She yelled at the man.

Her voice wasn't soothing now, no! It was like the echoing of low timbre. It was ghastly! However, Laine couldn't help himself as he erupted inside of the creature. It felt like a million explosions of his nerve endings going off all at once.

Scream. He would've screamed had he not just realized it was a dream. Laine bolted his head from the damp pillows upon which it nestled. His breathing was hard; his throat was dry. He could easily consume a gallon of water right now. There was silence in the bedroom and Laine briskly checked to see if there were any figures standing in the corner. Nothing. Laine listed to the heavy beat of his heart for several seconds and almost laughed in satisfaction that what he just experienced was only a nightmare. Still, it felt real.

Laine moved beneath his sheets and felt something cold and sticky all over his legs and lower stomach. When he placed his hand beneath the covers, he had discovered that he'd ejaculated all over himself.

-4-

Zander observed his sister, Catrina Taylor, for any sign that she may be waking. After two days of being in this hospital room, sitting next to the prone, comatose body of his sibling, Zander still couldn't believe that this was she.

He had thought about her many times, had wondered where she had gone, what she'd looked like, and what she was doing with her life. The only image of Catrina that Zander knew was of the time when she was just a child, before he made his 'exit stage' from their parent's house. He recalled the chubbiness in her face that, apparently now, had been lost through her adolescence. Instead, she donned a beautiful thin face. He reminisced about seeing her in pigtails—those two stubs of auburn hair that barely reached the nape of her neck. Now, Catrina's head, neck, and shoulders lay upon a pool of lengthy hair. Had she ever cut it? Had she grown it all this time? Had Mother and Father ever threatened to cut it as punishment, believing that only harlots and hippies kept their hair that long?

So this is the place she'd come to—Spook Valley. Zander was confused by the fact that Catrina would like small town life, given that the people were usually as strict as Mother and Father were. He would've thought that she'd at least move out of the state, not a mere eighty miles away.

And then there was that young man, the one with whom Zander encountered earlier, Stefan. Stefan claimed to be Catrina's best friend and Zander practically lost it. The young man had called him a 'beast' and that infuriated Zander. *How dare you say those things in front of my sister!* But Zander knew that would be the case when he felt that vibrant sensation upon shaking Stefan's hand.

Zander's mind was in a whorl of confusion. He knew that there had to be choices made, for Catrina's sake. Perhaps Catrina wouldn't have lapsed into a coma (which he still couldn't get answers as to why or how) had she gone some place further from Mother and Father's horrible grasp. Who were the true hosts for evil in this world? Perhaps, she would've liked New York City. All these questions and many more flooded Zander's thoughts. He had to go out and get some air. He had to get away, if only for a while.

The stillness of the night engulfed Spook Valley Medical Center and filled the place in silence. Most televisions were off by now and one could veritably hear the scrawls of pen on paper from the nurse on her graveyard shift who sat at the central station. As Zander passed by Catrina's bed, he studied her face. A single tear cascaded down her cheek. *I know,* Zander thought to himself, *the loss is unbearable.* Zander hoped that she would awaken soon.

-5-

Lucien battled with insomnia. The bed in the motel room was just as hard as the floor. He *wanted* to sleep, especially after working a double shift at

Laine's Music. Instead, there was something strange about the night. There was a weird stillness to it, a bizarre and unknown mute of the atmosphere.

As he arose from the uncomfortable bed, Lucien grabbed his sneakers and put them on. He opened the door to his motel room and stepped out into the night. Quiet. It was all so eerily quiet. There were neither pigeons cooing upon the rooftop of the motel nor snake rattlers emitting from the open desert across the street. The air was still, hot and muggy. A bead of perspiration raced over Lucien's forehead.

Lucien would take a walk. Yeah, that was it! Take a walk and burn some of the energy that was boiling within him. Then he could think about Stefan as well, concentrate on that precious face.

Lucien began walking the long and dark stretch of Violin Street, heading west toward the center of Spook Valley.

-6-

Stefan walked past the living room and quietly pulled out his journal. He wanted to make sure he didn't wake Aaron who had fallen asleep on the couch. He opened the journal to the next blank page…

From Stefan's Journal

I can't think straight. I keep imagining his face, his hands, and his body next to mine. I still can't believe that that woman, Lillian, destroyed Breckin. I think, perhaps, Breckin was right about Catrina and the others I accused him of hurting. Maybe it was Lillian who attacked Catrina instead of Breckin whom I had regretfully pointed a finger at. Why? Out of frustration? Or, maybe, I just can't cope in this world of horror where death and frightening creatures are all around me. I can't even distinguish who are the good ones, who are the bad ones, or who is out to get me. I still can't figure out why they just don't take me! Is there that much protection around me?

All I have left now is Catrina and I don't even know if she will ever awaken from her coma. Of course, there is Aaron, who I care deeply for. Still, I don't know him either. For all I know, he could be in on this whole thing, just pretending to like me. I don't know. I am so confused!! I need something; give me some type of guidance. Please!

I miss you Breckin. I'm sorry if I wronged you. I love you, Breckin. I'll make sure that woman pays for what she did to you…to us. I have nothing left to be afraid of because I've seen the most horrific thing already—your death. I will be your avenger and all of this will either be stopped, or the world as we know it will become a host for eternal evil. I love you, yes I do, and I remember the last glance you gave me, that face of yours in terrible pain, yet you still expressed that you loved me too.

As for Aaron, I find it very curious that he showed up just before Breckin was murdered. Was it to distract me? Oh, hell, I don't know whether to trust Aaron or—

Stefan's pen halted in mid script. A presence lingered behind him and he was too frightened to turn around. Stefan's heart raced and he jumped from his seat as a hand came down upon his shoulder. When he turned around, Stefan saw Aaron.

"You scared the hell out of me," Stefan snapped.

"I'm sorry, man. Are you all right?"

"Yeah, just great," Stefan said with sarcasm.

"It's all right to cry, man. I'm here for you, remember?"

"I said I was fine," Stefan hollered at Aaron. But it wasn't true and Stefan knew that. He wasn't fine; in fact, he was on the brink of snapping. All the while, Stefan continued thinking of Breckin's face. He imagined Breckin standing before him instead of Aaron. *Run to him and hold in your arms, yes! For there would be no better thing in the world. And plant butterfly kisses on his lips and run off together where nobody will ever find you. Make it all a fairy tale and don't forget to cry because it is all right to do so. Go ahead and release yourself.*

"Do you want me to leave?" Aaron asked.

Of course, Stefan didn't want that. He couldn't handle being alone with the thought of those creatures being right outside a window or the door or insidiously smiling at him from the other side of a mirror. "No. I want you to hold me." Stefan ran into Aaron's encompassing arms and began to let the tears fall heavy onto Aaron's shoulders.

Aaron, surprised by Stefan's reaction, held onto him tightly with both arms. *I could either hold you forever or hold you for God Damia,* Aaron thought. He felt an animalistic urge, an overbearing burning sensation between his legs, and led Stefan into the bedroom.

In the darkness of the room they kissed—lips onto suckling lips, tongues probing each other's mouth, faces buried at a side tilt and eyes closed. The passion between the two men was long overdue. This was now a time where fantasies had led to the real thing. And, the real thing, the truth of the daydream, with hearts racing in ecstasy, isn't it the grandest sensation in the world? No more imaginary desires to fulfill; no more thinking of the endless 'what ifs?'. No, this was the reality; this was flesh reacting to lustful flesh.

The two men broke the kiss and each tore off his shirt in a mad passion to expose his naked body to the other.

"I want you," Aaron spoke in between more kisses. He used his tongue and made a moist path down Stefan's neck. Aaron deliciously ran his tongue between the sculpted crevice in between Stefan's pectorals, making tantalizing circular motions around each of Stefan's dark nipples, and proceeded down to his firm stomach where he lapped at the soft chocolate hairs that made their own trail. From there, Aaron continued kissing Stefan's belly as he unbuttoned Stefan's jeans. The top button popped open and Aaron drew the zipper down slowly, trying his hardest not to rush this man as much as he wanted him. Aaron slid the pants down Stefan's slender hips and placed his mouth at the base of Stefan's solid cock. He licked at the salts beneath Stefan's organ, bringing the young man's testicles into his mouth for a brief moment, and then maneuvered his tongue up the long shaft to the perfectly rounded top that awaited consumption. Aaron lapped at the tip of Stefan's cock, felt the sensation of crushed velvet upon his lips, and then stood up to kiss Stefan's mouth again.

Stefan undid Aaron's pants, allowing them to fall around Aaron's ankles. He took Aaron's warm organ into his hand and gave it a few strokes to perk up Aaron's drive to take him here and now.

Aaron shoved Stefan on the bed behind and fell on top of him—two naked bodies writhing and twisting and experiencing the supple flesh of each other. *Melt. Could melt together if our bodies were any hotter!* Once again, Aaron went down on Stefan and, as he brought his tongue to Stefan's unyielding, pulsating organ, he swallowed it completely within his mouth. Stefan moaned. *Ahhhhhhh, the pleasure!* Aaron bobbed his head up and down the shaft as Stefan groaned in ecstatic gratification. Aaron's own cock was rock-solid and his animal instinct took over. Aaron viciously flipped Stefan onto his stomach and Stefan gripped the sheets of the bed. Aaron lapped at Stefan's shoulders, down to the small of his back, and parted his buttocks so that he could taste the forbidden desire that lay hidden in the body. Tongue probing, Stefan squirming and grunting, Aaron jumped atop of Stefan and shoved his organ deep into the young man. Thrust, push, slide out, repeat. Over and over again, he thrust into Stefan.

Stefan wanted to scream and attempted to discover that in between place, that parallel of pain and pleasure. *Stop. Oh god!* Yet it felt more wild and pleasurable than anything he had ever experienced. The agony became unbearable, those heavy drives of Aaron's cock, and Stefan yelped into the night. "Stop!"

Aaron didn't stop however. Instead, he pushed himself deeper within Stefan, pummeling into that animal bliss. And he growled! The animal within Aaron growled as he fucked like a beast and made love like an uncaring man.

Stefan heard the growl and it scared the hell out of him. What was Aaron doing? Furthermore, what the hell was Aaron? As much as he wanted to shove Aaron's body off his own, he hadn't the strength to do it. Aaron kept Stefan's hands pinned to the bed and continued to thrust.

Stefan didn't know whether to scream or laugh when his own cock ejaculated beneath his body, brought to the point of orgasm from what was happening and his organ rubbing upon the bed. He felt the liquid warmth seep beneath his stomach and slid upon it as Aaron continued pushing into him. Stefan felt Aaron's organ swell to enormous size within him as he thrust once more.

Aaron fell back, his breath erratic and heart speeding, as he orgasmed into Stefan. What shot into Stefan's body was a part of the love Aaron had for him and part of the animal that needed releasing. Still, beyond all selfish reason, Aaron cared a lot for Stefan. He shouldn't have taken it this far though, no! He should have stopped when Stefan said to. But that was when the beast within him took over and Aaron still had no control over that horrible creature that lay dormant in his body.

"Get the fuck off me!" Stefan yelled at Aaron as he flipped himself off the bed and got to his feet. Semen ran down Stefan's inner thigh.

"I'm sorry," Aaron attempted to apologize.

"What the fuck is wrong with you?"

Suddenly, Aaron felt enraged. Why did Stefan have to treat him as if he were not to be trusted? Hell, Aaron gave up a lot for this moment with Stefan. And he made this clear to him. "Don't disrespect me, man."

"Fuck off!"

"Do you know how easy it would've been to kill you?" Aaron rationalized.

Stefan didn't know what to do. His trust for Aaron was between being breached and confirmed at the same time. "Get out of my place," Stefan boldly hollered.

"I'll do that, man." Then, as Aaron began dressing, he directed his eyes that practically glowed crimson to Stefan. "I hope you can fight them alone."

Stefan trembled. Aaron began to exit the bedroom and, without warning, Stefan recoiled from the sight before him. Behind Aaron, transparent and hovering, was Breckin's body. Breckin glowered at Stefan and Stefan quickly called out to the man he had just told to leave. "Aaron?"

Aaron halted and pivoted toward Stefan. Perhaps an apology was already coming; perhaps Stefan realized that he couldn't fight the Nightworld alone. Maybe he needed Aaron more than he thought. "Yes?" Aaron softly asked.

Stefan gazed back at where Breckin's image had just been. It vanished into thin air in the same fashion it had when he was killed. "Nothing. Just leave."

Aaron walked out of the apartment and into the mysteriously pleasing night.

-7-

The Spook Valley Cemetery is located at the farthest, most Northern point of the town. There, it borders with a vast desert that may someday cradle the graves of the deceased in its hard barren dirt. The cemetery is traditional with mausoleums, high-arching tombstones, and sculptures marking the graves. The wind is still on this night and, even in this place of the dead, the air is warm and humid. Although the sky is clear of clouds, it is known that the monsoon will soon reach the area. With it, heavy rains will pummel upon the desert earth. Walls of dust collected from the desert floor will rise and sweep through the town. Some of the sculpted cherubs within the cemetery gaze up to the skies. They're chubby faces are either paused in a horrific scream or a playful laugh. Nobody knows, save for the artist or the sculptures themselves. Perhaps they are warning of a coming world that will creep from the desert and attempt to take over the realm of Earth. For tonight though, nobody is in the cemetery to decipher the faces of the statues save for one.

The man lurked from grave to grave. His back was hunched and his hands dangled down to where his knees are. The man knew he needed to feast.

He could feel that hunger in his stomach; his mouth watered at the thought of the forthcoming meal. He realized that his hair had thinned, his head wrinkled and bald and grotesque. His eyes were sunken into their sockets and the man's mouth was full of jagged, uneven teeth that protruded up and over his bloodied lips. The man comprehended that he was not the same man, nor did he resemble the same appearance of a man that arrived in Spook Valley only a day previous.

The man creature stalked each grave, paying attention to each tombstone, until he found the one bearing the name of Valerie Saunders carved into stone. She had only died a few nights ago; her body would still be fresh. With that, the creature tore at the earth, grabbing and digging at the dirt that marked the grave.

A half an hour later, a coffin was exposed, and the creature anxiously opened the lid. The girl's body that lay in the coffin was mangled; her flesh was pale and purple in areas. Decomposition was beginning to set in near her neck, where the maggots chewed away at it and left a tiny hole. This was of no consequence to the creature as he began ripping the flesh off the body and fervently stuffed it into his mouth. Chewy and tough, the creature continued to tear and shove the decrepit flesh into his hungry mouth.

The feast alleviated his hunger. However, during times such as this, the beast is reminded of that fateful rat.

-8-

Evil lurks in the shadows of your every move.

It waits.

What can you do to stop it now?

Maybe your love for him was that strong. Maybe love can transcend the realms of the afterlife. Surely, you believe it, for you saw his ghost. Yes, his ghost. You saw him watching you the way you were watching him, the two of you fascinated and in awesome wonder of each other's presence. What have you left now anyway? What is left but vengeance and hope that your friend awakens? And you will follow the guidance that has come for you, that same guidance for which you so secretly wished. You know it was him you saw; you know it was Breckin. Will you believe that though? Can you? You know you have no other choice but to believe. Just as you're thinking this, you see his image from the corner of your eye. Yes, there's that precious face, that face of a demi-god. And there are those emerald eyes and chocolate hair. Although his naked flesh is transparent, you can still view every curve of muscle and each carved feature of his body. Only you know what will happen should you go to him.

CHAPTER XIV

-1-

The soul, the transparent flesh on blackest night, spun and catapulted through the air like a bird gliding on wings forcefully rushed by a torrential wind. Freedom! That is what it felt like. To have no shell that kept your spirit grounded was unimaginable, to have no boundaries in and out of a world of dimensional rifts and bright colors was a revelation born. Where is it that one goes when the flesh has expired? Where do lonely hearts go after death, when there is so much love leftover from an untimely demise? They don't pass on to 'the other side,' no; for, although there is no flesh to keep the spirit roaming the earth, there is still the emotional tie that keeps one from passing. Perhaps they remain in this world, roaming the streets, in and out of others' skin and through closed doorways. This could be Heaven or Hell. It was this that Breckin realized as he hovered hundreds of feet above the town known as Spook Valley.

Spinning, plunging, and launching—his body was weightless. He observed the streetlights from above and they appeared as clusters of stars that were closer than the ones looming overhead. All those brilliant colors—the blues, greens, yellows, and whites—framed the bodies of the living. Breckin came to the conclusion that these were auras he was seeing. Over there, in the desert, the doorway to the Nightworld was pronounced with an overbearing ruby color that emitted several feet around its border in all directions. *Never want to be in that place again, no.* He projected horrific images of the netherworld in his mind.

Perhaps that was what haunted Breckin the most—that soon after his death, after Lillian had destroyed his body, his soul would be conjured by the Nightworld and he would be defenseless to keep it from being sucked in through the doorway and meeting with the tortuous laws of the fiery world. But that didn't happen. He was still here, in the Earth realm, treading on desires of the heart and unable to pass into *any* other world. Love held him to this place. Maybe love was stronger than evil; maybe the secrets of the heart kindled more power than the flames of destruction. Breckin was sure, however, that he loved Stefan. He had always loved Stefan, always gave Stefan his all. And that was why it hurt so much, sending convulsing jolts of invisible spasms throughout his transparent body, when Breckin had witnessed Stefan with Aaron, making love in the bed that Breckin and he had. Why couldn't Stefan comprehend the danger in knowing Aaron? Even in the afterlife, as a ghost of the Earth realm, Breckin still could not recall what beast lay beneath the supple flesh of Aaron Dabney. Stefan had disappointed Breckin—love still hurts when one is a ghost—and Breckin had to find a way to make Stefan see what Aaron truly was. Even still, Breckin hated Stefan for falling in love with Aaron. God, how he wanted Stefan to pay for his error in judgment.

So it was that Breckin was on the brink of making a decision, one that would either make Stefan open his eyes to the people around him or make him suffer for hurting Breckin. Breckin remained indecisive as he swooped down with enormous speed, and gracefully landed upon Stefan's front doorstep. Suddenly it occurred to him that, quite possibly, all of this nightmare could come to an end. But how far would the victims in this game of madness be willing to go? Where was the differentiating border between sanity and the unknown? Surely, Breckin knew. He proceeded through the solid door of Stefan's apartment and felt the tingling effects of his molecules contracting and expanding again. It reminded Breckin of passing through the doorway of the Nightworld.

-2-

A brisk, cold breeze passed Aaron and he shivered uncontrollably. He gazed up the length of the stairwell and to Stefan's front door. A few hours now, and Stefan still had not opened the door and invited him back in. Maybe Aaron was out of line when the primal beast within him took over as he made fierce love to Stefan. Aaron had no clue that Stefan would react the way he did, scolding him and making him leave the apartment that Stefan was so insistent he remained at earlier. All Aaron was trying to do was give Stefan what he wanted, give him what they both wanted. After all, the tension had been there since they had met. And what was it all worth? Was it worth it to defy the Nightworld and God *Damia* just for an attempt to *almost* make love to Stefan? Aaron cared about that young man, was hoping that he and Stefan could fight this battle together. Maybe they could win. Now all that was left were angry words that lingered in the air like a heavy, rotten stench. Nothing left now save for the consequences of Aaron's defiant actions.

Aaron longed to be far away from this new world, a modern world that he thought he could get to know and fit in. Instead, he was realizing how much he loathed it. He contemplated with his ever being attached to this place called Spook Valley when he had first emerged from the Nightworld. What's more, he struggled with his memory to go back to the time that he once lived, a time that had evidently occurred a few decades before this one. It seemed like only yesterday that the Nightworld had abducted Aaron. He recalled how he once had been interested in the occult and that was the way the Nightworld had gotten to him, the means for the doorway to open that had allowed the pack of wolves to attack him and carry him off into that horrible world of monsters. All like a dream, a past long ago that seemed to go by with the blink of an eye. There was one thing that bothered Aaron about the entire ordeal—how was it that he had been abducted almost forty years before and not aged at all? Was the *Nightworld* a dreaded fountain of youth overflowing with stygian waters? Furthermore, what about this pact? Was it true that the Order of Perennial Darkness would create an everlasting *crossworld* for their evil?

Aaron stood to his feet and gave one final glance to the shut door of Stefan's apartment. He recollected the first night he had emerged from the Nightworld and into the Earth realm. That first night, Aaron had stood naked in the surrounding brush of the Shadowood apartments and stared up into the window where the silhouette of Stefan had been. Now, Aaron didn't know if he loved the young man or would give the Nightworld what they wanted. There were no more definite answers; one's direction could change in a second. Aaron prayed he didn't have to make any more decisions, that everything in all the worlds would simply fall into place without his having to be the deciding factor.

The warm winds of the muggy, pre-dawn morning rushed over Aaron. A metallic, sweet-sour odor caused his nostrils to flare. What was that? The smell of blood, yes. It was the smell of blood and Aaron detected it quicker than anybody else could. After all, one of his lycanthropic qualities was that of having a keen sense of smell. Aaron's attention darted back and forth through his surroundings as wind gusts violently pushed past him. A storm was coming; there was the fresh aroma of rain in the air. As Aaron gave one final glance to Stefan's apartment, he bolted off in the direction of the Spook Valley Cemetery. With each bionic step he took toward the necropolis, the smell of gore grew stronger.

-3-

Lucien reached his motel room just in time. The winds had picked up during his midnight jaunt and, just before he arrived, sprinkles of raindrops were beginning to fall from the dark clouds overhead. He wondered if he should call off his afternoon shift tomorrow at Laine's Music and then decided that he wouldn't. After all, it would only be his second day working at the music store and he would finally get a chance to talk more with Stefan. Stefan had instantly mesmerized Lucien when he had gone by the man's apartment earlier and picked up the key to close the store. Lucien mentally begged that Stefan would be at work that next day; it would give him a chance to talk to Stefan and get to know him.

The young man had never had a boyfriend before. He had always felt timid by the thought of asking another man out. However, Lucien knew that Stefan was gay. He could tell when he went by Stefan's place and that other man was there. Something about that other man troubled Lucien. Or maybe, given the circumstances, he was simply paranoid. No, there was no paranoia, for that was only in that other place. This place, Spook Valley, seemed to alleviate the fears of paranoia. Lucien was glad to be in such a place and, perhaps, he could call this home. A place where nobody would ever find him.

Lucien closed the motel door behind him and switched on the light. He gasped at the horrid sight around him. Blood. Blood everywhere. Crimson rivers running down moist walls and splattered upon the white paint like a gory art deco. The lampshade was sprayed with droplets of blood and the light in the room was a ghastly pink. Lucien turned away from the bloodbath as his heart and mind raced. *No.* He turned toward the butchery once again, expecting it to be gone, but it was all still there. Blood dripped from the dresser drawers and splashed into thick puddles of liquid that soaked into the carpet. And there, on the bed, was the worst of the carnage. A swollen lump beneath the bloodstained sheets, black from the pool of blood that the cotton fabric had eagerly soaked up. *Oh God no.* Lucien's stomach convulsed, composing a dreaded rhythm of regurgitation. He trembled as he approached the bed. The edges of the mattress were stained in pink and grew darker toward the middle, toward the bulge that hid beneath the gory inkiness of life-giving fluid. The pungent odor made Lucien gag with each cautious step he made toward the butchery that lay beneath the sheets. Lucien picked at the corner of the sheet with his thumb and index finger, hardly wanting the blood on his hands. *Blood on pale skin is hard to wash away.* He hesitantly pulled back the covers, unveiling the slaughter. *Look what you have done you bastard! Damn you to hell, look what you have done!* As he pulled the sheet off the lump of butchered flesh, Lucien gawked with bulged eyes at the recognizable body beneath. *"Nooooooo,"* he wailed. He shut his eyes to the bloody horror and thought he could hear a million screams, all at once, tearing into the night. To both his shock and ease, when Lucien re-opened his eyes, the entire scene had dematerialized from the motel room. The walls returned to their off-white color, the sheets on the bed were clean and neatly folded, and the repulsive odor of death had vanished.

After a few minutes, Lucien's heart rate returned to normal and his stomach eased up. *Never want to see that again, not ever! They will not find me here; I won't allow them to find me.* Lucien was sure of this as he sat in the recliner and refused to think of the horrible scene any longer. He planned to stay in Spook Valley for a long time to come; he would make an effort to keep *them* from coming after him. Lucien would not give up at any cost.

-4-

Drifting in the realms of a sea of tranquility, Catrina Taylor glided toward Zander. She wanted to speak, god, how she wanted to ask him so much! *Where had you gone? Why did you leave me there with Mother and Father? I've missed you. I want to give you a big hug.* But the words would not come, not in this place. This was a place where words were not spoken with a mouth, but in her mind only. Sure, this was a serenity she had never felt in her life—a calmness and peaceful motionless that assured her safety from all the evil in the world.

Gazing over to Stefan, she recalled the images of the Nightworld. But that was a different place from this one; that was a world of torture and chaos. Monsters came from that unholy land, monsters that were hell-bent on capturing Stefan. Catrina realized she had to go back to reality. Was Stefan all right? Sure, he was standing before her right now with that cute, boyish grin. But wasn't this her own heaven? What was really happening to Stefan right now? And Aaron, the one who had saved her from the clutches of that demonic woman, was he all right? Still, there was Breckin. Breckin, the one she had grown to like and was happy that Stefan had fallen in love with.

A brilliant white light poured out from a rip in the skyline and beamed down upon Catrina as if to put her into its spotlight. The light was warm, inviting, and Catrina felt a hunger to go into that brilliant place of utter peace. *No,* the intuitive voice within distracted her from the bliss. *Stefan needs me. They all need me.*

Catrina maneuvered her body into a spin and directed herself away from the magnificent brilliance that caught her in its warmth. No longer was her mother, father, Lysander, or Stefan standing before her. Instead, there was a magnificent entity, perhaps half creature and half human. It flowed and its form rippled before her. Long locks of hair swam in the sea of air behind it and two horns emitted from the forehead of the being. The face was androgynous, neither man nor woman, but both. Its form was both lithe and muscular. *Beautiful Being of Light and Shadow, God and Goddess of my world. Cast your glory upon me and give me strength to fight this battle. I need to go back. Stefan needs me. Blessed Be that you will grant me this, for there is no other power in my world that is as strong as you are.*

The magnificent force did not speak, did not make a gesture with its mind. Catrina thought she had witnessed a smile. Then the image dissipated before her eyes and Catrina Taylor grappled for air as she began to fall from all that surrounded her.

-5-

Zander hastily walked through the electronic sliding doors of Spook Valley Medical Center and out of the rain. He strolled past the nurse's station, hair wet and dripping onto his shoulders and the floor. The attending nurse gave Zander a curious stare as he passed by. Zander commented, "It's starting to rain pretty hard out there." The nurse smiled, recognizing the well-mannered man as family to the comatose patient in Room 246.

As he entered the hospital room, Zander gave a hopeful stare to Catrina. He observed his sister tossing in her bed as if having a bad dream. Zander had yet to see her move in the past forty-eight hours and, now, it appeared that she was thrashing about. Just as he was about to call to the attending nurse, Catrina's body returned to its peaceful state once again. She called out a name though, and that name was Stefan.

Again with that name, Zander thought as he began to realize that maybe Stefan was telling the truth when the man had mentioned that he and Catrina were best friends. They must be close, surely, for she had to be dreaming of Stefan right now. And that look on Catrina's face was that of a content angel—a pursing of delicate lips, skin stretched masterfully over cheekbones drawn high from a smile.

Zander wished that his sister would wake from her coma, that she would come back to reality and witness the face of her brother looming over her, taking care of her just as he did when they were both children. On the other hand, the thought of her awakening frightened him. She hadn't seen him in all these years; her heart might burst in disbelief just from the sight of his face. The face of a man carved by the many years that he was absent from her life. Would she hate him for just leaving her like that? Still, there was a whole other set of options. Zander's trip to Spook Valley was not an accident. Local authorities contacting him in New York, as he had claimed to Stefan, didn't prompt his arrival. The only choice that was left to make now was between taking Catrina back to New York with him or to allow her to stay in Spook Valley, leaving her to the suffering of this wicked town.

A droplet of blood hit the polished linoleum beside Zander's foot. Pink raindrops dripped from Zander's brown locks and he wildly shook his hair dry. Judgment was coming soon, he realized. Perhaps it fell from clouds impregnated with blood.

-6-

Stefan lay on the sofa with his legs draped over the arm of the couch. He was exhausted, tired from the horror of his surroundings. Between Breckin's death and the sexual desires for Aaron, he experienced an emptiness within that seemed impossible to resolve. Hell, Catrina wasn't even around to hear him vent or give him solace. All that was left for Stefan came in languid images of his battle with the Nightworld—a hopeless battle that could not be fought. *You have lost, for it has taken everybody around you. Nothing is left; you should give in. And what would it mean to "give in?" Would it be terrible? Would it really be that bad to throw yourself into the arms of evil if those arms cradled you in comfort?* After all, he had nothing left. Then the guilt rushed over him in a suffocating wave—*it is because of you that all this is happening! Had you never gone to that desert, had you never been a hero and saved Breckin during his escape, had you been afraid then, you would have never felt the hands of dread that strangle and consume your life now. Everything would have been the way it was. Boring, sure, but without consequence and with an absence of madness. Give in; give them what they want. You can't though, can you? Even after your best friend's misfortune left her in a realm beyond reality and your lover's blood may as well been on your own hands. And then, the last person in the world you had your last chance to love forever, should that world of darkness clutch the Earth with its apprehensive hands, was run off by you. Now you have nothing.*

Stefan witnessed a brisk shadow dart from the corner of his eye. He practically jumped up from the sofa and followed the fleeting darkness toward the kitchen. The kitchen was without light and swallowed in a dimness that was only slightly touched by the illumination of the lamp from the living room. As he stared into the shady kitchen, Stefan could make out a movement of black on black. It was as if there was a form, an outline of a body upon the darkness of the room. Stefan's adrenaline began to rush throughout his body and his heart skipped a beat as he clutched his chest to feel the heavy pounding. What was there? Stefan imagined, with the sweat of trepidation swallowing his heated flesh, that the presence was something that emitted from the Nightworld. Another beast to bring hell into his life; another terrifying chapter in an unending novel of terror. And it was *truly* unending, was it not? Always, something new to face. There was never peace from that world of craze. *When was the last time you enjoyed a movie on the television in the darkness of midnight and sleepily snacked on junk food? When was it last that you created any poetry for the anthology that lent hope to your dream of being a poet?*

As he rose from the couch and approached the kitchen in cautious hesitation, the form that was crouched in the shadows began to emerge toward Stefan as if a mirror reflection that came closer with each step. Stefan came to a halt to alleviate the fear of coming face to face with the unknown force. However, the murky figure continued to draw near even after Stefan had stopped in his own tracks. Soon, the figure came forth from the dimness and light fell upon its presence, revealing its identity. It was Breckin! But it wasn't the Breckin that Stefan had made love to; it wasn't the body of flesh that had held onto Stefan on frightful nights. Instead, the body of Breckin appeared transparent, a glowing spectacle of dim light and dead flesh. It was Breckin's ghost! When Stefan realized this, he recalled the image of Breckin he *thought* he had seen earlier, before he kicked Aaron out of the apartment.

Breckin's features held no emotion. There was neither a smile upon his face, nor was there an impression of discontent. Breckin was simply straight-faced. His eyes were full as ever, yet the light in them had been long extinguished. The specter did not speak; he only glowered at Stefan with those dead eyes stained upon his powder blue face.

Stefan remained speechless and felt helpless, just standing there staring back at the one he had once loved so much, the man that he had saved from the Nightworld who had prompted this common disaster. "I'm sorry," Stefan broke the tense silence.

Breckin's ghost did not move or even gesture a response. However, a voice rang out into Stefan's mind and that voice mimicked the soft timbre Stefan recognized as Breckin. *Why Aaron?*

Stefan was shocked and his palms began to form sweat upon their surfaces. Breckin's ghost must have seen him and Aaron making love in the bedroom. Stefan could only imagine how it had hurt Breckin, as if a lover walked into a room to find his partner and another man together in bed. The pain Breckin experienced must have been phenomenal. Yet, Stefan could not answer the ghost before him.

There are things about Aaron you still do not know. There is a side of him that cannot be tamed.

"Tell me, Breckin," Stefan pleaded as the tears welled in his eyes.

I cannot.

"Then explain to me the power of the Nightworld. How can I stop it?"

I am unable to give you the answers, Stefan. I am no longer human; I am no longer a creature of the night. With my death, you claimed your human form again. This you must already know. I am specter to this world now and cannot give you answers; I can only warn. And I will not pass into peace until the wrongs done to me have been righted.

"I miss you, Breckin. I'm so sorry! There must be a way for me to bring you back," Stefan insisted.

The ghost of Breckin remained silent as it began to fade.

Stefan couldn't take the scene becoming. Would he ever see Breckin again? Why did this have to happen? "No, Breckin. Don't leave again! I love you." Stefan ran to the ghost with intent to embrace the supernatural creature. However, when he wrapped his arms around the transparent form, it vanished completely from sight.

Stefan fell to his knees and wept in the quiet apartment. He sniffled and wiped the rush of tears from his face as he lay on his side upon the floor where Breckin had stood.

He had to see Catrina tomorrow and tell her what had happened. She had to come back to him! Catrina knew a lot about the occult and she would be able to guide him. *Please let her come back*, Stefan mentally begged. He would visit her after work. He'd promised Laine he would be there tomorrow morning to open the store. Yes, that was the flicker of hope that burned away at Stefan—Catrina's awakening. For the rest of this early morning though, Stefan would sleep where he lay and cry from the haunting images of his a lover unable to be forgotten.

-7-

The rains of the monsoon had reached Spook Valley. The rain poured from the skies overhead, bouncing and dancing off the gray tombstones and marble cherubs that embraced the torrential waters without discrimination. The sod in the Spook Valley Cemetery was muddy and Aaron's feet sunk deep into the earth with each step he took.

Aaron Dabney's clothes were soaked and he shivered from the icy waters that continued to flood his view all around him. His nostrils flared as he continued to target the smell of rot, that smell of blood that had led him to this place. Aaron weaved in and out of the many tombstones and plots, making his way toward the back of the cemetery that bordered the welcoming desert beyond the cast iron fence.

The pungent odor was stronger than it had been as it permeated Aaron's senses and caused him to wince from the foulness in which the odor had mulled. Aaron came to a halt and scanned the perimeter around him. Another stench was detected, the scent of somebody or *something* that had recently been here. Three plots to the left of him, Aaron could see a grave that had been dug up. The mound of dirt next to the hole was now a small hill of sliding mud. Aaron made his way to the site and that is when he saw it.

A body had been half pulled from its grave. Locks of wet hair fell about the corpse's head and kept its identity a secret. The corpse itself appeared as if it had just recently been buried, yet it contained pockets of missing flesh.

Something had literally ripped chunks from the decayed corpse. What would do such a thing? The flesh of the corpse had been randomly gorged—a large hole where the back of the neck was, tears into the arms where the corpse's bones were visible, and rotted flesh from one hand had been ripped from the body completely.

Aaron stood appalled and quickly searched the area. Whatever had done this was now gone. Something inhuman…surely. Some creature from the Nightworld…definitely! Aaron briskly scanned the area around him. He was the only one standing there and anybody who may drive by would recognize him as the masochist of this corpse.

He approached the corpse to shove it back into its grave. With a shivering hand, he pushed upon the head and, as the corpse landed back into the hole from which it had been dug, the hair fell from the face of the corpse and revealed a decayed likeness that alarmed Aaron. It was *she!* Surely, it was *she!* Aaron gazed to the tombstone at the head of the grave. The name *Valerie Saunders* shot a pang into his chest. This corpse was that of the girl he had attacked nights ago upon transforming into a werewolf and selecting his prey. Although he had mauled her body, he was not responsible for all of the desecration he had just witnessed. Why this body? Who was to blame for taunting him with this sick game? And that face, that innocent face that had once been Valerie Saunders haunted Aaron's conscious. It was bad enough that the blood of her death was on his hands. But now, he still couldn't escape the reminder of his horrible affliction.

Aaron fell flat on his back into the welcoming mud and howled curses to the Heavens. Over and over again, the howling would echo inescapable pain through the pummeling rain until the coming dawn.

CHAPTER XV

-1-

Within the shadowy, cavernous atmosphere of the Nightworld, the chants that had composed a symphony of destruction had come to a halt. All six of the Order of Perennial Darkness, each cloaked in dark-hooded fashion, had lowered their hoods as the roars of *Damia* became present. Beyond the silence and beneath the Order's hymn to the underworld, the crackling of fires blazed in the background and the thunderous steps of their God caused the immediate foundations to tremble from his gigantic monstrosity.

Saint Trace fell to his knees, bowing before his lord, and soon, the others followed their leader's gesture. "To what bidding do you ask, oh divine God of the night?"

The god-beast stood before the Order of Perennial Darkness, silent and still. Soon, he lifted his head into the air and the reflection of the fires of the Nightworld shimmered off *Damia's* curlicue horns that extended high toward the heavens. A vicious snarl emitted from *Damia's* mouth, exposing a set of jagged teeth that appeared so sharp they could chew through metal. The deafening roar quaked the Nightworld and the members of the Order were certain that this was the voice of anger and of rage untamed. *The time has come! I want to cross into the Earth realm! The doorway must remain open now and for all eternity!*

Saint Trace kept his head bowed, fearful of the great God before him. "God Damia, the pact will be initiated upon Stefan's capture."

There was a boisterous moan of despair coming from the God of the Nightworld.

"I beg of you, God Damia, it will only be a short time before the doorway between the two worlds is open for all time," Saint Trace assured his leader. "The one they call Catrina, the witch that aided Stefan, has still not awakened."

Saint Israel eagerly added, "And Breckin…Breckin has been destroyed!"

"Stefan is practically defenselessssss," Saint Batiste murmured.

Saint Dante joined the group in reassuring *Damia.* "And, Lillian, the demon child, she is seducing the man that Stefan slaves for; he could provide an alternative to the plan if Aaron doesn't come through."

SILENCE! Damia bellowed. As he took in a breath, the sounds of a wild cougar emanated from his lungs. *Aaron will not fail us. He knows of the consequences should he do so. I have perfect faith in Lillian; she is of no concern. And the other; he is there to make sure NOBODY fails. Something troubles me however...*

"What is it, God Damia?" Saint Dante asked.

...There is a force in the Earth realm, a force that could prevent the pact from being executed. I saw it in a vision, this force. I know not if it is male or female, yet it is strong. We must capture Stefan and initiate the pact before this force grows more powerful. Damia's mind shifted without notice. *Breckin! Why is it that I do not have Breckin's soul in my Garden of torture?*

Saint Trace's crisp flesh grew stiff from *Damia's* utter determination to persecute the man who had escaped the grasp of the Nightworld. "He has been destroyed, God Damia. His soul has not yet arrived."

ENOUGH! the voice boiled in disgust. *His body was destroyed. His spirit remains in the Earth realm.*

Saint Collin burbled, "His spirit is lost."

Love holds his spirit to that place! Damia corrected the Saint Collin. *I want his soul and, when I get it, I'm going to eat it over and over again! I want another to pass the threshold immediately.*

"Sire," Saint Cassius reminded them all, "we must harness the power to have another pass. It is too soon."

Initiate the pact, Damia demanded. *Only one more must cross and then, the six of you. Once that has come to pass, then we will make the sacrifice and I, along with the rest of my Children, will be able to cross into the Earth realm. I can smell the flesh of innocence already.*

"What can we do to quicken the process, God Damia," Saint Trace took control of the conversation once again and gazed high above into the dark eyes of his lord.

Capture Stefan immediately! Once he is within our grasps, all hope and strength will be stripped from him. Chaos must make its way into the Earth realm NOW!

Damia barreled away, leaving the Order of Perennial Darkness to their defenses. The plan was put in place—do whatever had to be done to keep the doorway open, to initiate the pact—the traps were set. If Aaron couldn't imprison Stefan with his entire lusting demeanor, then there was always Laine, the owner of Laine's Music, the place in which Stefan worked, the owner in which Stefan confided. Lillian would hold true to her word of executing Stefan's capture regardless of the casualties. And if that failed, if the demon child of the Nightworld could not come through with, yet, another of her malicious plans, the other creature would make sure not to foil the rites of the pact. The other was just as vicious as Lillian was and would prove, with all his deceptive malice, to be crowned in the coming world of evil. Nevertheless, there were three creatures in Spook Valley hell-bent on capturing Stefan and making the pact a reality. The Order of Perennial Darkness grew confident in this. Little did they expect that Stefan would be within the grasp of the Nightworld sooner than they anticipated.

-2-

The dream haunted Laine Young. Actually, it wasn't so much the dream that disturbed Laine than the woman who starred in it. Lillian…or,

Lily…as Laine wished to remember her by, was a wet dream never expected. After all, he usually geared toward having sex with other men. However, something about that fantastic lady infatuated him. *But wait…didn't she turn into a creature?* Laine's mind suggested. But, for some reason beyond explaining, it didn't make a difference; the excitement of the sex was just as intense. Laine reminisced about the diva, recalled every part of her body as if it were timelessly captured in a photograph of a supermodel to which he could masturbate and fantasize about in the darkest hours of the night, when the entire town slept and illusions of the most perfect body came to life, awakening his organ with long, unstoppable strokes. Oh, how he remembered her—long raven hair spilling down her back, skin soft as rayon beneath his fingers, silky breasts of unmeasured size within the cupping of his hands, slender hips riding him up and down, voice so delectable, smooth and sensual. 'Join us,' the voice had said. 'Bring Stefan,' the desirable woman had demanded.

What did it mean? What did any of it mean? Perhaps his psyche was working overtime, recapturing the lust he'd felt for Stefan a long time ago when he'd initially hired the young man. Still, there was a type of determination in Lily's voice, an obsessive inflection in her request. Laine shrugged it off. He was happy to find that he was still capable of wet dreams given his forty-something age.

Laine sat up in bed and felt the sheets beneath him. There were spots of the sheet that were crisp from his dried semen. He studied them to assure himself of the dream. Yes, it did happen.

Sunlight poured through the gaps between the vertical blinds. Another day had visited Spook Valley; another night had passed. However, Laine reminded himself that last night had proven better than the many others had. It was true; usually Laine's nights consisted of gay porn videos or fantasies of making love to a particular pick of married men that visited Laine's Music or, even in his most wildest of fancies, thoughts of sodomizing Stefan Powell. Yet, it wasn't a man who permeated Laine's lustful mind. Instead, it was a woman by the name of Lillian.

Laine gazed to the opening of his bedroom door and his sight was instantly locked. It was she! It was Lily standing in the doorway, precious, naked, and innocent as a porcelain doll waiting to be dressed for the coming teatime. The hair between her legs was the color of mocha; it was trim and neat as if it were just placed there by adolescence. Her stomach was flat and her breasts were perked in magnificent fashion. Laine was convinced he must have been daydreaming.

"Lily?" he called out to the exposed woman.

"Laine," she said, and she did so in a tongue that melted his heart and created firmness within his loins.

"Am I dreaming?" he curiously queried. *How does she know my name*? Laine drastically stressed.

"You're not dreaming," Lillian confirmed.

"What is this?"

"I want you, Laine."

"You want me?" Laine spoke unconvinced.

"Oh yeah," Lillian said in tones that made Laine's flesh crawl.

"Are you real?"

"I want Stefan. Wouldn't you love to fuck Stefan?" Lillian bemused.

"Well…uhhhhhh…" Laine was at a loss for words. What did Stefan have to do with this? What was this anyway?

"Join us."

Join us? Join who? What the hell was Lily speaking of?

"I want you to do something for me," Lillian requested.

Laine shut his eyelids tightly. *This has to be a dream!* he convinced himself. When he reopened his eyes, the comely figure that stood before him was gone. "Get a hold of your self," Laine scolded. Within his mind, however, the sound of Lillian's voice repeatedly echoed. *Join us*, it said. Laine shook his head quickly to rid the voice and the striking image of Lillian.

Still, dammit, Laine couldn't understand Stefan's involvement in this fantasy. As he gazed at the clock upon the nightstand, Laine realized that Stefan would be opening the store by now. Perhaps he should give him a call and make sure everything is copasetic. Not to mention, Laine wanted to make certain that the new kid, Lucien, had zeroed out on his Register the night before.

As Laine Young began dialing the number to Laine's Music, the image of Lillian continued tantalizing him. When he heard Stefan's voice, his organ grew excited almost immediately.

-3-

Stefan Powell could always tell when something was troubling his boss, Laine Young. The concern in his voice accentuated each word that came out of his mouth in a low tone. Laine's attention was always distant during times in which something disturbed him. It was no different this morning, when Stefan's boss called to make certain the store was open. There was a deep distress in the older man's voice. Stefan asked if Laine was feeling all right a couple of times, but Laine dismissed the concern Stefan emitted by discussing the condition of the store this morning.

Stefan was shocked that Lucien had closed the store the night previous. The boy must have won over Laine's trust in an instant. After all, Laine hadn't entertained the idea of Stefan being in the story by himself until he had reached his six-month anniversary. But, hey, people do change.

Stefan had only seen Lucien on one occasion. That was when he came by the apartment to get the store key from Stefan. It was before that horrible creature named Lillian murdered Breckin. In that short time, in the mournful day that filled the space between Breckin's death and coming to work this morning, Stefan attempted to fit Lucien into the puzzle of the Nightworld. Had Lucien been a distraction for Lillian's arrival? Lucien *is* new to Spook Valley. Where did he come from? And what about Aaron? Was Aaron harboring some malefic secret as Breckin's ghost suggested last night? *Breckin. How I miss you! How I wish I could love that sweet body of yours and be able to kiss those precious lips!*

Within Stefan's mind, a whirlwind of chaos afflicted him. He felt that work was the last place he should've been. Instead, he should have been getting answers and searching for every possible resolution to stop the Nightworld and all its minions. After all, evil doesn't halt until it has conquered. There's no greater feeling than hopelessness. And that's how he felt: hopeless. There was no Breckin to hold and love, no Catrina to confide in, and, Aaron, he didn't know what to think of Aaron after what had happened in his bedroom back at the apartment. Hell, where was Aaron? Had he scared off the young man from ever coming back? Somebody had to have the answers; Stefan only wished it were he. Still, why couldn't Breckin's ghost supply the answers? His only hope lay in his best friend, Catrina Taylor. And she was comatose. Nevertheless, he planned to visit her after work that afternoon.

Stefan picked up the phone and dialed the number to Spook Valley Medical Center. He asked the receptionist how the patient in Room 246 was doing. She had relayed to Stefan that there still wasn't any change and Ms. Taylor's health was stable. The receptionist also added that the patient's brother was seeing over his sister. "OK," Stefan somberly replied, then hung up.

The patient's brother: Zander. Stefan had the same uneasy feeling about Catrina's alleged brother that he had about Lucien. *Funny how they both arrived at the same time*, Stefan thought. And Catrina never mentioned having a brother, Stefan reminded himself once again. Catrina must have the answers! His best friend always had a keen insight, especially when it came to the world of the occult. She would be able to reveal if Zander was telling the truth or if he was an insidious imposter. Stefan felt that Zander might have been sent by the Nightworld to keep watch over Catrina, make sure she didn't wake. Stefan had to visit Catrina soon; there was no doubt about it.

Stefan, a voice called out. He immediately recognized it.

As Stefan turned around, he observed Breckin's transparent form standing in the open doorway of the break room located near the back of Laine's Music. He wanted to start bawling right then and there, but held back the tears. "Breckin," he called out. The store was completely empty save for the two of them. "Why are you doing this to me?" Stefan scolded the specter as he approached it. "I can't stand to see you like this; it's tearing me apart."

Breckin's ghostly gaze fell to the floor. *I have no choice, Stefan. I'm trapped here until the time comes that my death is avenged. I'm here until you stop holding on to the love we shared. Let go, Stefan.*

"No," Stefan boldly commented as he wiped away a tear that welled in his eye. "I need answers, Breckin. My entire life was turned upside down when I saved you from that place and I need to know how to stop it."

I cannot give you the answers, Stefan.

"Won't the Nightworld ever give up, for Christ's sake?"

As I told you before, they will not stop until they have you.

"What about the pact?" Stefan rubbed at his forehead in frustration.

That is for you to learn. You're heading in the right direction.

"Right direction? Everybody around me is disappearing from my life! You're gone, Aaron's gone, and Catrina's almost gone."

You'll learn of Aaron soon enough, the ghost addressed.

"Tell me about Zander…or Lucien for that matter?"

My tongue is bound from giving you the answers, Stefan.

"Goddammit!" Stefan broke down and fell to his knees. None of this drama was worth figuring out. None of this terror deserved to be bestowed upon his shoulders. He wept. Stefan wept on the linoleum floor of Laine's Music. "Why'd you have to leave me?" he cried. "Why can't you just be alive? Why can't everything go back to normal?" As he wiped at the rivers of tears that poured down his face, Stefan looked up to find Breckin's ghost had silently vanished. Sniffling, Stefan briskly rose from the floor when he heard the bell over the entrance announce the day's first customer.

Only it wasn't a customer who'd entered Laine's Music, it was Lucien. After the young man had closed the door behind him and approached the break room to drop off his backpack, he noticed Stefan. Stefan was getting to his feet as if he'd fallen onto the floor. Though his features were striking and were the epitome of lust tamed in Lucien's mind, Stefan's eyes appeared swollen and red.

Lucien gently released his backpack to the ground and advanced to Stefan. "Are you all right?"

That voice, Stefan thought, *how bemusing. How subtle.* "I'm fine," Stefan assured Lucien and began advancing toward the back of the counter. "Make sure you don't clock in more than five minutes before your shift," he instructed.

Lucien ignored the last statement. "You don't look fine."

"I said I'm all right."

"You've been crying, haven't you?" Lucien acknowledged.

Stefan didn't think it was that noticeable but, apparently, it had been. Still, he was flabbergasted by Lucien's instant kindness toward him. Not to mention, his ability to bluntly make Stefan's business his own. "Yes, I've been crying. Do you feel better knowing that now?"

"No. Not at all." The boy dressed in black approached Stefan and stood stock-still before him. Lucien gazed into his eyes, studied Stefan's features up close as if Stefan were a rare specimen. How splendid Stefan looked! How comely and fantastic, and Lucien began thinking that love at first sight was possible.

Though Stefan felt slightly intimidated and baffled by Lucien's face-off, he refused to back down. He didn't know if this was a way for the boy to test him or initiate him as a friend. Stefan studied Lucien the way the boy studied him—at first, he simply glared into Lucien's shimmering jade-colored eyes, and then Stefan observed the fine milky texture of Lucien's face. So Victorian, that face; so smooth, as if it were crafted from porcelain.

"What are you doing?" Stefan broke the calm between them.

"If you need somebody to talk to…I mean...I know you don't know me that well, but—"

Stefan interjected, "You're right. I don't know you that well." Stefan could easily sense that Lucien felt uncomfortable.

"I mean…if…well, hell, if you need a friend, I'm here for you." Lucien took a sigh of relief. Breaking the ice was tougher than he'd thought, especially since he felt so attracted to Stefan.

"I don't need another friend. I have enough friends already," Stefan said callously.

Lucien turned and waked to the break room. His lips peeled back as a frown emerged on his face.

Stefan felt stupid for being so cold to the boy. Instant guilt, for his words spoken to Lucien, overflowed his conscience. Still, he didn't know Lucien. For all he knew, Lucien could be one of those creatures from the Nightworld. Stefan really had no way of knowing; yet, he didn't want to get close to another person only to find that they were harboring horrible secrets. Lately though, that seemed to be the pattern in Stefan's life.

The day at Laine's Music went by slowly. There weren't as many customers since the Hellfire frenzy last week. Now that the band released their second single on broadcast radio, the true fans of the group had already made their rush to the music stores to purchase the new disc.

There was little talk between Stefan and Lucien, the kind of talk that exists only with mutual enemies or lovers harboring tension between them. Every now and then, Stefan would show Lucien the correct way to do something—replacing the Register tape, signing in the new freight, and reiterating which discs didn't go on the shelves until the designated "street date." Other than that, there were no friendly words between the two, though Stefan realized that Lucien was still hurt by the way he'd snapped at him earlier.

Stefan's focus was concentrated on Catrina Taylor and had been for most the day. Now, five minutes before his shift was over, as he counted down his till and was about to hand the key over to Lucien, the eagerness to get to Spook Valley Medical Center had his stomach turning somersaults.

Before Stefan left Laine's Music, he walked up to Lucien, ready to deliver an apology. "I'm sorry about earlier."

Lucien said not to fret over it.

"I'm just going through a lot right now."

You're not the only one, Lucien kept to himself. "Why don't you get going; I'm sure you've had enough of this place for one day."

Stefan smiled and, for the first time, he witnessed his co-worker don a grin.

Lucien could not keep his eyes off Stefan as he made an exit from the store. He studied every step Stefan took, every twitch in Stefan's face, until he was completely out of sight.

*****

Aaron Dabney appeared a wreck. His clothing was still somewhat damp (the only reason they'd dried thus far was because he'd spent the late morning and early afternoon beneath the sun's rays) and his hair was disheveled. His flesh was splotched with dried mud from the wet sod the night previous.

Aaron had remained in the Spook Valley Cemetery all night and throughout most of the day. His mind drifted in a sea of terrifying catatonia from the discovery he'd made the night before. Valerie Saunders. Once before, just another name, a nameless face that meant nothing to him. And now? Now the name brought a whole new meaning to Aaron's life. Perhaps it was due to his own guilt for murdering the young woman when he had transformed into his werewolf alter ego nights previous. Perhaps it was the sight of her mangled body that he viewed as a human—such a fragile girl, such delicate flesh, and so defenseless. However, although the remorse ate away at him like a ferocious, unrelenting cancer, Aaron assured himself the result of the indescribable remains of Valerie Saunders, when he'd discovered her late the previous night, had not been completely inflicted by the beast that he had become. No, something else had done that to her. Something else had desecrated her grave and feasted upon her flesh. But who? And, more importantly, to whom could he explain this strange phenomenon? Certainly not Stefan!

As far as Aaron was concerned, Stefan was done with being seen around him. Stefan made that clear the night he threw Aaron out of his apartment. Aaron has scolded himself many times for his actions; he had prayed for absolution for the way he'd almost raped Stefan. Raped? Yes, raped! Aaron had practically overpowered the young man of his desire and when Stefan begged Aaron to stop, Aaron proceeded. Stefan was definitely out of the question. On the other hand, Stefan *did* want answers about the Nightworld and, now that Breckin was gone, the only person Stefan could rely on was Aaron.

The Nightworld. That awful horrible place! How Aaron loathed the thought of that otherworld, that place where the dead scream incessantly and are never at peace. And God *Damia*! God *Damia* would soon find that Aaron wasn't executing his plans as instructed. In fact, Aaron was doing the opposite! And when God *Damia* finds out that he was in the midst of having a love affair with the object of their capture, there's no telling what the master of the Nightworld would do to him. Torture…that's all there was to do with a traitor of the Nightworld…endless and eternal torture! Aaron feared that more than he feared that Stefan would never speak to him again. He was just as defenseless as anybody else who resided in Spook Valley. *Will this nightmare ever end? Remember back, a long time ago, when flower children grazed the plains and the only worries you ever had were if the beats of classic rock n' roll could top the ones of the band you'd heard before. Remember the parties, the music, the drugs, the psychedelic colors, and the orgies?* In that instant, in that fleeting moment of a memory rekindled and extinguished, Aaron reminisced about that place, about that time. *His* time! A time that'd passed only four decades before; a glimpse back over the years that brought him joy. It all happened before the wolves came. How he longed to forget about everything following that.

In the distance, near the entrance of the cemetery, a Volkswagen Jetta pulled in. Aaron made his way past the plot of Valerie Saunders, away from the disgrace left by some creature as an intentional foreboding to haunt Aaron. He scaled over the wrought iron fence and almost caught his jeans onto the spears that pointed upward. *Heaven*, Aaron thought. But Heaven wouldn't have him now, not after all the chaos and carnage he had committed. Sure, God may forgive, but there had to be a line drawn somewhere. When it all came down to it, Aaron Dabney felt hopeless. There was no hope for him, no God to save him, no love with whom he would grow old. He had hurt many and the guilt panged him over and over again.

As he reflected upon it all, he realized that Catrina Taylor brought on a big chunk of that guilt. She was the only one who knew that Aaron was a werewolf. Hell, he rationalized, he had tried to warn her in the beginning, but she continued fighting for the safety of her friend Stefan. Though it was foolish of her not to heed the gory warnings he had left her in her apartment on two occasions, Aaron also found it courageous that she fought to the end. The end came when she followed Aaron into the desert that night. Damn the girl for following him! He remembered how she'd called out to him, he in all his wolfen form ready to strike, and Catrina had broken through the barrier, said she understood the love he kindled for Stefan, said she knew what Aaron was.

Unfortunately, Lillian had been there as well and, when Aaron ran off into the desert, afraid to face Catrina and all her splendor, that was when Lillian attacked the woman and practically killed her. Now, Catrina lay comatose in a hospital.

She'll probably never wake again and it's my fault. Hopeless. There was nothing left for Aaron and it was of this that he was sure. His only hope lay in the consequences of his actions and that God *Damia* would take him back with open arms and make his torture less than what he deserved.

As Aaron made his way across the humid desert, he detoured before he reached the town. He was on his way to the doorway, to the Nightworld. It was time to take the penance for his failures.

-4-

Falling.

Catrina Taylor stopped grappling for air; it was useless. There was nothing to grab onto after all—the clouds were high above her body and she effortlessly plunged though the cyan blue of her dreamscape. It was so strange, the way the colors high above were brilliant yet, as she fell further (into what she did not know), everything became darker, more aged and polluted. The brilliant yellows and whites gave way to sky blues, the sky blues gave way to turquoise greens, then emerald—all around her the most precious emerald—

then came the purple, and Catrina felt as if she were bathing in a pool full of rich wine. Now, everything around her was cyan blue, that shimmering blue that reminded her of the waters in the deepest of oceans, beyond royal, but not quite midnight-colored. What a beautiful experience!

The whole experience was so amazing that Catrina had a hard time coping with it as her heart raced, slowed, and returned, once again, to rapid beats. She was coming back, surely. She was on her way to the world of the living where there were tasks in desperate need of being executed. Stefan needed her. She was there to help Stefan battle the evil of the Nightworld—she knew that for certain. Of course, there were other things she knew, many things she recalled before she was attacked by that horrible demon. She knew of Aaron, or rather, the creature of which Aaron could transform. Yes, she had seen it with her own eyes that night! Aaron Dabney was a werewolf, a creature of the night, and, subsequently, that made him a creature of the Nightworld. However, Catrina didn't scare from Aaron or his bestial counterpart; for she realized he didn't want that, he couldn't! Aaron had feelings for Stefan and there was no denying it. The only problem with that was Breckin. Breckin wasn't a bad guy though; she had learned that as well. Breckin had rescued her, probably saved her from her own death, and Catrina looked forward to thanking him for that.

Beyond the recollections before the attack, Catrina was reminded of what she had experienced here, in this place that could not be described to anybody unless they'd also visited it. She recalled the peacefulness, the serenity that filled her being, and the power of the witch she had so much attained to be in the real world. There was Zander, of course. Zander—how she missed her brother! And here, in this place, he was grown and a man, handsome as ever. Then, there was the God and Goddess. Oh, Great One of all her waking moments, how she had yearned to be face to face with her makers in all the years she'd spent in this life. And, in this time, in this very special place, she had the chance to do such. They were the force that sent her drifting; they were the One that rejuvenated her body. *Praise thee, God and Goddess.*

As Catrina Taylor continued falling, she could barely make out the sounds of voices as if heard at the other end of a tunnel. Catrina smiled. *I'm on my way, Stefan.*

-5-

"Have the doctors given any indication that she'll wake soon?" Stefan was flustered by the entire period of waiting. Will she come to or will she be a vegetable all her life?

Zander observed Stefan's frustration and glared in revulsion at the young man's inability to be calm. "You have to be patient, Stefan."

"I've been patient for days now!"

"There's no need to take your anger out on me," Zander casually replied.

"I'm not taking it out on you," Stefan lowered his tone an octave. "And who are you to say I can't be angry?"

"I'm her brother that's who," Zander snapped. Instantly, he brought his voice down to a calm level once again. "I don't want her upset in her state."

"Where were you then?"

"What?"

"If you're Catrina's brother, then where the hell have you been all this time?"

Zander clenched his hands. He would have struck Stefan right then and there if not for the passing nurse whose silhouette floated past the window. "I am her brother, Stefan. I think it might be best if you leave."

Zander's wiry figure grew closer to Stefan and loomed over him. Stefan's heart skipped a beat at the monstrous size of Zander. Although intimidated, Stefan collapsed near the edge of the bed, grabbed Catrina's hand, and bowed his forehead onto the mattress. "Oh God, Catrina, please wake up. Please! I need you, Catrina. I need answers. Please, help me fight this battle."

Zander stood still as he studied Stefan sobbing at Catrina's bedside.

There was silence for almost a minute.

Stefan wept, whispering for his best friend to return. Stefan glanced up to find that Catrina remained in her unconscious state. "Fuck," Stefan roared as he stood. His slumped shoulders and bowed head told of his defeat.

"Get out," Zander demanded with an authoritative voice.

Stefan pushed past Zander, glaring at the tall man with an evil eye, and exited Room 246.

Not more than fifteen seconds later, Catrina Taylor began mumbling, shaking her head, and it appeared that she was coming to.

Zander briskly rushed to the hospital room door and locked the deadbolt. Catrina didn't need to be bombarded by people right now.

-6-

Stefan drove erratically. He sped over the sidewalk at the corner of Main Street and Violin Road, racing past Laine's Music, and maneuvering the whining vehicle to the furthest reaches of Firehouse Road, that would pass the darkest area of Spook Valley: the outlying desert.

Enough was enough! He had to start somewhere. He couldn't get answers from Breckin, Catrina wouldn't wake to his calling, and Aaron was nowhere to be found. A fury had grown out of control within Stefan. If it was he the Nightworld wanted, then so be it. He was disgusted of this whole ordeal. He was sick of the heartache, the horror, and the chaos that had encroached upon his once normal world. He was determined to make an attempt at breaking this code of evil once and for all.

Stefan Powell pulled his car off into the darkness, along the stretch of Firehouse Road that had only known daylight, and ejected from the driver's seat. He began his walk into the night, into the desert where this entire dreadful nightmare had begun.

-7-

She had felt Stefan's hand cupping her own. The warmth and the bliss of a best friend holding your hand!

Everything became instantly bright and it had been dark for so long. The cyan blue led to black, and there was nothing but darkness for a good portion of the fall, until Catrina viewed the light before her…

She fluttered her eyelids open. Everything was so bright, so blurry. She immediately shut her eyelids again to escape the instant blindness. The hand that held her hers squeezed gently. "Stefan," she called out, but her voice was hoarse.

"Catrina," the voice responded, but it wasn't her best friend's voice at all. The voice was deep, alien. Yet, at the same time, it sounded familiar.

Catrina attempted to open her eyes again. This time, it felt like a hundred pins driving deep into her eyeballs and putting immense pressure on her brain. Determined, she kept her eyelids open. Slowly, the blur cleared save for the area around the edges of her vision. The face that was revealed was that of her long lost brother. "Zander?" she asked excitedly.

"Yes, Catrina."

"How? When? You're alive." She wanted to jump from out of her bed and hug him; however, her energy was depleted. She rationalized the situation with the only explanation she knew. "No, I must still be dreaming."

"No, Catrina, you're not dreaming. It's me, your brother Zander. Thank God you're alive. You're much prettier without the pigtails."

All thoughts of Stefan rushed from Catrina's mind as she began bawling uncontrollably.

-8-

Aaron felt himself getting closer to the doorway of the Nightworld. The static hum of the doorway's presence was within proximity. Yes, he needed to do this. No longer would he cause harm to another person. As if any person wanted him. Aaron halted. Sagebrush rustled near him. Aaron drew back behind the tall lithe form of a saguaro cactus that loomed mightily.

Aaron waited. Perhaps his mind was playing tricks on him. Or, maybe, it was that bitch Lillian, come to greet his entrance into his world of consequences. Peering from behind the cactus, Aaron was aghast by the image he witnessed step from out of the shadows and into the direction of the doorway: Stefan.

Stefan had thought of other ways, but this was the only one that seemed feasible. Sure, it was crazy. Sure, he might die, but what was left anyway? Still, there was that one slim chance that he could find a way to destroy the Nightworld. Better yet, what if he could find a way to bring Breckin back?

Stefan Powell came to a complete stop. He peered at the space before him and he was sure he had found the entrance. Here, in the heart of the desert, beyond the town of Spook Valley, stood the doorway to the Nightworld. The buzzing was constant, electrical. A step closer and Stefan saw the shade of black on night. The doorway was monolithic, four times his own height, and, as Stefan took another step closer, the audio of the entrance became hypnotic and alluring. There was a certain freedom beyond this doorway, a certain terror to be fulfilled; there was something for everybody waiting in this dark and desolate netherworld. Louder, the drone grew. Stefan could see the ruby-colored outline of the doorway. All left was to take another step.

"STEFAN!"

The terror. The evil that had impregnated his nights with horror. The malice that had been bestowed upon him and all his friends. It all began here.

"Stefan," Aaron called out.

Stefan heard the voice, thought it rang a familiar tune—a lover he'd spoken to in long conversation but could never have, a friend trapped by a fate that would not allow her to listen.

The whirring of the doorway enraptured him. Stefan placed his right hand within the door between reality and madness. It disappeared before his very eyes, swallowed by what lay ahead. The tingling sensation began crawling up his arm. It tickled. It hurt. It was utterly invigorating.

Aaron began running for Stefan in an attempt to keep him away from the doorway.

Stefan turned his head to view all of Spook Valley behind him and witnessed Aaron Dabney. How he wanted him so badly. Before Stefan could resist the power of the doorway, it sucked him in like a hurricane and swallowed his body whole.

"NO STEFAN," Aaron screamed. He ran with all his might, eager to jump in after Stefan.

By the time Aaron had reached the doorway, it had sealed shut.

PART II

Mysteries of the Nightworld

"The gate of Hell are open night and day; Smooth the descent, and easy is the way; But, to return and view the cheerful skies; In this, the task and mighty labor lies."

- John Dryden

CHAPTER XVI

-1-

At first, there was nothing save for the incessant buzzing around his entire being, as if a thousand killer bees were on the attack. The undying hum became a part of Stefan's body—the monotone vibrations filled his stomach with giddiness, his limbs with flightiness, and his head faltered in and out of a disorienting state. Blackness was in this place—an inky, jet black that was thick as fog. Its weight was just as heavy, as it rushed all the air from Stefan's lungs. There was an uncanny atmosphere between his flesh and bones, beneath his blood and above his muscle. It separated his body from other parts—his face was below his knees, his chest above the point where his head should've been, his hips far off from the rest of his body, as if they watched in thrusting wonder at his acclimating form. That static hum kept everything together, though his body disintegrated in the darkness of this in-between portal. It was as if his body were falling apart, limbs drifting in zero gravity, but, at the same time, was attached by invisible threads that would pull it all back together in due time. Folding and twisting, Stefan felt like a mathematical jigsaw puzzle of creepy, geometric design. This was the entrance! This was what they all felt as they entered and exited the Nightworld.

There was a momentary lapse of reason to all of this, a much-needed doubt of the inexplicable, that perplexed Stefan beyond the possibility of a whole other world where madness governed the land. He was entering a world where monsters existed, a place only attained in the most horrific nightmares of the mind. But this was real! This was all so real, and, if it wasn't, may he wake and find Catrina at his bedside explaining how he'd tossed and turned all through the night. And may she question his convictions of men named Breckin and Aaron and of a dreaded, dark dimension known as the Nightworld.

Though his conscious mind was constantly arrested by the static sounds, that haunting reverberation like a tearing that never ceased, Stefan managed to maintain his focus on retrieving the answers from this netherworld. His life, Catrina's life, perhaps Breckin's soul, the residents of Spook Valley, even the population of the world, all depended upon his quest to stop the unspeakable evil that was growing more powerful with each passing night. *I must keep the pact from being performed*, he reminded himself as his insides spun out of control. *Yes, the pact must be stopped.* The Order of Perennial Darkness, as he was reminded of the term Breckin had used, must not make the sacrifice! And who exactly was the sacrifice? Himself? Catrina? Had the pact already begun without his knowing? *No…there couldn't have been thirteen that had already crossed over the threshold of the doorway*, Stefan deduced. In this place to come, this alien land in which Stefan knew little about, he prayed that he would resolve Aaron's identity and discover a way to bring Catrina from out of her coma. Still, there was a piece of him that was determined to free Breckin's soul, if not bring him back to the world of the living.

Stefan's body began to become whole again. He watched aghast as his flesh collected itself into the being that he was before he stepped into the doorway of the Nightworld. Stefan held his hands in front of his face to assure that his body was intact. The buzzing that drowned all the sound around him, developed into a high-pitched whine that began to fade. It gave off one last echo that punctuated the end of the resonance.

From out of the darkness, a new visual wonder appeared before Stefan. His feet were firmly on the foundation and Stefan quickly turned around to find the monolithic doorway that appeared as it did when he came through the entrance. He was on the other side of the doorway. This is where the doorway led! Stefan had made it to the Nightworld.

The atmosphere of this entire world shimmered in orange and red. Stefan thought it looked like a gigantic open cave, though the jagged rock and cliffs seem to go on forever. He stood over the large valley of unknown terror, indecisive of his next move. As Stefan proceeded forward, his body retreated to a halt from the echoing of screams. Men, women, and even children, were bellowing in agony. Dark shadows loomed over the crevices of the many cliffs; the shadows proved inhuman beasts with horns and pointed tails and, the one over there…it had, what appeared to be wings, upon its back. Stefan couldn't comprehend how Lillian and the others who had crossed over into Spook Valley could live in such a place of dread.

Stefan cautiously continued forward and studied the rivers of fire to the West of the Nightworld. Near the banks of the flowing glow that made fiery paths through the center of the Nightworld, Stefan gazed at the outlines of creatures that had congregated there. To the East, the netherworld was dim as if it had not yet been developed.

The terrifying sound of galloping hooves jolted Stefan's heart. He took refuge beside a large boulder that hid him from the oncoming terror. Crouched out of site, Stefan observed a passing horse that breezed by. The flesh and muscle were absent from its form and Stefan took a double take at the dashing structure of bones. Sweat trickled from Stefan's forehead; his heart raced in frenzy and his stomach turned somersaults.

Making sure he no longer heard the hooves of the skeletal horse, Stefan returned to the path he had begun walking. He took one more glance at the doorway that lay hundreds of feet behind him—just another view to make sure it still remained, just in case he couldn't take any more of this world. The door was still there and Stefan's tense muscles relaxed a bit. However, he did realize that the further he went from the doorway, his chance of hope for retreat diminished.

Somewhere, in that horrible place, Stefan was bound to find answers. He trod upon the dirt that was like crushed petrified rock. As the doorway disappeared from his sight, his ears perked to the sound of chanting, like that of a group of monks. *The Order of Perennial Darkness*, Stefan realized. He vigilantly weaved in and out of the landscape, from one red rock to another, intending to do so until he reached the group of men. When he got there, he still wasn't sure what he would do.

-2-

Aaron Dabney had failed. His legs folded beneath him and his knees landed to the floor of the desert as he wept. His sobs echoed through the dry landscape like the cries of a frightened child who'd lost his or her way and feared the howls of the distant coyotes. If only he'd run a bit faster and grasped onto Stefan before he vanished into the doorway. If only, in the worst scenario, he would have been sucked into the doorway with Stefan. Then, at least, Stefan wouldn't have to navigate himself through that horrible place alone. After all, Aaron was a child of the Nightworld, and he knew that place more than he had ever known the place from whence he was abducted. In his mind, he pictured the rivers of lava, the untamed beasts that roamed the land, and God *Damia* himself. Aaron's heart almost burst from his chest just thinking about the gigantic god of the Nightworld—the inferno that burned in *Damia*'s eyes, those monstrous, jagged teeth, and the robust body etched in armor form that loomed at least fifteen feet above the other minions under his power. Aaron winced, his tears coming to an end just thinking of the world he so much abhorred.

There had to be a way to rescue Stefan; there simply had to be! Stefan was alone in that place, and, if he were caught, there was no telling what God *Damia* would do to him. Yet, none of it made sense. None of it meshed together as the ultimate plan the Nightworld had prepared for. The pact didn't work like that. It was true; Aaron had overheard the Order of Perennial Darkness discussing the pact many times. The one gift the Nightworld did bestow upon him, when it created him into part man and part beast, was the ability of sensitive hearing. Aaron knew that there were thirteen that had to cross into the Earth realm. The Order of Perennial Darkness counted as six. The six of them made up the thirteen. Aaron wasn't sure how many others had already crossed. There was he, Breckin, and Lillian. That was all he knew of. Surely, there had to have been others! The Nightworld didn't expect Stefan to willingly cross the threshold to it. Nobody had ever done that before!

Aaron's mind raced in confusion, unsure of what to do next. He soon realized the only person he could turn to, the only person he entrusted with the secrets of the Nightworld. Catrina. She was in a coma though, Aaron recalled. Still, it was his only shot in this entire nightmare. That's what it was, wasn't it? A vicious nightmare that had no end?

With the only hope flickering in the distant, Aaron made his way through the darkness of the desert and headed toward Spook Valley Medical Center.

-3-

She still couldn't believe it. All this time and here he sat right before her, consoling her. Catrina Taylor hadn't seen her brother in over a decade, not since he'd vanished from their parent's home in Phoenix when she was just a child. And now, here he was! But how did he know this had happened to her? Mom and Dad probably sent him, Catrina rationalized. They didn't even know she was in a coma. Or, did they? There were too many questions in Catrina's mind for her to sort out and answer. What mattered was that Zander was here. Of all the people in the world she'd expected to see as she regained consciousness, he was the last. Her tears were finally beginning to subside.

"When did you get here?" she asked with as much excitement as she could muster. It was difficult for her to move around much, given her condition.

"A few days ago," Zander replied. "I came in from New York."

"New York? That's where you've been all this time?" For a moment, Catrina wanted to scold her brother for never contacting her. Mom and Dad had trouble coping with Zander's disappearance and had convinced themselves that he was dead as a way of bringing closure to the emotional situation. Catrina decided to bite her tongue. She didn't want to burn a bridge that hadn't been crossed yet. No matter what Zander had done, he was blood; he was family. Catrina, of all people, was adamant on forgiving others.

Zander nodded his head. "I'm sorry I never called or wrote. I…there was too much going on in my life."

Catrina didn't know where to start, what to say, or how to approach a brother she hadn't seen in so long. She studied the luster of his almond flesh, his chocolate-colored hair, and trim goatee. He was so handsome. "Look at you," Catrina said, grabbing at the hairs on his chin.

Zander smiled. "I know. When you last saw me, I was practically a child."

Her happiness subsided.

"You look the same as I remember," Catrina smiled. Suddenly, the Nightworld and all that had happened rushed over her in a terrifying wave of realization. "Stefan," she'd said.

"Oh, your friend. Yes, he has been here almost every day. He seems to be a very kind man. In fact, you just missed him; he was here no more than a half hour ago." Zander's voice became serious. "Catrina, what happened to you?"

She couldn't begin to explain it to her brother, although she recalled it all as if it'd only happened minutes before. She reminisced about her attacker, that evil demon named Lillian. In her mind, Catrina relived the pain of her claws that burned her flesh and the way Lillian had almost gotten her way with Catrina. If not for Breckin, she would have never survived. Now, her brother wanted answers and, although she'd missed him so badly, she refused to give them to him. There was no reason to put Zander in harm's way by getting him involved in this battle against the Nightworld. "I don't remember," Catrina lied.

Zander explained, "The doctors said you may be a bit leery of the facts at first. I'm sure it'll come back to you. Speaking of doctors, I should let one of them know that you're awake from your beauty sleep."

Catrina managed a grin.

"You don't mind if I leave you alone for a while do you?"

"No," Catrina voiced with concern. "Where are you going?"

"Well, now that I know you're alright, I'm going to go get myself some real food."

His sister's brow shifted in wonder.

"The food in this place is terrible," he smirked.

Catrina gathered her strength to rise from the bed and hug her brother. She flinched from the scratches upon her back around which Zander's arms had wrapped. "I missed you, Zander." She almost began to cry again.

Zander pulled back, stared into Catrina's eyes, and gently kissed her forehead. "I know; I missed you too."

Catrina watched as Zander left her bedside and exited the room. She prayed to the God and Goddess for a quick recovery and that she wouldn't be bed ridden for too long. She had to find Stefan and Breckin as soon as possible. There wasn't much time left and there was no telling what else had crept through the doorway in the desert as she had lain in her coma.

A nurse entered the room. She was older; however, Catrina recognized a youthful glamour in the way the nurse had strutted like a twenty-something vixen. Her hair was auburn and tightly curled and her face, though the signs of middle age were revealed by the wrinkles accentuating her eyes, was luminous and smoothly contoured. The nurse had checked the heart monitor, made a few notes on Catrina's chart, took Catrina's pulse, and commended Catrina for being brave and having pulled through her coma. "Not many people handle it this well," the nurse had remarked.

"How well?"

"You seem to be very relaxed."

Relaxed? If she only knew, Catrina thought.

"You also seem to be the latest sensation around here," the pretty nurse added.

"How do you mean?" Catrina gazed at the nurse in utter puzzlement.

"Well, if you're up to it, there's another visitor here to see you."

Stefan! "Send him in," Catrina voiced desperately.

"Alright," the nurse said in motherly fashion, "but only for fifteen minutes. You've got to get your rest young woman."

Catrina suddenly felt as if her mother were allowing her to watch the Late Movie although she had to report to school the next day.

The nurse left the room and in the time before her "visitor" entered, she had run her fingers through her hair and pulled the lengthy locks behind her shoulders. She refused to show defeat to anybody.

She studied the door, anticipating with each rushed breath, for Stefan's entrance. To her shock and dismay, it wasn't Stefan who sauntered into her room. Instead, it was Aaron.

When he'd appeared, she was at a loss for words. She stared at him, just as he stared at her with those eyes; eyes she'd remembered being ablaze in ruby shade. This time, however, his eyes were dull of life; they bled sadness and Catrina could almost make out tears that weren't quite there.

"Catrina," he broke the silence.

"Aaron." She knew she had to get it out in the open. She knew it all came down to this proverbial breaking of the ice. And she knew that he knew; it showed in those same sad eyes. "I know who you are, Aaron. I know *what* you are."

"I know," Aaron collaborated.

"You're a werewolf, aren't you?"

Aaron's eyes bolted downward as if to dodge the accusation. There was no use denying though, not to her. She was in the desert that night. She called his name to the beast on four legs into which he'd transformed. "Yes, Catrina."

"You're one of them; a creature from the Nightworld."

Catrina's words made it sound so horrible. To her, he must have been a horrible creature amongst a throng of evil minions that would stop at nothing to bring chaos and disorder to the world. Aaron felt he was losing a battle already lost. "I am from the Nightworld. I was abducted years ago. I can't go into details right now. There are more important things I need to discuss with you. I'm not here to harm you, Catrina."

"I know that," Catrina mocked. "You tried to warn me. You were the one who—"

"Yes," Aaron interjected as he briefly recalled his bloody warnings created in Catrina's apartment. "Catrina, we don't have much time."

"Where's Breckin? Has he figured out that you're not here to harm us?"

Aaron was bemused. It took him a minute to register how much Catrina had missed while in her coma. Now, he, Aaron Dabney, was the one who would become the bearer of bad news. And more than she could imagine.

"Breckin saved me," Catrina commended, trying to force a smile into the conversation.

"He's gone, Catrina."

"What?" Catrina attempted to react by bringing her body into an erect state; however, her lack of strength got the best of her.

"He's dead."

Catrina fell silent. She brought her hands to her face to cup the coming tears from her messenger. After a few seconds, a long sniffle emerged and she wiped the sides of her eyes with her index fingers. "How?" Her voice was strongly monotone and determined.

"Lillian." That was all that had to be said. Aaron was shocked by Catrina's response.

"That bitch! I'm going to make her pay!" She bellowed with conviction she had never felt. It was as if she'd never been any stronger than now. Quickly, thoughts of avenging Breckin's death subsided as she realized what Stefan must have been going through. "What about Stefan? Oh god, he needs me. Is he alright, Aaron?"

The concern that shifted her comely eyes into a squint penetrated Aaron. He didn't want to tell her the horror he had witnessed. There was no use covering it up though. She had to know. And time! Time could be running out as they spoke. Aaron spoke the words clearly, so that he need not repeat them. "He crossed into the doorway, Catrina. He's in the Nightworld."

Catrina's body abruptly jolted in one enormous, nervous tick. She was lost amongst all thoughts of their conjoined battle of evil. There was once the three of them, three souls determined to conquer the coming of the Nightworld into their own. And now? Now, she was the only one left. She was the last person standing in this ultimate battle. Surely, this had to be the end. There was no other way to defeat the inevitable. The Nightworld had won. "We have to go after him," she announced.

"No, Catrina. We can't."

Catrina didn't understand why. "Aaron, I don't care about the consequences. We have to get Stefan back."

"The doorway has closed."

Catrina's eyes darted in panic. "It's over? No, it can't be over! Aaron," she'd begun weeping, "please tell me it's not over."

"I don't think it is over," Aaron simplified. "That's why I came here. I know a little about the pact and it doesn't seem to make since. When Stefan crossed over into the Nightworld, I think it changed things somehow. This isn't the way it was supposed to work. Also, if it were over, if the Nightworld had truly won, we would know."

"How?"

"All the creatures of the Nightworld would be able to enter this world. Do you realize how much chaos would be in the Earth realm?"

Catrina nodded. But, *Earth realm*? That was the first time she'd heard that term. That's what the Nightworld called this place? It was strange to hear, considering Catrina knew of no other worlds. *Earth realm.* It sounded like something in a science fiction novel.

The silhouette of the attending nurse was in view on the other side of the door. "I think they're going to keep me here overnight," Catrina added. "Visiting time's over."

Aaron observed Catrina's mind at work, as she remained silent but mouthed words to herself. Aaron felt confident that she was already working out a plan. In his hesitation to speak, Catrina's voice rang out. "Go to Stefan's apartment, Aaron. Stay the night there. That's the only place that is partially safe from the creatures of the Nightworld."

Now it was Aaron's brow that knitted in confusion.

Catrina continued. "Stefan and Breckin had prepared the place against demons, vampires, and warlocks. It should have no affect on you. After all, you've already been there before. It should keep you somewhat safe.

"There's a key above the door. Use it to get in. I'll meet up with you there when they release me tomorrow morning. I'm sure they won't keep me any longer than that. We have to work this out, Aaron. The two of us are all that is left to get Stefan back and stop the pact from happening." She reached to her right to grab the small, spill proof cup of water.

"Will you be all right?" Aaron asked.

When Catrina turned up to assure Aaron that she would be, her words came to a halt and her face froze in wonder. An inverted star shown upon Aaron's face. Two of the five points reached high above his eyes and one point aimed directly south, ending at the bottom of his chin. It appeared like war paint, crimson and streaked as if were applied by a cursed finger. The pentagram was even and precise. *It could even be blood*, Catrina thought to herself.

"Will you be all right, Catrina?" Aaron repeated himself.

Catrina snapped out of the enigmatic daydream. The image upon Aaron's face had disappeared. "Uh, yeah. I have Zander with me; he should be back any time now."

"Zander?"

"Oh, my brother."

Aaron approached Catrina, at first unsure if he should make the gesture he was about to perform. However, Catrina had already held her arms wide-open and taken Aaron to her as if one of her own. They hugged. Catrina whispered, "Be safe, Aaron."

With that said, Aaron strolled out of the room. Catrina closed her eyes, still puzzled over the mark that had adorned Aaron's face. She hadn't a clue what it meant, but it was obviously some kind of warning. But of Aaron himself or of impending danger to Aaron? For now, Catrina attempted to get some sleep. Tomorrow, their battle would begin.

The automatic doors of Spook Valley Medical Center slid open and the atmosphere of Spook Valley welcomed Aaron Dabney with the same open arms Catrina had. He was to get to Stefan's apartment immediately and await Catrina's arrival tomorrow. So that was the plan thus far. Aaron knew Catrina would have an answer to this; he realized that he could count on her and was glad he decided to show. The way in which she hugged him—she trusted him. That was one less thing for him to worry about, that being to win over Catrina's trust. He felt better than he had earlier. At least now, he felt that there might be a chance to save Stefan. Maybe, even his own soul.

Walking through the parking lot, Aaron came to an abrupt halt. There was a tingling sensation in the pit of his stomach, a whirring in his head. His hand began to shake uncontrollably. Another from the Nightworld was around! That trademark sensation—Aaron knew it all too well. He rushed past the few cars that rested in the parking lot, and by the time he had made it to Firehouse Road, Aaron used his animal agility to get to Stefan's apartment.

-4-

Laine Young had spent the entire day with a bottle of scotch. He entrusted the store to Stefan and Lucien. He didn't leave his house once. It was rare that Laine would do this—not leave the house and drown himself in a bottle of Glen Livet. If fact, the last time he did such was over a decade ago when he'd been denied the loan for his store while still residing in Phoenix.

However, today was different. Laine couldn't get that beautiful woman off his mind. The monstrous creature into which she'd transformed. *Another shot.* Lillian comprised each and every thought in Laine's fragile mind. How he wanted her! How he'd wished that she shown up during his drinking frenzy and he would take her right there! Yes, he would fuck her like an animal and take her over and over and, blessedly, over again. Yet, she never came. In fact, Laine deduced, she only appeared in his dreams. But his woman was no conjuration of his mind. He had sex with her and it was real.

Now, as Laine lay sprawled out on his bed, empty bottle by his side, Lillian made her entrance into his world once again. She emerged from beyond the bedroom door, a naked beauty of luminous flesh accenting the darkness of night. He wanted to reach up to her, take her in his grubbing hands. Lillian appeared at the foot of his bed, unbuckled the belt of his jeans, and tugged them down to Laine's ankles.

"Oh, baby," he grunted.

Lillian was speechless. Her head made its way to Laine's inner thigh. Her tongue lapped at his hairs there and maneuvered toward his organ already grown erect. She took it into her mouth, swallowed it deep, and, after a few of his thrusts into her mouth, she pulled up and glowered at Laine with her obsidian eyes.

"Ah, don't stop," Laine requested.

"Why didn't you invite Stefan over?" The comely woman asked. Again with Stefan. "Why? You want us both don't you?" Laine chuckled. "You're a kinky one aren't you?"

"I want you to bring him to me?"

"When? How?"

"He works for you doesn't he?"

"The store's closed right now, baby."

"I want to see your store," Lillian mused as if in excitement.

"You do?"

"Yes. Tomorrow morning."

Laine realized Stefan would be opening the store the next morning. Although he didn't know where any of this was leading to, he grew more excited with the idea of the three of them there the next morning. This fantasy was becoming so intense, so sexually charged, and Laine had never thought he would've been part of the ménage trois the woman was suggesting. And, in his own store of all places! "OK," Laine agreed.

"Good," Lillian kissed at his stomach, "don't be late." Her lengthy tongued fell from her mouth, tipped like that of a snake, and took a long lick of Laine's erection. As instantly as she had appeared, she was gone from the room.

Laine remained in bed with the biggest smile he'd ever donned grazed his face.

-5-

Harold Shevers, owner of the generically titled *The Gun Shop*, had been in business for twenty years. In all that time, he had always closed his shop at five and reopened for business at ten the following morning. Harold was a senior citizen and needed his rest. Not to mention, his business didn't have any competition in the entire town of Spook Valley, so he didn't worry about the store hours he kept.

Today, Harold had received the strangest call ever. The gentleman on the phone had made a special request. Along with it, a certain time he would be by to pick up his specialty made item. In fact, the time he said he would come by was ten o'clock at night. At first, Harold immediately dismissed the man's request. However, the man had offered him an extra three hundred dollars in addition to the price of the item. Harold was old, but he was no fool. It wasn't often that a price like that had been offered to him.

When Harold closed today, he made his way to the back of the store. He had heated up the kiln and tossed in a couple cubes of the precious metal he was surprised he'd had. After the substance had melted, he diligently poured the metal into a casting iron where it would instantly cool into the mold. It wasn't that tough actually; he was done within an hour. Instead of going home for the day, Harold did some extra cleaning around the shop as he waited for the special customer.

The man showed up on schedule and Harold unlocked the door to his shop. The gentleman was young, handsome. Harold didn't recognize him. "You're not from around here, are you lad?"

The gentleman shook his head. "No, I'm not from around here." The stranger pulled the money from his right front pocket and handed it over to Harold.

Harold rushed back behind the counter and produced the item sought for upon the countertop. "Took my time with this one," Harold remarked. "Got to say, it's probably my best work to date."

The dim light of the store gleamed off the silver bullet. The stranger picked it up from the countertop and studied it. "You did a good job," the gentleman commended.

The old man chuckled, "I thought so too!"

They both shared a quick laughter and then the stranger thanked Harold as he left the store.

As the man sauntered down Main Street, into the encroaching twilight that would bring another witching hour to Spook Valley, he observed the curves of the silver bullet he'd purchased. The hardened silver was cold between his fingers. For a moment, it reminded him of the gelid stone of mausoleum walls from years back. He shook his head, quickly dismissing the memory.

Now, he had only to find his target.

CHAPTER XVII

-1-

Stefan crouched behind a formation of jagged rocks. It was the only thing that separated him from the group of cloaked men he conceived to be what Breckin had called "the Order of Perennial Darkness." Beyond the rock formation in which Stefan remained hidden by, the six hierarchy of the Nightworld stood with bowed heads, chanting unintelligible words, words that could only be some incantation or prayer in a tongue only known to minions of this dark and hellish place. Between the ghoulish chants that emitted from the Order's mouths and the fiery landscape of the Nightworld, Stefan eyes remained fixed on the scene before him. Still, it all felt so inconceivable. Once again, it was like a nightmare from which one could not awaken. At the same time, Stefan knew it had to be real! Yes, this place did indeed exist. Perhaps that was another reason he decided to cross the threshold—not only to find the answers of Aaron's part in this horrible ordeal, but also to see if the Nightworld was in fact a real place. Before, in the awesome hesitation to coming horrors, Stefan's mind harbored doubt of such a place. But not now, no. The Nightworld was as real as he was. This was the place he saved Breckin from on that fateful night; this is where all of his troubles emerged. This was the source of every evil that had touched him, along with Catrina and the other innocent people of Spook Valley. This was the home to evil.

Stefan remained oblivious to his next move. So he was here, now what? When would the answers come? What of Aaron, which Breckin forewarned? And Breckin—was there any way to bring him back to the world of the living? Furthermore, there was the infamous pact that was spoken about between the creatures of this place and the living humans of the real world. With the latter thought in mind, Stefan observed the sextet of creatures before him as they pulled scrolls from within their cloaks. Stefan's mind recalled something Breckin had briefly mentioned about such scrolls held by the Order; they contained the words of the pact that would allow the doorway to be opened permanently. And what hellish diction would be inscribed on such papyrus? What possible inscriptions could force the Nightworld to prevail over the Earth? Stefan uncontrollably shivered at that very thought and, as he did so, he was reminded of Breckin's words once again. The six member of the Order were a piece of a whole. If he could just get one of those scrolls and escape this place! Stefan peered behind himself to recall how he had gotten from the doorway to this central point of the Nightworld. Yes, it was possible. It would take courage, but it was indeed possible. He imagined seeing himself emerge from the rock formation, swiftly and cunningly running past one of the Order as he grasped for any of the scrolls with which any of them held, and making his way back toward the doorway. The plan seemed full proof. *That would be too easy though*, Stefan doubted himself. Surely, it couldn't be that simple. Then again, he had come this far, what more could he lose?

Losing sight of his imaginary plan, Stefan gazed back through the small crevice of the rocks to the gathering of the Order of Perennial Darkness. Something was amiss! There were only five of the six congregated in the clearing and, although their sixth counterpart was absent, they continued their alien chant. The words cut like a catastrophic tornado upon a peaceful day. Their tones were ominous, crackling whispers that foretold of danger. Of an impeding threat, surely! The chant enveloped Stefan's mind, as if the voices of the Order were all around him. His heart quickly jolted into panic. As Stefan turned around, a voice that hissed like that of a snake met his eyes. A member of the order loomed over Stefan. His obsidian eyes burned a hole into Stefan's soul. "Within the bowelsss of our preciousss world, and who would have thought that your capture would be difficult."

Stefan was aghast with fear. As he sprung to his feet, the creature raised his hand containing a red rock of the landscape. He brought the rock down hard upon Stefan's head with the weight of a hammer hitting a nail. Stefan felt himself fall to the embracing dirt of the Nightworld and, as his sight of the subhuman blurred and contorted, his vision went black.

-2-

Who would have thought that after days and nights in a state of comatose, one could sleep?

Catrina Taylor did just that.

She fell to sleep shortly after instructing Aaron to take refuge in Stefan's apartment.

However, the images of her dreams were not like that of those in her coma. No, there were no messages given from a brilliant force known to her as the God and Goddess. There were no friends here—no Stefan, no Aaron, and certainly no brother Zander. Instead, the image whirring in her state of dreaming was that of a foreboding and grisly monster.

The creature was inhuman and kneeling near a tombstone in a cemetery, not more than thirty feet from where Catrina stood. Of course, she couldn't see her body. She only remained aware that she rested away from the creature, at what was easily a safe distance and yet close enough for the abomination to notice her. The stooped monster's flesh was pale green, bordering on gray, and its entire body appeared as a bloated suit of rubber. Catrina could not see what the creature was doing, nor was she concerned with its actions. However, in her conscious mind, the part of the mind that tells one that he or she is asleep and they are only experiencing a dream, Catrina came to a realization that there was a reason for this unusual nightmare. Perhaps a sign; maybe a warning like the similar experience she had days previous when she had viewed the beast in her dreams that turned out to be Aaron Dabney. In that dream, Aaron was trying to warn her, attempting to scare her away from Spook Valley before all the chaos had begun. However, whether it was ignorance, bravery, or even an unhinged curiosity, Catrina had remained in the town. Just as Aaron had predicted, Catrina came face to face with evil. In fact, it had almost killed her if not for Breckin coming to her rescue before the demon known as Lillian mangled Catrina's body.

Catrina continued to observe the creature in her dream. Its movement was like that of a wild animal, untamed and vicious. As that thought of the creature preyed on her mind, the monster turned toward her and carved revulsion upon her face. Its features were horrifying, completely otherworldly even though it walked as a human on two legs and had two arms. The creature's eyes were sunken back into its head; they were like two caverns of darkness that emitted no sign of a soul, no signature of goodness. Its chin was unusually long and came to a point and its cheekbones were sharp and erected beyond its face, as if they antennae to Heaven. The mouth of the creature was stained in crimson all about where its lips should have been and a meat of some sort dangled from that bloody grimace. Catrina recoiled and peered to the creature's hand where elongated blue-black nails that appeared sharp as razors gripped onto a human arm. Catrina's stomach folded inward at the disgusting sight. The creature had been feasting on the human arm! In fact, Catrina grasped in utter apprehension, this creature was of a known species; there was a name for such monsters. What stood before her, in all its horrific evil, was a ghoul, a beast that robbed cemeteries and fed off the dead!

The ghoul studied Catrina, tilting its head at first toward the right and then the left. Catrina felt her body cautiously backing away from the beast, taking notice of the tombstones and granite statues around her, and mentally forming an immediate exit from the impending danger that stared her down. Catrina was ready to make her escape. However, her body remained frozen, her limbs paralyzed by the beast that was taking slow and diligent steps toward her. *Run*, she desperately instructed in her mind. *Run from it, Catrina!* Still, the adrenaline bursting throughout her body kept her stock-still. The ghoul was dangerously close; the smell of rot filled Catrina's nostrils. Unable to move, she stood her ground as the ghoul was practically in her face. It opened its mouth and Catrina's insides cringed at the sight of its irregularly pointed teeth that protruded in various angles. Its teeth were stained pink from its unholy feast and pieces of the corpse it had fed from were stuck in between the fangs of its mouth. Drool dripped like waterfalls all about the creature's mouth and that is when Catrina produced a terrified scream that jolted her awake.

Zander's face—that was the first thing Catrina saw as she awoke from the nightmare. Her brother's visage was etched with concern; his age showed up close in the lines that appeared penciled at the corners of his russet-colored eyes. Still, although age had taken its toll on Catrina's brother, his face remained as youthful and innocent as it did when they were kids. "Are you alright, Catrina?" he spoke in calmly smooth inflection.

Catrina took immediate notice of her surroundings. The hospital. She was still in her room at the hospital and not in a cemetery facing down that repulsive beast. *Alright? I'm alright now.* "I'm fine; I just had a bad dream."

"Do you want to talk about it?" Zander attempted to console her.

He would never understand, Catrina told herself. As much as she wanted to confide her troubles and all the horrible things the Nightworld had brought to the quiet town of Spook Valley, she knew better than to involve another innocent person. Especially, her brother of all people. "No. I'll be fine. It was only a nightmare. I was just a little scared."

"Well, in that case," Zander stood to his feet and sat in the chair next to her bed, "good morning." He smiled and Catrina felt love in that precious grin.

It had been so long since she saw her brother last. And, now, he'd walked back into her life, obviously knowing she missed him. Now that he had returned to her life, Catrina didn't want to lose track of him again. Catrina reminded herself once this whole ordeal was over, she would plan to make happy memories of her and Zander, memories that would take place of the absent ones she had in her years of growing up without her brother.

"Today's the big day," Zander announced.

At first Catrina was confused by what he meant, but then it immediately became clear to her. Yes, today was the day she was being released from the care of the Spook Valley Medical Center. Catrina quickly recalled Aaron's visit the night previous. She was to meet him at Stefan's apartment. They were to congregate for their battle against the Nightworld and their fight to get Stefan safely back from the netherworld's grasp. Her mind writhed in the act of making up excuses to Zander to keep him from going with her. "Where are you staying, Zander?"

"At a motel on the edge of town for now? But I figured, once you were well enough to leave this place, you might consider leaving with me for New York."

Zander's eyes were so expectant of her positive answer and she felt guilty when she brought on the news of her staying in Spook Valley. At first, Catrina tried sugarcoating the subject. "What would I do in New York?"

Zander pondered the question for a moment, his eyes darting back and forth in consideration. "Well, you could get a job; you could live in my condo with me for the time being. I think you'd like it there, Catrina. I mean, it's much bigger than Spook Valley, but there is so much opportunity for you there."

Catrina's glance felt the guilt already began to instill itself within her mind. "Spook Valley is my home, Zander." She studied the hurt look stamped upon his upturned smile. "I have an apartment here. I have friends here, Zander, friends I love dearly."

"How about this?" Zander compromised, "We'll discuss it."

"OK," Catrina agreed.

Zander jumped to his feet in excitement. "Let's get you checked out, little sister."

"Zander?"

"Yeah?"

"Can I ask a favor of you?"

"Of course you can. I'm your brother. Hell, after all this time I've been away, I figured I owed you one, if not two or three."

She laughed. "Well, I need to go see a friend; it's really important to me. Once I get out of this place, can you drive me back to my apartment? I'll take my car from there."

"Sure, I'll go with you," Zander invited himself.

"Actually…this is something I want to do on my own."

"I understand," Zander said in a monotone that obviously derived from despair. "What about me?"

"I can meet up with you later. Give me the number to your motel and I'll give you a call when I'm done. Deal?"

"Deal," he settled. Zander exited the room to fetch the attending nurse and prepare for Catrina's discharge.

The drive from the Spook Valley Medical Center to Catrina Taylor's apartment complex took fifteen minutes. In that time, as she gave directions to Zander at every turn and each stoplight, she acted as a tour guide to her brother. At the most northern point of Main Street that connected with Yucca Lane, she gestured for Zander to turn left. Here is where Main Street began, she had explained to him, and it ran through the entire center of the town. As they approached Saguaro Street, Catrina pointed out the historical courthouse that loomed over the town center in all its granite and marble wonder. Across the way from the courthouse, on the opposing side of the town square, Catrina showed Zander the white-lattice gazebo that contained the bronze statue of Jamison Spook, the town's founder. Catrina noticed that Zander hardly seemed that amused by Spook Valley and all her hopes of a possible permanent stay for Zander faded. As the two turned onto Firehouse Road, Catrina took a secret glance at Laine's Music, the store where Stefan worked. A closed sign remained dangling in the window. Catrina wished that Stefan were unlocking the doors. She longed to imagine Stefan there, in her world, that everything was all right, and he was just getting to work. A tear formed in her eye.

Zander dropped off Catrina at her apartment and she got out of the passenger seat, only after giving her brother a hug and a kiss on the cheek. "I'll give you a call later," she promised him. Zander continued to watch her until she unlocked her apartment door and stepped inside, closing it behind her.

It felt like she was in someone else's apartment at first. Everything seemed unreal, as if she hadn't been there for years. She glanced around her apartment, relishing the surroundings as if they an old friend she'd almost forgotten about. The pictures on the walls reminded Catrina of her craft—a painting with a unisexual entity brilliantly floating in the midst of a darkened universe (the God and Goddess) and another with the lithe form of the hunter Diana holding her quarry proudly in one hand and an arrow in the other. These were images of her Wiccan world, a place where Catrina Taylor was at peace with herself. The study of Wicca made her whole. It made her the powerful and magical person she was today. And, she enforced the thought in her head, it was the one trait she could use in the upcoming battle against the Nightworld. For, she too, had powers beyond the normal; she only needed to harness the magic more powerfully to defeat the Nightworld. She had no doubt that she could do such a thing.

She entered her bedroom; the smell of jasmine and sandalwood still permeated the air. The red light upon her answering machine flashed in quick succession. She pressed the button and began listening to the messages left for her as she went to her closet and gathered some clothing to take to Stefan's apartment.

There were many messages left for her by her employer, Andy Sullivan, owner of the Violin Street Tavern. He had asked why she never showed for work on a particular day, proceeded in a following message by saying that he needed to know where she was and why she didn't show again and, finally, with a voice composed of smitten anger, informed her not to return to work because she was fired. And he made sure he yelled the word "fired" into the answering machine. *Oh well*, Catrina calmed herself, *he was a pig anyway.*

She went to the edge of her bed when she heard two other messages on the machine. There were both from her mother. "Catrina, this is your mom. Your father and I want to speak to you about moving back to the city." Another message followed, time and date stamped a couple days later. "Catrina, please give us a call. Are you doing all right? Call us as soon as you can. God bless." *God bless? Please, not the religious riot act again.* Catrina would call her, but not right now. She had to get to Stefan's apartment and meet with Aaron. That priority took precedence over all other things.

Catrina finished packing her clothes, grabbed her tarot cards, locked her apartment door behind her, and made her way to her Acura. The car purred to life and Catrina began her drive down Firehouse Road, eager to meet with Aaron and plot their plan of rescuing Stefan. "Please, God and Goddess," she said aloud, "let him be safe."

-3-

On the other side of Spook Valley, where Violin Road extends to the edge of town before merging with Interstate 87, Lucien awoke in a sweat. He immediately jumped from the bed, tearing at the sheets upon the mattress, as if searching for something lost. However, he was simply assuring himself that the nightmare wasn't real.

A large lump of dead flesh beneath the white sheets of the bed. The unrecognizable and gory crimson pool oozing beneath the covers. You Bastard! You'll pay for this; look what you've done! Death in the air. Rotten flesh.

Just a dream, Lucien eased himself. *Not like the other night at all. No, that happened when you were awake. It was only a dream.* Still, Lucien knew there was more to the images of carnage that haunted his waking and sleeping moments. He drowned the thoughts from mind as he scanned the clock on the wall. Shit! After nine o'clock and he was late for work! Hopefully, Stefan was already there and had unlocked the place.

Lucien briskly jumped into the shower and cursed at it as the cold water splashed against his flesh. Toweling himself off, he ran his fingers through his jet-black hair and dressed quicker than he'd ever remember doing. In no time, he was out the door of the motel room and made his way to Laine's Music.

-4-

Laine Young couldn't believe she was there! Lillian had made the promise that she'd be at his store that morning. However, he wasn't sure of how much the conversation they'd engaged in the night previous was fantasy and which part was reality.

When he arrived at Laine's Music, he expected the door to be unlocked and the first morning's customers to be perusing the shelves for the latest hits by their favorite artists. However, it appeared that Stefan and Lucien were running late. The glass door was still locked and Laine retrieved his keys and locked the door behind him. To his amazement, Lillian had been in the store. His mind was flushed with confusion as Laine tried to crack the mystery as to how Lillian had gained entrance. Yet, his libido got the best of him as the puzzle faded from his mind and the voluptuous woman of his dreams stood before him, naked flesh and smooth contours begging for his attention.

"You're here," Laine said, bemused.

"I told you I would be," she whispered in that sultry voice that turned him on. That beautiful voice of an angel.

"Oh, Lily." Laine advanced to her, unbuttoning his shirt and pressing his flesh against her. The nipples of her breasts were hard and Laine knelt slightly to meet them with his mouth as he began sucking on them. He pulled his hand up the vixen's thigh and into the crease between her legs where he could feel her warm juices flowing. Oh, how he wanted her as if it were his first time meeting her. Every time with Lillian made Laine feel as if it were the first. He lost all self-control with this woman; she'd captivated him beyond lust.

"Where's Stefan?" Lillian asked as she pulled back and brushed her fingers along Laine's neck.

Laine broke from his sexual hunger, as he recalled Lillian's request to have both he and Stefan meet here. The thought of Stefan involved in their forthcoming ménage trois caused Laine's cock to stiffen harder than he could imagine. "I think he's running late. He should be here anytime though. Why don't the two of us get at it in the meantime?"

Lillian chuckled as she brought her hands to Laine's chest and threw her lithe body against his. He fell back to the floor and Lillian unbuttoned Laine's pants and pulled them off.

Laine closed his eyes, ignoring the iciness of the polished floor beneath him, and moaned in ecstasy as Lillian gently eased herself onto his organ. She slid it into her with an expertise he had never known any other woman or man to do and began to ride Laine. Laine's passionate grunts grew louder with every push of himself into her.

Lillian's plan had been put into action. She needed only to wait for Stefan to arrive. Once the young man got there, she could make the capture. As for the man beneath her buckling hips, he was expendable. After all, she only used Laine so that he could bring her closer to Stefan.

Lillian's demon mind was projected out of her euphoric state, though she continued to move in sexual rhythm with the man beneath her. The sounds around her had all faded, and the tones of static acted as a barrier between the Earth realm and the Nightworld. Once her mind broke through that barrier, she heard the roaring voice of her God within her head. It spoke aloud as it had done with them all. *Damia* knew all, he knew of all his minions whereabouts, and he could telepathically communicate with them whether they in the Nightworld or any other world for that matter. *Lillian*, his voice echoed in her head.

Yes, God Damia, she mentally answered.

Stefan has been captured.

Lillian's mind raced with pure enjoyment. The time was forthcoming! The pact would be initiated soon and then Lillian would take to God *Damia*'s side as Queen of this conquered Earth realm. *Then I shall return to the Nightworld immediately. Open the doorway.*

Laine felt a tickling sensation at the base of his cock. He thought he could burst into orgasm at any moment. Laine opened his eyes to view why Lillian had stopped pleasing him. "Is there something wrong?"

"Yes," she paused, "something is terribly wrong for you."

Laine was taken off guard. He didn't understand what just happened. Why did she stop? Was she waiting for Stefan? "Hey, baby, I told you Stefan should be here anytime."

"He won't be here, Laine. Not ever! And, I'm afraid to say that you won't be here any longer either."

"Wha—" Before Laine had a chance to react to her statement, his eyes grew in amazement as the woman atop of him morphed into the creature he'd believed his mind had tricked him into seeing before. The rough and leathery texture of her flesh cut at Laine's own and her sexual grip on his organ tightened. Her eyes filled with inky darkness over the white of her sclera and Laine's heart sped in panic as Lillian's fingernails and the teeth in her mouth protruded in monstrous transformation. He could feel her tail slither back in forth between his legs and he used all his strength to buck off the demon. However, it was to no avail; for the creature's power was ten fold his own strength. Laine tried to scream but not a sound could escape his throat. Lillian threw back her head and shrieked toward the Heavens. Laine experienced the god-awful pain of pressure on all sides of his cock. Instantly, he felt Lillian's sex close around his organ and sharply tear upon all sides as she lifted her body off his. The agony intensified; the pain shot through his stomach and down his legs like a million razors cutting in unison. He produced a stifled cough as he gazed down to the bloody black pool where his cock should have been. The last sight of Lillian he saw was her mouth full of wretched teeth that shot downward, viciously tearing through his chest and to his heart that he prayed would seize before she got to it.

Lucien pushed at the door to Laine's Music. "Shit," he yelled. "Nobody's here yet." He pulled out his key, inserted it into the deadbolt, and heard the bells overhead announce his entrance. He decided to leave the door unlocked. After all, the store was supposed to be open by nine o'clock.

He immediately made his way toward the back of the store to retrieve the cash till from the safe. Lucien stopped in his tracks when he heard the slurping sound. It sounded as if a dog were eagerly lapping at a bowl of water it had been neglected. Lucien looked around the store for the source of the sound. His eyes darted to the left and right as he made slow steps toward the back room. "Hello," he called out. "Stefan? Laine? Are you guys here? I'm sorry I'm late, but I…"

Lucien stood motionless as he gawked at the gory scene before him. There was some sort of hideous creature burrowing its mouth into the chest of what appeared to be his boss, Laine. Crimson puddles concealed the floor around the attacker and its prey. The sight alone, along with the pungent stench of decay, caused Lucien to gag.

No, he tried telling himself, *this isn't happening. It's another one of those horrible images just like you had in your dream this morning. It's another MEMORY of what happened.* As much as he willed the forbidden scene from his mind, the slaughter remained before him. What made Lucien realize that the horrendous crime before him was taking place, what ignited him to turn and bolt out of Laine's Music, was the creature taking notice of his presence. Its obsidian eyes threw daggers at him and Lucien sprinted as a constricting lump swelled in his throat.

"Traitor to your kind," the monstrous voice snarled, "come back to me!"

Lucien took no notice of the monster's words and the bells over the entrance of Laine's Music jangled loudly as he dashed out the door. Behind him, he could hear the creature shrieking; it pierced his ears and he felt his head would explode.

At the corner of Firehouse Road and Main Street, Lucien stopped to catch his breath. What the hell just happened? He knew he couldn't call the police. There was no way he was going to lead *them* here! Lucien anxiously stared behind him to see if the creature had followed him out of the store. Soon, an answer formed within Lucien's panicked mind. He took off along the lengthy stretch of Firehouse Road. As the morning approached early afternoon, Lucien mentally prayed that Stefan would be home.

Stefan opened his eyes to the circle of beastly men surrounding him. At first, he wanted to dismiss it all for a dream. But it was no dream. He was here in the Nightworld. A member of the Order had caught him. That's when he blacked out. He had been knocked out. The Order loomed over him, looking down upon Stefan with their black eyes and parchment faces.

Stefan felt light-headed and groggy, as if he'd been drugged. He reached for his head and when he pulled his hand back to his face, he saw that his fingers were covered in blood. He had been hit hard in the head and now he was faced with an even bigger dilemma. How the hell was he supposed to escape?

"Don't fret, young man," Saint Trace spoke. Stefan noticed his voice was powerful and echoed throughout the immediate area. "You're not dead yet."

Another piped in. His voice was like that of a snake, if snakes could speak with their forked tongues. "Yessssss, Sssstefan, not yet."

"You're needed alive for now." This was Saint Dante.

"You're needed to initiate the pact," Saint Israel finished, as if completing Saint Dante's thought.

Stefan gazed to each of the Order of Perennial Darkness and noticed that they were the size of normal men. Although they were not monsters, they were ancient, old beyond time. One of them cackled. Stefan had to fight! He couldn't just let this happen. "I won't let you win," he stated with authority.

"You have no choice," Saint Trace counterattacked. "You've already lost, foolish young man."

Stefan took a momentary gaze at each member of the Order. "I'm going to stop you."

All six of the Order guffawed in amusement. Their voice, in unison, was like a choir of horror—hissing deeply, high-pitched and low-moaned. Saint Collin burbled his own addition to the conversation. "It's no use to fight us, Stefan."

The ground Stefan lay upon began undulating beneath him. It felt as if a tremor had stricken the Nightworld. Soon after, a roar of massive strength was ignited and echoed throughout the entire atmosphere.

"God *Damia* is coming," Saint Cassius announced.

God Damia, Stefan's mind raced in horror. *I have to escape now!*

As Stefan stood to his feet, Saint Dante quickly tended to the young man. He gripped both of Stefan's arms. Stefan felt the frail fingers of his adversary grasp with very little strength. "You're not going anywhere, Stefan. You're going to stay and face God *Damia.*"

Stefan almost broke into tears. This horror was far worse than anything he had been exposed to in the Earth realm, even worse than the sight of watching Breckin die before him. He had to act quickly and that was what he did.

Remembering where the Order had stored their scrolls from earlier, he immediately reached into Saint Dante's cloak and grasped for the rolled papyrus. He felt Saint Dante's slimy flesh but refused to recoil. Once Stefan pulled out the scroll, he used all his energy to push over Saint Dante. As he fleeted, Stefan practically trampled and tripped over the toppled member of the Order.

"Get him!" yelled Saint Cassius. "Don't let him escape!"

Stefan refused to look back. He ran forward with all his will, each fateful step comprised of forced strength and every thought of Breckin, Catrina, and Aaron composed his yearning to escape that awful place. Stefan heard the pattering of feet in the distance and would not chance to slow down his pace toward the doorway. As he ran, he gripped the scroll in his hand as tightly as possible, digging his fingernails into the flesh of his palm. There was a massive sense of eagerness and accomplishment in knowing he held a piece of the pact. *Now, if only to get through the doorway!*

The roars of wild animals and ungodly shrieks filled the air around him. The doorway was only beyond the red, dirt path upon which he was backtracking.

The humming.

The static hum like the tearing of the universe.

The doorway was near!

Stefan's legs grew heavy, but he couldn't give up! Like an atomic blast, the explosion of a monstrous bellow shook the entire foundation of the Nightworld. It was the most frightening and inhuman inflection Stefan had ever known. It had to be God *Damia.* Stefan's side began aching in piercing agony; he wasn't sure if he'd make it or not. Yet, just as doubt of his strength set in, just as the throbbing in his head got so intense that he felt he would fall over any second, he saw the illumination of the doorway ahead.

Stefan slid to a halt as he saw the form emerging from the doorway and, at the same time, he noticed a second doorway near the one that something was already using to return to the Nightworld. To the left, there was a third doorway! *Oh my God!* Stefan's mind screamed. The form from the doorway took shape and he immediately recognized it as the demon responsible for taking Breckin away from him. It was Lillian! Oh god, it was Lillian in her monstrous form. And those eyes! Those horrible black eyes had taken him into their target. Lillian shrieked in harrowing fashion, baring her teeth and clenching her gruesome nails in hopes of grabbing Stefan. With his last ounce of strength, Stefan leapt into one of the other doorways as he felt one of Lillian's nails tear into his hand that held the scroll.

The sound of static was more welcoming than ever. The same dissipating and disembodying feeling Stefan had experienced while entering the Nightworld was mimicked by the same sensation as he exited. Molecules broke and reformed, the incessant buzzing of the black limbo in between, the gory dissection and regrouping of his cells and his flesh—going through the doorway was like watching an abstract picture form upon a canvas.

Earth.

He fell face first as he emerged from the doorway. He rested. His chest heaved. His hand still held onto the scroll. He could sleep now, surely; his heart could slow down to a normal rate. He had done it! Stefan had escaped the grasp of the Nightworld!

In the distance, the sound of music could be heard. A voice yelled something unintelligible into a microphone. It sounded as if a concert was being performed. Stefan pulled himself to his feet and gazed into the distance. *What the hell?*

Before him, there was a throng of people upon grassy knolls. Some were naked; some were laughing as if the event were a party. They were all there for a concert though, for there were multiple stages and bands. The music they played seemed familiar too. Like something Stefan may have heard a long time ago.

Where am I? Stefan's perplexed mind asked. *Where did Spook Valley go?*

Stefan took small steps toward the congregation of people, puzzled but glad to have escaped that place of terror and monsters. As he advanced toward the loud and riotous throng, Stefan's mind repeatedly reminded him of one thing: *There is no end to this nightmare.*

CHAPTER XVIII

-1-

The man had watched her every move, studied each course of action she had taken from the moment she was discharged from the Spook Valley Medical Center. Of course, he was quite assured that he exercised caution and Catrina Taylor hadn't noticed. He imagined what she did once she entered her apartment and was shocked at first to see her exiting, carrying a duffle bag and a backpack that were probably stuffed with clothes. Where was she going? Had she been scared enough to leave Spook Valley? What's more, was Catrina Taylor that easy for the Nightworld to remove from their master plan? Had the dark netherworld known this, he probably wouldn't have had to monitor her and prevent her from interfering with the pact.

However, the man trailing Catrina Taylor knew better than to assume she was leaving town. God *Damia* would torment him forever should he make a mistake and she remained. So he had followed her as she sped down Firehouse Road. Within the vast deserts that bordered the road, beyond the saguaro cacti and the various other desert shrubs that impregnated the dry landscape, the door to his home existed. How he longed to go home; how he wished this would all end.

His instinct to follow Catrina proved relieving and made him realize he wasn't wasting his time. He had a feeling she wasn't that weak; a woman such as she would put up a battle to the very end. This woman was somewhat feared by the Nightworld and they sent him to the Earth realm to ensure she remained out of the way. Even if it meant her death.

She turned into an apartment complex that hailed the name *Shadowood Apartments*. She was going to Stefan's home, the man realized. But why? After he studied her walking up the concrete steps and entering the apartment, the man hid in the green shrubbery where he studied the window high upon the second floor and gauged Catrina's next move.

Strangely, he felt the tingling sensation that marked another of his kind within proximity. He had a good idea he knew who that person was. And, as the man remembered Aaron Dabney's human face from the Nightworld, he reached into his shirt pocket and admired the sheen of the silver bullet he had specially purchased for their meeting.

-2-

The morning hours were eclipsed by the coming of the afternoon as Catrina Taylor and Aaron Dabney discussed their plans. Aaron had been awake and waiting for her when she walked through the front door of Stefan's apartment. He had greeted her with a hug and Catrina couldn't believe that she once feared this man, this man whose ominous ruby-colored eyes announced his transformation into a werewolf. Still, as Aaron had explained, he wanted to break free of the Nightworld; he insisted on helping her fight the present darkness that loomed over their lives.

Catrina had brewed them both some tea and she let Aaron spew all the information he knew of the Nightworld. His explanations ran on for hours as he described to her the landscape of the horrible world—the endless darkness, the rivers of fire and lava, the many minions that stormed the land in hatred and chaos. He clarified for her how the Nightworld preyed on believers of the occult and how they'd abducted hundreds if not thousands of such believers from the Earth realm.

Of course, she had already known some of this from the conversations she had had with Stefan when he was still a vampire and under Breckin's spell. *Breckin.* How she once loathed the man and, ironically, he was the one who'd saved her from Lillian. She never had the chance to thank him, never had the opportunity to ask for his forgiveness for thinking him evil. Catrina felt her instincts were way off these days. First Breckin, then her fear of Aaron (who was now her only friend she could confide in). She had to focus more on her gifts, had to entrust in the powers that be for the guidance they would deliver. Catrina made her new beginning as she thought this. She interrupted Breckin's detailed and traumatic account of the time he'd spent with Stefan before Stefan crossed the threshold into the Nightworld. "Aaron?"

"Yeah?"

Catrina pulled her lengthy locks of auburn hair behind her shoulders so that he could see her entire face. *Nothing to hide behind.* "I just wanted to apologize if I treated you unfairly."

Aaron gave Catrina a queer look, confused by her apology that came out of thin air as if she hadn't heard a word he was saying. "Unfairly?"

"Yeah. There was a time that I treated you differently because I was scared of you. I thought you were going to hurt me, or even worse, Stefan."

"I was trying to—"

"Warn me," Catrina finished Aaron's sentence. "I know that. Thank you. But, for what it's worth, I'm glad I stayed in Spook Valley and held out through what's happened thus far."

Aaron grinned. "Me too. Don't worry; I forgive you as long as you forgive me for making a mess of your apartment."

Catrina couldn't help but laugh. Tears of happiness welled in her eyes. Perhaps the first tears of joy she'd shared with Aaron.

A moment of silence followed their laughter. It was the kind of silence shared by friends, the type of quietness in which one could briskly reflect on his or her memories, but only the pleasant ones. It was a golden silence.

"So," Catrina changed the subject again, "what do you know about the pact?"

Although Aaron felt he was oblivious to the answers, after he voiced all he knew aloud, it began to make sense. In fact, when spoken aloud, he realized he knew more than he thought he had. Aaron gave Catrina the details of the Order of Perennial Darkness; how they were connected to the pact and that they held the scrolls to initiate it. He made a mention of "one" being sacrificed in the final process to keep the doorway open for all time.

"That must be Stefan," Catrina added.

Aaron's brow knitted in confusion as he waited for Catrina to explain herself.

"It has to be Stefan. The sacrifice," she began rationalizing. "Think about it, Aaron. You said that the Nightworld preys on believers, right? Well, wouldn't it made sense that the sacrifice would be the one who opened the doorway in the first place? Otherwise, the Nightworld could initiate the pact at any time. And it seems logical to say that that is why the Nightworld wanted Stefan so badly."

"I think you're right," Aaron agreed. "I'd never looked at it in that way before. In fact, I wasn't sent here from the Nightworld to kill Stefan. They made precise instructions for me to 'capture' him so they could cross over and initiate the pact. They also sent me to destroy Breckin, though my conscience got the best of me."

"Exactly," Catrina beamed as they cracked the puzzle. "Stefan was never in any true danger of being killed. Only the people around him were in harm's way. Still, there's one thing I don't understand." Catrina paused for a moment, trying to figure out how to word her concern. "Why didn't the Nightworld want you to bring Stefan back onto their turf? I mean, wouldn't it seem more sensible that if one were to use another as a sacrifice, they would keep him in their world until the time came to initiate the pact?"

Without warning, Aaron jumped up in excitement by his own answer to Catrina's question. Catrina was startled by his sudden anticipation. "No. That's not how it works, Catrina. Thirteen have to cross over; that's part of the pact. Which means, they have to initiate the pact in the Earth realm; they can't do it in the Nightworld."

"Wait a minute," Catrina mentally scurried through all the facts to assure she had this right. "You mean as long as Stefan is in the Nightworld, the pact can't be initiated?"

Aaron eagerly nodded his head. "Thirteen have to cross through the doorway, Catrina. And the pact has to be initiated here, in the Earth realm. In Spook Valley where the doorway was opened."

"Thirteen have to cross," Catrina repeated. She began recalling the creatures they had come up against thus far in an attempt to figure out how close the pact was to being initiated. "Okay, first there was Breckin. That's one. Then, the two men that came through and tried to capture Stefan and kill Breckin that first night. There's you, of course." She couldn't help but smile at Aaron.

"That's four," Aaron kept count. "Don't forget our favorite succubus Lillian."

"Five."

"The Order makes eleven," Aaron added.

Catrina's mind thrust into shock from this statement. "The Order of Perennial Darkness?"

"They have to cross to initiate the pact, Catrina. There are six of them. I would imagine they're the last to crossover. But they do count as part of the thirteen."

"Great," Catrina threw up her hands as if in defeat. "How are we going to stop this? Eleven have crossed over already and Stefan's trapped in that horrible place."

"I don't think he'll be there long, Catrina. The Nightworld can't perform the pact with him on their ground. They'll have to force him out in some way. By the way," Aaron corrected Catrina, "I think I have number twelve."

"Who?"

"There's something else that has crossed over. The other night, when I was in the cemetery, I found a corpse dug up from its grave. It looked as though something had been tearing or eating at its body. It gives me reason to believe that there is another creature in Spook Valley."

Catrina's mind catapulted back to the night previous, to the dream she had of the ghoul that confronted her in the cemetery. "Oh my god; you're right, Aaron. I thought it was a nightmare, but it must have been a vision. I know of the creature you're speaking. It's a ghoul, a feeder of the dead." Catrina shivered at what she'd just said. "But, where is it? Don't you have some insight into others from the Nightworld, Aaron?"

"There's this…sensation I get when another is around."

"At least we have some way of knowing. Still, that makes twelve. Only one more entity needs to cross over to make this pact a reality." Catrina gazed over at the digital clock, noticing the afternoon hour. "We have to make plans before nightfall, Aaron. And we have to know if Stefan's alright." She stood up and proceeded toward the kitchen to retrieve another cup of tea. "Do you want another cup," she called aloud.

"No, I'm fine," responded Aaron. But was he fine? Aaron reflected on the entire conversation and, although he didn't want to be pessimistic with Catrina, he admitted to himself that the odds were against them.

'…*It's very far away-- it takes about half a day to get there*
If we travel by my dragonfly...'

Aaron's ears perked to the sound of the music. *Hendrix,* he thought. It had been a long time since he'd heard that song. That was a song from his time, from decades previous, and it took his memory back to the days of long hair, peace, and love. Was it coming from a car stereo outside? "Catrina," he called out.

"Yeah," she replied as she walked back into the room with her cup of tea.

"Do you hear that?"

"Hear what?"

"Listen."

Catrina stood in a still silence. A minute later, she said, "I don't hear anything."

"Oh," Aaron spoke gingerly.

"What do you hear?" she asked.

"Jimi Hendrix live." Aaron chuckled at his ridiculous observation.

"That's strange; I don't hear a thing. Can you still hear it?"

"Yeah, and it's one of my favorite songs. *Spanish Castle Magic*." Aaron grinned.

Catrina sat, remaining quiet so that she may hear the same thing. However, she didn't hear music at all. The only sounds were that of the passing cars on Firehouse Road. She observed Aaron as he mouthed the lyrics to a song she barely knew.

-3-

Firehouse Road extends for miles. The two-lane road makes a beeline that runs from one edge of Spook Valley to the other. For some, it's a quicker route to the other side of town, a road where stoplights are non-existent and speed limits are ignored. The road was originally named during a time when the Spook Valley Fire Department once existed where the Shadowood Apartments now stand. The road gave quick access to the other side of Spook Valley, should a fire be reported, and made it easier for the fire trucks to appear on the other side of town without having to get caught up in the vehicle and pedestrian traffic of the town center.

Come twilight, the lengthy stretch of Firehouse Road is bathed in the shadow of night. The street is surrounded by desert, and it is common for one driving the road at night to run over rattlesnakes slithering along the warm tarmac (especially in the winter). However, during the daylight, in the midst of an unseasonably warm summer, the road could prove dangerous for those who walked its length. There are no businesses along Firehouse Road, no convenience stores for a pedestrian to stop at and grab a bottle of water to prevent his or her body from dehydrating. Nothing exists along this stretch of road; nothing save for a dimensional doorway hidden in the desert some eight hundred feet from the edge of the asphalt.

Lucien had to get to Stefan's apartment. He had to tell him what happened at the music store. He only prayed that Stefan hadn't already left en route to the store. *God forbid he'd have to see that gory scene*, thought Lucien. And that woman, that awful creature that snarled at him as he ran—Lucien had a difficult time getting that face out of his mind.

The sun's rays beat down upon Lucien's jet-black hair; his head felt as if it were on fire. *Black attracts heat;* Lucien made a mental note that came out of nowhere. Perhaps it was a way for him to keep his mind off that crazy woman-beast. *Don't think of her.* When he thought of her, his mind instantly recollected the other bloody scene, the one in which the large lump of crimson stained the white sheets of a bed. *Don't want to think about it! Can't remember that.*

His walk had slowed to a shuffle; this road was longer than he'd thought. Although, he couldn't see the structure of Stefan's apartment complex, Lucien knew it couldn't be much further. When he had driven Laine's truck to Stefan's that first day he'd met the ravishing young man, the drive seemed to take only ten minutes. Lucien dragged his feet upon the asphalt as he felt the heat soaked in by the road in the soles of his shoes. Sweat rolled off his head and along the small of his back. He was thirsty; his throat had grown dry, his mouth unable to produce saliva.

A whirring sound brought Lucien to a halt. The drone was constant and gave off no space for a beat or a rhythm—just an infinite buzzing that seemed to emit somewhere from within the desert with which he walked along.

A buzzing. Like that of static on a television set, once all the shows have gone off the air for the night. Oh God, blood on the screen of the television! Blood on the lampshade; blood on the bed. No, don't look beneath the sheet. You know what's under there, don't you? You did it, Lucien. You bastard, the voice echoed in his head. *How could you do this? Oh, Christ, look what you've done!*

Lucien panicked and his heart raced in his throat. The buzzing sound continued. Lucien cringed from the whirr that grew louder. What was going on? Lucien shot a glance behind him, only to see a vacant ribbon of black asphalt that was known as Firehouse Road. Lucien didn't like what he was hearing; it brought back the memories. Though his body had very little energy, he began jogging the remaining distance of Firehouse Road, anticipating Stefan's greeting. However, the pessimist within him clearly conveyed that he was already too late.

-4-

Stefan approached the gathering of people that formed upon the grass. Some sat and rocked back and forth to the music blaring from the stage. '*The clouds are really low and they overflow,*' the singer on stage claimed as he bellowed the lyrics into the microphone. There was laughter all around him, screaming women flailing their hands in the air and running around naked as if at a party. The skies were overcast in this place; clouds billowed overhead and thunder collaborated with the sounds of the band on stage. '*With cotton candy and battlegrounds red and brown,*' the song continued.

Perhaps it was shock; yes, that had to be it! Stefan could think of no other rational reasoning for any of this. It was the shock of exiting the Nightworld, surely. He must have hit his head on the ground when he fell back into his world. So, what did it mean then? Why was he in this place, in the middle of nowhere? There were no buildings, no asphalt, and no traffic. There was no sign of Spook Valley whatsoever. There was only celebration, a concert of humanity. No danger existed in this place, for everybody was having a good time.

Stefan glanced at the people around him—couples kissed and danced to the music, groups gathered in laughter, and others held up cardboard signs that announced 'peace' and 'love' in the beautiful bright colors produced by magic markers. The men had long hair, the women wore braids, and Stefan even spotted a few children whose laughter matched that of their parents. The skunk odor of marijuana permeated the air. People were getting high, celebrating, and hailing to the black man on stage with the Afro hairstyle. *'But it's all in your mind -- Don't think your time on bad things -- Just float your little mind around…look out.'* This place was like a refuge for hippies. The telltale signs were all around him—the long hair, the nudity, the peace signs, the classic rock blaring from the stage, and, not too mention, all the pot smoking going on.

This didn't feel real. Stefan felt that either he was going crazy or this was a trick of the Nightworld. And, he'd bank that it was the latter, for he had seen too much already to be just going crazy now.

Remembering that he still held onto the scroll he had taken from one of the members of the Order of Perennial Darkness, Stefan unrolled the parchment paper so that he could view the words that were part of the ominous pact. He studied the ink that appeared blood red; the letters appeared as sharp angles, like calligraphy. Just as Stefan had expected, the diction was in another language, probably a language from long ago. If only he had a way to decipher it! Still, Stefan realized, regardless if he could read the information on the scroll or not, he anticipated that his having possession of this part of the pact meant that the Nightworld could not go through with their ill-omened plan.

A shoulder bumped past Stefan and put him off balance. "Excuse me," Stefan said to the man rushing by.

"Watch where you're going, man," the guy responded as he continued walking.

Looking all around his surroundings, Stefan observed the crowds of people gathering around him. He was practically in the middle of the throng now; people brushed against him, laughter and flesh consumed his world. He had to get out of this place, but where the hell was he? How was he supposed to escape when he didn't even know where he was? Still, just to get out of the crowd before it got any crazier, just to seek refuge in an isolated area where he could figure some of this out.

Stefan had stopped a woman who stood by herself and twirled locks of her long brown hair around her finger. She was wearing round, coke-bottle sunglasses (just like John Lennon wore in more of his famous posters). Laine's Music had quite a few posters of the classic rock legend. "Ma'am?" Stefan queried.

The skinny woman didn't look any older than Stefan did. She giggled uncontrollably. "Ma'am?" she countered as she drew the word out in a long pronunciation.

"Where are we?" he asked.

"Where are we?" she mimicked. "Wow," she continued chuckling, "do you have anymore of the stuff *you're* on?" She began spinning in small circles and laughing.

"This is hopeless," Stefan whispered as he passed the woman who was obviously higher than a kite.

He spotted a secluded area upon a small knoll and began approaching it. Once he got there, he sat upon the soft, green grass and immediately felt relaxed. He attempted, once again, to figure out where the door to the Nightworld had led him. Stefan experienced a certain sense of loneliness. Although there were people all around him, they were too taken by the concert and the events around them. Not too mention, a majority of them were either too drunk or stoned to know where they were, let alone explain to him.

The music continued to ring through the atmosphere:

'*...Hang on, my darling, yeah*
Hang on, if you want to go
It puts everything else on the shelf
With just a little bit of Spanish Castle Magic
With just a little bit of daydream here and there...'

Gazing at the crowd and the vast open landscape with which provided them the ultimate of parties, Stefan caught the sight of another man who sat only ten yards away. He rocked back and forth to the beat of the band as he read a book that rested open upon his lap. Stefan stared at the man; something about him was vaguely familiar. The man's hair was blonde, somewhat long but not like some of the other men who raucously yelled and danced with the crowd. Stefan quickly turned away from the young man as he glanced back at Stefan. In Stefan's mind, the face looked exactly the same. It looked just like *him*! But no, it couldn't be!

With nothing else to lose and answers to be gained, Stefan got to his feet and approached the young man who continued reading his book. As he got closer, Stefan slowed his pace. After all, he didn't want the stranger to think he was going to victimize him or anything like that. However, everybody here *did* seem free-spirited and appeared not to care about anything save for the band on stage and the drugs that were being passed around.

Stefan loomed over the young, blonde-haired man, and when he crouched on his knees, Stefan was greeted by a shock that sent shivers down his back. The young man who stared back at him was Aaron Dabney! *But it can't be*, Stefan eagerly rationalized in his sane mind. But it looked just like him; everything was an exact likeness to Aaron—from the hatchet-sharp face, to the bee-sting lips, to those inviting pools of eyes. And, then, the voice.

"Can I help you?" the young man asked.

"Aaron?" Stefan hesitated.

"How do you know my name?"

"Aaron Dabney?"

"Yes. How do you know my name," he asked again with a face gone completely rigid.

"It's me, Aaron. It's Stefan?"

"What are you on?" Aaron asked, a smile forming on his face.

"Aaron," Stefan repeated with frustration, "It's me."

"I'm sorry, man. I don't know you."

What was going on? What had happened upon Stefan's exit from the Nightworld? "You do know me, Aaron. You do."

"Sorry," Aaron said as he began to look toward the stage again.

"You're from Los Angeles. You're a songwriter." This grabbed Aaron's attention.

"Hey, that's pretty good, man. How'd you know?" Suddenly, like a child who has just discovered a new toy, Aaron beamed in enthusiasm. "Hey! Are you one of those mind readers? You know, like, read minds and tell people about their futures?"

"No, Aaron."

Aaron ignored Stefan's denial. "I'm reading a book on that type of stuff. Well, you know, a little about the whole occult world." He held up a large hardcover book that was generically titled, *The Occult.*

Stefan was completely perplexed. None of it made sense. But wait, he reminded himself. Didn't Breckin mention something about discovering Aaron's identity, some secret of some sort? *Breckin.* How that name brought back memories of love and horror. It felt as if he and Breckin happened forever ago. The memory of Breckin and Stefan's frustration with all the confusion swirling around him caused him to cry in defeat.

Aaron spoke up to console him. "What's wrong, man? Hey, why are you upset?"

Stefan made a feeble attempt to refresh Aaron's memory. "Aaron, I met you in a music store. Laine's Music; the place where I work. Don't you remember anything?"

"Back in L.A., you mean?"

"No," Stefan snapped in disappointment. "In Spook Valley."

"Where's that?"

"Spook Valley, Arizona."

"I've never been to Arizona. I think you got the wrong guy, man."

"Aaron, it was only a few weeks ago. Why can't you remember?"

Aaron's face became etched with bewilderment. "Sorry, man."

Stefan gave up. "Fine, then just tell me where we are."

"You don't know where you are?"

"Please."

"We're at the biggest event in the world, man, and you don't know where we are?"

"Humor me," Stefan said in monotone, defeated by the attempt of jarring Aaron's recollection.

"New York, man. Woodstock. See that guy on stage," Aaron pointed at the black entertainer. "That's the great Jimi Hendrix and he's singing my favorite song. *Spanish Castle Magic.*"

Woodstock? Stefan's confusion was on a downward spiral and his journey was only taking him further away from his fight to save his friends. But why hadn't Aaron remembered him? All of a sudden, Stefan knew the truth. Perhaps Aaron didn't know him because he hadn't met Stefan yet. There was only one more question to ask and then Stefan would have an idea of the new horrors he was up against. "Aaron? What year is it?"

Aaron chortled to the skies. "1969."

A lump swelled in Stefan's throat. *Oh my god. I've somehow gone into the past. The doorway to the Nightworld. No,* he corrected his mind, *the doorways. There was more than one!* Stefan immediately knew he had to escape this place. That meant having to return to the Nightworld and going through the doorway that took him back to his own time. So much terror awaited him, this he couldn't deny.

Beyond the sound of the music and beyond the screaming of the crowd, Stefan heard a loud pounding as if somebody was eagerly knocking on a door. Intense and hard hollow thuds sounded as if they were beating in the sky above and all around him. "Aaron?"

Aaron's attention broke from the stage as he gazed over at Stefan. "Yeah."

"Do you hear that?"

"Hear what? The band?"

"No, there's another sound. Like somebody knocking on a door. It's very loud though."

"All I hear is my favorite song being played live." With that, Aaron shot his attention back to Jimi Hendrix on stage.

Stefan lay on his back and wished nothing more than the Earth to swallow him within its grassy embrace. The echoing raps invaded his mind until that was all he heard. Stefan Powell prepared for the worst. Surely, he had lost against the unstoppable forces of the Nightworld.

-5-

The Order of Perennial Darkness congregated before the two marble columns that reached high into the pitch-black heavens of the *Nightworld.* All six were on their knees, awaiting the arrival of *Damia.* Five of the six elders formed a horizontal chain behind their leader, Saint Trace. The fires around them grew large and the orange glow elongated their kneeling shadows against the gigantic body of *Damia* as he appeared. The god-beast roared in disapproval and the grounds beneath the Order of Perennial Darkness knees undulated.

"How could you let him escape?" he scowled in awesome fury at Saint Trace.

"He overpowered me God *Damia.* I didn't expect him to react that way."

"None of usssssss did," Saint Batiste added.

"He has taken one of the scrolls!" *Damia* scorned in thunderous inflection. "I would make your suffering one unforgettable if it weren't for the pact, Saint Trace."

"We tried to capture him," Saint Cassius explained.

"ENOUGH," *Damia* announced. "I want no poor excuse for this ignorance. The pact will be initiated. We will take over the Earth realm. I will conquer that world and nobody is going to bring a halt to my coming kingdom. I want the one called Stefan captured immediately!"

From out of the shadows, Lillian emerged in her demon façade. She gazed up into the glowing eyes of her god, her king that she may one day sit beside as the Nightworld reigned over the Earth realm. "He cannot be captured, God *Damia*. Not now."

"What's this, demon-child?"

"He has escaped to a world already conquered," she explained in disgust. "He didn't cross the threshold into the Earth realm. He has gone into a parallel. We must let the world play itself out and wait for his entrance back into the Nightworld."

The foundation quaked in awesome tremors as *Damia* wailed in almighty tones that deafened all throughout the Nightworld.

"I am part responsible," Lillian explained to her God after the echoes of his anger became distant. "I tried to get hold of him as I was re-entering, but he was already gone into the parallel. I pray for your forgiveness, God *Damia*."

"There is no need to apologize, demon-child. You are not at fault. If we cannot enter the parallel, we will wait for Stefan. I want the Order to guard the doorways immediately."

"Yes, God *Damia*," Saint Trace obeyed as he bowed his head.

"And what of this powerful witch of the Earth realm, the one they call Catrina Taylor? What of her? She has become more powerful since her awakening. Why isn't she dead yet?"

Lillian took control of the conversation, answering for the Order of Perennial Darkness. It almost appeared that Lillian was now the leader beneath the ranks of *Damia*. "One has already been sent, God *Damia*, and he will not fail us. He has kept her in his sights as well as the traitor, Aaron. He plans on taking both their lives and delivering their souls to you, almighty master."

"Excellent. Once the pact is initiated, you will prove a generous asset beside my throne, demon-child."

Lillian writhed in pride, baring her jagged teeth. "I will not fail you, God *Damia*."

"Be certain that you don't!"

God *Damia* trod the rigid landscape of the Nightworld, the ground quaking with each step made by his hooves. The fires of the world breathed like the heartbeat of a human. Near the doorways, the Order of Perennial Darkness took their places and prepared for Stefan's re-entry.

-6-

Catrina and Aaron were both jolted from the couch by the heavy pounding on the door. Catrina's heart practically burst in her chest from the unexpected knock. As for Aaron, he leapt nearly three feet over the arm of the couch and stood back observing the locked door. The two of them stood in silence. They looked to one another for some answer as to who could be standing on the other side of the door. But the hammering away of the door would not cease. It continued, the person on the other side of it eager to get in, producing chaotic and uneven beats that played out an abstract symphony of frenzy and anxiousness.

Although the fleeting seconds felt like minutes, Catrina Taylor's realization of what was happening ignited her mind and her courage. *Stefan, it must be Stefan! He must have escaped and those creatures are probably right behind him!* Without further delay, Catrina advanced toward the door.

That's when Aaron felt it. The vibrating sensations began at the small of his back, crept up his spine, and gnawed at the base of his skull. The awkward feeling consumed him momentarily; it froze his body and the perspective of everything happening around him was put into a cadence of slow motion.

Catrina Taylor stood at the door now. She was oblivious to anything else save for unlocking the door. She turned the deadbolt and through the drumming beat upon the door, the lock produced a click that veritably echoed over all other sounds.

Aaron hollered, "Catrina, don't!"

It had been too late though. Catrina had twisted the lock on the doorknob and the door violently flew open, coming inches from striking her. The young man that barged in was drenched in sweat and began to yell as he flailed his arms in panic. "Stefan! Where's Stefan?"

Catrina stood shocked from the young man's powerful entrance. His hair was jet-black, his features like that of a child. The guy continued yelling for Stefan, directing his request to Catrina who remained speechless. From behind Catrina, a horrible growling sound emerged. She observed the young man become speechless as his body went to stone.

Trembling as she spun on her feet to identify the horrid sound emitting from behind her, Catrina Taylor jerked from the monstrous sight she had recalled witnessing before. Aaron's eyes were glowing ruby, his teeth grew into inhuman fangs, and the area of his forehead pulsed and appeared to shift beneath his flesh. He was in the midst of transforming into his werewolf form and Catrina was flushed with confusion. Although she knew he wouldn't harm her, the sudden fear that enveloped her mind couldn't distinguish whether to feel protected or scared.

"Back away from him, Catrina," Aaron snarled. His inflection was ominous, a mixture of beast and man.

Catrina shot her glance toward the young man who stood stock-still. He gawked at the events unfold before him with a slack jaw and eyes that bulged with apprehension. With utter caution, Catrina began to take small steps backward.

Turning to gaze back at Aaron, Catrina noticed the coarse, dark hair forming on the tops of his hands, replacing the fine, blonde hairs of Aaron's human makeup altogether. He growled once again. It sounded more like the howling of the beast into which he was morphing. "He's here to kill us, Catrina. He's from the Nightworld."

CHAPTER XIX

-1-

The sun shone high overhead, beaming its fiery light upon Spook Valley, and the heat couldn't have been much worse. This was the time of year when the monsoons were the talk of the town, not to mention, the entire metropolitan areas of the Southwest. With the temperatures climbing into the one hundred-degree range, it was difficult for anybody to believe that rain had poured in thunderstorm fashion within the last seventy-two hours. Although, there was still a trace of humidity in the air, a muggy sensation brought with it the sticky sweet smells of the yucca and saguaro plants that laced the encapsulating deserts. It was days like this that the residents of Spook Valley remained tethered to their domestic lifestyles accompanied by oscillating fans and air conditioner thermostats set on seventy-two degrees. On days like this, children refrained from playing in the park near the Town Square and, instead, sought refuge in the comforting and cool waters of backyard swimming pools. Days like this caused irritability to anybody, regardless of his or her rank in the public eye. Nobody was immune to the powers of the sun; instead, people tolerated it. For that was all one could do. To escape would mean to relocate to the North where snow and icicles would have recently melted away. Still, some were trapped in this town. Whether their lives were magnetized to it and they felt homesick from a simple trip to Phoenix, or destiny called to them, or, even, if their life was dictated by a career that would carry them to their grave.

Officer Colburn, one of Spook Valley's "elite" realized that he would never leave this town. He would never make it in the city, especially as a police officer. He had grown up in Spook Valley, remembered Grandma's gingerbread snaps that were always slightly overcooked, and he knew that would be one of many memories that would seal his life in Spook Valley. Officer Colburn was assured that he would remain here all the days of his life. After graduation, he immediately enrolled in the police academy. The training took place in Phoenix for twelve weeks. That was the first time he had experienced the uncanny feeling of homesickness. His stomach was upset every evening, he had trouble sleeping, and he called his mother and father practically every day. He even took up smoking during his weekend leaves from the academy. After graduation, he immediately returned to Spook Valley and became a police officer at the local station.

The one thing Officer Colburn was assured of more than anything was that Spook Valley proved a quiet town compared to Phoenix. The burglaries, rapes, and auto thefts were saved for the city. In Spook Valley, an officer of the law dealt with drunken residents, speeding teenagers, and domestic violence. Officer Colburn's worse trial was when he and Robert Salinger almost got into a brawl when the officer had to escort him out of the Violin Street Tavern for getting so intoxicated that he pissed on Pearl Lubbock's brand-new loafers she'd just purchased. Old Man Salinger tried taking a swing at the officer; however, the policeman hardly felt threatened enough to pull out his mace, let alone his gun. In fact, Officer Colburn never had to pull his piece for any reason save for target practice. Certainly, Spook Valley wasn't home to serial killers or child pornographers.

Officer Colburn's thoughts changed that theory on this very day.

Officer Colburn wiped the sweat forming at the roots of his dishwater blonde hair. Between the heat and the carnage before him, his nerves were on edge. He still couldn't believe that the bloody mess before him was Laine Young, owner of the only music store in Spook Valley. It was true, Officer Colburn had never formally spoken to the owner; however, he had always come to the store to get the latest Kenny G or Celine Dion CD's upon release. He had always thought Laine a hippie, a long-haired nobody like the bullies that picked on him in school. Yet, Laine was somebody. He had run his own business and, not to mention, had picked a prime location for it. But the man known as Laine Young, the hippie who had gotten off his ass and pursued the dream of going into business for himself, lay massacred before the officer.

Who would do something this awful? Officer Colburn's mind was at unease by the gory corpse.

Sarah Rogers, Spook Valley's hippest grandmother, who had skipped bingo to party with her daughter and wore tight jeans as if she was still seventeen, discovered the body when she entered Laine's Music to get her daughter a birthday gift. Though she was upset to find the owner's body mutilated on the floor, she had managed to make a description of a young man who had run out of the store as she pulled up in her Cadillac.

Black hair. No, "jet black hair." Pale skin. Five foot eleven inches. Maybe one hundred and fifty pounds. The description didn't match any of the town's troublemaking ruffians.

This was a true investigation. This was a homicide no doubt. The man had been sliced and diced with a knife, razor, or some other sharp object. The suspect had even removed Laine's genitals. For the first time in his career, Officer Colburn had a killer on his hands.

The business was taped off with yellow crime-scene ribbon and Officer Colburn began looking around the store as he waited for the town coroner. He began checking the logs of the store sales and was making his way toward the employee files that were stored in the bottom drawer of a back office desk. He was determined to make sure that Laine's murder didn't leak to the public. God forbid the residents of Spook Valley learn about the owner's untimely demise. *They would have a field day with this one*, he thought. He had to investigate this murder and have the suspect in custody immediately.

Officer Colburn's instinct informed him that he must start with the employees of Laine's Music. Perhaps they may have some insight to any enemies the owner of the store may have had.

The officer wanted a cigarette but held back from the craving that always revisited him when under stress and pressure. The investigation was under way.

-2-

Lucien stood aghast. His limbs were unable to recoil from the awe-inducing sight before him. Lucien's mind raced with reason, attempting to justify the extraordinary man before him. No, not a man; it wasn't a man at all! Maybe it had once been a man, but now it was a thing. Something inhuman; a creature or, perhaps, some freak born of human deformities. At this point, Lucien felt anything but sane. He had experienced this insanity before, this awesome jolt of the mind that caused him to lose control and become dangerous.

Where was Stefan during all of this? Perhaps Lucien was too late, perhaps Stefan had already left, and Lucien wasn't sure which fate were more undeserving for the man he had grown to adore—that creature at the store that murdered Laine, or the one presently before Lucien; the monstrous abomination directly across from him that was covered head to toe in thick hair and whose eyes emitted a brilliant and bloody red. And the woman, the one the creature referred to as 'Catrina,' what was her role in this chapter of uncertainty?

"Leave the room, Catrina," the half-transformed werewolf demanded.

Catrina Taylor didn't know what to make of the scene becoming. Sure, she and Aaron had spoken all day of the dangers of the Nightworld and the minions that had crossed the threshold. In fact, she and Aaron were targets of that dark place filled with rage. But now, she mentally scolded herself for not being prepared. She didn't imagine that the creatures would come for them so suddenly, and in the midst of the daylight no less. And, then, another thought enveloped her mind and preyed on her fears: what if she was the only human the Nightworld wanted? What if Aaron had lied to her the entire time and this whole scenario was a setup for her demise? Catrina pushed the doubts from her mind; those thoughts were ridiculous. Not too mention, her doubts had placed her in perilous situations before. Still, with everything happening so fast, her thoughts were torn between the creature Aaron was becoming and the young man who stood petrified.

"Leave, Catrina!" Aaron growled.

Catrina made no further move to leave the living room. Strangely, she experienced a tickling sensation that ran between her fingers. A subtle static jumped between the gaps of her digits, and when Catrina glanced down at her hands, she swore she saw arcs of electric blue that danced within the spaces of her fingers. Once that was noticed, Catrina felt assuredness in her limbs and in her feelings. No, she need not leave the room. There was nothing of which to be afraid.

Aaron ignored Catrina's unwillingness to leave and directed his attention toward Lucien. His growl was one long and constant, like that of a threatened panther ready to pounce on its prey. If he were to fully transform into a werewolf, if his human legs were to fold back and place him on all fours, Aaron would be unable to speak the tongue of a human. He fought the transformation with all his will so that he may get answers from the intruder. "Who are you?" Aaron's eyes grew a brighter shade of red to intimidate the stranger.

Lucien was shaken; his trembling body was confused of what to do in the midst of fight or flight. "Please, let me leave." Lucien's voice was reduced to a whimper, like that of a frightened child.

"I asked who you are!" Aaron's voice roared in authority, his eyes beamed fiercer and burned a hole through the young man's emerald irises. Aaron began to walk toward the stranger, his arms outstretched before him with hands that produced rigid, brown claws.

Lucien knees folded beneath him. He brought his hands over his head and morphed his body into a fetal formation.

"Aaron," Catrina piped.

"He's from the Nightworld, Catrina!"

"How do you know?"

"The sensation," Aaron explained. "The feeling that links the creatures of the Nightworld. I feel it so strongly." Aaron focused on the young man again.

"I don't think he is one of them, Aaron." Catrina gave into her instincts, something she had not fully relied on before.

"Trust me, Catrina. I get this feeling only when others are near."

"Then why is he so frightened of you, Aaron?" Catrina gestured to the young man who remained curled in his defensive position.

"It's an act. He's here to harm us."

With an unexplained and newfound bravery, Catrina approached the young man. "I'll be the judge of that, Aaron," she said with assuredness in her voice.

"What are you doing?" Aaron's growl exclaimed in protection for her.

"Stand back, Aaron. If he is from the Nightworld and decides to turn into some hideous beast, I'll jump out of your way and you can finish him off."

"It's not a good idea, Catrina."

"Stand back. I know what I'm doing."

Aaron felt threatened by Catrina's bravery. Or perhaps it was envy; for he had never witnessed a human willingly succumb to another of the Nightworld, save for Stefan. He cautiously retreated with small steps.

Catrina reached her hand out to the young man whose head was covered by his arms. She grabbed one of his wrists and the stranger instantly recoiled. Still, Catrina held onto it, felt the shakiness that consumed the man's body. "I promise, I will not harm you," she said in a soothing voice like that of a mother tending to a hurt child. The young man's eyes glanced out from behind their cover. "What's your name?"

"Lucien," he warily stated with a quaver in his boyish voice.

"My name is Catrina." She pulled at his hand and folded her fingers around his palm. "I will not hurt you, but you have to promise the same, OK? And if you do try to hurt me, I will not give you the chance." Lucien nodded his head. "Stand up, Lucien."

Aaron observed the scene before him, stunned by Catrina's courage. This wasn't the Catrina he once knew, a young woman in fear of his own bloody warnings scrawled throughout her apartment. Instead, Catrina more sure of herself than ever. Something had changed in her from the time she was attacked by Lillian to the time she had recovered from her coma. Still, Aaron remained poised for the attack, should this man named Lucien attempt to victimize her. *Lucien.* Aaron tried to place the name among many others that he'd encountered while a prisoner of the Nightworld. Although he was unsuccessful, he couldn't deny the sensation that existed within him, even now.

Lucien stood before Catrina. He was a bit taller than she was, but that didn't prevent her from gazing into his emerald eyes. The young man's locks of black hair appeared beautifully soft and gave off a healthy sheen; his porcelain face was unmarred and delicate to her touch. Catrina grabbed at either side of his face and placed her hands flat against his temples. She noticed Lucien's eyes darting beside her toward Aaron. "Don't be afraid, Lucien," she spoke.

God and Goddess, Catrina mentally prayed; *give me the strength of insight.* However, Catrina was confident that she needed not pray to gather this ability. After all, her hands tingled with a power that volunteered itself all its own.

Aaron continued watching Catrina work on Lucien. Reluctantly, Aaron's body began to transform back into its human state. He couldn't figure out why his supernatural consciousness gave way to his fleshly form in the wake of harm.

The images instantly came to Catrina in quick, camera-action succession. *Blood. Crimson gore upon the walls of a room. Rivulets dripping in slow motion upon solid plaster. Blood. Upon a blank television screen. A puddle of gory art, from that of a madman, upon the sheets of an unmade bed. Blood. Flesh strewn across the bed; a lump of carnage hiding beneath the white sheet. Blood and the stench of rotted meat, an acrid odor aged and metallic. Blood and screams, awful shrieks into the midnight hours of twilight.* Catrina's hands briskly retracted from Lucien, causing him to jolt from her reaction.

"What is it?" Aaron's human voice panicked.

Lucien's eyes bulged in wonder at Aaron's human form.

"He's not here to hurt us. At least, I don't think he is."

Aaron's eyes darted back to Lucien, then to Catrina again. She appeared upset by something. "Well, then why the hell is he here?"

"I came to find Stefan," Lucien volunteered. "I have to warn him."

Catrina walked to Aaron's side and both of their eyes fixed upon the young man named Lucien.

"How do you know Stefan?" Aaron asked.

"Warn him about what?" Catrina dug for answers.

"Laine's dead. Our boss. There's a woman…uhhh…she's not a woman though. She's a…."

"Lillian," Catrina announced.

Aaron nodded his head to confirm her fears.

"You know her!" Lucien sounded repulsed by their knowledge of the creature he had seen.

"Where did you come from?" Aaron began his interrogation. "How did you get to Spook Valley?"

"You don't understand," Lucien flailed his arms in frustration. "We have to find Stefan!"

"Don't worry," Catrina attempted to alleviate Lucien's fears. "Stefan is safe for now." As much as she didn't want to believe that, she knew it to be true. The logic that came out in her conversation with Aaron, before Lucien had broken their discussion, proved that the Nightworld could not perform the pact without Stefan being on this side of the doorway. "Sit down and tell us all you know."

Lucien experienced a sense of comfort from Catrina. She was a gentle woman who was in control of situations at hand. He crossed over to the recliner and sat on its edge.

Catrina's thoughts of Lucien weren't quite the same. As he began telling her and Aaron of his coming to Spook Valley, Catrina couldn't shake the awful images she had sensed when she had come into contact with Lucien's mind. There was something strangely frightening about the young man that didn't show in Lucien's physical stature. There was a rage within him that could kill and mutilate.

-3-

Outside the perimeter of Stefan's apartment, the man continued to linger in the shadows, hidden by the landscape of the Shadowood Apartment complex. He had observed the young man who ran up the stairs to the apartment and made his way in. At first, the man thought the other to be one of his own kind. For the young man's features were like that of the undead. However, the fact that such undead could roam the Earth during the daylight hours was rare and he immediately dismissed the idea.

The message had clearly come to the man as he observed his surroundings. God *Damia*'s voice was like that of his inner mind come to life. What God *Damia* wished, the minions of the Nightworld were expected to carry out. Unlike Aaron Dabney, who had escaped the Nightworld and had betrayed the race of creatures. The man's soul starved to witness Aaron crumble before him.

God *Damia* made his instructions clear: another was on the brink of joining those who were against the pact's initiation. The good side was growing stronger and now was the time to diminish it. Of course, the man was also warned of the consequences should he fail. The man understood. It was finally time to end this whole charade, time to pull the masque and reveal his true nature.

The late afternoon was leading way to the orange and purple tinges of evening. The man ejected from his hiding place and approached the stairwell that led to Stefan's apartment. He began to ascend the stairs.

The battle was about to begin.

-4-

Aaron had passed out. Stefan had no clue as to why the man sitting beside him had suddenly gone unconscious. At first, they were discussing Stefan's credibility that he had known Aaron in another year, the *present* year. Aaron mocked Stefan at first and then began to reference his book of the occult. Soon after, Aaron fell back and Stefan loomed over him in an attempt to awaken him.

The throng of people continued their bellows all around them. Rains poured from the skies and made puddles of mud all upon the landscape beyond the stage. The hippie audience was peeling off their clothes to expose their naked bodies; they danced and slid in the mud as if put under a trance by the band on stage. Nobody seemed to question Aaron's passing out on the nearby knoll upon which they sat. They probably attributed it to drugs anyway.

"Aaron. Aaron," Stefan continued to call, shaking Aaron's chin. Stefan's hair was drenched and drops of water slid off his locks and fell all about Aaron's face. "Aaron." Soon, Aaron's eyes fluttered open, eyes that Stefan remembered being fierce with passion on a night not too long ago. The night after Breckin's death and before Stefan's entrance into the doorway of the Nightworld.

"What was that?" Stefan asked. "What just happened?"

"I don't know, man." Aaron sat up. "Sometimes I have these…blackouts, I guess."

Blackouts? "When do they happen?" Stefan anticipated finding a way back to Spook Valley. He realized that he was here for a reason and that reason being to discover the "true identity," as Breckin's ghost had stated, of Aaron. Perhaps once he had discovered that, he would be able to return to his own time. His instant recollection of Catrina almost brought tears to his eyes. He had to return to her. He had to crack this puzzle and stop all of this chaos.

"I don't know," Aaron feebly explained. "I usually get a headache right before it happens. Sometimes they last for a few minutes, sometimes longer. I think the longest one I've ever had was for fifteen minutes."

Stefan continued to nod his head as if understanding, though he truly felt lost.

"That's why I bought this book." Aaron gestured to his occult book that remained hidden beneath the cover of his shirt. "There are a lot of interesting things in this book, man."

A thought occurred within Stefan's mind that grasped for answers. Breckin had told him long ago that the Nightworld fed off "believers," people who believed in such creatures. With Stefan, the doorway had opened during his dedicated time of writing his dark anthology of poetry. Stefan's beliefs gave the doorway power to emerge. *That is when all of this began.* What if the same thing happened to Aaron? What if Aaron had opened a similar doorway in this time from his avid inquiries into the world of the occult? After all, Aaron existed in Stefan's own time, and appeared the same age as he did now. Furthermore, Stefan had crossed the threshold and had spanned some forty years without his own physical body being affected by age. The Nightworld was timeless, a bridge that appeared to gap over time and space. That would be the only explanation of Aaron's existence in Stefan's present. This meant that the Nightworld had also abducted Aaron! Stefan panicked with fear at this thought: was Aaron sent to Spook Valley to kill him? Was he a creature of the Nightworld? The enigma began to piece together like a jigsaw puzzle of which a completed picture would reveal a world of chaos and mayhem.

"Did you know that blackouts have been linked to documented cases of demonic possession and lycanthropes?"

"What?" Stefan snapped out of his mental deductions.

"Lycanthropes. You know...werewolves."

Stefan's stomach was panged by dread and unease. "We have to get out of here."

"You want to leave the most celebrated festival of love and peace?" Aaron's voice was filled with astonishment.

"I have to talk to you, Aaron. We need some time to discuss some things that have to do with that book." Stefan knew this would grab the man's attention.

"There's a motel not too far from here. They'll probably have a room since everybody's out here for the last day of the Festival."

"Good, let's go then." Stefan stood up and extended his hand to Aaron.

"You're a real strange guy, you know that?" Aaron said this, smiling.

Stefan couldn't dismiss that smile. It was a smile all too familiar to the one he had seen only days previous in a time decades in the future. "Well, things are going to get a lot stranger."

-5-

They had no choice but to tell Lucien everything—the doorway, the pact, and Stefan's abduction into the Nightworld. With each moment that passed, a new chapter in an unending tome of horror was created. This horror not only affected Catrina and Aaron, but now a new person had been initiated into the secrets of the Nightworld.

Lucien remained speechless. He continued to peer around the apartment in attempt to find a camera and waited for a group of producers to emerge and tell him that he had been the subject of a televised stunt. However, no such thing occurred. The end result was that he was, once again, in the center of a world of fear and chaos. The main reason he had left Tucson in the first place, that balmy June evening, was to escape a similar situation that continuously haunted his being. Now, some hundreds of miles away from his home city, Lucien was faced with murder once again. This time, however, it was charged with supernatural qualities.

Aaron sat back the entire conversation, adding in occasional details of the Nightworld that Catrina had left out. He gauged Lucien's reaction to Catrina's telling of their trials. The sensation of another from the Nightworld remained picking at Aaron's mind the entire time. Even if Aaron dismissed that sensation, that definite feeling that was undeniable, he still had his reservations about Lucien. There was something not right about his coming to Spook Valley the same time as all that had occurred.

"I don't want any part of this," Lucien said.

"It's too late," Catrina explained. "You know about the Nightworld and they will assume you a target."

"I didn't want to know!"

"You can chalk it up to being at the wrong place at the wrong time then," Aaron retorted. "Regardless, the choice is yours. You can walk out that door right now. Just remember to watch your back. You've seen what those creatures can do to people. You can hope that you make it out of town before they get you."

"Well then what am I supposed to do?" Lucien glared back at Aaron and then to Catrina for guidance.

"You can stay with us. You can help us. I don't think you realize what is at hand here, Lucien. The entire world. I know that's hard to believe, but it's true. When Stefan first told me, I was in utter disbelief. And I'm an open-minded person," Catrina smirked. "I learned the truth quick enough when that demon bitch Lillian attacked me."

"So now what do we do?" Lucien's question voiced to Catrina and Aaron that he had now been inducted into their quest to keep the pact from being initiated.

"We have to stop Lillian," Catrina answered. "She's getting more deadly by the night. If we can get her out of the way, that will help us in our fight."

"And how do we stop a woman who can turn into a demon and tear a person up the way she did Laine?" Lucien's realization of the impossible held the conversation in thrall.

Catrina turned her attention to Aaron for the answer.

"We dismember her."

"What?!?" Lucien asked as if he hadn't heard Aaron right the first time.

"We dismember her," Aaron repeated again. "The Nightworld preys on those who believe in such creatures. Therefore, the creatures of the Nightworld have to play by the rules of Man and his legends of destroying such creatures. The only way to destroy a demon is by dismemberment. You decapitate the creature and cut off its limbs. That's the only way."

"And who's supposed to do that?" Lucien couldn't believe the fantastical things he had heard thus far. Did they all share the same nightmare?

"You don't even have to ask *that* question," Catrina voiced. Catrina stood from the couch and crossed to the kitchen where she turned on the light. She did so because the room was slowly diminishing into darkness from the lack of light emitting from the setting sun. "I'm going to check my messages at home."

Catrina dialed her home number, waited for her machine to turn on, and punched in the access code to hear her messages. Once again, her mother had left another message for Catrina to return her call. "Damn."

"What's wrong?" Aaron asked, concerned with Catrina's despair.

"I have to call my mom before she decides to show up in Spook Valley. That's the last thing I need."

"That's fine; I'll make us something to drink while you do that. Lucien, would you like to help me out in the kitchen?" Aaron was hoping he could get more information from Lucien to expose the young man. Aaron still didn't feel comfortable around him.

"Sure," Lucien said as he rose from the recliner. "I'm dying of thirst."

The two men passed by Catrina as she began punching the buttons on the phone to connect her to her mother's house. She hung up. This time, she dialed a one before the number, forgetting to do so the first time.

The knob of the living room door slowly turned.

Catrina got a busy signal. She mildly laughed at the fact that her mother was so old-fashioned in her ways that she didn't believe in having call waiting. Once again, she pushed down the receiver, waited for a dial tone and, this time, tapped the phone number to her mother's house in slow fashion.

"Put down the phone, Catrina."

At first, she was startled by the voice. Aaron and Lucien were in the kitchen that connected with the living room from where the voice emerged. Then, she felt somewhat at ease by the familiar voice. It was Zander. Then, another startling feeling filled her being. How did Zander know where she was? "Zander," she said. "What are you doing here?"

"I said, put the phone down, Catrina." His inflection consisted of a seriousness she had never heard him speak before.

"What's wrong, Zan—"

He cut her off with his actions. From within his jacket, Zander pulled out a revolver. He pointed it directly at his sister and cocked the hammer. The click echoed in dread through Catrina's head. "Hang up the phone."

She did as she was told, slowly returning the receiver back to the cradle. Bewilderment flooded her eyes with tears. "No, Zander," she wept. "No, please don't."

At first, Aaron had thought Catrina was talking on the phone, but when he emerged from the kitchen with a tray of glasses, he knew otherwise. The tray dropped from his hands; the glasses shattered to the floor below. Without warning, Aaron's eyes were accentuated by an intense glow of ruby color. Aaron experienced the pain of his vertebrae as it began to constrict and contort into a painful arc. Coarse, dark hairs shot from his follicles and his breathing became erratic. "Lysander," he exclaimed, and he couldn't believe he didn't piece it together any sooner. *My brother Zander*, Catrina had told him back at the hospital.

"From out of the depths of the Nightworld, we meet once again Aaron," Zander had announced.

"Oh my god!" Catrina was enveloped by staggering revelation before her. "No! It can't be! You can't be…"

"Yes, Catrina," Zander admitted. "I'm one of the creatures you are attempting to defeat."

Aaron face became waxen and flushed as his eyes were gulped by his facial reconstruction. His nose and mouth began to flatten and then stretched outward in an improbable shape-shifting metamorphosis.

"No, Zander," Catrina objected. Her love for her brother betrayed the obvious that stood before her. "You're my brother."

Lucien froze out of sight of Zander. He observed Aaron's transformation for the second time today. However, unlike earlier, Aaron was morphing into a full wolf. Lucien had nowhere to run; the enclosing walls of the kitchen trapped him. His only escape would be to pass the werewolf before him and run into the room where more danger was on the brink of forming. Lucien's heart raced in apprehension of all that was occurring. He pushed his body hard against the Formica counter, as far as he could from the monster in front of him. His mind sped in mystification and frustration; his bordering lack of control gave way to insane answers.

Zander was unfazed by the process of Aaron's transformation. He was aware, having seen such creatures in the Nightworld before, that the process of metamorphosis in such beasts could take minutes. Then he would destroy Aaron. Until then, he would entertain Catrina with the truth he knew would twist a knife into her heart. "The part of me that was your brother died long ago Catrina. It was almost a decade ago, shortly after I left you in your bed with your precious curls, that I was abducted by that with which you now wish to stop."

"Please, Zander," Catrina implored as the tears flushed her face. "You can help us to stop all of this. You can get away from that awful place."

The timbre of Zander's guffaws echoed throughout the apartment. "Away from that place? Do you know where I was before that *place*?" A drop of a tear form in his eye. "I stayed in a mausoleum, a crypt in the middle of a cemetery. A cold cemetery in New York in the middle of winter! I ate a rat to try to survive, Catrina. A fucking rat!" Zander regained a composure that eclipsed the last of his self-pity. "No. That *place* is my home and, soon enough, we will make the Earth realm a part of that same home. You can't stop us with your witchery, Catrina, and neither will the one who betrayed us." Zander gestured to Aaron whose legs folded at the knees and caused him to fall onto his hands. "You should have died already, Catrina. And I have been sent to make sure that it does happen this time."

Catrina took in two stuttering breaths.

"Oh, don't worry, Catrina. I wouldn't dare shoot you with this. I have saved this special bullet for Aaron. You're death, I assure you, will be much slower and painful. Damn you for trying to stop us!" Zander changed his direction to Aaron. The wolf's claws ejected from where Aaron's fingers once were. "But first, Catrina, I have one more surprise for you."

Catrina jolted from the scene of trepidation that practically brought her heart to a complete stop. Her eyes bulged in disbelief as Zander began his own transformation. The hair on his head was sucked into his scalp, revealing a leathery baldness that appeared monstrous. His chest bulged and ripped out of his shirt and jacket. Zander's legs did the same thing, tearing his pants as they freely fell to the carpet. The fingernails that once looked human grew black and jutted outward. Catrina cringed as she imagined their razor-sharpness tearing at her flesh. The monster forming in front of her was horrifying and reminded her of the dream she recently had. However, this was no nightmare. This was reality twisted into a nightmare fantastic!

The face that once contained the angelic features of her brother shriveled up into a wrinkled deformity. Its eyes were filmed over with white and sunk deep into its sockets; its chin grew long and pointed; and its teeth…oh god the teeth!…protruded in every direction, uneven and jagged. It was then that Catrina realized the significance of her recent dream. It was indeed a vision and not a nightmare. The creature before her was a ghoul. Zander was a ghoul!

It spoke. Its voice was hoarse and animalistic. "I'm going to enjoy eating your body, Catrina."

Catrina sunk back as far as she could against the wall.

A howling impregnated the night.

Zander looked to Aaron, who was now fully transformed into a creature of the moon. "And, now," the ghoul spoke, "it is time to meet your destiny, werewolf."

The gun had remained in Zander's hand during his entire transformation. His monstrous finger brought pressure to the trigger.

The silver bullet didn't get a chance to escape its casing.

The werewolf let out a fierce roar as it pounced through the air and landed before the ghoul. The ferocity of the werewolf gripped the ghoul's wrist with a mouth full of anxious teeth. Aaron's bestial alter ego locked onto the ghouls arm and powerfully wrestled at the limb within its tight hold. The revolver fell from the ghoul's grasp and glided onto the floor, spinning into the corner where two walls met.

The ghoul counterattacked as he brought his own mouth full of jagged teeth onto the werewolf's hide. Its teeth sunk deep into the flesh of the werewolf and an instant yelp discharged from the beast that was Aaron.

"NO!" Catrina screamed. She glanced over to the kitchen where she found Lucien peering around the corner of the wall at the monstrous battle. The two were so consumed by the horrific tussle that they were unable to make any movement.

The ghoul and the werewolf struggled to the floor, an ultimate battle of good versus evil. The creatures' claws dug into each other, creating bloodshed about the apartment. They bit at each other with avid mouths and synonymous convictions in attempt to prove each the stronger of the two. The horrid growls and yelps of the creatures played on as a symphony of terror, a concert enrapturing the frightened mind in an unending landscape of dread and fantasy. As the werewolf tore into the leg of the ghoul, the ghoul took both of its arms and viciously grabbed the fur and flesh of the werewolf's body. The ghoul stood to its feet, the werewolf in both of its hands, and it heaved the body of the canine species far across the room.

Aaron's werewolf body hit close to where Catrina stood. She caught her breath from the near miss of the creature hitting her body. Looking back to the ghoul, an inhuman form that was part of her bloodline, Catrina examined the creature's movement toward the gun that had been ripped from its hand. She peered back to the werewolf that was coming about its senses and decided that Aaron wouldn't have enough time to get to Zander before he had the gun in tow.

Lucien had lost his sanity completely. His entire being became warped with rage and uncertainty. He bolted toward a series of drawers near the sink and eagerly opened each one with a strength that caused them to fall to the floor. Silverware clashed with the linoleum, producing a clanging beyond the horrific growls and screaming from the other room. As he pulled open an opposing drawer, a dozen sharp knives collided with the floor. Among them, a large butcher knife gleamed in the light and brought back the memory that would be relived on this night.

Catrina cried out in an unmatched screech as she lunged across the couch and at the ghoul. One of the lamps was brushed by her foot and crashed to the floor. The light bulb gave a quick flash as the filament gave way to the force of its fall and left the room dimmer than it had been. She landed near the foot of the ghoul; it's back turned away from her as it fumbled for the revolver. Catrina pulled herself up by grabbing onto the ghoul's waist and used all her strength to wrap her arms around the creature's neck. Distracted by the sudden nuisance, the ghoul spun around and threw Catrina off its back. Catrina's jaw went slack and her eyes grew wide before it landed a backhand upon her face. The force of the strike sent Catrina flying through the air and crashing her weight into a wall.

The ghoul knelt back to the ground and picked up the gun.

The werewolf had its target locked and prepared to pounce forth.

Lucien ejected from the kitchen with the handle of a butcher knife gripped tightly in his hand. His heart and stomach were as one; a familiar rush of adrenaline devoured his body and took over his actions.

Catrina shook off her collision with the wall and watched the finale of the battle at hand. It happened so fast, that the entire scene appeared to be going back in time in slow motion.

The werewolf charged the ghoul as it leapt into the air. The werewolf's mouth was stained in red and salivating in hunger for its prey. The ghoul gave pressure to the trigger of the revolver, and, as it did so, as the bullet launched from the gun and the hollow thud echoed into the night, Lucien appeared behind the ghoul and pummeled the butcher knife into the monster's back.

Catrina's undivided attention went to the battle of Zander, the ghoul, and Lucien. The ghoul shrieked and attempted to turn around and face his assailant. However, Lucien held tight onto the handle of the knife and used all his might to pull the blade downward, making a center split that divided the creature's backside in half. Lucien toppled onto the ghoul as it fell to the ground. He extracted the knife and rolled over onto the top of the monster that lay on its back and screeched in agony. Lucien brought the knife high into the air and pummeled it down into the chest of the ghoul. He pulled it out and repeated the action. Over and over and over again, the knife dug into the monster's flesh as if chipping away at a block of ice. Harder and faster and with more aggression, Lucien continued digging the gory-stained blade into the flesh of the beast beneath him. Lucien began screaming over the ghoul's ungodly cries that were high-pitched with trauma and pain. "Damn you! Damn you!" Lucien reproached. All of Lucien's energy was being used up with every drive of the knife. Blood spewed about Lucien's face and neck, and his arms were covered in crimson. Finally, after knifing the creature over forty times, Lucien retreated and fell to the floor beside the ghoul. Lucien gasped for breath and he made no movement as the ghoul, known to Catrina as her brother Zander, disintegrated into dust. As it dematerialized, the creature's last wail waned into silence.

Lucien brought his arms to his face. *Blood. Oh my God! Look what you've done! You bastard! Blood!* The memory sent Lucien into a traumatized shock. Catrina got to her feet and winced from the pain in her back where she had met with the wall. Beside Lucien was nothing but ash. There was no ghoul anymore. There was no Zander. The only sibling she had known to love had been beaten and destroyed.

"Aaron," she called in an exasperated breath. She walked over to where the werewolf had lunged. But there was no werewolf at all. Instead, there was Aaron in his human form, lying on the ground and losing blood from a wound made by a silver bullet.

"Noooooooooo," Catrina screamed.

The apartment wept bloody tears of its own from the first true battle brought on by the Nightworld.

CHAPTER XX

-1-

Twilight consumed Spook Valley. The blue-black skies produced a plethora of stars, moons, and all the planets of the universe that were seen by the naked eye as nothing more than a series of shimmering pinpricks upon a vast canvas of shadow and virgin texture. Streetlights illuminated the asphalt that weaved in and out of the small Arizona town. The playful squeals of children were absent from neighborhoods, as they prepared for home cooked meals at dining room tables. From beyond the silence of a town approaching slumber and all its magnificent design, an eastbound wind howled through the branches of trees in full bloom.

On this particular night, the animals refrained from speaking their cryptic language. The sparrows ceased to chirp, the pigeons kept from cawing, and the powerful howls of wild coyotes had not made themselves present. Near the Town Square, upon a gazebo that housed the bronze statue of Jamison Spook, a murder of crows congregated. The sheen of their black feathers brushed against each other as their movement came to pause. Their muted cacophony was an eerie story of horrible things to come.

Catrina Taylor gulped for a deep breath, her mouth dry as the desert from the quick, short gasps that rushed over her lips. Panic infiltrated her body, her breathing beyond erratic from the battle that had just taken place between two creatures of the Nightworld. An alien sound emitted from her throat, a mixture of sobs and screams that produced an inhuman whine. "No," she wept. "No, Aaron, please." She studied Aaron's unmoving body and the blood on the wall above him that marked where he had been hit by the silver bullet. Aaron's eyes were closed, his lips pursed; a peaceful look adorned his face. *But he can't be dead*, Catrina denied the scene.

"Lucien," she hollered over to the young man who lay upon the other side of the living room, next to the ashes of the creature they had defeated. "Lucien!" Catrina ran over to Lucien's body and loomed over him.

Lucien stared at the blood on his hands in awe. He was conscious and his eyes were wide open. However, he paid no attention to Catrina; he appeared to be in shock of his attack on the ghoul, Zander. *Blood! Look what you've done, you Bastard!* Crimson stains upon his hands, *the blood of that whom you have murdered.* The revisiting memory blended into his current reality. *Have to leave,* his mind raced in fear. *Have to leave this town and don't look back. They're going to find me!*

"Lucien," Catrina cried his name in frustration. "You have to help me."

Leave this place. Leave before they come and take you away. Don't let Father know. Don't let Father see. No. Just kill yourself. Take the knife to your own wrists. More blood. Blood, and you're going to Hell! I can't go; I am in Hell. This is my Hell and I can never leave it behind. I can't hide from it. Everybody is a monster here!

"Ca—tri—na ," a weakened voice sputtered from behind where she stood to get Lucien's attention.

"Aaron!" She rushed to his aid, leaving Lucien in his own world of trauma and shock.

Aaron pushed his back up against the wall, wincing with the slight movement of his body.

"Aaron." Catrina's inflection was delighted in the aftermath of battle that had occurred. She reached down for his shoulder and Aaron instantly recoiled, hitting the back of his head against the wall.

"Where…is—" the man before her took in another uneven breath. "Where is…he?"

"He's dead, Aaron. Lucien stopped him. Are *you* all right?"

"The bullet got my shoulder," he said as he glanced down to the pool of blood that jutted from the wound.

Catrina's eyebrows twisted in confusion.

"Silver in the heart," Aaron said. "Have to get a werewolf in the heart to stop him. Don't worry, this will heal," he assured her.

Catrina produced a half-smile and, with the knowledge that Aaron was safe from the attack on his inhuman body, she threw her attention toward Lucien.

As she hovered over Lucien, once again, she reported the news. "Aaron's going to be all right, Lucien."

Lucien's mind couldn't comprehend Catrina's words. It was flooded by its own horrendous images and babble of insanity. He held his hands in front of his face, examining the thin rivulets of blood that trickled over his palms and down the length of his pallid arms. His vision caught a glimpse of Catrina's visage; it mimicked the features of a porcelain doll, and her hair flowed about her shoulders. It was as if an angel hovered above him or was floating high above a mountainous range. Lucien's attention made out another hand among his two that were stained red. It was Catrina's; she extended her arm out to him. Lucien's instinct and a sense of flying to safety propelled him to grasp the inviting hand. He could feel her warmth as she pulled him from off the ground.

-2-

Aaron's body flew into the air of the motel room and made a hard landing onto the ground.

"Aaron," Stefan yelled at the sight of the strange occurrence. His being briskly grasped for an explanation to justify what had just happened.

They had checked into the motel on the outskirts of Woodstock as planned. Not five minutes after they escaped the drowning rains outside and entered the room, Aaron was ejected off the ground by an unseen force and thrown across the length of the room.

"Aaron," Stefan bellowed as he ran to his aid.

"Holy shit, man," Aaron managed to say in a weakening voice.

"What just happened?"

"I don't know," Aaron announced as he gripped his shoulder. "It was like, I was walking toward the window and something hit my shoulder hard."

"You flew across the room," Stefan exclaimed in disbelief.

"My shoulder is killing me, man."

"Let me check it out." Although Stefan didn't have any experience in medical assistance, his gesture was comforting nonetheless. He assisted Aaron to slip out of his shirt. Stefan couldn't help but notice the robust form of Aaron's smooth chest that he'd recalled from the night in his own time that they had almost made love. Breaking his mind from the lusting thought, Stefan observed Aaron's shoulder. He applied pressure to the shoulder at which Aaron had flinched as if in pain. "Can you move it?"

Aaron gave a faint shrug to the shoulder. "Yeah, but it hurts like hell, man."

"I don't think it's broken." Stefan made a closer study of the front and back of Aaron's shoulder. "There's a small bruise here though."

"Damn, that was weird."

"You're right," Stefan agreed, "it was."

"And now I'm feeling so drained."

"Why don't you take a rest on the bed?"

Aaron got to his feet and began walking to the bed that was centralized in the room. "What about you?" he asked as he lay down.

"Can I look through that occult book of yours?"

Aaron nodded.

"I'm going to read over some things." *There have to be some answers in that book*, Stefan convinced himself.

-3-

Officer Colburn had remained at Laine's Music the duration of the afternoon and through the setting of evening. The crime scene had bothered him the entire day; the investigation not warranting any leads whatsoever. There had been no money stolen from the register or the safe. In fact, nothing appeared to have been tampered with. Even the compact discs appeared to be in order on the shelves. Nothing in the store had been broken and nothing, to the officer's naked eye, had been taken. He only had a dead corpse, that of Laine Young. This frustrated Officer Colburn; it picked at his deductive reasoning until he began forming impossible motives. After clearing his mind several times, Officer Colburn decided that the motive was as simple and concise as a hate crime. The only reason a man laid slain on the floor of his own business was because somebody wanted him dead. Somebody had hated the man so much that they'd decided to take him out in his own workplace. That was it, plain and simple. Upon the officer's further investigations, he was unable to produce a murder weapon or any abnormal fingerprints that weren't already throughout the rest of the store and made by the employees of Laine's Music.

Sitting in the dim lights of the Spook Valley Police Station, Officer Colburn lit the end of his second cigarette of the evening. The mouthful of smoke didn't affect his throat as the first cigarette had; it wasn't as harsh. And, unlike his first cigarette he'd smoked earlier, this one didn't make him feel as light-headed. Taking in the carcinogens of the cigarette, Officer Colburn felt a sort of psychological ease, the kind that only a smoker can know—the deceptive mentality of each drag relaxing the body, the calmness of exhaling a smoky stream, and the security of the cigarette clenched between two fingers. Officer Colburn didn't realize how easy it had been to turn back to cigarette smoking after years of being free of the drug. Yet, with his frustrations mounting in the murder case before him, his battle was lost. He had purchased a pack of Camel filters before arriving at the station.

The station was empty of all other police officers. Officer Colburn scanned the folders and papers that flooded his desk. He had discovered the employee files in the bottom drawer of a back-office desk at Laine's Music. There were only two. One belonged to a Stefan Powell, the other to a man named Lucien Matthews; both their names were scrawled in felt tip pen upon the top of manila folders. The contents of the folders were strange to Officer Colburn's investigative eye. Whereas Stefan's folder contained tax information and an application for employment, Lucien's was empty. Officer Colburn went through all the other paperwork in front of him—store logs of the inventory, quarterly tax information, business licenses. Within the mounds of paperwork, he was unable to locate any information on the employee named Lucien Matthews.

The officer had come to a dead end in his investigation, and he knew there wasn't much more he could do this evening. With that, he made his way out of the station and toward home. He reminded himself that he *did* have a lead though. Stefan Powell. His application for employment had listed his address, and Officer Colburn would make his way there in the morning. Perhaps Stefan would be able to give some information as to where his co-worker resided. Still, there was something bothering Officer Colburn about the man named Lucien, something beyond the strange name. As the officer cruised down the length of a vacant Main Street, he chocked it up to an investigative hunch.

-4-

In the realms of the Nightworld, where darkness and hatred curled and folded into each other in an ultimate design of madness, Lillian entered *Damia*'s chambers. Another minion had never before entered the dark lord's chambers. In fact, the creatures of the Nightworld were reluctant to travel the solitary path that led south to the engorged cavity in which *Damia* resided. The path grew deeper in red tint as it ended at the large compartment, the brightest of fiery lava hissed on either side of the trail; this section of the Nightworld was at, what would be called in the Earth realm, sea level. However, instead of the calm blue and green waves that composed such seas, the Nightworld consisted of blazing, violent lakes.

As Lillian entered *Damia*'s chambers, the furious god immediately faced her. His form was gigantic; the hooves of his feet were practically the size of a human head, his impossible height loomed over her, and he buried his obsidian eyes into her soul. At first reaction, Lillian winced from the angry lord.

"Why is it that I am always failed by my disciples?" *Damia* roared this more as an angry statement than a question.

"God *Damia*," Lillian apologized, "I do not know why Zander failed."

"Aaron continues to live! The witch Catrina lives!" *Damia*'s voice caused the rocky walls surrounding them to tremble.

"I'm sure there is an explanation, God *Damia*. Zander must have been taken off guard."

"Enough of these pathetic excuses!" A sonic wave emitted from the humongous being of God *Damia* and struck Lillian, forcefully throwing her to the foundation. She withstood the punishment and scampered to her feet. "There is no explanation. I have already taken Zander's soul and it is suffering the consequences of eternal damnation as we speak. Need I do the same to what soul you have left, demon child?"

"No, master," Lillian pleaded. "We must send another into the Earth realm. One who thrives on chaos and cannot be beaten by such humans."

A snarl like that of an infuriated panther emitted from God *Damia* as he directed another wave toward Lillian. Just as she had done after the first punishment, she immediately stood to her feet. The minions of the Nightworld knew better than to show defeat or weakness in front of their god. "Another CANNOT be sent! A space must be reserved for the *thirteenth* to cross or the pact cannot be performed. Only those who have already crossed can enter the Earth realm."

"Then I will go, God *Damia*," Lillian immediately volunteered.

"Yes," he agreed as if his mind was made up before Lillian volunteered. "You will go there, demon child. You will destroy that witch and Aaron. And you will NOT fail. The consequences of your failure will far more exceed that of those who have ever crossed my path."

Lillian's naked human form morphed into her succubus shell. Her tail slithered behind her in the molten dirt. "I will not fail you, God *Damia*," she hissed in a forked tongue.

"Are the Order on guard near the portals?"

"Yessss."

"Give them my instructions to continue waiting for Stefan's re-entry. At that time, they need only to ascertain the scroll, and send him back to the Earth realm. Once that is done, we will initiate the pact."

Lillian bowed before her god and left him to his thunderous meditations. As she made her way toward the portals of the Nightworld, her mind burned in fury. She could not fail her lord. A rage bubbled in her like that of the gurgling seas of fire that surrounded the landscape. Lillian had never experienced this much chaos within her monstrous shell. In fact, she felt so enlivened by the evil mounting within her that she felt like a god herself.

-5-

Past the midnight hour, Stefan's apartment was silent. Catrina had laid Aaron and Lucien to rest on the two couches in the living room. They both needed their sleep. Aaron was obviously drained from the battle with Zander. As for Lucien, he had been mentally drained and in shock by his killing of the ghoul. She had sat in the living room, with all the lights extinguished, until she knew they had both drifted to sleep.

Catrina knew Aaron would be able to get through this latest of trauma in their lives. As for Lucien, Catrina wasn't sure how it had affected him. She'd only met him earlier in the day. Lucien, the young man with the pale face of a vampire and the jet-black hair to match. Nonetheless, the images she had seen within the young man's mind left her in mystery. They were visions of the violent coming to pass, or perhaps memories of a monstrous act committed by Lucien. She had no doubt that Lucien was human. Aaron's trademark sensation when encountering another from the Nightworld had obviously been triggered by Zander's stakeout of the apartment. Since Zander's death, Aaron felt this sensation no more. Still, something about Lucien troubled Catrina, and she just couldn't shake the foreboding feeling that she was in the company of danger.

Catrina lay in Stefan's bed, the door to the bedroom shut. It was impossible for her to get to sleep. Especially after seeing Zander get massacred before her eyes. Or, the monster that Zander became. She had been so joyful to see him when she awoke from her coma. His face, that long lost face that use to comically cringe from her childhood 'I love yous' she'd always announced to him. That beautiful man who had abandoned her, that man whom she never thought she would forgive for doing such. But she had forgiven him, hadn't she? She had embraced him with arms that appeared to belong to a mother who had just won custody of her son. She wouldn't let go; she wanted to hold him in that hospital forever. And she would have, if not for the immediate circumstances surrounding Stefan and the Nightworld. Why couldn't she have him? Why couldn't it have been as it appeared? Why couldn't she love him again and hold him; why couldn't they spend nights discussing Mother's strict Christian rules and the childhood games they'd once played?

Catrina sniffled. Her eyes welled in tears as she took in a trembling breath. "I love you, Zander," she cried the whisper into the darkened room. "Why did you have to leave me?" She broke down into full sobs.

"*That thing wasn't your brother, you know.*"

The soothing voice broke the sounds of her crying. At first, Catrina almost jumped from the bed. However, soon enough, she recognized the voice. Upon the wall she faced, Catrina viewed the reflection of an illumination that came from somewhere behind her. As she rolled over to face the sound of the voice, she saw *him* standing there, hovering over the bed. It was Breckin. But

Breckin was dead, Catrina realized, and as she studied the being that stood near her—its translucent flesh that shimmered in the darkness, its wavelike motion as it hovered above the ground—she knew it to be Breckin's ghost.

"Breckin!" A smile ignited her features and tears of happiness quickly replaced the tears that mourned the loss of her brother. She sat up in Stefan's bed and wiped away the downpour upon her face.

"*Catrina,*" he said. "*You know that wasn't your brother, right?*"

"Breckin. I miss you," she stated, as either person didn't acknowledge the other's conversation.

"*I miss you, Catrina. But I have to let you know that the creature posing as your brother was nothing more than a monstrous abomination from the Nightworld.*"

"I'm trying to tell myself that. It's just...it looked just like him Breckin."

"*But it wasn't,*" Breckin's spirit confirmed. "*You have to be stronger than that, Catrina. You are very powerful and you must save your strength for the battle that is coming.*"

"The Nightworld," her voice tapered off.

"*Yes, Catrina.*"

Catrina knew the laws that bound ghosts to the Earth plain. She couldn't help but wonder why Breckin hadn't moved on to the next level of spiritual achievement.

As if he had read her mind, Breckin's spirit answered. "*I am bound here until the things that had wronged me have been righted.*"

"The Nightworld," Catrina voiced again. Unless the Nightworld was destroyed, Breckin would always be bound to this earthen state.

"*You must destroy it,*" Breckin voiced. "*The battle is beginning.*"

"But how?" Catrina asked, bewildered.

There was no answer from his ghost. Breckin's transparent form began fading, his ectoplasmic molecules dissipated and blended into the blackness of night, appearing as pinprick lights.

"Breckin!" He couldn't leave already. "I never had a chance to thank you for saving me," she called out.

Before the outline of Breckin had completely vanished, he had said four words that catapulted her into a state of fright that sent a jolt through her body. "*Catrina,*" the voice had echoed. "*Beware the succubus.*"

The door to the bedroom had creaked open. Startled by Breckin's words and the events taking place, Catrina leapt from the bed.

She glanced at the silhouette that came toward her. It was Lucien. He was walking toward Catrina with the same knife he had used to kill Zander. He extended the blade toward her and came to a halt. The knife pointed to her as if it were her accuser.

-6-

Stefan was right. He extracted a lot of information from the occult book he perused as Aaron slept. The book was inclusive of almost any creature that may have existed in the Nightworld. Vampires, witches, spells for the dead and the undead, secrets of alchemy, symbols like that of pentagrams, ankhs, inverted crosses, and werewolves—it was all contained in that book. The one bit of information Stefan couldn't find in the tome was any mentioning of another world like that such as the Nightworld.

However, there were a few brief passages on something deemed as "parallel time." The book had given into the theory that past, present, and future were all happening at the same instant, that the only difference lay in the *timespace* and setting of each. Essentially, the text of the book went on stating that if one were to cross the threshold of such parallel, he may have an affect on any, if not all, of the time frames in question. Hence, someone that lived in the present, if crossing into the past, could perform some action in the past that would immediately affect the present. The book had even given a name to this: a *timequake*. Still, where was the Nightworld in all of this? The only thing Stefan could muster in his tiring mind was that the Nightworld was timeless. It knew no boundaries of time and space. Though he remained puzzled by this reasoning, he couldn't help but feel he was on the right path.

Stefan went through each page of the book. All the while, he had the scroll from the Nightworld unrolled upon his lap. He attempted to locate any information that may help in deciphering the text on the scroll, any possible alphabet that cracked this cryptographic piece of the pact. His search was to no avail. He had read about old languages used in occult dealings, such as Latin, but there was nothing that came close to resembling the diction on the piece of parchment that he possessed.

Stefan recalled Aaron's earlier mentioning of lycanthropes, evidently the scientific term for werewolves. He studied the books contents on werewolves and read of two "real-life" accounts. Both involved men that claimed to have transformed into wolves. They complained of having "blackouts and headaches" before the metamorphosis began taking place. Aaron had complained of similar symptoms. What if Aaron's dabbling into this book of the occult had opened the doorway to the Nightworld? What if Aaron was a creature from the Nightworld in the present time? Perhaps a werewolf? The answers were striking Stefan left and right; it overloaded his knowledge of everything he'd known. And it would make sense, right? Stefan remembered how Aaron had acted in bestial fashion that night back in his apartment. Was Aaron a werewolf? Is that what Breckin meant when he'd told Stefan about discovering who Aaron truly was? But how would that explain Aaron flying through the motel room the way he'd done earlier? Or the loud pounding Stefan had heard at the concert? Unless…

Stefan closed the book shut. He gazed over to Aaron who was sound asleep upon the bed. Aaron's stomach was flat, concave; his flesh was luminescent and appeared virgin to the touch. *This was the man that had professed his love to me after Breckin's death*, Stefan thought. *This was the same man I fell for when I first saw him in Laine's Music. Those eyes, those beautiful emerald eyes.*

As he rose from the recliner, Stefan set the book and the scroll next to each other on the nearby end table. He made slow steps toward Aaron's motionless and peaceful body. Stefan stood above Aaron. He reached down with his fingers and grazed the smooth flesh on Aaron's chest. He ran his fingers down to Aaron's stomach, along the path of fine golden hairs that disappeared beneath the waistband of his pants.

Aaron's eyes fluttered open and he was speechless. He stared into Stefan's eyes, enjoying the touch of Stefan's hand upon his flesh. Aaron extended his arms toward Stefan, placed his hands behind Stefan's neck, and pulled him down to where their lips met. Their tongues probed into each other's mouth; Stefan's hands were on Aaron's chest as Aaron tugged at the bottom of Stefan's shirt. In turn, as they continued kissing into one drawn out gesture of passion for each other, Stefan unbuttoned Aaron's pants and repeated the action to his own pants.

Soon, the two were nothing more than naked bodies in a time long past. Their bare and silken skin writhed against each other, the velvet textures of their excited organs brushed, and their bodies moved in a sync of subtle undulation. This passion would go on through the night, these kisses of past, present, and of undeniable future.

-7-

Aaron squirmed upon the couch. He could feel the hands on his chest, beneath his shirt. The hands traveled alongside his stomach, teasing the flesh that was so sensitive there, and made their way down to his rigid organ. He felt the hands jerking at his cock, the ecstasy bubbling at the base of his organ and sending a tingling sensation throughout his body. The lips pressed against his, and, as he attempted to kiss them back, they were invisible. Then he felt the mouth of his ghostly lover make a path down his neck, upon his chest, next to his stomach, and then onto his sensitive cock. Oh, the pleasure. "Oh, Stefan," he called out to the vacant living room.

In Stefan's bedroom, Catrina took cautious, backward steps from Lucien. He held the knife outward and Catrina feared the worst. *The young man has snapped*, she mentally assumed. She thought that he would attack at anytime now. All he needed to do would be to rush her with the blade of the knife. As much as this troubled her, she tried speaking calmly. "Lucien. It's all right."

He shook his head no.

"Lucien?"

As he spoke, a tear escaped his eye. "This is like the knife I used to kill my Mother."

CHAPTER XXI

-1-

Catrina Taylor dare not move. Her posture was straight and still to Lucien's advance. She wanted to scream Aaron's name, yet she hesitated. After all, he was only in the next room and, if Lucien attacked her with the knife he wielded, she could easily scream quick enough for Aaron to be there in no time flat.

"Lucien," she gently said, like a mother consoling a child. "Put the knife down, Lucien."

The young man was a mess. His inky hair was tangled, sweat poured all over him and flushed out all color there could have been in a face that pale. His hands shook uncontrollably in involuntary spasms. The tears continued to stream from his eyes. "But you don't understand," he whined.

"Tell me, Lucien. What is it?" Catrina maintained her composure, though she was at wits' end with all that had recently occurred. Between Stefan's capture, her brother Zander's deception, and this new enigma that unraveled before her eyes—Catrina remained strong-willed. *Just like any practicing witch of the Craft,* she internally assured herself. She held out her arms to the young man. Although Lucien pointed the blade of the knife toward her, as he had apparently done with his mother—*this is the knife I used to kill my mother*—Catrina stuck to her first instinct that was one of welcoming the young man into her arms. *Envelop him; bring him into your world of safety. Save this lost soul.* These internal voices were either that of her own subconscious talking to her or the *higher powers* she referred to in part as the *God and Goddess.*

Lucien's eyes squinted in a desperate plea; his lower lip quavered. Catrina wouldn't hurt him, no. Lucien envisioned her as a ravishing angel. Ever since he had begun experiencing the terrors in Spook Valley, she had been there during his times of trauma; times when his mind collapsed and the insanity crept in like a cancer. *Go to her*, he heard a voice that came from somewhere around him. Panicked, Lucien's eyes darted around the room. For a momentary lapse, he swore he saw a man as transparent as a glass of water, a beautiful man he'd remembered when he came to Stefan's apartment that day to retrieve the key to Laine's Music. The first time he'd met Stefan. Had it been Stefan's lover? Where was he now? In a fleeting instant, the outline of the image evaporated into the air.

"Tell me, Lucien," Catrina continued to counsel. "Give me the knife." She made a bold move toward the troubled youth. As she stood only inches away from the tip of the blade, Lucien turned the butcher knife around and placed the hilt into her hand. Catrina reached back and placed the blade on the nightstand behind her.

Lucien fell into Catrina's arms, hysterically sobbing.

"Shhhhhh," she whispered as she enclosed him in her arms and ran her fingers through his matted hair. "Sit down with me here on the bed," she gestured.

The two sat next to each other and Catrina grasped Lucien's trembling hand. Lucien's sniffles broke the silence in the room. "I know," Catrina comforted. "I know; this is all so horrible. But you can tell me anything, Lucien. I'm here for you. We're all in this nightmare together and we have to stay strong."

Lucien's glance met with hers.

"You know," she continued, "this isn't what life is normally like." Catrina realized how young Lucien was. She studied the baby soft contours of flesh around his puffy eyes. "Everything seems like a dream, doesn't it? I kept telling myself that what I was seeing wasn't real, but I cannot deny that anymore. This is real, Lucien. And we are being tested. We're the ones who were chosen to fight this; none of us had a choice. We are simply survivors of our own surroundings. But we can't fight or survive if we're at each other's throats. I will be here for you and you can trust me to do my best to protect you, OK?"

The young man nodded. His insides were filled with an alien comfort he had never experienced. "I killed my mother," he confessed to Catrina. "In Tucson. That's why I came here; to get away from all of that."

Catrina had already known. For Lucien had stated that the weapon he had in hand was what he'd used. It all made perfect sense when Catrina pieced that statement together with the visions she had seen when she'd first met Lucien. *It all makes sense, but why did he do it?*

As if Lucien read her mind, he began telling his account of a young boy who was nothing more than victimized throughout his childhood and adolescence. He explained to Catrina how he'd lived the reverse of a traditional family. Mother was the breadwinner of the house; Father was quiet and reserved. Mother had always said how Lucien was worthless, how he was a "bastard child," and how he would never amount to anything. Father always watched, only voicing a warning if Lucien talked back to her after Mother had repeatedly slapped him. Lucien was a boy who grew up without friends, one whose own life was limited to the blank walls of his bedroom—Mother would never allow him to put up pictures or posters, God forbid there would be holes in the walls made from tacks or small nails. "Friends will only hurt you," Mother would say, "because they know you are a bastard child; they know you are a freak."

Catrina listened in awe, her mouth falling agape to the description Lucien gave of his mother's beatings and unwillingness to let her son be like any other normal teenager. She wanted to ask why his mother was that way; what terrible childhood did the mother have while growing up to inflict such upon her son? However, Catrina knew that Lucien wouldn't have an answer to this. The young man was an innocent victim to the lifestyle of a family full of anger and nothing more. He was a man who could never talk back, never disagree with any of what his mother said, and never able to escape any of the pain by leaving and hanging out with friends. It could only build up to a point. That's exactly what happened—one who allows such things to build up within himself, without having any type of outlet, eventually explodes

Lucien explained, in detail, how Mother had finally forced him over the breaking point. She had had a bad day at work, he explained to Catrina. She took it out on him. Hitting him, while Father had been picking up dinner. She beat him repeatedly, took a swig of her third beer in the past half hour, and then said, "I wish you'd never been born." That did it for him. All that had built up was on overkill. That night, as Father watched television in the living room, Lucien had crept into the kitchen, grabbed the largest butcher knife the family owned, and went to Mother's bedroom. Mother was passed out drunk, sprawled on the bed, clothed only in her lingerie. He gently closed the bedroom door behind him. She would pay for her abuse. The first plummet of the knife went into Mother's throat, so that she wouldn't scream. Her eyes had flickered to life for a brisk moment. The dying yelp that emitted from her mouth was nothing more than a subtle gurgle. The gleam in her eyes had dulled at that point and tears of pain raced from the corner of her ducts. But there was too much rage in Lucien, too much pain from all those years. He had extracted the blade of the knife from Mother's throat and thrust it, once again, into her chest where he knew her heart was black. He repeated the action and pummeled the blade into her stomach from whence he was born. Then again. Each thrust of the knife broke apart all of Mother's flesh, the sounds like that of digging a grave with a shovel. Over and over and over again, just like each of Mother's beatings. Once for the time she'd slapped him across the nose so hard that it had bled for an hour. Once for the time she'd kicked him in the side and he couldn't walk straight for days. Another time, when she'd pulled him by the hair and cracked his skull on the coffee table. Too many times. Lucien would make her pay for each time with another plummet of the knife. He had stabbed her so many times that there was blood all over the walls, all over the lampshade, and the television screen that was four feet away from the bed. The carnage on the bed was unrecognizable as the cruel woman he had known all his life; it was a puddle of gore and strewn flesh, a festival of murder. Blood—all over his hands, his face, and soaking into a crimson pool that was once a mattress. After he had stabbed her countless times, he had pulled a white sheet from the closet and thrown it over the butchery that was once his Mother's living shell. The sheet had instantly soaked in the bloodshed, impossibly hiding the gory lump of the dead corpse. It was at that point that Lucien finally realized what he had actually done. He had to escape now; there was no other way! He had committed a crime, whether it from insanity or countless years of premeditation.

As he was exiting through the bedroom window, Father had walked in. The horrors that awaited Father could make him do nothing more than scream and yell. *"You bastard! How could you do this?"*

Catrina sat shuddering, her body in shock by the retelling of Lucien's once shady past that was unraveled in the course of ten minutes. Of course, she had heard of and seen the horror that grazed her world, thriving on the town known as Spook Valley. Those fantastic horrors, how they were filled with imageries like that of a troubled horror writer! However, in Lucien's case, things were different. There were no supernatural aspects to his story. There was only a pained human avenging himself against the wrong actions of another human. Still, Catrina couldn't distinguish which was more terrifying—the supernatural world that had recently enveloped the lives of her and her friends or Lucien's psychotic actions against his own kin. There was a certain apprehension to the idea, a certain dread that revolved around the thoughts of bloodshed when it came to human nature. Dahmer, Cunanan, Jack the Ripper—but Lucien was no serial killer, right? He reacted, and reacted harshly for that matter. The side of Catrina's mind playing the Devil's advocate couldn't help but voice itself: *What if he tries it again?* She instantly shut out the thought. Instead, she enclosed Lucien in her arms and told him that things would be all right.

"They're going to be after me. I'm sure they're coming for me," Lucien words were shaped with concern.

"Who?"

"My father…I'm sure he contacted the police. I'm sure they'll find me in no time."

"Listen," Catrina rationalized, "you can't hide in fear all your life. We'll worry about that when it happens." She didn't want to come off as sounding selfish, but she couldn't sugarcoat it any other way. There were other things at hand besides Lucien's recent confession. There was the safety of Spook Valley on the line. Hell, the entire world for that matter! Most importantly, there was Stefan, a man Catrina had known for years. She and Aaron had to rescue Stefan and stop the Nightworld. That was the first priority. Unfortunately, Lucien had come to the wrong town in which to find a savior from what he was running from.

"Will you help me?" Lucien was like a confused child that couldn't make up his mind for himself.

"I will do my best," Catrina said. "Right now, we have to focus on Stefan and the Nightworld. We have to stop all of this!"

Aaron burst into the bedroom. "Stefan!"

Catrina jumped to her feet in expectation. "Is he here?" She couldn't help the anticipation of elation propelling her body into joy.

"I felt him," Aaron said.

"What do you mean *felt* him?"

"I could feel him…kissing me."

The look on Aaron's face was exploding with happiness. Catrina thought she saw tears in Aaron's eyes. Too much was going on. There were too many factors in this nightmare, too many things that were so unclear to Catrina Taylor. She prayed for immediate guidance, for something in the form of answers, whether they be logical or irrational. "Gather around," Catrina told Lucien and Aaron as she reached into her bag for her Tarot cards.

The three of them sat on the bed. Lucien was still somewhat upset and Aaron's gaze fixed on Catrina as she shuffled the cards. Her eyes were closed as she fumbled with the cards. She continuously whispered something over her lips that was inaudible to both Aaron and Lucien. The first card was placed face up on the mattress.

The World. The cartoon-like image of the card donned an androgynous woman, a dancer with a scarf covering her sex, who held a wand in either hand. An oval wreath framed her figure. The beasts that represented air, earth, fire, and water were illustrated along each corner of the card. *A card of all humanity, of involution and evolution,* Catrina thought to herself.

The card she placed across the first was that of *The Lovers.* This card represented the obstacles along the way. The picture was that of a man and woman, standing hand and hand, naked, and the God and Goddess, a looming figure above them indistinguishable of gender, looking down upon them. Catrina read back the formation of the cards to herself as the attention of both Lucien and Aaron were fixed upon her reaction. *The World...and that card is crossed by the card of The Lovers.*

Catrina continued turning over each card, meditating on each one as she did so, until the formation she made was that of a *Celtic cross.* In the placement for the card that represented the current that was coming into play was *The Tower. A card of chaos,* Catrina mentally defined. The card that represented fears was *The Devil. Damia,* she quickly recognized. Among some of the other cards in the formation were *The Moon* (which she attributed to being Aaron's card), *Strength* (which she hoped she continued to maintain), and *Death* (could that be their failure in stopping the Nightworld?). The last card she turned up, the card that she knew as the *Destiny card* and of things to come, was the *Ace of Swords.* The picture on the final card sent shivers up from the small of Catrina's back to the base of her skull—it was that of a hand emerging from the clouds, holding a double-edged sword, topped by a crown. *The crown of victory?* She only hoped. *The battle is about to begin.*

"What's it all mean?" It was Aaron who asked this.

For a moment, Lucien's locked gaze on Catrina broke and addressed Aaron.

"It means that we have to prepare ourselves," Catrina answered. She was still looming over the formation of the cards and trying to derive an exact meaning. Catrina stood to her feet. "I want to try one other thing."

"What?" Aaron asked.

"A séance."

Lucien couldn't believe all he was hearing.

-2-

Stefan lay next to Aaron in bed. They were both naked, their bodies exhausted, and their hands interlaced in between the space of their bodies. The sounds of Woodstock grew more silent; the concerts were ending. Rain tap-danced upon the roof of the motel in chaotic fashion.

"Wow, man," Aaron said in an exasperated breath, "I've never done anything like that before. I mean…with another man." Aaron didn't know what came over him. It was as if he had no control over his body whatsoever and he gave way to the guiding force within himself.

Stefan noticed the slight blush in the form of rose-tinted cheeks on Aaron. "You're kidding," Stefan laughed. Laughter. Why couldn't it have all been laughter, all this time?

"I'm serious. I don't know who you are; maybe you're my guardian angel."

Stefan chortled again. "If I'm your guardian angel, you better hope another one gets assigned real quick!" What was happening anyway? What had prompted him to make love to Aaron? Sure, he had felt that once before, back when he and Aaron almost made love in Stefan's apartment. *Back when? Or is that forward when?*

"I was reading through that occult book of yours," Stefan went back to focusing his attention on the issues at hand. "How long have you been into that?"

Aaron stared at the ceiling that looked like cottage cheese with all it spackle and rough texture. "I don't know; for a while now. I got it because I have a real interest in lycanthropes."

"Right," Stefan remembered, "werewolves. When were you born?" Stefan curiously asked.

"October 8, 1941."

Stefan was amazed by the date. It brought him to the realization that this was *truly* the year 1969. It also caused him to conclude that, technically, the Aaron he had been around in Spook Valley was over sixty years old, though he didn't look a day past thirty. "What do you know about parallel time?"

"About what?"

"In that book of yours, it mentions a concept called 'parallel time.'"

"I don't know, man. Like I said, the main reason I got the book was to study the origin and accounts of the lycanthrope."

"Do you think it's possible that two times are happening at the same time?" Stefan shivered from hearing the words emit from his mouth.

Aaron shot Stefan a queer gaze, one obviously filled with befuddlement.

"I mean. Do you think it's possible that this year, 1969, and a year decades into the future are happening at the same time, only on different levels of perception."

"I'm not sure."

"Do you think a person can exist in two times at once?"

"No," Aaron immediately answered.

"Why not?"

"Because, man, if you were in two places at once, it would create a sort of…paradox."

"I'm not following you." Stefan continued his attempts at making sense of this whole madness, this dream within a dream. Surely, there had to be an answer!

"Well," Aaron explained, "let's say that you are here with me and, as you claim, the future. Well, wouldn't your actions here affect what happens to your body in the future? The same applies: if you did something in that time, wouldn't it affect what is happening in the here and now?"

Stefan became frustrated. When the discussion got going, it became more illogical and confusing than what he'd bargained. "But I'm not saying *I'm* in that year and this year at the same time." A minute of silence had passed. "Did you follow me through the doorway?"

"What?"

"The doorway. Did you come after me once I went through it?"

"Is this the same doorway that brought you to my world?" It almost sounded like Aaron was making a mockery of the entire situation.

"It's the doorway into the Nightworld. Once I escaped though, there were three other doorways."

"Now you've completely lost me!" Aaron gave off a puzzled laugh.

Three doorways, Stefan thought.

"Maybe you picked the wrong doorway," Aaron entertained the idea. "Maybe you picked the one into the past."

The hairs upon Stefan's arm stood on end. *Three doorways. Past, Present, and Future.*

-3-

All the lights in Stefan's apartment had been extinguished. In their absence, two pillar candles stood upon the dining room table at which Catrina, Aaron, and Lucien quietly sat. Their faces gave off a yellow tint brought on by the illumination of the dancing flames before them. Silence… and they could hear each other's deep breaths—stuttered breaths over quavering lips—as they prepared to speak to the dead.

Catrina had shown Lucien and Aaron how to make an unbreakable circle around the table with their hands. Thumb to thumb, fingers outstretched, and pinky fingers connecting to the pinky fingers of the person on either side of them. She had warned them about breaking the circle, and not to do it at any cost. To break the circle would cause a "rupture" in the spirit world; it could be quite destructive and cause the spirit at hand to become trapped. Although she had studied Wicca for the past four years, all Catrina Taylor knew of séances was limited to book knowledge. She had never conducted one before, never gave a second thought that she would *have* to be a part of one. But she needed answers.

They all needed answers.

The trio remained silent for five minutes, their heads bowed and their breathing beginning to match in rhythm. Catrina lifted her head and opened her eyes from her meditative state. "I ask that the Archangel Gabriel protect us all in our dealings with the spirits we call upon who have passed to the other side," she announced. Lucien and Aaron lifted their heads and gazed at Catrina as she began.

"I call upon a spirit lost, a fresh soul that has recently passed. I call upon a soul of the Nightworld, one who has seen the evil at hand and knows of its workings. Breckin, I call upon you Breckin, soul trapped in this world, lover of Stefan Powell. I bid you to aid us in our workings this evening." Catrina's voice echoed throughout the apartment, each word loud and completely clear.

Lucien gasped as he studied the glowing that started as a small light and grew into the form of a man. His entire being shuddered and Catrina quickly addressed him. "It's all right, Lucien. Don't break the circle."

Aaron sat amazed. He was bewitched by Catrina's power to call the dead, amused by how much more powerful she had gotten since her awakening from the coma induced by Lillian. It was at that point that he realized how much he envied her—for her ability, for her undying love for Stefan, for all her strength.

Furthermore, Aaron couldn't believe his eyes. It was indeed Breckin who was forming before them. Aaron had recognized him quickly. The Roman face, his thin but defined limbs, the chocolate-colored hair, and those emerald eyes—they were his finest features, just as recognizable in his transparent form. Breckin—a man Aaron had seen many times in the Nightworld—a youthful soul, a recent abductee murdered at the hands of Lillian. *Stefan's first true love,* Aaron reminded himself.

Lucien was aghast and sat in fear, his body trembling by the haunting events that unfolded before his eyes. Still, he had faith in all that Catrina said. She wouldn't let anything happen to him. She promised, and her words were made of gold.

Breckin's ghost spoke, addressing the entire room. *"Why have I been brought to this spectacle?"*

"We need answers, Breckin." This was Catrina.

"It is you who needs answers, Catrina. You are the vessel that carries the strength for all the others in this battle. Yet, you are not immune to the evil." Breckin's ghost began circling the three, curiously glancing at Lucien who timidly looked away, and stopping beside Aaron. *"Wolf,"* Breckin announced. *"You are the only piece of the Nightworld that continues to exist in the Earth realm, unscathed. Do you know Stefan is falling in love with you?"*

Aaron shook his head no.

"Of course you do. You've dreamt of him tonight, haven't you? You dreamt of his making love to you."

Aaron nodded. "Yes, a dream of him."

"It was no dream." Before Aaron had a chance to respond to the confusion, Breckin's ghost merged with his body. Aaron jolted in numerous spasms as the transparent body of the ghost dissipated into a million tiny-sparked particles that showered his flesh and wormed their existence within him.

Lucien practically screamed. "What's happening Catrina?" He forced himself to lean as far away from Aaron's convulsing body as he could. He barely managed to keep his fingers touching Aaron's, about ready to break free of the delicate flesh.

"Stay calm, Lucien!" Catrina yelled. "Don't break the circle. Relax; I think Breckin's going to use Aaron's body as a vessel to speak through."

The candles flickered wildly, creating silhouettes of the trio that danced upon the walls. Lucien did his best to remain still through it all. He closed his eyes. It was like being on a roller coaster ride right before it hits the summit where it will plunge hundreds of feet downward. Lucien's heart violently fluttered within his chest and he began gasping for air as the lump in his throat grew to proportionate size.

The spasmodic thrashing of Aaron's body briskly came to a halt. Lucien attempted to relax, though it felt as if somebody were pinching at his shoulder.

Catrina was right; Breckin was using Aaron's body as a tool through which he could speak. She had known how spirits would use a living person as a "mental medium" through which to speak. After all, it takes energy to exist as a ghost, even to speak. With the combination of the strength in Aaron, Breckin would be free to hold long conversations if he so chose.

When Aaron's face looked up across the table at Catrina, she immediately recognized the emerald-colored eyes that she looked into. Breckin was in Aaron; he had successfully possessed Aaron's body.

The voice spoke, but it wasn't Aaron's voice. Sure, it was Aaron's mouth that shaped the words, but it was Breckin's voice that came out. The whole thing was like madness warped. *"What is it you ask of me, Catrina? You already know that I am limited to the information I can give you."*

"Breckin," she began, "Stefan's life is in danger."

"We are all in the midst of danger, Catrina. Stefan's life as well as yours. Even this young man beside me." Breckin's eyes shot a sideways glance to Lucien. Lucien made no movement; he only gawked at the entire spectacle.

"The Nightworld, Breckin. We need answers. We need to know how to stop it. I need to find out where Stefan is, if he is all right."

"Stefan is alive, I can tell you that. As for the other answers you seek, they lay before you. You already have the answers, Catrina."

She wanted to throw her arms up in frustration, but knew she couldn't break the circle they had formed. "No, I don't have the answers! I don't know what to do!"

"You know of the Pact."

"I know of a sacrifice, and I'm sure that is supposed to be Stefan. After all, he opened the doorway. I know of a thirteenth that will cross the doorway and activate the initiation of the Pact. Who is the thirteenth?"

"Stop looking further into the enigma than you have to, Catrina. Stefan's whereabouts are right in front of your eyes."

"Aaron?" she queerly asked.

"Yes. Aaron knows of Stefan's location. It is time that is your enemy, Catrina. Stefan will come home soon."

"I wish he could hear me," Catrina said in despair.

"He hears me speaking through Aaron right now. He hears Aaron. Aaron is the key. Aaron. Time. The wolves. The wolves will come for him soon. Their howling is the dreaded beginning."

"I don't understand. You're not making sense, Breckin."

"Stop trying to understand, Catrina. Nobody will ever understand the many faces of Evil or how they function. Evil has a face here in Spook Valley; its features are made up of the Nightworld." Aaron's body began to convulse again.

Catrina knew Breckin's ghost was ready to make its exit. It had used all the energy Aaron's body could give it without bringing Aaron to the brink of death. Catrina gripped Aaron's hand tighter. "Thank you, Breckin. Thank you for saving me that night." *I am finally able to say it.*

"Set my soul free, Catrina. Right the wrong that has destroyed my life. Let me be in peace." The luminous force within Aaron's body began congregating into a brilliant ball of light behind him. As it lifted and disappeared before all their eyes, Breckin's voice gave one last warning. *"Catrina, beware the succubus…"* The words trailed off into a haunting echo.

Aaron squinted; he appeared as if he had just awoken from a broken sleep. "Oh god, I'm so sore," he complained.

"Breckin used you to speak though," Catrina explained.

Lucien went to stand.

"Wait!" Catrina shouted. "I have to close the circle."

Lucien sat back down and Aaron let his head droop.

"Thank you for protecting us, *Gabriel.* As we close this circle, we expel any and all other spirits who have not made themselves known to us. You may no longer exist through this ritual. Blessed Be." Catrina got to her feet, pulling her hands back from Lucien and Aaron.

"That was weird," Aaron said. "I heard everything you two were talking about, only, it was like I was a spectator, watching from behind the lines."

"Then you heard what he said?"

"Yeah."

"Tell me everything you know about the Nightworld, Aaron."

"I already have."

"What about the wolves? Tell me about the wolves. What does that mean to you?"

The wolves, Aaron thought. His abduction. He recalled the day when he had been carried off by a pack of wolves, that terrifying last day of his human existence that gave way to night. That horrible day! He remembered screaming—oh, those ungodly wails into the night—as he lay upon the many backs of a pack of wolves that carried him off into the doorway of the unknown. "It seems so long ago but, at the same time, it only seems like yesterday. I always had an interest in werewolves, in lycanthropes (that's the scientific name given to them). I purchased an occult book, because I was having blackouts, what I thought to be symptoms of documented cases of werewolfism. I took it with me to Woodstock…"

-4-

It was difficult to explain the existence of the Nightworld to anybody. As Stefan made an attempt to describe everything he knew of the dark netherworld to Aaron, his memorable accounts of the Nightworld were rich in detail, like that of a fictitious novel he had read over and over again. Each time Stefan told anybody of that forbidden place, he was able to add more detail. In fact, it reminded him of a revised urban legend that got more intricate as it was fueled by time.

Time. Trapped in this time. To Stefan's amazement, during his conversation with Aaron, a barrier had been broken; a rift in time had given him answers. And those answers came from the two voices he had missed the most: those of Catrina and Breckin.

Stefan couldn't believe it. Surely, his reality was one in which dreams formed within dreams, nightmares that were triple fold; only, there was no waking up. No matter how much he had wanted to escape the terrors that came in the form of monsters and time travel, he had no choice but to live through it all. *Try to live!*

As he spoke of his voluntary entrance into the Nightworld, Aaron cut off his words. Only, it was not Aaron who spoke; instead, it was the long lost voice of his lover Breckin. *How was it possible? How was any of this happening?* With excitement and apprehension exceeding levels previously unattainable, Stefan made a mighty attempt to talk to Breckin, Breckin's voice that spoke with Aaron's features. It was of no use. Aaron's body was in some sort of trance; it was unable to react from Stefan's touch or hear his words. Stefan could only listen to the voice, unable to make much sense of what it meant, or exactly of what it was speaking.

'*You know of the pact,*' the voice had spoken. It was tough not addressing Breckin's voice from Stefan's standpoint. It appeared as if the voice was speaking to him.

'*Stop looking further into the enigma than you have to, Catrina…*' Catrina! Yes, just to hear her name! And then, he heard her *voice* as if it were traveling through a narrow tunnel that separated her and Stefan only hundreds of feet away.

'*Aaron,*' the voice had echoed in a muffle. She was alive; she had awakened! Stefan's body was unable to sit still, the excitement brought on by Catrina's recovery brimming within him.

'Yes. Aaron knows of Stefan's location. It is time that is your enemy, Catrina.'

'I wish he could hear me.'

"I do hear you, Catrina. I'm alive! I love you," Stefan voiced to Aaron who was the portal for the voices.

Breckin's voice continued a conversation that didn't exist in Stefan's here and now. *'He hears me speaking through Aaron right now. He hears Aaron. Aaron is the key. Aaron. Time. The wolves. The wolves will come for him soon. Their howling is the dreaded beginning.'*

Stefan peered around the motel room, shivering from Breckin's statement. There was a nervous strike of his veins, a monumental trepidation of all forebodings given that Aaron was still and Breckin's voice came from his throat, along with Catrina's in the distance.

Seconds later, it had all ceased. Aaron's eyes blinked him back to life and Stefan called his name three times to ensure that Aaron heard him. Stefan studied Aaron, waiting for some explanation, some iota of reality stemming from the strange freakshow he had just witnessed. "What just happened?" That was what Aaron asked instead.

"I was about ready to ask you the same thing. Did you blackout again?" Stefan thought, given Aaron's previous connections with blackouts and the unexplainable that might have been the case.

"No," Aaron paused, trying to make sense of all that just occurred, "I heard everything."

"And what do you make of it?" Stefan burned holes into Aaron with his eyes, waiting for the key that would return him to Spook Valley. *The key*, that's what Breckin's voice had said. *Aaron is the key!*

"I'm not sure what to think." Aaron turned his head toward the window of the motel as he watched the droplets of rain that began forming on its surface. "But…"

"But what?" Stefan excitedly asked.

"I feel like I know the girl named Catrina."

Stefan gripped for his chest to feel his heart knocking hard against it. Oh God, when would it all end? Time. Aaron, the key. The wolves.

Stefan almost choked on his own breath when he heard the howling. In the distance, the yelping of wolves filled the night.

-5-

The doorway leading from the Nightworld into the Earth realm vibrated and pulsed in its bloodstained, ruby tint. Along the purple backdrops of a coming dawn, the black doorway shimmered in the desert beside Spook Valley. Coyotes cocked their heads and stared in wonder as jackrabbits sped off with hind legs high in the air. The rising sun forced snakes to slither back into their holes into the hard desert floor and an undying whir permeated the immediate area.

Lillian surfaced from the black pits of the doorway. Lillian, a demon enraged by all her fury to stop those who would keep the pact from being initiated; a succubus fueled by the consequences of God *Damia* should she fail. Her inhuman body sweated a slimy substance, the scales along her neck throbbed in lusting power, and her tail slid back and forth upon the desert land. Upon viewing the sunlight, she shrieked. Throughout the entire town, the residents of Spook Valley would hear her siren song.

She immediately fell back into the realms of the portal to the Nightworld, the darkness embracing and comforting her until her arrival later that evening. The black dimensional corridor eclipsed the sun that peaked just over the mountains. It led her back to a place she called home. She would wait until nightfall.

-6-

When Aaron had finished telling Catrina of his abduction, she remained silent, her eyes upturned as if looking to her brain, or even the heavens, for any possible reaction to what had just been said.

"Tell me what's going on in that head of yours," Aaron voiced.

"Oh…damn…I'm not sure how it all fits together yet," Catrina answered. "Breckin said that Stefan would be coming back soon. As for the thirteenth crossing, that must not have happened yet or else things wouldn't be this calm. What is it that you know, Aaron? Breckin said that you are the key!"

"I don't know what to say," Aaron exclaimed in an exasperated sigh. "I've already told you everything."

Lucien sat in the living room, upon one of the couches, as he observed the sun coming up over the mountains. Without warning he announced, "I want to leave; I want nothing to do with this."

Aaron turned and gave him an angry look. Catrina gestured for Aaron not to say a word. "You can't just leave," she told Lucien. "We're all in this together."

"I didn't ask to be!" Lucien's voice was short of a condescending yell.

"Neither did I," Catrina retaliated with her own angry inflection.

"What do we do then?" Now, Lucien's tone was soft and forgiving.

"I'm not sure yet; give me a minute." Catrina left the room and entered Stefan's bedroom. The Tarot cards remained on the bed in their cross formation. She studied each one. *The World. The Lovers* crossing *The World.* Wait a minute…*The World* crossed by *The Lovers!* That was it! Aaron and Stefan were the lovers and that world had definitely been crossed. Was Stefan in Aaron's old time, his past that continued to haunt him? The pieces of the puzzle began making a bigger picture. "Aaron," she desperately called.

Aaron came running into the room as if she were in danger. When he arrived, he saw Catrina staring at the cards. Her eyes came up to meet his. "What was the name of that song you kept hearing? The one that you said was your favorite but I couldn't hear anything at all?"

"Spanish Castle Magic?"

"Yes, that one! When did you hear it last before then?"

"I heard it last at…"

"Woodstock." Catrina completed his sentence. "And you also said that you could feel Stefan making love to you tonight."

Aaron gave a queer expression to Catrina, not sure where this was going. "Yeah, but that was probably just a dream. A very vivid dream."

"No," Catrina protested. "It wasn't a dream. Breckin said it wasn't! He also said that Stefan was hearing us as we spoke. Breckin was speaking through you!"

"What are you saying, Catrina?"

"Now I'm not sure, but I think that Stefan is somehow trapped in your past."

"What?"

"It makes perfect sense! You're experiencing what Stefan is experiencing, what the Aaron of the past experienced. Even though you're here, he still sees you in the past."

Aaron was completely flabbergasted and shook his head in disbelief. "Are you trying to tell me that I'm in two places at once?"

"Not necessarily *you* per se, but your old self is back there with Stefan. You're the connection between the now and the past. I think he somehow went into the past. However, Breckin said he would be coming soon and I think we should make the necessary preparations and meet him at the doorway."

"What about Lillian?" Aaron asked in disagreement. "You heard what Breckin said."

"Yes, I know." Catrina need not be reminded again of those awful words that sent shivers in in many directions upon her body. *Beware the succubus.* She looked to the Tarot spread again and, taking closer glance at the *Destiny* card, the *Ace of Swords*, she said, "I think I know what I have to do."

Aaron slowly exited the bedroom, unable to keep the confusion brimming in his mind to a minimal. He thought of all she had to say and then he thought of more words that Breckin had spoke through his own mouth. *'You are the only piece of the Nightworld that continues to exist in the Earth realm, unscathed. Do you know Stefan's falling in love with you?'* At that point, Aaron knew what he must do as well. If not for Stefan, then for the two of them.

As the morning dawn revisited the town of Spook Valley, Catrina, Lucien, and Aaron began preparing for Stefan's arrival. Little did they know, this would be the last morning they would witness in serenity before the ultimate battle would take place.

CHAPTER XXII

-1-

As the light of dawn enveloped Spook Valley, it was eclipsed by the slate gray of cloud cover. The large cumulus clouds billowed in the atmosphere and appeared pregnant in their bulged size. The cluster of clouds came in from the West and one could almost imagine that the congregation of stormy colors—tombstone gray, deep purple, and even black in some areas—had slowed down their velocity as they approached Spook Valley. The animals of the desert remained silent; the only sound was that of the morning commuters on their way to work.

Officer Colburn peered out the window to his home as he took a drag off his cigarette. He watched the nightly news religiously, especially the meteorologist's report. He hadn't recalled the weatherman mentioning anything about a storm; today was supposed to be sunny, highs in the lower 100's. Then again, all weather anchors were known for being wrong from time to time. Perhaps the storm clouds would pass Spook Valley altogether.

Officer Colburn stubbed out his cigarette and opened the file of Stefan Powell that lay on the kitchen table. He copied the young man's address information off the application in Stefan's file onto a Mead notepad and then stuffed the small pad into his breast pocket. He knew exactly where the Shadowood Apartments were. It would take only fifteen minutes to get there.

The officer quaffed his cup of black coffee and clipped on his holster. He grabbed his badge off the counter as he exited and locked the door behind him.

-2-

In another place parallel to the time continuum of Spook Valley and the rest of the Earth realm, darkness shrouded the land and the night was filled with the howling of wolves. The howls refused to cease; they were a continuous loop of an eerie composition composed of insidious yelps and drawn out cries in the dark.

"What the hell is that?" Stefan asked aloud, a slight tremble to his voice.

"Good, you hear it too," Aaron confirmed. "I thought I was going crazy."

Stefan's eyes bulged in the realization of what was apparently coming. "Oh my god, Aaron."

"What?" Aaron had jumped off the bed from Stefan's hurried concern.

"Wolves. It's wolves; can't you hear them?"

In the spaces of the two men's pauses, in the midst of acknowledgement from one man to the other, the howling grew louder and fiercer.

"You're starting to freak me out, man," said Aaron as he glanced out the small window of the motel room.

The pieces of the puzzle were beginning to fit into the enigmatic full picture that relentlessly haunted Stefan's mind. "You said you knew Catrina, Aaron."

"Catrina? Oh, that girl's voice that I could hear off in a distance?"

"Yeah."

"I said that I felt like I knew her."

"You *do* know her Aaron. But, you haven't met her in this time because you know her in the future, in *my* time." Stefan contemplated telling Aaron anymore of his deductive logic for fear of creating a possible "timequake" (as Aaron had deemed it) in the future. However, it didn't make a difference. What was happening now had already been; the pages of the past had already been written and there was no changing them. Or, at least, that's what Stefan's newfound convictions had told him.

"This is getting too weird for me, man." Aaron continued to crane his neck and focus his vision on what was beyond the window, on the animals that made those horrific cries in the dark.

Stefan grabbed for the scroll that rested upon the nightstand. He unrolled it, briskly observing the bloody scrawl of words from some cryptic language, and handed it over to Aaron. Perhaps, since Aaron was into the occult, he would be able to decipher it. "Have you ever seen anything like this?"

"Well, it's obviously an old scroll of some sort."

"Besides that," Stefan said, frustrated by the unending howling that brought goosebumps to his flesh. "Do you recognize the writing or…the language it's written in?"

Aaron studied the piece of parchment for a minute, turning it upside down and holding it up to the light. "It's not Latin; in fact, it's much older than Latin. See these script marks, the way the ink of the pen takes a sharp curve?"

Stefan moved in closer to Aaron and took notice of where his finger pointed. "Yeah."

"Some of the formations of the letters are taken from Latin text. You see, look at the 'S' and the 'W'."

"And? Do you think you can decipher it?"

"Not at all." Aaron's answer was simple and to the point.

"Why not, you seem to know what Latin looks like?"

"Right, but you have to understand something. This has been encrypted like I've never seen before. You can't even find a book that would describe this type of encryption. There are numbers in the middle of the words, not too mention half of the text is written upside down. It would be difficult enough to decipher one word let alone the entire thing. What is this anyway?"

Stefan took in a breath of hesitation before explaining the scroll's origin. "It's from the Nightworld. There are five others like it. They belong to a group known as the Order of Perennial Darkness. Each of the Order has a scroll that is part of a bigger piece to a pact they plan to initiate to take over the Earth. I grabbed this one during a struggle, before I arrived here. You see, they need that scroll to initiate the pact. As long as I have it, they can only wait."

"Wait? Why don't they just come and find you?"

"I thought about that myself. I couldn't figure out why they just didn't follow me through the doorway and get the scroll. But I realized, after hearing the voice of Breckin and Catrina speak through you tonight, that they can't. This place doesn't exist."

Aaron laughed in craziness, his body bouncing up and down in hysterics. "Now you're trying to tell me this entire place—this motel room, the concerts, myself included—doesn't exist?"

"I mean. It did back in its time, back in 1969. But, now, it's just like watching a movie. The same thing happens over and over again. I'm just a spectator."

"A spectator to what?"

In the background of their conversation, the howling grew closer. Stefan feared for what he knew would happen. He wasn't sure how to stop the phenomena, or if he should sit and watch Fate take its toll. "The Nightworld preys on believers to open its doorway, Aaron. Just as I opened the doorway in my own time, with my constant thoughts of demons for my poetry, I think that you opened the doorway in this time. But, you have already opened it, Aaron. The doorway was opened in your own time and that's why you exist in my time…because the Nightworld abducted you back here. I am witness to your abduction, Aaron."

"Abduction?" Aaron threw the scroll at Stefan. This was too much; surely, this was all a dream growing into nightmare proportions. Aaron was sick of hearing any more from this man. At first, he allowed the young man to entertain him with the enigmatic talk of time travel. But, now? Now it was getting too much out of control. "My abduction? Abduction from what, Stefan!?! Aliens? Or, I see, by the Nightworld, right?"

Stefan could tell that Aaron was emblazed with anger. He didn't blame him. He had put himself in Aaron's shoes, imagined what it would be like hearing about any of this without having some type of knowledge of the situation as it'd played out in the present. Stefan nodded his head. "Yes, Aaron, I fear that to be the god-awful truth. The Nightworld has abducted you. But you escaped, Aaron! You are with me in the present. We can stop this! Don't you see? You're the key to all of this."

"Then how did I open the doorway? I didn't ask for any of this!"

"I think it was your research of lycanthropes." Stefan paused before continuing because he knew how insane it would sound and of what fears it would project in the man he had learned to love. "Aaron…you're going to become a werewolf." It was the truth, and this Stefan knew. It was why Aaron acted the way he did that night in the apartment—the beast within him was trying to escape. It's what Breckin meant when he'd told Stefan that Aaron wasn't the man he appeared to be. And it came down to this. The truth had finally come out; a truth Stefan was willing to accept because he had traveled decades into the past to find it.

Aaron stood flabbergasted; his eyes bulged at the idea and tears flooded his ducts. He cringed when he heard the wolves' howls that appeared to be emitting from the parking lot of the motel.

-3-

Catrina was in Stefan's kitchen preparing toast; she felt as if she hadn't eaten a thing in days. As she buttered the toasted bread, Lucien wandered in and stood near the breakfast nook, simply staring at her. When she turned around, she was almost startled by the quiet young man. Almost. She had seen so much unexplained phenomena and witnessed so much chaos in the last few days that she had become immune to presences just suddenly being in front of her.

"I made some toast; do you want some?" She offered this to Lucien.

Lucien shook his head. "Do you know what we're going to do? Where do we go from here?" A troubled concern etched Lucien's eyes.

"We're going to fight," she said plain and simply. "There's no other way. We need to rescue Stefan from the grips of the Nightworld. I need to stop by a place in town and then I'm going to have Aaron show me to the doorway out in the desert. I have a feeling that Stefan will be coming through soon. I'd like you to go with us, Lucien."

Lucien contemplated everything that had just been said to him. Fight against a force called the Nightworld? His distinction between fiction and reality, between monsters and human, had been eerily twisted by seeing the monstrous demon in the music store killing his boss, Aaron's and Zander's morphing into wild beasts, and the appearance, during a séance no less, of a ghost named Breckin. Stefan. He would love to see Stefan again; he would love to put his faith in Stefan the way he had with Catrina and tell Stefan of what brought him to this place called Spook Valley. Would Stefan console him as Catrina had? Would Stefan keep Lucien from harm's way and hold Lucien when he cried from his haunting past? "No," Lucien said, "I want to stay here."

"It's your choice, Lucien. I think you would be safer with us though."

"Are you…" Lucien couldn't finish his question.

"Am I…what?"

"Are you from that place?" His gaze fell to the floor, embarrassed by his question.

"The Nightworld?" Catrina gave off a small laugh. "No, Lucien, I'm not from that place."

"But Aaron is, right?"

"Yes, Aaron is from the Nightworld."

"Then why is he trying to help save Stefan?"

Catrina felt like a mother trying to explain the fundamentals of life to her uninformed child. "Because Aaron is not like the others from that place. There were those who were abducted from their normal everyday surroundings. Surely, those people were normal at the time. I suppose that some of them joined the Nightworld, and some fought against it the entire time they were there. Aaron is one of those people, Lucien. I think it's brave of him, don't you? To fight against such a dark force while having to remain in their evil place for all that time?"

"Oh," Lucien muttered as he nodded his head. "I guess so."

Catrina could see the aura of dark colors that surrounded Lucien's being. The young man was so depressed, so somber in his everyday life. She wished that he could be happy; she prayed that, someday, he would put his bloody past behind him. She was sure that his smile would be so precious. "Lucien, is there something else bothering you?"

"Does Aaron really love Stefan?"

Catrina meditated on the question for a moment before answering. Is that what this was about? Did Lucien have feelings for Stefan? "Well, I can't say for sure," she answered. "I think he does. I know he really cares for Stefan. If anything, I'm sure he loves him at least as much as I love Stefan. Stefan's a really good man, Lucien. I don't want to lose him and I'm sure Aaron feels the same way."

There was a dreaded silence between the two, a silence that couldn't be measured by seconds or minutes.

"Why don't you get yourself some toast, Lucien. I'm going to go see what Aaron's doing?"

"I think he's sleeping in Stefan's bedroom," Lucien stated as he passed her by. As Lucien watched Catrina exit the kitchen, he thought of Aaron. There was a part of him, the part he couldn't control the night he'd endlessly stabbed his mother to death, that wished Aaron wasn't around.

Catrina pushed open the door to Stefan's bedroom to find Aaron lying on his stomach. Aaron's elbows propped up his upper body and he was writing something on a piece of paper. "Hey," he said as he glanced up at her.

"Hey," Catrina repeated. "I thought you were asleep."

"Nah."

"What are you doing?" Catrina gestured to the paper and pen he held.

"Oh, just working on something. Actually, I'm finished." Aaron folded the paper into thirds.

"I want to stop by *The Gun Shop* in town and then have you show me where the doorway is."

Aaron sat up. "What are you going to do, Catrina? Go in after him?"

"Of course not," she replied. "But Breckin said that he'd be returning soon. I thought we should wait by the doorway."

"That could be dangerous."

"That's why I want to stop by *The Gun Shop* before we go out there."

"A gun isn't going to stop half of those things in the Nightworld, Catrina."

"I know Aaron. I'm not getting a gun. Do you think you'll be ready in a little bit?"

"Yeah. What about Lucien? Is he coming along?"

"He wants to stay here."

"He'd be safer with us," Aaron offered.

"I tried to tell him the same thing, but I think he feels a little intimidated by you."

"By me?" Aaron frowned at the idea. "Why?"

"He asked me if you loved Stefan. I think he has a crush on him."

"Do you think I love Stefan?"

"I think that as long as we all get out of this alive and Stefan is happy, then I'd be happy for him, regardless of who he's with."

A loud rap at the front door sharply echoed throughout the apartment. Aaron briskly jumped to his feet and Catrina's heart began racing. Knocking on the door. A visitor. It had always meant a visitor, and Catrina couldn't help but wonder if the visitor would be another creation of the Nightworld.

"I better go answer that," she hesitated. "Stay here, Aaron. If I need your help, I'll yell for you."

"Be careful," said Aaron. As he watched her leave the room, Aaron slid the piece of folded paper beneath the mattress.

The rapping came again as Catrina made her way into the living room. Lucien met her at the door. She whispered, "Go back in the kitchen." He did as she instructed without another word.

"Who's there?" Catrina called through the close door.

It was an older man's voice, a strong voice. "Officer Colburn with the Spook Valley Police Department."

Catrina was instantly baffled. She pulled her hair behind her shoulders and composed herself. What did the police want?

Catrina opened the door just enough to get a glimpse of the man in the black police outfit. He donned a silver badge. The last name Colburn was embroidered into the fabric of his police uniform. Catrina opened the door wider and stepped into the space of the doorway. "Can I help you?" she softly asked.

"Hi there," the man said. The officer's hair was cropped short in military fashion. His form was overpowering; he was at least six foot one with broad shoulders and a husky build. "Can I speak to…" he paused as he looked down at his notepad, "Stefan Powell?"

"He's not at home right now." Butterflies tickled Catrina's stomach.

"When do you expect him back?"

Catrina wasn't sure what to say. Her hands began to tremble. "Actually, he's out of town for a few days; he went to Phoenix to visit family. I'm apartment-sitting for him."

"What's your name?" Officer Colburn asked as he grabbed for a pen from his breast pocket.

"I'm sorry," she said laughing, "I'm Catrina Taylor; I'm his best friend." She extended her hand to the officer and then retracted when the officer didn't meet her gesture. Instead, he had apparently written her name down on his pad."

His crystalline gaze met with hers and his eyes eclipsed his overbearing stature. "Do you know a Lucien Matthews?"

Back in the kitchen, Lucien heard the entire conversation. When he heard his own name, he immediately rolled up into a ball upon the kitchen floor and hid himself in the corner. *Please don't say it! Please God, don't let them take me away!* He silently whimpered.

Her heart sank. What did Lucien have to do with this? Suddenly she recollected Lucien's words. *They're coming for me.* "Lucien Matthews?" Catrina rolled her eyes in her head as if trying to recall the name from her lying memory. "No, I don't."

"Has Stefan ever mentioned the name to you?"

"No," she shook her head. "I've never heard him say it once.

"When's Stefan expected to get back?"

"A couple more days," she lied. "He said that he might be longer."

The officer put his notepad back into his pocket. He pulled out a business card and extended it to Catrina. "Please have Mr. Powell call me as soon as he returns. It's urgent that he get a hold of me."

Catrina grasped for the card and she knew that the officer was observing the trembling of her hand. "OK."

"Is something wrong, Ms. Taylor?" The officer's eyes met hers.

"Oh, not at all," Catrina smiled. "I quit smoking two days ago and I think the withdrawal is kicking in." She reveled at her ability to make a quick, viable excuse given the pressure she was feeling.

I know the feeling, thought Officer Colburn. "Make sure you tell Stefan I stopped by."

"I sure will. Have a nice day, Officer."

"You do the same Ms. Taylor," he said as he turned around and descended the stairwell.

She closed the door and locked it. As she turned around, Lucien and Aaron met her in the living room. Lucien's eyes were flooded with tears. "Thank you," he sobbed. He embraced her in a giant hug as Catrina's eyes met with Aaron.

"Calm down, Lucien. I told you I would do my best to help you."

Given the new turn of events, Lucien realized that he wouldn't be safe in Stefan's apartment. He wiped away at his tears with the back of his hand. "I want to go with you guys," he announced.

"We can't leave for a while," Aaron said. "Not with the police looking for him and Stefan."

"We'll go in a couple hours," Catrina resolved.

-4-

"You're freaking me out, Stefan." Aaron was pacing back and forth in the motel room. He refused to shield his nudity as he did this; the last thing on his mind was concealing his naked body. "Werewolf? You're saying I'm going to become a werewolf?" His voice was loud in the midst of confusion and anger.

"It shouldn't come as a big surprise to you, Aaron. You told me yourself that you were researching lycanthropes because you thought you had the symptoms of so called documented cases." Stefan was trying his best to calm Aaron. He reached out his hand to touch Aaron's shoulder.

Aaron immediately flinched and recoiled. "Don't touch me! No, none of this is happening. Those wolves out there, those fucking wolves! Why don't they stop? What do they want?"

The howling was all around them. Long, drawn out yelps and barks created no escape for the two men. They had surrounded the motel room. The creatures could be heard all around.

Stefan didn't know what to do. Surely, this is what happened to Aaron. And, without doubt, there was no way to change that. This was how Fate had planned it for the young man. This was how the Nightworld had abducted him. Stefan was powerless to change it. But he couldn't make Aaron understand that. He couldn't rationalize the thoughts of terror to a person who was already petrified beyond belief. Stefan cringed from each howl that impregnated the night.

Aaron began to weep. He stopped in his tracks and flailed his arms in the air. He began to yell and spin in a circle to address the walls of the room surround him. "Leave me alone! Leave me alone!" he cried to the wolves. Then he fixed his gaze upon Stefan. "You did this, didn't you? You caused this to happen."

Stefan was speechless. He identified with Aaron's bewilderment and the longing that made him accuse those closest to him of this horror. After all, Stefan had done the same thing to Breckin before he knew much of the Nightworld.

"Leave! I want you to leave!" Aaron was enraged. His scowls were mixed with tears.

"I can't leave, Aaron," Stefan attempted to justify. "The doorway is closed. I'm stuck here with you."

"No," said Aaron. He grabbed Stefan by the shoulder and forced him to the door of the room. As Aaron was about to unlock the door, that's when the scratching sounds began. At first, it was barely audible amidst the wolves' cries. But within seconds, the scratching came from all sides of the room. The wolves were trying to get in.

Aaron's heart jolted into a horrific panic as he cringed from the door. There were no walls he could back up against. The fierce scratching enveloped his world and, collectively, sounded like a large charge of static electricity that was nothing less than a constant in his foreboding world. Aaron fell to floor in the center of the room. His body convulsed in shock and his eyes were fueled by dread.

-5-

There was something suspicious about the way the girl named Catrina Taylor had reacted to Eric Colburn's line of questioning. He had questioned and interviewed many suspects and witnesses to crime over the years, and he could always tell when they were lying to him. Officer Colburn had learned to observe how their bodies reacted and got uncomfortable under certain questions versus others. The girl, more than likely, had told the truth about Stefan Powell being out of town. However, her reaction when asked about Lucien Matthews was that of a scared rabbit. Her hands had begun to tremble and she seemed distraught by the way she avoided eye contact with the officer. She was definitely lying about knowing Lucien Matthews. Now, the question was why? Was she trying to protect him? Was he her boyfriend? Still, the only thing linking Lucien to Laine Young's death was the testimony of an eyewitness who'd claimed to see a young man running from the scene. There was no proof that young man was Lucien Matthews because there was no way of knowing what Lucien looked like. At least, not until Officer Colburn questioned the young man.

Officer Colburn stubbed out his cigarette and exhaled a stream of smoke before opening the door to the Spook Valley Police Department. The phones were quiet today, and one of the dispatchers waved to him as he passed. As he approached his desk, another officer was walking toward him with a file in his hand. It was Officer Trexler.

"Hey James," Eric Colburn called out.

"How's the case going, Eric?"

"I can't seem to locate either of the two employees of the store. It seems that one of them is out of town and the other one seems to have disappeared off the face of the planet."

"Well, I think I just got the break you were looking for," Officer Trexler said as he handed Eric the folder in hand.

"What's this?" Colburn opened the file and was shocked by the gruesome pictures within—a body on a bed that had been maimed beyond comprehension.

"This came in from Tucson after I ran those names for you. It seems that our Mr. Lucien Matthews is wanted there for the murder of his mother."

"They want him for questioning?"

"No, Eric; the father witnessed it, saw his own son leaving out the bedroom window."

"Oh, god; how horrible." Officer Colburn closed the file and dropped in onto his desk. He knew there was something strange about this case. He knew that one of the employees of Laine's Music was involved. His hunch had served him well again.

Officer Colburn began walking away from his desk.

"Where you going?" Officer Trexler asked.

"I'm bringing in a girl for some *formal* questioning." Eric Colburn was convinced that Catrina Taylor wasn't telling the full truth, and, now, he had more questions for her given the new evidence that had surfaced.

-6-

The trio had left Stefan's apartment at 3:30pm, although the cloud cover outside made it appear to be dusk. Thunder rolled throughout the clouds and lightning was flashing all around Spook Valley. The storm would hit at any time.

Catrina instructed Lucien to lie down in the back seat and remain out of view as they traveled down Main Street. The last thing they needed was that officer from this morning spotting them with Lucien in the car. When Catrina maneuvered her Acura into a parking place in front of *The Gun Shop*, she told Lucien to remain in the vehicle and that she and Aaron would return in no time. Lucien did as he was told, his breathing heavy and his heart pounding from the idea of being arrested.

"I still don't know what we're doing in a place that sells guns," Aaron remarked as they entered the store.

"They just don't sell guns," Catrina stated as she waved at the shopkeeper behind the counter. Harold Shevers was an old man, but Catrina Taylor had seen him from time to time around town. He was the kindest man she had ever met in Spook Valley, very courteous and nice.

"Can I help you kids," Harold called from behind the counter in a weakened voice.

"Just looking around, Mr. Shevers," Catrina informed him.

Harold Shevers adjusted his glasses and took a harder gaze at Catrina. "Do I know you?"

"I've seen you around town, Mr. Shevers. My name's Catrina Taylor."

"Oh," he snickered, "Catrina. How you doing sweetie? Still working at the Violin Street Tavern?"

"Definitely not. That guy's a womanizer."

Harold laughed even harder. "Good girl," he commended.

The walls were lined with locked glass cases of handguns, shotguns, stun guns, and just about any type of gun one could imagine. The three aisles consisted of various types of knives. Aaron couldn't believe how many different styles there were.

From off the wall, Catrina pulled a claymore sword. The sword was over half the height of Catrina and must have weighed a good ten pounds, if not more. The double-edged sword gleamed beneath the store lights and Catrina held the hilt in both hands as she extended the sword in front of her. *Ace of Swords.* "This is what I need," she called to Aaron.

Aaron came around the corner of the aisle and was stunned by the sight of Catrina holding the claymore. "Wow," he said.

"This should do the trick if anybody decides to interfere."

Aaron was awestruck by the warrior posture Catrina maintained.

They purchased the sword and briskly made their way back to the vehicle. Lucien told them that it seemed like they were gone forever.

"Now where?" Aaron asked, ignoring Lucien's remark.

"Show me to the doorway, Aaron."

He directed her to get on Firehouse Road. Sprinkles of rain began coming down upon the windshield of the Acura as she started the vehicle.

-7-

It came as no surprise that Catrina Taylor was no longer at Stefan Powell's apartment when Officer Colburn knocked on the door for the second time that day. She'd probably gone to warn Lucien that the officer was asking about him.

Eric Colburn lit up a cigarette as he got back into his patrol car and made his way toward the Town Center. As the patrol car cruised down Main Street, Officer Colburn spotted Catrina Taylor and another young man leaving Harold Shevers' shop. Who was the other man, the one with the blond hair? Was it Stefan Powell? Had she lied about Stefan being out of town?

By the time Officer Colburn turned the car around, the two had already left. The rain began to lightly fall, and Officer Colburn spotted taillights down Main Street turning onto Firehouse Road. He sped his police cruiser down Main Street.

-8-

"This is where it is," Aaron announced.

They were no more than fifty yards into the desert that stretched to the East of Firehouse Road. Catrina had parked the car off the side of the road and rushed Lucien into the desert to avoid his being spotted by any passerby. Now they stood where the doorway apparently was. However, nothing was visible to the naked eye.

"I don't see anything," Catrina said, holding the claymore in her right hand.

Lucien kept looking all around the surrounding desert. He shivered from the large cold droplets of rain that fell upon him.

"It's cloaked during the day, but I know this is where it is."

"What's that buzzing noise?" Lucien asked.

"That's the sound of the doorway," Aaron answered.

A wind gust collected dust from the floor of the desert and threw it up in their faces. Catrina squinted past it.

"What are we going to do now that we're here?" This was Lucien who continued surveying the landscape in paranoid fashion.

"We're going to wait for Stefan," said Catrina. "I know he'll be coming through, and if anything tries to follow him, we're going to stop it."

Aaron shook his head in attempt to free the sounds that were haunting him. The howls and yelps were so loud he clasped his hands to his ears.

"What's wrong?" Catrina immediately acknowledged Aaron.

"I keep hearing wolves howling."

-9-

"You have to help me, Stefan! You have to do something! I can't stand it! That sound; that horrible howling!" Aaron was crying on the floor of the motel room. The scratching at the foundation of the room grew louder.

Stefan felt so bad for Aaron. At the same time, something seemed horribly wrong. They were trapped in this room and there was no way out. Not without the wolves outside getting them. And if the wolves made it in, what would happen to Stefan? Stefan yelled over the fierce howls and incessant scratches. "I don't know what to do, Aaron."

"Please!" Aaron hollered. "Don't let them get me! Make them stop!" Aaron's face was flushed red; the area beneath his eyes was swollen from his constant tears.

The scraping at the door continued; the claws of the beasts beyond it were eager to get at Aaron's flesh. The scratching sounds came from all sides of the room along with the yelping and howling. Without warning, the foundation of the motel itself began to quake. The walls were folding in and out, the glass to the window broke inward, and the floorboards undulated beneath Stefan and Aaron's feet.

"OH MY GOD," Aaron screamed. "OH GOD! WHAT'S HAPPENING!?!"

Suddenly, the door to the motel room exploded open. The pieces of the wooden door knocked Stefan to the floor.

Silence. Everything went silent. The quaking had ceased. No longer was there any howling, let alone eager scraping upon the wooden walls of the room. Aaron sniffled and gazed over at Stefan. "Stefan," he called. And he was amazed at being able to hear the sound of his own voice. "Stefan?" Aaron began to crawl on his hands and knees toward Stefan. The floorboards creaked beneath him. Aaron halted. He craned his neck toward the open doorway to the motel room. In the darkness outside, Aaron squinted to make out a dozen pair of eyes that emitted a crimson glow. In a flash, the pack of wolves burst into the room. Aaron shrieked as loud as he could over the anxious growls of the beasts that lunged toward him. He had no chance to breathe, for his shrieking didn't end. His screeches continued into the night until they were nothing more than silent screams.

-10-

Catrina, Aaron, and Lucien stood with their backs to Firehouse Road. The wind was at a constant speed now and they had to squint through the dirt that incessantly whipped past them.

Dusk had come. The clouds grew purple and black above them.

Lucien gasped at the sight of the doorway to the Nightworld appearing and almost backed into a cactus.

The doorway was monolithic in size, and the three that watched it appear before them were entranced by the ruby outline that pulsed.

"This is it," Aaron told Catrina. He gazed over at her.

Catrina was stricken with awe. *This is where Stefan went through,* she thought. *He's in there somewhere. He's coming back.* Catrina observed every particle of the black doorway, every bit of its size that was triple that of her own. The whirring sound of the doorway filled the evening as Catrina raised the sword in high into the air.

"Hold it right there," called a voice from behind.

Catrina turned to find Officer Eric Colburn poised with his gun in hand.

"Lucien Matthews," the officer called.

Out of instinct of hearing one's name unexpectedly, Lucien turned toward Officer Colburn.

"Put your hands in the air, Lucien."

Lucien made a quick glance toward Catrina who remained speechless. Aaron inched toward Lucien.

"Don't make a move, young man," Officer Colburn instructed Aaron.

"Officer," Catrina tried to explain. "It's not what you think." She began approaching Officer Colburn, her sword in tow.

"Drop it! Drop the weapon. Ms. Taylor." He had the gun pointed directly at her and alternated his gaze between her and Lucien and Aaron.

"I'm not going with you," Lucien cried out.

Aaron jumped in front of Lucien. "Stay behind me," he yelled back.

"One more move," the officer warned, "and you'll give me no choice but to use this gun." He shifted his attention to Catrina. "I said drop the weapon, Ms. Taylor."

Catrina threw the sword down to the ground.

Aaron's eyes grew red and a low growling emitted from his mouth. Lucien stood behind Aaron's form.

"What the hell is going on here?" Officer Colburn asked as he witnessed the sight of the doorway behind the three.

"Catrina," Aaron yelled, "the doorway!"

She pivoted and turned toward the doorway. The buzzing sound intensified and the black outline of someone or something coming through could be seen.

Officer Colburn was shocked by the phenomena and his mouth fell at the unexplainable sight.

"Stefan," Catrina called out to the figure emerging from the doorway.

The figure came into view. It was Lillian in human form. She stepped onto the desert floor as the rain came down and trickled onto her flesh. All four spectators watched as she morphed into her demon counterpart—her mouth erected forward baring sharp teeth, the scales of her back lumped up as slime slid down her legs, a tail fell from her lower back and slithered in the dirt, her obsidian eyes grew large, and rigid, blackened brown nails ejected from her fingers. The leathery exterior of her russet flesh had shriveled.

Catrina grasped for the sword near her feet but, before she had a chance to do so, an unseen force emitted from Lillian and sent the sword soaring into the air. The sword plunged into Officer Colburn's chest. Lucien gasped as the officer fell to the ground, the claymore buried halfway into him and blood oozing over his lips.

"Witch!" Lillian shrieked to the heavens. "Witch!" The drawn out siren sound of her scream pierced their ears and infused the atmosphere.

Catrina took a step back, looking toward Aaron and Lucien.

Lightning illuminated the blackened sky. The roar of thunder created a sonic boom that echoed into the night.

CHAPTER XXIII

-1-

The heavens cried in the dawning of battle—tears in the form of gigantic droplets fell heavy to the Earth. Once the rain made contact, it'd become saturated into the dirt floor of the desert that enveloped Spook Valley. The thunder had followed with its echoing roars like that of an excited audience playing spectator to the confrontation that was about to begin. The heavens ached. The cracks of thunder were sharp and shrill as if the sky had been torn in places. If the sky were a living entity, if there were truly angels beyond those billowing clouds, then there were also demons that cast their applause in the form of lightning that zigzagged throughout the darkened skyline.

This is what it had come down to—Catrina, Aaron, and Lucien standing in the heart of the desert before a portal that transcended all time and space. And, unexpectedly, what had emerged from the monolithic doorway was not Stefan as Catrina had anticipated. Instead, it was Lillian, demon child of the Nightworld with whom Catrina had come face to face on one other occasion. Only, during that confrontation, Catrina was rendered powerless; the demon had maimed her back and sent her traumatized body into a coma.

Beware the succubus! Beware the succubus! Breckin's ghostly forebodings relentlessly raced through her mind. This is what he'd meant; this was the confrontation Breckin had warned her about. But she had come prepared, hadn't she? She had come to the doorway wielding a large claymore with intent of dismembering Lillian's demon body should she come in between Stefan's arrival. But it was to no avail. Lillian had sent it airborne and into the chest of Officer Colburn. Catrina knew Lillian was powerful, however, the realization of just *how* powerful Lillian was struck her with unmeasured fear.

The hideous shriek that emitted from Lillian's mouth had echoed away from the proximity. Catrina Taylor's heart galloped within her chest and a suffocating lump emerged in her throat. She gawked at Lillian in her succubus form—the leathery skin, the protruding fangs, the creature's tail adorned with overlapping scales, and the eyes. Those obsidian eyes! Catrina could feel the dread that shot like daggers from Lillian's eyes into her own. This creature had no conscious, it knew of no love; the succubus was horror unscathed.

Lillian began a slow approach to the trio who had grouped together in single file. Catrina stood in the front. "Witch," the demon spoke with a disgust that sharply etched the single word. A gust of wind shot past Lillian and she ignored it. All of her attention was dead set on Catrina.

Lucien was immersed in apprehension. It was she! It was the same creature he'd witnessed the day he'd entered Laine's Music. That awful creature! Lucien instantly recollected the scene of her atop of his boss, slicing away at the man's chest with those rigid and horrid claws that were her nails. "That's her," he yelped over the thunder.

Catrina heard Lucien's accusation come from behind; however, it was like any other distant sound. She had practically tuned out everything around her save for the howling wind, the thunder, the rain that began to pellet all around her, and Lillian. Yes, Lillian! And why was she backing up from the sight of the creature? After all, this was what she'd prepared for; this was Catrina's battle. Most importantly, this confrontation was the crux of her convictions to stop the Nightworld. Isn't that what she'd told Aaron she would do? Isn't that was she'd convinced Lucien there was no other option but to do? Stop the Nightworld and save Stefan. Catrina halted in her steps. To her surprise, Lillian also came to a complete stop that left a ten-foot gap between the two of them.

"That's her!" Lucien announced once again. Except this time, he ran off into the bushes like a scared rabbit.

Lillian's eyes darted toward Lucien's escape. "Run, child," she roared. "Soon, there will be no place left to run."

From behind Catrina, Aaron made a low growling sound. And, although the sound of Aaron slowly morphing into a werewolf brought on a slight startle to Catrina, it was nothing compared to the disgusting creature before her.

Catrina Taylor closed her eyes, extended her hands to either side of her, and tilted back her head to pray. *God and Goddess, give me the strength is this time of battle.*

Lillian's insidious cackles permeated the night. "Pray to your false Gods, witch. It will do you no good. My god has been here since before the Earth realm was developed into existence. It is my god, God *Damia*, to whom you will fall to your knees and beg. Beg him to devour your soul, witch."

The succubus' words brought on the reality of how powerful the Nightworld truly was. Still, Catrina would not tremble from the demon's awful commands. Catrina's heart returned to its steady beating and the adrenaline that coursed through her veins had slowed. She suddenly felt empowered, emblazoned by vigor. Fall to her knees and beg? "The hell I will!" Catrina hollered to Lillian.

Lillian took a step toward Catrina. "Then it is I, witch, who will become your destroyer."

Catrina felt two hands from behind grab at her palms. It was Aaron. The course hairs she felt pricking at her palms signified that his body was transforming into a werewolf. Yes! Catrina had a plan and knew in her heart and soul that Aaron was on her same wavelength. Time, she needed more time for Aaron to fully morph.

"Aaron," Lillian announced, "I see you back there. You are one of God *Damia*'s children, but you have defied him, haven't you? He has plans for you, Aaron."

"Your god is a joke," Catrina yelled. "Your god knows nothing of love, only hatred. You can't even summon him to this place, can you? You can't call on him for strength, can you? He can't even step foot or have any type of presence here until the pact is initiated. That makes your god weak."

A hoarse moan emitted from Lillian as she took another step toward Catrina.

"Your god is nothing," Catrina continued.

The moan of the succubus was replaced by a snarl as Lillian took another step.

"Your god is shit!"

"Die, witch!" Lillian screeched as her steps gave way to a full charge toward Catrina.

Catrina felt Aaron's claws dig into her palms and a fierce howl made love to the thunder overhead. Aaron used Catrina's hands as a springboard and pushed off them as he launched into the air. Catrina ducked as the werewolf leapt over her, aiming its landing onto the succubus rushing toward her.

Before Aaron's came down upon his target, Lillian pushed her hands in front of her. "Wolf!" she screeched as she forced her hands towards the werewolf's descending leap upon her. Lillian's hands contained a powerful, invisible force. When she extended them toward her attacker, Aaron's soaring leap shifted directions, sending him flying the opposite way and into a desert garden of large sagebrush.

The werewolf howled as it tried freeing itself. However, Lillian forced her magic upon the bushes, willing the branches with her mind to wrap around each of Aaron's limbs. Although the werewolf clawed and howled in panic, the flexible branches continued to encompass his entire body. The branches made continuous loops around the werewolf's arms and legs, around its torso and neck, until the encircling branches consumed every bit of the werewolf's body. Aaron was rendered powerless.

As Catrina studied Lillian using her powerful magic to trap Aaron, she saw her only attempt to go in for the attack. Catrina rushed toward Lillian and, as she did so, made her right hand into a hard fist. She landed a heavy blow onto the succubus' right cheek. The creature barely flinched as Catrina saw the blood forming on her knuckles when she pulled her hand back.

Lillian pivoted toward her. The creature's tail slithered back and forth with charged anticipation. "Your time has come, witch." Lillian backhanded Catrina who immediately hit the ground from the forceful blow.

-2-

Stefan fluttered his eyes open to an eerie silence, a silence that somehow informs one that something is amiss. His head throbbed and he immediately brought his hand toward his forehead where he discovered a swollen lump at the hairline. What had happened? His mind instantaneously replied in hopeful answers. *It was all a dream! Yes, a dream. There is no dark world battling against you. Everybody is fine and you can go home now!* Home. Where was home? Stefan wrestled with his thoughts. He felt like the victim of a drunken blackout who forgets all he or she has done.

As Stefan stood to his feet, a wave of light-headedness rushed over him and he quickly sat upon the bed that lined the wall of the room. He surveyed his surroundings and took notice of the wooden debris that flooded the floor. As his eyes made their way to the open space where there was once a door, he had made the first of many recollections. The door had exploded open, he recalled. Yes, that's what happened. The floor had swelled beneath him and the walls had quaked. The wolves! Their howls were constant and louder with each passing minute. And Aaron—his screams—oh god, how Stefan recalled such cries of dread from a man infused with his ultimate fear!

"Aaron?" Stefan's voice echoed throughout the motel room. Stefan examined the room, expecting to find Aaron hiding in a corner. However, something wasn't right. The wolves had ceased their howling and the surroundings were still.

But it made since, didn't it? A pang went off in Stefan's stomach as he pieced together the events that had occurred while he had been knocked out by the blow to his head. The Nightworld had abducted Aaron; that's what had happened. After all, this time period was the past; this was the place in which Aaron had first been abducted and taken through the doorway. Stefan remembered telling Aaron that his reason for being here was to witness Aaron's abduction and Stefan couldn't have been more accurate with his logic. This is where it had happened—this run-down motel near Woodstock—a location in the heart of nowhere. But, that couldn't be it, could it? It couldn't be over.

Emptiness consumed Stefan's being. What was he to do now? This place; he was in this place and now he was alone. He didn't have to convince Aaron of the Nightworld or Aaron's future meeting in Spook Valley any longer because his past mind would now merge with his current self. There was a bit of mystery in thinking of such a thing. Was this deemed "parallel time" as Stefan had read in the occult book? What happens when there is such a drastic change in one time? How does it affect the other half of the person in the present? Do they become aware? Stefan took the time to ask himself the next question, not wanting his mind to formulate an answer to it. Would Aaron remember everything that happened once Stefan met up with him again? Would his mind be ignorant to it all—the long talks in this time, the shared laughter that was so brief, and the night of making love right here on this bed? What's more, how the hell was he going to get back to Spook Valley, to the present? Stefan refused to believe that he was trapped here, the silence his enemy and the endless questions creating a madness unmeasured.

"Stefan!" The voice reverberated from far away. "Stefan! Help me!"

Aaron! It was Aaron's voice! Stefan jumped to his feet and made a fleeting movement toward the broken doorway of the motel room. "Aaron," he hollered back. He scanned the emptiness of the motel parking lot. To the East was the vast and unfilled area where there was a concert and throng of fans only hours previous. Now it was all clear of any living soul. Were they ever even there?

"Stefan!" The voice was a distant peep in the night and emitted far from where Stefan stood.

Stefan's scan focused more fervently, determined to find Aaron, as he rushed out of the motel into the parking area that was nothing more than a vacant lot with a dirt foundation. The skies were covered with the slate gray of clouds, the same clouds that had produced the rains they had made love to earlier in the evening.

Stefan waited to hear the voice again, poised to shoot his gaze in the direction from whence it came. Soon enough, the cry for help impaled the silence of night. Stefan looked further to the East, over to where the grassy knolls were upon his arrival in this timespace. At first, when he had pinpointed Aaron, Stefan was perplexed and stood frozen.

Aaron appeared to be floating a few feet above the air, his prone body flying further toward the East. But, with further observation, Stefan saw the truth. It was the wolves! A pack of wolves were running side-by-side, carrying Aaron off toward the doorway from which Stefan had emerged. Stefan could only watch the horror as Aaron's naked body bounced up and down upon the wolves' backs and to the rhythm of their dreadful gait. Aaron screamed for Stefan again and this caused a tear to come to Stefan's eye. This was how it had to happen. This was Aaron's abduction as it had already been written in the annals of time and Stefan was powerless to rescue Aaron from his fate. Stefan could hear Aaron's diminished cries; he could veritably feel Aaron's horrific panic as to what was happening and why. It must have been so dreadful, this unknown evil of the Nightworld as it swept one away from their normal lives and plunged them into a world of chaos and darkness, a world where monsters roamed the heated land and every waking moment could only feel like an unending nightmare. This was true horror and no maniac in the world could compare to such apprehension.

The sheen glow of Aaron's naked body grew further away as Stefan gaped at the scene. Soon, the whimpers for aid were practically inaudible. Yet, Stefan could still view, in the distance, the bouncing of Aaron's body upon the backs of the wolves. Stefan wanted to turn away. He couldn't watch anymore. However, a shriek ignited the stillness of the night and Stefan grew more attentive to what was happening. He watched as the pack of wolves—their bodies black upon the gray night—launched into the air, propelling Aaron, skyward with them, into a deep cavern of death, a tomb of a twisted and chthonic nature. One by one, the wolves, along with Aaron, had disintegrated into the middle of the atmosphere. One by one, they were crossing into the doorway of the Nightworld. Their capture had crossed over the threshold with them.

The doorway! It was open! Of course! Suddenly, a sense of freedom exploded into Stefan's being. The doorway was open and he could return. But what happened if the doorway were to close before he got there? Stefan refused to entertain the idea and began to run from the parking lot of the motel. He came to a brisk halt when he realized he didn't have the scroll from the Nightworld. The scroll! Was it still in the motel room?

Stefan raced back toward the motel; all the while, his thoughts composed a lament for Aaron. *Aaron taken to the Nightworld.* What was it like to live in that place for four decades? The horrors he must have witnessed! And Stefan could imagine the awesome freedom that must have rushed over Aaron when he had crossed the threshold into the current time and arrived in Spook Valley. How did he escape the Nightworld? Unless…he was sent to Spook Valley to abduct Stefan and recapture Breckin. Yes, it made sense; everything was now making sense! But he must have retaliated against the Nightworld. Otherwise, he wouldn't have tried to save Stefan from crossing the threshold in the first place. Surely, Aaron must have realized what it was like to live in a normal world once again when he crossed over into Spook Valley. Yet, the normal world was just as chaotic as the Nightworld. There was no denying that. There were monsters everywhere, only they hid behind the façade of a human body.

Stefan burst into the motel room, eagerly searching for the scroll. His actions were brisk and feverish as he flipped over debris from the door and ripped the sheets off the bed. Where was it? He had searched almost everywhere when he found that the scroll was right on the nightstand where he'd originally left it. He grabbed the rolled parchment and immediately bolted out the open doorway of the motel room.

As instantly as he had hit the dirt of the parking lot, a thunderous rumble shattered the silence of the world that encompassed Stefan. The roaring emitted from the West and Stefan turned to face the resonance that grew uninterrupted. The gray skies cracked in zigzag fashion and then began ripping away; tearing as if the sky had seams. Chunks of the atmosphere were falling off into an unknown oblivion, leaving only the black space of nothingness. The landscape far to the West fell apart as if breaking away from its foundation and being consumed by emptiness. As each part of the atmosphere fell away, it left nothing more that a darkness unmatched by any other. It was as if this entire world was being erased, and Stefan's eyes bulged at the foundation in the distance as it broke away, creating an undertow of undoing.

"Oh my God," he uttered, frozen with disbelief.

-3-

Aaron was suffocating.

He attempted to wriggle his arms and legs, but the unyielding branches tightly constricted his body. Aaron was practically paralyzed and movement was virtually impossible. Still, he had to breathe. The rough texture of sagebrush that conformed around his head covering his nostrils and mouth, kept him from taking in breath.

Aaron maneuvered his lips up and down, just enough to make a space for his jagged teeth to bite at the branches. The taste of the thin twigs was sweet and dry, and he continued to chew through the tough texture of the plant. A few pieces of the branches had filled Aaron's mouth; he tried hard not to swallow them for fear of getting them lodged in his throat.

Within minutes, Aaron had formed a small hole, just tiny enough so that he could breathe. He could taste the rainwater on his tongue that dripped in through the opening that was made. But he couldn't stop there, no. He had to free himself and help Catrina. Poor Catrina, out there with Lillian. Lillian was a powerful force and Aaron couldn't deny this. Her power held him captive, mummified in sagebrush. Aaron prayed that Catrina would overcome the demon.

He could hear the hollow sounds of their battle twenty feet away.

Catrina's cheek was flaring and she could feel her blood rushing into her face as the welt began to swell. She told herself not to focus on it. She reminded herself that there was a battle at hand, one that she intended to win.

Pulling herself to her feet, Catrina spotted Lillian behind her. She faced the demon, repulsed by the slimy shell of its body. And when Lillian spoke, Catrina cringed from the sight of the jagged teeth that jutted in all directions within the demon's mouth.

"You are no match for me, witch!" Lillian brought back her open hand. Her sharp brownish black claws were prepared to dig into Catrina's flesh.

As the demon powerfully swung its hand toward Catrina, claws targeting Catrina's neck, Catrina ducked and watched as the demon swung its body around full circle. Catrina rushed the demon, steadily holding her hands out in front of her, and used every ounce of strength to push at the demon's stomach.

Lillian went flying and landed flat on her back. The shrieking roar that emitted from the demon created gooseflesh all over Catrina's body. She had to stop this horrible creature; she knew that this battle would be to the death and she wasn't ready to give up. *No, I have to save Stefan; I have to see him again. I have to stop the Nightworld! I will not give up!*

The only way Catrina knew how to stop Lillian, or to kill any demon for that matter, was to dismember her. That is why she had brought the sword. *Ace of Swords.* Catrina glanced over to where the claymore remained embedded in the dead Officer Colburn's chest. If only to get to that sword! If only to use it to kill Lillian. But Catrina came to the dreaded realization that she didn't have enough time to run to the policeman's body, extract the sword, and use it before Lillian would be at her back. Still, she had to find a way!

Catrina observed Lillian getting up from the ground. The look on the demon's face was gruesome—thick drool dripped from the creature's mouth and its obsidian eyes tore through Catrina's and into her gray matter.

"I tire of these games," Lillian warned. "Be gone with you, witch!"

Catrina witnessed Lillian positioning her hands in front of her, and when the demon opened its mouth, Catrina gasped at the flames that had launched from within. As the flames rippled like a flowing stream from Lillian's mouth, Catrina stood awestruck and frightened for her life. She had underestimated Lillian altogether. Lillian, demon of the Nightworld; Lillian, a powerful creature with the temptation of a succubus and the powers of a wizard.

The stream of fire made its way into the atmosphere, heading straight for Catrina. The falling rain sizzled as it grazed the fire. Catrina took in a deep breath, reaching further into herself that she ever had before, going beyond the inner self and into a region where gods and goddesses filled her with their strength and love. *Powers That Be*, she called in her mind, *reach into me your powers so that I may defeat this evil.* As Catrina re-opened her eyes, she witnessed the flames of the approaching fire billowing towards her and heard that god-awful shriek from Lillian.

Catrina exhaled all of her breath to the point where her body felt empty of oxygen and her head felt light. As she did this, Catrina watched in amazement as a torrent of brilliant blue ice spilled outward from her own mouth. The ice and fire collided right in front of Catrina, and the clashing of the elements created a large body of water that was airborne for but a couple of seconds before splashing to the dirt.

Lillian was instantly aghast by the witch's newfound power.

The fear that had once consumed Catrina was eclipsed by an assuredness she had never felt. "I want Stefan back," Catrina demanded to the demon.

Yet, Lillian wouldn't budge. Nor would she belittle herself to such bargaining from one who resided in the Earth realm. "If you want him, go and get him." Lillian gave a fleeting nod of her head, a nod that came with an invisible power of controlling physical matter.

Catrina felt herself being lifted off the ground and was thrown toward the doorway of the Nightworld. She gawked at the monolithic entrance. The immense black opening could have easily devoured her whole. The incessant whirring of the doorway infiltrated Catrina's surrounding world. Suddenly, there came a force which begun to drag her toward the doorway. It was as if the Nightworld was sucking her into its clutches, into its appetite of chaos. Catrina clawed at the ground, the muddy dirt of the desert floor rolling beneath her fingernails. Glancing up at her adversary, Catrina studied Lillian as she screeched a sound that could only be that of victory into the rushing winds that enveloped their surroundings.

Catrina maneuvered her hand so that it faced Lillian. As she felt the power of the doorway on the brink of swallowing her body, Catrina focused all of her will into the brisk movement of her hand. Just as Lillian had directed Catrina with a wave of her hand, Catrina had done the same, catapulting Lillian toward Catrina's body where Catrina grasped onto the creature's leg.

Lillian hit the floor of the Earth as Catrina held onto her leg in an attempt to keep the Nightworld from consuming her body. Lillian kicked her foot wildly, trying to escape Catrina's grip. A white flash shot through Catrina's vision as the demon's foot made instant contact with her face. It didn't matter though. If Catrina was to be taken into the doorway, she was making sure that Lillian went with her.

Catrina's feet were on the edge of the doorway, just inches from entering the portal that she knew could only take her to the darkest place she had ever imagined. No, she wasn't going in there!

The rain began to pellet and the stinging drops were like pinpricks to Catrina's face. She held on to Lillian's leg with all her might, knowing that if she let go she would be wisped away into the doorway. Without warning, a searing pain ignited her hand. Lillian was scratching at it with her hideous nails. The pain! How she remembered that particular agony all over her back during the last confrontation with this demon. Her hand began to feel numb. The contagion of the demon's acidic scratches flared her wrist and crawled up to Catrina's forearm. *Bitch!* Catrina scorned in her mind.

Strength. Yes, she needed strength. Catrina called on it from within herself. Within only a few seconds, as she willed her mind to conjure all of her strength, physically and mentally, the world around Catrina Taylor went mute. The heavy raindrops were silent as they hit the ground, the buzzing of the doorway directly behind her had immediately ceased, and the inhuman growls of the kicking demon to which she clung were unable to be heard. Catrina shot a glance over to the sword that seemed to give off a shimmer, though the sky was composed of an overcast gloom. *If only to get it.* But she couldn't force her mind to extract it from the officer's flesh.

Instead, she reached up with her other hand and grab Lillian's free leg. Although the pain in her wounded hand continued to burn, she gripped onto the demon tightly, digging her nails into the hard exterior of Lillian's flesh. Lillian had kicked with both legs. However, Catrina clung to her like an incurable disease. Gradually, she grabbed with each hand as she climbed on top of the demon. With each grab of the demon, Catrina deeply dug her nails into its flesh. Soon, Catrina was grabbing onto either one of Lillian's shoulders and was positioned directly over the demon's body that continued to buck beneath her in attempt to throw her off. Face to face with the creature, holding onto it for dear life, and, if they were lovers, this is how they would have kissed.

Catrina gazed into the obsidian that clouded Lillian's eyes. Now, to push herself off. But now it was Lillian who refused to let Catrina go. Lillian's full mouth of teeth snapped at Catrina who buried her face into the demon's chest to avoid the deadly bite. Catrina couldn't contain the demon's flailing arms any longer and, as they broke free of the weight of Catrina's body holding them down, Lillian's nails scratched down the length of Catrina's back. Catrina screamed into the winds that howled around the two. The agony of the creature's scratch had sliced open the scar tissue made previously by the creature. Another scratch—another long and deep penetration of her flesh—

from the demon's claws. It burned! Catrina's flesh sizzled as the awful agony swathed her entire body. *Oh the pain! Oh god, let this be over*! But Catrina was reluctant to give up.

Catrina used her hands to push the demon's jaw upward. Then, with all her vigor, she burrowed her mouth into the space between Lillian's shoulder and neck. Catrina opened her mouth wide and clamped down on the demon's flesh. She bit into its jugular, clenching her teeth together as hard as she could like a venomous snake. Catrina could taste the rough meat of the demon's flesh as the creature's body below her wildly bucked.

The creature's feral convulsions sent Catrina bouncing up and down upon her adversary. To the right and toward the left, but still, Catrina would not let up her bite. A slimy substance that was the demon's blood was cold against Catrina's lips. Another scratch upon her back, and Catrina bit as hard as she could, feeling the tough exterior of the demon skin tear beneath the force of her teeth. Lillian shrieked and a powerful force threw Catrina soaring into the air some ten feet away from the wounded demon. As she hit the desert earth, Catrina quickly clambered to her feet.

Lillian stood up as well, gauging Catrina with fierce eyes that pierced through Catrina's being. It roared; the demon roared with ferocity unmeasured by any other creature of the *Nightworld*, save for *Damia* himself.

Making a sideways glance to the corpse of Officer Colburn, Catrina measured Lillian's next move. But her peeking gesture at the claymore buried within the officer had been noticed by Lillian, and now there was no use in keeping it a secret that Catrina had every intention to sprint for the sword in a last ditch effort to expel Lillian from the Earth realm.

Catrina bolted toward the dead officer's body and, just as quickly as she made her dash, Lillian leaped into the air and landed on Catrina's back, causing them both to hit the moist dirt once again. However, now it was Lillian atop of Catrina. And the demon had no remorse for this human; there was no conscience left in the creature that was hellbent on destroying one of the only people that could come between the pact of the Nightworld taking over the Earth realm.

Lillian grabbed a handful of Catrina's wet, auburn locks and pushed her face into the dirt. Again, she pulled at Catrina's hair and forcefully bounced Catrina head off the floor of the desert.

Catrina yelped from the demon's pulling of her hair. Her shouts were instantly muted as her face continuously hit the earth. The gritty, bland dirt filled her mouth with a vile and dry taste. Catrina reared her hips so that she may throw the demon off; however, Lillian had Catrina pinned. The creature's knees held down Catrina's forearms in the same fashion that Catrina had used earlier on the demon. She bucked again, in between each breath shared with the agony of her hair being ripped at the roots.

"Die witch," Lillian screamed over the howling winds.

The winds. So violent now. The winds whipped the plants all around them, pushing the sagebrush and century plants into an awkward bend that

Catrina witnessed each and every time that Lillian pulled her head back. Another time, her face into the dirt. And yet another. Catrina's mouth swelled. She could feel the sharp pain of her teeth cutting into the backside of her lips. Gusts of wind brought heavy dirt into her eyes. A puddle of water and blood was forming beneath Catrina's head. Still, she kept rearing up her back and her hips.

Catrina's energy was depleting fast.

She called to the God and Goddess, attempted contact to that inner self that she had only just discovered, but it was to no avail. Her head continued to meet with the dirt. And the pain, oh god, the pain! Surely, her nose was crushed; numbness consumed it. Surely, the pebbles of the desert floor would leave lasting contusions and scars. Everything was going blurry. *No! Keep fighting.* But then it all seemed lost when she felt the searing slices of Lillian's dreaded nails as they tore at her back. *No, not that pain again!*

Blurry...

Pain...

I'm dying, she thought.

-4-

What was happening? Stefan remained astonished at the sight before him. The sky was tearing. It was being sucked into some terrifying darkness. And the foundation! The land itself was being swallowed by that same enigmatic darksome. What would warrant such disaster, such a maddening phantasm of nature? Where was it all going? Into nothing. The entire world was going back into the nothingness from whence it had emerged. It was the unmaking of a world; birth of the Earth in reverse. And Stefan bore witness to it.

That was it wasn't it? There was no more need for this time. Aaron had left and this place was no more real than that of a historic house and all its ghosts. Yes, Stefan assured himself, this was the unmaking of this world. What was had already occurred. What was left? Simply nothing. The existence of this world that must have rung in the year 1969 a hundred times over in the furthest dimensional outreach of the Nightworld, had now been "played out." There was nothing left for this place and now it would be consumed into the mysterious equations of time and space.

So wonderful! Stefan was mesmerized by the marvel. So destructive and, at the same time, so beautiful. It was in the way the sky tore open and disintegrated into a black nothingness. It showed in the landscape and how it broke away from the whole, propelling into the blackness. Away with the trees being sucked into the darkness. So powerful! Away with the dirt roads as they shifted upwards and tore from the Earth, leaving gaps that one could fall into on a journey through an endless descent. Endless. Time stopped moving out there in those outer limits of the Earth; time no longer existed and neither did anything once material. Material—whether it be land, buildings, or even…human. It made no difference to this unnatural event, this hungry Nothing.

It was at that point that the apprehensive reality struck Stefan. This entire place was being consumed, bit-by-bit and fragment-by-fragment. The road leading to the motel was being erased, eclipsed by pitch black and smothered by timelessness. The doorway! Yes, he must run to the doorway! That was the only escape; that was his only refuge from becoming victim to this unbecoming world.

Stefan's body convulsed from another thought. *What if the doorway closed? What if you are stuck here with no escape and you will be wisped away with the rest of this? What if you fall endlessly into that same nothingness that is devouring the land?*

Refusing to give into any other thought, Stefan made a break for the knolls in the East. His heart wildly thudded in his chest as he looked behind him and saw the hungry Nothing eating everything in its path. His attention went forward again as he plodded up the hills of grass that would soon be nothing. Shortness of breath. But he must continue; he must tread the knoll and escape that chaotic force with the insatiable appetite for everything that came within its path.

Stefan peered behind him once again. The hungry Nothing moved faster, with quicksilver speed, as if it had smelled the human meat that ran away from it. The emptiness was taking away the base of the hill, devouring it like some ardent creature out for its prey. When Stefan turned his attention in front of himself once again, he could see the ruby outline of the doorway. A sensation of relief infused his heart and fueled his drive. His eager feet got the best of him as Stefan lost balance and fell to the grass. The wind was instantly knocked out of him as he gasped for deep breaths. He flipped himself to his back, scurrying up the small hill where the portal to the Nightworld awaited his re-entry. Stefan pushed with his feet and grasped at the sod behind him as he witnessed the blackness coming for him. Nothing was beyond the knoll. The sky had been torn and shredded, the landscape eaten away. The motel was no longer in sight; it had gone into that great black hole of neverwhere.

As he grabbed for the next patch of earth, the scroll had slipped from his hand and began to roll downhill. The darkness of the hungry Nothing crawled up the slope of the knoll, shifting the sod and taking away everything around it with a violent flowing motion. Stefan quickly reached down to grab the scroll, before it was out of sight. He crawled to his feet and feverishly raced toward the visible doorway.

Stefan gave once last fleeting look at the collapsing knoll, one final glance at what was becoming nothing more than empty black space.

The portal was before him and Stefan halted. What awaited him on the other side? He panicked from the fear of not knowing. However, the roaring of the emptiness consuming this world left him no other option. He couldn't look back now, for he feared the darkness was within arms reach. If he hesitated one more moment, he would become feast to the empty black space that had taken everything in this place in the course of a few minutes.

Now! Jump in now!

The echo of the roar dissipated as he leaped into the doorway. The undoing of his molecules couldn't have felt any better as Stefan transcended dimensions for, yet, a third time.

-5-

Lucien stopped running. He couldn't leave Aaron and Catrina back there with that horrible monster. After all, Catrina had vowed to keep *him* safe. And what if everything they had discussed was true? What if this world would become a playground for chaos and monsters? He had to go back. Not to mention, Catrina had said that Stefan was returning. Lucien had to see Stefan. Oh, how he longed to see that man again!

Lucien redirected himself and went back to the clearing where that terrifying creature had emerged from the black doorway. The driving rains and the rushing winds caused him to squint as he maneuvered through the desert. His trail led him around cacti and sagebrush. It was a frustrating and long obstacle course of the desert, and it would ultimately take him back to Catrina, Aaron, and that creature.

It had seemed like minutes that Lucien ran; each second had gone slowly as he tread through the muddy desert. All the while, Lucien had told himself, *this wasn't happening*. But the sheer reality reared its ugly head when Lucien came around the corner of a large saguaro cactus to witness that terrifying creature attacking Catrina.

God, no, his mental scream brought the adrenaline in his body to fleeting speed. Lucien heard Catrina's own cries. Her cries—so innocent, yet horrific. Catrina's cries projected the pain she was feeling into Lucien's body. Sympathy pains accosted him; his back seared from gawking at the demon scraping upon Catrina's flesh.

He had to do something! Where was Aaron? It didn't mater how scared Lucien was, for his body shot immediately into action. He ran to the dead officer whose prone corpse was stuck into the ground by the large sword buried within his chest. *The sword, yes! That was it! The beast could be stopped by being dismembered,* Lucien recalled Aaron's haunting revelation. At the time, it had sounded utterly preposterous. But now, in the face of terror, Lucien was willing to try anything to keep that creature from killing the only person willing to help him.

Although the hilt was wet and slippery, Lucien used a double grip, grabbing the gold-colored handle with both hands. He pulled with all his might, while gazing back at the scuffle behind him. The sword wouldn't budge. Lucien pulled harder, pushing his entire weight against his hands in an upward motion.

First, a tearing sound…and then, there was gurgling from the wound that pooled with blood as the sword was extracted from the officer's corpse. Now, Lucien held the claymore with both hands. He felt powerful holding such a weapon and visions of *Excalibur* came to mind.

Now that he wielded the large weapon, he made a run toward the creature atop of Catrina. Catrina was still flailing her arms and legs in attempt to escape the demon's evil grip. Thunder crashed overhead as Lucien brought the sword back and made one sweeping movement that landed the blade into the demon's side.

The creature's yelp was high-pitched and louder than the thunders in the heavens above. It threw up its arms and stood to its feet, turning to face Lucien who had taken a few steps back. The demon roared in obvious pain and, before Lucien could bring the heavy sword back to strike the creature once again, Lillian had backhanded him so hard that there was a loud popping sound that cracked into the evening.

Lucien went soaring some fifteen feet away from the demon, hollering as he did so, and landing against a large cactus. He winced in agony as his entire back was pricked by hundreds of needles all at once. His entire backside went numb from the multiple pinprick sensation and he slumped to desert floor.

Catrina had seen it all—Lillian approaching Lucien, Lucien trying to swing the sword, and a fantastic blow against Lucien's face. The sword. It had fallen to Lucien's feet before he was launched into the cactus. And Lillian. Lillian was beyond the claymore and approaching Lucien who writhed on the ground in pain.

This was the diversion Catrina needed.

She got on her knees, cringing from the sharp flaring of her flesh. Catrina crawled toward the sword, watching each one of Lillian's steps toward Lucien. When Catrina reached the long blade, she used it to pull herself from off the ground and then weighed the sword in her hands.

This was it. This would be the end.

With every bit of verve left in Catrina, she ran with the sword toward Lillian. Catrina sliced the wind and rain with the pulling back of the weapon. She cried out as loud as she could, her voice in control of every element around her as she brought the sword around to a full swing and buried the blade into Lillian's neck. Lillian's head disconnected from her body and somersaulted into the air. A thick stream of black slime bubbled and burst from the demon's neck, shooting high into the air like a geyser of carnage and gore.

The demon wasn't silenced by the decapitation. In fact, it bellowed a shrilling siren song that acted as its lament. As it did this, Catrina brought the sword high over her head and slammed the blade against the right arm of the creature's headless copse. The sharp edge separated the arm from the demon's shoulder. Strewn pieces of rotted flesh swayed in the heavy winds. Still, Catrina was far from done. She pulled her wet hair back behind her shoulders as she took another swing at the creature's leg. And then the other leg and the other arm. Over and over again, bringing the blade down hard upon Lillian's body until all that was left was a gruesome jigsaw puzzle of body parts. The tail was still attached to the torso and it slithered in the bloody mud beneath it. "DIE, DAMN YOU!" Catrina yelled as she made one final blow with the claymore, dividing the torso into two.

Screams! The essence of the beast emitted terrifying and haunting screams that mimicked a resonance like that of a hundred babies squealing all the air from their tiny lungs. Catrina fell to the ground, still keeping a tight grip on her weapon as she studied the phenomena of Lillian's dying body. The pieces of the dismembered corpse were peeling at a fast rate, flaking off into the wind as they fast-forwarded into a rapid state of disintegration. Soon, just as all of the screams of the demon died out, the body parts twisted and turned as they broke apart and wisped themselves away into black ash. The ash collected itself in the form of a mid-air stream, gliding in snakelike fashion through the pouring rains and back into the doorway of the Nightworld.

Catrina had defeated Lillian. The battle was over and, at the same time, it had only just begun.

Catrina Taylor rolled to her side and began crying in victory as the rain cleansed her wounds.

PART III

The Pact

"An event has happened, upon which it is difficult to speak, and impossible to be silent."—Edmund Burke

CHAPTER XXIV

-1-

The Nightworld quaked. It was as if some modern weapon of massive destruction had struck the foundation of the dark underworld in an attempt to bring it crumbling down. Boulders broke free from their petrified surfaces, pummeling the orange dirt of the netherworld. Lava sloshed over the banks of the fiery rivers, sizzling as it disintegrated the loam surrounding the boiling rushes of magma. The monsters that resided in the ominous setting scurried and sought refuge in dark crevices as the tremors came, at first, one by one, and then, all at once. A fear unfathomed induced all of their souls; for the creatures of the Nightworld knew that the cataclysm shaking the environment was far from natural. It was *Damia.* Their god was infused with rage.

Damia arched his back and outstretched his arms. The ferocious bellow that raced past his lips was like that of a hundred snarling panthers in the midst of attacking their prey. *Damia* slammed his fists on either side of his cavelike sanctuary. The resonance of the booming thuds bounced off the foundations of the Nightworld and could be heard all across the shadowy land. As the echo of his roar diminished, he followed it up with yet another snarl that infiltrated his surroundings. So much rage in his animalistic holler; so much hatred for the witch named Catrina Taylor; and so much contempt for Lillian, who had failed in protecting the Nightworld from those who could find a way to stop the Pact. Yes, Lillian, demon of the Nightworld and evil temptress of the Earth realm. Lillian, the creature that vowed she would stop at nothing to keep the witch and the others from interfering. She gave her promise to him! Lillian pledged that she would stop them and one shouldn't make such convictions to his or her god if they can't be carried out. No, one should never dedicate his or her life to destruction and chaos, and then fall weak in the name of his or her god. Lillian had failed *Damia*; she had broken her word given to her god. But *Damia* refused to let this failure go unnoticed.

Lillian's body had been broken in the Earth realm, disintegrated into nothing save for wisps of black ash that acted as a transport for her soul. After all, her soul had always belonged to the Nightworld; her black ashes could never deny that. *Damia* was mentally linked to practically every creature of the land he ruled and Lillian was no exception. *Damia* was aware that she would hear and see his every action as he sentenced her soul to everlasting damnation.

The cylindrical form created by Lillian's whirling ashes slithered over the great lake of fire outside of *Damia*'s domain and came to a halt mid-air, near the vortex of the spewing ocean of flames. *Damia* glared at the spectacle, if only for a moment. No, there was no pity for this one either. She had betrayed him surely as she'd betrayed her world and all she stood for. *You have failed me*, his mind roared, addressing the side-winding ash. *Damia* was deaf to the begging

pleas that were the mental response of Lillian's soul. No sympathy for this wicked creature, no. "I damn you into the Hellfire evermore!"
With that, the ash spun into a downward spiral and plummeted into the fire-breathing center of the ocean of flames. The black residue of Lillian's remains sparked upon entry. A sharp and haunting shrill impregnated the Nightworld. It was the last breath of one who would be known to the future children of the Nightworld as nothing but legend. And *Damia*'s actions as a result of her failure would be told like a ghost story around the fires that breathed within the Nightworld. Let this be their lesson, all of them. Let them be aware to the fact that even the most vicious of creatures that resided in the Nightworld were not immune to his unearthly and terribly strong power.

"May your tortured soul incessantly sear, demon child."

Soon after he administered Lillian's punishment, a sensation inched throughout *Damia*'s body. One of the doorways had been activated. Stefan was coming through. An insidious smile etched his monstrous face.

-2-

As Stefan Powell's molecules collapsed and began rebuilding his body's chemical makeup, his immediate thoughts gave way to exasperation. Free of that place, yes! Away from the nightmare come real of being in a foreign place, and during a different era of time; away from the hungry Nothing that almost swallowed him as it took the world into its dark embrace; and away from Aaron. *Aaron.*

Thoughts made fleeting passes though Stefan's becoming mind. They were the kind of flashing thoughts that, in a normal world—a world without chaos and monsters—one may easily take for granted. The flesh of his arms began to reform in front of his eyes. His body was gluing itself together again, piece-by-piece and hair-by-hair. A giddy feeling caused his stomach to turn somersaults. *One step closer to home*, he reflected. He needed only to make a break for the doorway to the left of this one as he re-entered the Nightworld. There was no need in seeking out the Order of Perennial Darkness and trying to discover secrets that would allow him to stop the Pact's initiation. After all, he had one of their scrolls. *The scroll.* The yellow piece of parchment had formed in his hand before he had a chance to give a cautious thought of its whereabouts.

Yes, back through the other doorway. *And, then home.* Back to Spook Valley. To Catrina and Aaron. Oh, how he missed Catrina; how he longed to hold her tightly in his arms and vow to always protect her from this terrible place. And Aaron...would Aaron remember their night at Woodstock? Would he recall the brief passion they'd spent together? Stefan had to see Aaron. He had to have the chance to love a man again. And it was Aaron he loved. Sure, he still harbored feelings for Breckin—passionate feelings that he would always carry in his heart for the young man. However, after discovering Aaron's concealed werewolf identity, Stefan felt he knew Aaron much better now. Many things were beginning to make sense. The way they always do in the midst of danger and at the brink of terror.

Stefan's body was becoming whole. He wiggled his toes against the soles of his shoes. Whole again...and he would cross into the Nightworld any minute. He reminded himself, setting his plan of escape into action, that he would immediately jump through the doorway to the left of the one from which he would emerge. To the left—an exit from the Nightworld and an entrance to Spook Valley. Stefan's heart fluttered at the thought of what unknown presence may be standing on the other side of the doorway. Why did none of the Order ever come after him? His curious mind wouldn't allow a moment entertain the idea any further.

The buzzing was everywhere around him. The atmosphere made a whirring song like that of a thousand cicadas brushing their wings together. The darkness around Stefan lightened to a midnight blue, then to a slate gray. *Almost there.* Soon, he felt the warmth of an alien foundation seep through his shoes. He had made it.

Stefan emerged from the doorway that led him into the Nightworld. At first, he stood gazing at the shimmering orange and red dirt beneath his feet. But as he looked up at this hauntingly familiar place, he discovered that the Order awaited his arrival.

All six of the Order circled Stefan, closing in on him so that he had nowhere to run. One of the hooded figures attempted to snatch at the scroll in Stefan's hand, but Stefan's reaction was quick and he shoved it down the front of his shirt. A hand from his left side grabbed at his shoulder. Another hand grabbed at his arm from the right.

"Sssssssso glad you could join us again," Saint Batiste spoke into Stefan's ear.

"Yes, we've been waiting for you," Saint Collin snarled.

One of the cloaked figures before him began to approach. He bent slightly on his knees to reach Stefan's height. Stefan could veritably see the empty darkness for eyes that remained concealed behind the hood. "And we've waited long enough," Saint Dante added. "You've lost already, foolish man. There's no use in fighting."

"Then let me the hell go," Stefan demanded through clenched teeth.

"Oh, we will. We don't want you, Stefan. At least, not yet. It is true; you are the sacrifice that will merge our worlds. However, all will come together in due time. You have something that is ours."

Stefan's jaw fell slack. He had heard it from the voice of the member of the Order. It was true! He, Stefan Powell, was the sacrifice for the worlds to merge. Sure, he had always been fretful of such, had somewhat entertained the idea. But now, it was set in stone. "The scroll," Stefan mumbled.

"Yes, give it to us," Saint Cassius yelled from behind the others.

"Yes, Stefan, give us the scroll and we will allow you to live until your time comes."

"The fuck I will!" Stefan began resisting the hold of the Order members on either side of him. He jumped up, moving about like a lunatic trying to shake the cloaked men off him. One arm broke free and, soon, the other followed suit. Stefan searched for the doorway that would lead him home and bolted toward it. He felt for the parchment in his shirt, making sure it still rested against the flesh of his stomach. As he made a hesitant attempt to leap into the doorway, a hand grabbed at his ankle and sent him flying face first to the ground. He flipped onto his back and began kicking. Before long, the other five of the six member of the Order were upon him, trying to extract the scroll from Stefan's possession.

In a matter of seconds, as the Order of Perennial Darkness viciously fought to take the scroll from him, Stefan was smothered by all of their fabric and concealed rot.

-3-

Any glow that remained in the evening hours, as the sun descended into the western skies, was eclipsed by the billowing purple and black clouds that held strong over Spook Valley. The pouring rains gave way to a sprinkle that, in turn, created a mist that fell over the town. Still, the thunder roared in the heavens above and the skies wept for the wounded.

The pain infusing Catrina was almost unbearable, though the rains had refreshed her flesh and cooled the burning sensation that crawled all over her skin as a result of Lillian's fierce scratches. Lillian, demonic creature from the Nightworld; she was now gone. Yes, she was truly gone! Catrina had won. There was a sense of relief in her knowing this. Yet, Catrina was well aware that the battle was not over. Through the pain within her and the fatigue of the battle she'd just fought, she couldn't help but charge her ego with the thoughts of triumph.

It had all happened so quickly—each blow, powered by minutes condensed into seconds. In the end though, Lucien had given her the opportunity to slay the demon while attempting to slaughter Lillian himself. He, in a sense, had rescued her from the demon's deadly grip.

The cool sensation of a raindrop rushed down her cheek and along Catrina's neck.
She hadn't remembered seeing Lucien. The last thing she recalled concerning the young man's presence was that he bolted from the entire scene. But then, from out of nowhere, Lucien showed himself, courageous as ever, and came at Lillian with the claymore.

Catrina had underestimated him. Then again, she couldn't put it past Lucien. After all, he *was* a killer. Still, she couldn't thank him enough. As she fluttered her eyes open, not wincing from the agony that was either subsiding or beginning to go numb, she had the chance to.

Lucien called her name, a wounded tremor in his voice. "Catrina? Catrina, please be alive."

His tearful plea caused her to lift her head and reach out her arm towards his standing body that loomed over her. "Lu—cien," Catrina hoarsely spoke the name. "Thank you."

"Oh god! Catrina, you're OK!"

She flipped onto her back and pulled up her knees. "No. I feel like I got the shit kicked out of me," she laughed and immediately flinched from the pain of the chuckle that placed pressure on her chest.

Lucien knelt to her side. "You're going to be all right, Catrina," he reassured her. "I'll make sure of it."

She managed a smile. Funny how one could feel a shred of happiness in the face of horror. Catrina reached her hands out toward Lucien so that he could stand her up. "Aaron," she said. "Is he all right?"

Lucien pulled Catrina to her feet in one swift movement and they immediately turned toward the sagebrush that had ensnared Aaron by Lillian's will of mind.

The branches moved about, left and right, as Aaron squirmed free of their hold. Catrina and Lucien rushed toward Aaron and began breaking off the tough branches of the sagebrush. Aaron didn't appear to be wounded, save for the scratches upon his face as a result of the branches that he'd been entangled within.

Aaron gasped for air as he rose from the ground, still trying to untangle his feet from the desert plant. His eyes shot back toward the doorway of the Nightworld and around the perimeter. "Is she dead?" he hurriedly asked. "Did you destroy her?"

"*We* destroyed her," Catrina replied as she smiled over to Lucien and leaned against him to maintain her balance.

Aaron was somewhat shocked by Catrina's claim. Not so much that Lillian had been defeated as much as the fact that Lucien had assisted in the matter. Reaching out his hand toward Lucien, Aaron said, "Thanks for sticking around."

Lucien, feeling more honored than he'd ever felt in his entire life, blushed at Aaron's kind and warm gesture. "But what do we do now? Where do we go from here?"

Catrina immediately answered. "It's not over yet. We have to get Stefan out of that place."

Suddenly, Aaron's mind whirred with excitement. Stefan, yes! He had an immediate urgency to see Stefan again. He felt so much closer to him. Ever since…no, that was just a strange feeling during an act of survival. Still, it was something that made him feel more different than before Lillian trapped him in the sagebrush. Something happened while he was subdued. A strange sensation had rushed over his body, coursed thought his being. Aaron was certain it had something to do with Stefan and…

…"The wolves."

"What?" Catrina was befuddled by Aaron's words that came from out of nowhere.

"The wolves. I don't hear them anymore."

Lucien cocked his head in bewilderment and looked at Catrina who'd felt she missed the last five minutes of a conversation she hadn't been attentive to.

Aaron began to clarify the confusion. "Before Lillian came out of the Nightworld, I heard wolves, remember? I don't hear them anymore. Catrina, something happened when I was trapped in all those branches, something strange."

"What?" she asked, eyes fixed on Aaron.

"I'm not sure, but there was this feeling I got…a feeling of wholeness or oneness. It's rather hard to explain. It felt as if my past had been completely clear to me. What was even stranger is that I got a good sense that I had spent time with Stefan in my past."

"How could that be?" Lucien jumped into the riddled conversation.

"I don't know, but I think it has something to do with all the times in the previous days I was hearing various sounds that you two weren't."

"The music," Catrina piped in. "That song. Remember, Aaron? Remember what I told you about Stefan somehow being trapped in your past?"

Aaron nodded, remembering the whole conversation. At the time though, he had thought Catrina was grasping for straws, seeking out some way of connecting everything together in the midst of anticipation. But now, he was beginning to believe. Aaron had seen some amazing things in his existence. It wouldn't be that far-fetched to give credence to Catrina's theory.

"You said the howling of the wolves had ceased and you felt a 'oneness' with yourself. I think that your past self and your present have merged. And that can only mean that Stefan is no longer trapped in you past. I think he's coming home."

With that, the trio turned to face the doorway. Always that doorway, the one that brought nightmares to their daytime realities. The doorway—monolithic in size, a portal to transcend worlds, the edge of its borders pulsing in ruby red, and the means for anything to come into the Earth realm, whether it be Stefan or some dreaded creature.

Their hands were tied now. There were no answers, no direction as to what action to take next. Either one of them could cross the threshold or wait. They chose the latter as the skies thundered above and a flash of lightning illuminated their world.

-4-

Stefan wrestled on the ground of the Nightworld with the Order of Perennial Darkness. Although the hooded creatures were the chosen ones to carry out the initiation of the Pact, they weren't as strong as Stefan surmised. If anything, they were weak, like old men. They were more like watchers than fighters; they were the keys to the Nightworld. Still, had there not been so many of them, all clawing and trying to keep Stefan subdued so that they could grab the one scroll that could merge their world with his, Stefan would have been able to easily escape.

Stefan kicked at them and began to throw punches. However, as one would be thrown off him, another would take that one's place. Each of the members of the Order snarled as they battled with Stefan. Their fetid breath and pungent smell of decay had practically asphyxiated him. Two of the Order grabbed for Stefan's shirt in attempt to extract the parchment from beneath it. Stefan pushed at them both, turning over onto his stomach. However, that kept him from being able to fight them off. In an instant, all six of them were upon him—at his legs, grabbing for his arms, and at his hair.

Looking forward, Stefan saw the doorway back to his world, back to Spook Valley. With as much strength as he could channel, he made a weak crawl toward the doorway. He couldn't allow them to have the scroll, no! To do that, would surely put the control of initiating the Pact back into the Nightworld's hands. If only to get to that doorway that was a mere five feet away! Stefan used his entire body, the six creatures upon his back trying to reach under to his front side. When his hands were grabbed at by one of the Order, he nudged his body forward, making every effort to reach the doorway. It was no use. There was no way he could cross the threshold with all the Order members upon him like this.

Stefan allowed them to flip him over. With every ounce of vitality left in him, he brought his knees back to his stomach and forcefully pushed his legs forward, catapulting two of them into the air. Immediately, he began throwing blows again, hitting one of the monstrous men beneath its hood and making contact with the leathery texture of its face that felt like part withered flesh and part bone. He bucked up his hips, he threw more punches, and he kicked with all his might. There was a moment, a brief second, that Stefan had the chance to briskly get to his feet. He took the opportunity and, without giving a second glimpse, tripped toward the doorway.

Face to face with that chemical darkness again.

Stefan lunged forward; ready to cross the threshold once again. But it was too late. One of the creatures was already at his back again, hissing as it ripped a portion of his shirt. The scroll fell to the ground and was instantly picked up by another of the Order. Stefan pivoted and threw out his hand to grasp at it, but another of the beasts grabbed at his arm.

"Thank you," one of the hooded creatures said.

"We'll be coming for you sssoon, Ssstefan," another announced.

"But, you are no longer needed here." This was the leader of the group, who walked up to Stefan. "You are useless here and we need you in order for the Pact to begin. We look forward to cutting out your heart and seeing your world. But first, you may enjoy your pathetic Earth for one last time."

What were they saying? Stefan was being positioned in front of the doorway. Did they mean to return him back to Spook Valley? Why? Why was he rendered useless to them here?

Two of the Order were on either side of him when they grabbed at each of his shoulders and then heaved Stefan into the doorway.

Once again, Stefan felt his flesh begin to deconstruct and his molecules detach and swirl about. There was one last thought that came to mind before the process of transcending worlds paralyzed his brain activity. *Home.*

-5-

Catrina, Aaron, and Lucien stood ten feet from the doorway. Catrina had felt somewhat refreshed from the battle she had with Lillian. The pain inside of her was beginning to heal and her strength was slowly returning. She needed the time to recover. But most of all, she needed to know that Stefan was safe. The things he has seen. What horror did they subject him to in that awful place? A place full of darkness surely. Would he be the same Stefan she once knew? The kind, brave, and friendly Stefan with whom she'd spent her days and nights. Or would their friendship be marred in some way, a product of his experiences with the Nightworld? Could they have changed him?

"So what are we doing now?" This was Lucien who curiously asked as he glanced back at the dead Officer Colburn who sank slowly into the muddy earth. "What's left to do?"

"We're waiting," said Aaron.

"For Stefan?"

"Yes," Catrina confirmed.

"What if he never comes back?"

Silently, in their own minds, Catrina and Aaron refused to give credence to such a thought. *No, he will return.*

"He'll return," Aaron assured. "They can't use him in that place."

"What do you m—" But before Lucien had a chance to ask any further questions of Stefan and the battle with the Nightworld, the whirring of the doorway became shriller and the ruby-colored pulse around the doorway became more erratic.

The full attention of the trio was on to the doorway as if they were about to witness a miracle. No sooner than their excited thoughts got a chance to develop, did they see Stefan Powell emerge from the doorway. He looked as if he had been to Hell and back—his hair was disheveled, his face dirty, and his shirt torn—and he probably had. Still his appearance didn't make a difference. He was alive!

Catrina made a limped run up to him, screaming his name in joy.

Stefan took a quick look at his surroundings, making sure he indeed was back in Spook Valley, and a smile ignited his face as he saw an obviously injured Catrina run toward him. "Catrina," he yelled.

The two came together and their outward appearances were of no consequence. They eagerly embraced each other, holding strong to the other and weeping tears for their reunion. Their hearts beat in a rhythm of love as if they hadn't seen each other in years. Catrina's warm tears brushed against

Stefan's face. And he held her. He held her so tightly that he had to ease his embrace for fear of pushing all the oxygen from her. He, too, shed his tears that ran freely like an unstoppable waterfall.

After minutes of hugging and rocking with each other beneath the overcast, nighttime skies of Spook Valley, Stefan pulled back from his best friend and studied her wounds. "Are you all right?"

Catrina chuckled. "Yeah. So much has happened since you've been away." And she was right. So many monsters, so many answers discovered, and so many worries of Stefan's return.

"I know. Last time I saw you, you were lying in a hospital bed unconscious. What happened to you? You weren't this beaten up when I saw you last."

So much to explain. "It was Lillian. We went rounds just before you arrived."

Stefan raised his brow in wonder. "And…" he studied the darkened perimeter, "…where is she?"

"We killed her."

We? Stefan looked past Catrina and saw Aaron. "Aaron!" He walked with Catrina to where Aaron stood. Aaron—those emerald eyes; that blonde hair. Aaron was unscathed, save for a few scratches on his face. "I thought I was never going to see you again."

Aaron approached Stefan and wrapped his arms around him. Oh, to hold this man again! It was like a blissful dream come true; one in which nothing else much mattered save for their happiness.

Stefan brought his lips to Aaron's ear and whispered, "I know what you are now."

"I know you do," Aaron smiled and placed a small kiss of adoration upon Stefan's lips.

Lucien wanted to weep. His heart had fluttered when he first saw Stefan emerge across the threshold. But now he was in pain. Look at them, the way they held onto each other and shared that kiss! Lucien wished that it were he in Stefan's arms. With a sad face that showed defeat, Lucien turned away from the scene.

Thunder cracked the sky, as if it tearing it apart, and everybody flinched from the overbearing sound. Lightning flashed and Stefan saw the young man with his back turned toward them. "Who's that?"

Lucien revealed himself with a turn toward the three. "Hi Stefan. Remember me?" He felt awkward by his greeting.

Stefan's reaction was almost cold. Yes, he remembered that young man. Lucien, wasn't it? The one who had begun working at Laine's Music and had pestered Stefan with his longing to console him. What did he have to do with any of this? "What's he doing here?"

"Don't worry, Stefan." This was Aaron who spoke. "He knows about everything. In fact he saved Catrina tonight from being ripped to shreds by Lillian."

Catrina acknowledged this by nodding her head.

Aaron continued. "And, he saved us both from Zander who had almost killed me and was working on killing Catrina as well."

"Zander?" Stefan asked with amazement. "You mean—"

"Yes, Stefan," Catrina finished his sentence. "My supposed brother."

"So I was right. He was sent by the Nightworld."

"I don't want to talk about him right now, Stefan." Catrina's attention was divided by thoughts of Zander. *He was alive at one time. He was a good person.*

"I've been waiting for your return too, Stefan," Lucien announced. "We all missed you." Lucien went up to Stefan and threw his arms around the man for whom he held a deep passion.

Stefan hugged back, shocked by Lucien's attachment to him. What was it about this beautiful young man? However, all the while, Stefan smiled and kept his focus on Aaron. He still had a chance to love this man who had already escaped him once tonight in a world that was years away.

Lucien held tight to Stefan and kept his eyes closed. He imagined himself with Stefan in a far away place, just the two of them, with no worries of the danger that had them locked into its grip.

-6-

Deep into the center of the Nightworld, where creatures hissed and cackled, and the screams of the tortured innocent bellowed in a foreboding symphony, the Order of Perennial Darkness gathered in their ritualistic circle. They knelt when *Damia* made his way before them, his thunderous steps a warning that he was coming.

"It is done, God *Damia*," the head of the Order, Saint Dante, affirmed.

"And what of the scroll," *Damia's* booming voice emitted authority.

"We have it in our possession, once again, my God," Saint Cassius spoke.

"Where is this 'Stefan?'?"

"We sssent him back to hisss own world, God *Damia*." This was the hissing voice of Saint Batiste.

Damia roared in accomplishment. "Then it has come to pass. The Pact shall be initiated immediately!"

Saint Collin interrupted with a question. "What of the witch, Catrina?"

Damia's guffaws were like that of a hundred thunderheads snapping all at once. "Catrina may have destroyed the demon-child, Lillian, but her meager spells are nothing compared to our power." *Damia* knelt down from his monolithic size to meet with the head of the Order. Saint Dante held out both hands in which *Damia* placed a curved stiletto that gleamed from the light of the fiery land. "To you, I give the sacrificial dagger."

The others were wide-mouthed and searching to see the double-sided dagger that had been bequeathed to Saint Dante. It was an honor to receive the dagger from *Damia*, and, throughout the entire ordeal of making the Pact a reality, each of the Order of Perennial Darkness secretly looked forward to being the chosen one to strike down the sacrifice with this particular weapon. But it was Saint Dante who was chosen. Saint Dante would bring down the strike that allowed both the Nightworld and the Earth realm to unite.

"Thank you, God *Damia.* This is truly an honor. It is so magical, so bedazzling."

"Yes," *Damia* bellowed. "This weapon is made of nothing but pure silver and evil. It will take nothing to cut into the heart of Stefan." *Damia* took in a heavy breath as he stood to his true monumental size once again. "Now, I order you all to cross over and initiate the Pact. Make the sacrifice. Join our worlds and allow me to cross over into my new kingdom." A boisterous booming shot from *Damia*'s mouth as the Order of Perennial Darkness proceeded to the doorway that would lead them to Spook Valley.

They stood before the doorway, in single file. Each grabbed for his scroll and unrolled it in preparation of reading the incantations that would soon bring the two worlds together.

-7-

Lucien felt Stefan pull back from their embrace, though, in Lucien's mind, he wanted to scream for letting him go. Still, Stefan wasn't gone. He was here, right here with Lucien and the others. There was a heartbroken feeling of jealousy as Lucien watched Stefan walk toward Aaron's side.

"There's so much to tell you, Stefan," Catrina said. "Perhaps, too much."

"Yeah," Aaron added, "to sum it up for you, Catrina awoke from her coma after you left, Zander turned out to be a ghoul whom I fought to the end with, Lucien came to us after escaping the music store where Lillian murdered Laine—"

"Wait a minute," Stefan interjected, "Laine's dead?"

Aaron nodded. "Yeah, Lillian has been on a killing streak and Laine wasn't her only victim." Aaron gestured over to the corpse of the officer.

"Who's that?"

"He's a cop who was searching for Lucien."

Lucien went red with embarrassment and hatred. *No, don't tell him about my past! Don't give him a reason to hate me! I need him, for a reason I don't even know yet, but I need him!* Lucien's mind was fueled by pleadings to Aaron.

Stefan's expression was etched in lines across his brow. There was so much he didn't understand. "Why are the cops searching for Lucien?"

This is where Catrina came in to defend the young man. Not to mention, there were other pressing matters at hand, other situations that couldn't be obscured by this reunion of friends. "It's too much to go into now. We'll talk about it later." She stared at Aaron in a secret code that could only mean for him to be quiet about Lucien's past. There was no need for Stefan to feel that he couldn't trust the young man. They had already been through that hadn't they? "There are more important things we need to discuss. Like how we plan on putting an end to this entire nightmare."

As if on cue, the skies flashed a streak of fierce lightning and the echo of thunder filled their ears. The rain began to drive down.

"I had one of the scrolls," Stefan explained. "I thought that if I could get back here with it, that the Nightworld would be unable to perform the Pact. But the Order got it from me, just as I was coming through the doorway. Now, I'm not sure what to do! When I originally crossed the threshold, I was hoping to get some type of answer on how to stop it all from happening."

Catrina didn't want to bring up what she said next, but it was inevitable. Stefan had to know. "Stefan, we think that you may be the sacrifice they speak of upon the process of bringing the Pact into reality."

Stefan anticipated. "Yeah, they made that clear when they pushed me back here."

"Pushed?" Catrina's voice was twisted into confusion.

"Remember what I said, Catrina?" Now Aaron was explaining things. It seemed that, even though not one of them had all the answers, each of them harbored certain knowledge that would bring about the truth. "Stefan was of no use to them there."

The heavy rain gave way to a drizzle again. Not voicing anything in the conversation, Lucien studied the dark laden skies that appeared to glow. He searched for the moon.

"That's what the Order told me," Stefan agreed with Aaron. "Damn, if I could have escaped with that scroll, it might have changed everything!"

"I have to ask you something Stefan," Aaron veered off the immediate subject. "Where were you when you entered the Nightworld? Did you see anything else?"

"Funny thing is that I wasn't in the Nightworld that long. Only long enough to take a scroll from one of the Order and head back this way. But I went through the wrong doorway. There are *three* doorways!"

"Three?" Catrina's mind swam in amusement. How many other horrors were connected with the Nightworld? How far did the trail of madness go and where did it end?

"Yeah, three. I went through the wrong doorway and somehow ended up in the past." Stefan turned to face Aaron. "I ended up in your past, Aaron. I saw how you were abducted."

Aaron was speechless, but he knew it to be true. Now that it had been confirmed, it only made his entire life with Stefan seem that much more precious. That night, in what he thought to be his dreams, it really happened didn't it? How he recalled Stefan's hips brushing with his own and those delicate kisses that were like silk to his touch.

"We spent so much time together, we—"

"I know," said Aaron. "I remember it, Stefan."

A tear wanted to escape from Stefan's eye. A tear of joy, perhaps, in the knowledge that Aaron was well aware of the night they shared. Stefan's fears were no longer when it came to Aaron's memory of the events. Aaron knew. Aaron recollected the entire account. And it didn't matter to Stefan as to how Aaron knew or how his present self had felt Stefan making love to him. All that mattered was that Aaron was aware of the passion and they were both here together.

Lucien shot a quick glance of disapproval at Stefan and Aaron as they melted into each other's eyes. He continued to gaze up into the sky, searching for the illumination of what had to be a full moon igniting the radiant atmosphere.

Catrina had given the two men their chance to relive the time they shared. But, time, wasn't it running out? Shouldn't they get a move on their plans to stop the Nightworld? "Sorry to break up the memories you two, but I don't understand why they would push Stefan back to this place if the Nightworld was ready to go forward with their Pact."

"Well," Aaron answered with his logic, "with Stefan here, then that puts everything in place. All that needs to happen now is for the thirteenth to cross the threshold."

Catrina craned her neck to view the doorway. "Then where is it? Why haven't they sent the thirteenth through the doorway yet? What are they waiting for? And what are we going to do to stop the Pact from happening?" Catrina was beginning to get frustrated by all the questions her mind summoned from her fearing consciousness.

"I have a plan." Aaron gazed directly into Stefan's eyes. *You know I love you, don't you?* "I think we should get back to the apartment and get it in order."

In the dark skies overhead, Lucien spotted a patch of cloud that gleamed with a brilliant purple hue. It appeared to strobe, from a light orchid-color to a deep and mesmerizing cross of blue and black. It hypnotized Lucien, that luminous piece of sky. It was like a heartbeat, as if the sky had a pulse. Thud, thud. Lucien peered at it in awesome wonder as the edges slowly expanded in all directions. Beautiful. Purple. Heartbeat. The beaming light travelled across the atmosphere.

"Let's get going then," Catrina said, trying to quicken the process. She knew they didn't have much time before the thirteenth cross. Then it struck her. "Aaron?" she called forward. Aaron and Stefan had already begun exiting the desert clearing. "Could it be that the god of the Nightworld, this…*Damia*…could be the thirteenth to cross?"

Aaron halted and waited for Catrina to catch up to him and Stefan. "Impossible," he remarked. "*Damia* is unable to cross the threshold until the Pact is coming to close. He wouldn't cross until the sacrifice was about to be made; the actual act itself."

Stefan shivered just thinking about his own moment of death and what would result because of it.

Catrina's mind was eased by Aaron explaining that to her. She felt that none of them had a chance against a powerfully evil creature such as *Damia.*

They began their trod through the mud again, when Catrina noticed Lucien's absence. She called back for him, yelling for him to join their departure.

That cloud. So purple. And glowing. So beautiful. No, not the cloud. It was the sky. The sky was glowing purple. And it kept expanding! It was becoming globular, beginning to reach along the entire horizon around Spook Valley. *So beautiful. No. So strange. But still beautiful. Her voice. Catrina. Something's happening. Something terrible.*

Falling from his hypnotic delirium, Lucien turned to find the others had already left. But he heard Catrina's voice. She was calling for him. He targeted the source of the voice and began to walk between two cacti, away from the clearing.

A buzzing. An awful whirring growing louder. Lucien knew what that meant. Somebody, no, *something* was coming through the doorway. He briskly pivoted in his tracks, turning toward the monolithic structure that towered the cacti. Pulsing. The doorway pulsed in a ruby color that matched the rhythm of the purple sky.

A silent scream emitted from the young man's throat as he witnessed the first one of the Order of Perennial Darkness emerging from the black pit of the doorway. It was Saint Dante, cloaked in his brown robe, holding an open scroll in one hand and a gleaming dagger in the other.

Lucien ran through the desert, sloshing through the muddy terrain until he made it to the others. He was almost out of breath. The run and his speeding heart made him practically collapse at their feet.

"Lucien!" Catrina was freaked out by his sudden appearance. He was more pallid than ever; he looked like a ghost.

"They're coming!"

"Who?" Aaron asked.

"Something in a robe…and…he's holding a dagger!"

"The Order?" Catrina shot a questioning gaze to Aaron.

Aaron nodded, just as perplexed as Catrina was.

"But how?" Stefan queried with anticipation raising his voice an octave.

"Oh shit!" Catrina was beside herself. "The thirteenth! Oh, I can't believe we didn't figure this out any sooner! Stefan's the thirteenth!"

"What?!?" Stefan didn't want to believe it. It couldn't have worked that way. Everything was rushing toward chaos too quickly.

"She's right," Aaron backed Catrina's theory. "You went into the Nightworld, but you never crossed into the Earth realm. They needed thirteen to cross into the Earth realm, Stefan. Your coming back has activated the process."

Suddenly, an irrefutable guilt rushed over Stefan. Instantly, he realized that coming back to Spook Valley was the biggest mistake he could have made, let alone trekking into the doorway of the Nightworld in the first place. He should have stayed back in that other place; he should have allowed himself to be consumed by that hungry Nothing. Now, he was putting everybody at risk. Oh, dear God, how could this be stopped now that it's been started?

"We have to leave," Lucien yelled.

Catrina dismissed the young man. Although he was right, they had to act and act fast! "Aaron, you said you had a plan."

"Yeah, but…"

"We don't have anymore time."

"Let's make a break for the car and get back to the apartment."

"We can't run away from it!"

"Do you have any better ideas right now? We're not prepared to stop this, Catrina!"

Aaron was right. They needed to buy more time, even if it was two minutes. It seemed now that time was of the essence.

The four raced out of the desert and to Catrina's car. Officer Colburn's squad car was right behind hers. Catrina jumped into the driver's seat and turned the key to the ignition. However, nothing happened. The engine wouldn't turn. "What the hell?" She glanced up the road where she saw a vehicle in the opposing lane. But it was simply there, without movement.

"C'mon," she hollered to the others. "Let's flag down this car."

When they got to the vehicle, they discovered something even more frightening than they had witnessed. The car was not running and the driver of the vehicle, an older man who appeared to be in his sixties was sitting stock-still, eyes still staring at the open road in front of him and mouth agape. "What's going on?" Aaron called out.

Lucien looked back to the Heavens. "The sky," he muttered. "Look at the sky!"

All of them turned their attention to the sky as their hearts pounded in their chests. The entire sky was a gleaming purple color. As they studied the curves of the purple tint that pulsed in dome fashion above them, Catrina felt a solid strike of trepidation infuse her body. "We're trapped. The Nightworld has stopped everything in Spook Valley except for us. We're under its power now! It's beginning!"

CHAPTER XXV

-1-

Spook Valley was still. An eerie silence ensnared the entire town. Silence—on a night like this when, normally, a residual traffic could be seen at the intersection of Main and Saguaro Streets, in the town square. However, it wasn't that the town was absent of traffic. Rather, traffic was at an uncanny standstill—vehicles adorned the streets, transmissions in 'Drive' yet unmovable, just as the citizens operating their vehicles were. The residents of Spook Valley were just as still as the absent current of wind that had peculiarly vanished, although the vortex of a vicious storm hovered over the town only minutes previous. Families sat in their homes, paused in entertainment on their couches, in front of televisions; patrons at the Violin Street Tavern appeared as statues on barstools before their cocktails; and if one were to stumble upon this scientific eureka, he would be unable to distinguish the still form of the populous from the bronze statue of Jamison Spook, the founding father of the town, that stood in its isolated gazebo within the town square for over two decades.

However, this biological oddity would go unnoticed by the rest of the world. For Spook Valley had been isolated from the remainder of the Earth. The edges of the town's asphalt and desert borders would not permit any visitors nor allow anybody to escape the town limits. A heinous and unnatural force held Spook Valley captive within a dimension all its own. And perhaps that is why the patrons of the town were motionless; perhaps they weren't experiencing this wayward slipstream of dimensional frenzy that held the town in throe. They were here, yet they were not; time existed and moved, yet time stood still. And beyond this paradox, in cities and towns across the Earth where evil and monsters didn't exist, the night gave way to the witching hour.

The streets were still wet with water, glimmering like a trove of jewels from the bizarre, purple atmosphere that encapsulated the town. The deserts were still muddy from the storm. Although the storm had appeared to cease, it continued beyond the radiant glow of the purple dome. The spherical border of the dome could be seen by the naked eye as it curved through the atmosphere. Beyond the purple tint, flashes of lightning reflected off the glasslike environment that covered Spook Valley. They were stroboscopic flashes beyond the purple hue, as if one were staring deeply into the magical and hypnotic cosmos of an undiscovered galaxy.

Along the isolated stretch of Firehouse Road, four people were immune to the spell cast over the town. They were well aware that the source of this strangeness was accredited to the dark desires of a place called the Nightworld. What's more, they wished that they were as oblivious as the rest of Spook Valley's population; for they were the ones fated to fight this horrific battle of monsters and madness. And now it had all begun.

The Pact was being initiated at that very elongated second that refused to pass into the next.

-2-

"It's starting," Catrina yelled at Stefan, Aaron, and Lucien. The three men stared in awe at the mesmerizing purple of the sky. *Such beauty in the gloaming.*

A wave of nausea hit Catrina and her body felt as if it were going to fall over. She wanted to faint, but Stefan caught her before she collapsed to the asphalt. *In his arms*, she thought; *I get to feel those arms again.* And how she missed Stefan's embrace as she recalled every goodnight hug that seemed to have been eons away in a distant past. Stefan had returned, their golden friendship rekindled, and now Catrina would be able to revisit those very arms that had consoled her in times of need.

Catrina's energy had depleted to a dangerous level and she knew it. There was simply no time to rest. Out of the hospital and into the ferocious battles of the Nightworld. Her body ached. Oh, if just to sleep! But she couldn't take that risk. She had destroyed Lillian and now she had one last battle to do with the Nightworld. Not exactly battle, for it was Stefan they were after. But she would be there to aid him in stopping his being sacrificed. So tired! She realized that the energy she had spent running with Stefan, Aaron, and Lucien was nothing more than a second wind created by the adrenaline of seeing Stefan again. Now, there was nothing left—no nourishment to fuel her energy, no rest to let her body regenerate. Catrina couldn't help but to fall; her legs flared in agony. Yet, Stefan stood next to her and supported her veritable dead weight.

He spoke to her in the same words of solace he had back in the days when the weight of the world was bringing them down. "Are you going to make it?"

"I don't know how much longer I can hold up," Catrina spoke in a weak voice.

Aaron took his gaze of the flickering spectacle that mutely shot across the sky. "Maybe we should take her back to the apartment, man."

Stefan nodded to Aaron.

Catrina instantly refused. "No, I have to be here! I'm going to see this thing to the end."

Now it was time for prayer. It seemed she was doing that a lot these days—praying to her God and Goddess, asking for their protection and strength to get her through. To get them *all* through this ordeal. However, something was amiss. Catrina's mind focused on the genderless being of light, yet she couldn't bring the vision of her redeemers into view. But with just a bit more concentration…no, it wasn't happening. And the tingling sensation that would overwhelm her entire being when she connected to the God and Goddess failed to infuse her body. Catrina now knew that she was beyond weak. No, she had to focus!

Stefan gazed back to Aaron who arched his eyebrows as if it were up to Stefan if Catrina were fit for the battle.

Time was running out.

"Aaron," Catrina called subtly, "you said you had a plan. What is it?"

Aaron looked down at the ground. Yes, he did have a plan, just not a full-proof one. If he spoke of his plan to the others, there was a possibility that they would find it a risk they'd rather not take. How was Aaron to know that the plan he had formulated, after the battle with Catrina's brother, would even stop the Nightworld? Actually, his strategy to bring this nightmare to an end was rather simple. Perhaps, too simple. Then again, the Pact itself was no elaborate process either. It only involved the Nightworld having to make their sacrifice—the reading of the scrolls and the plunge of a sacrificial dagger into the heart of the one who'd opened the doorway, Stefan Powell.

Aaron's eyes met with Stefan's—emerald hues locked to brown as if it were the end of the world and this was their final day. Aaron felt a selfish urge to grab Stefan and take him away from this ominous setting. He yearned to take him back to the apartment and make love to him. That skin, so soft and those lips, so delicious. Aaron was taken back to a night over three decades previous when the two of them had shared their bodies with each other in lusting rhythm. Aaron felt somewhat aroused by the thought of Stefan holding him, the flesh of their bodies hard against each other, and the hot breath of Stefan's against the nape of his neck. Oh, how he could be in that moment forever, how he could easily forget all of this that was happening. That's right, forget it all! It could be just he and Stefan pulled together through time and love, surviving on velvet kisses and warm embrace. However, the sky told of a different story with its foreboding purple tint, a story of one final battle to overcome and a story of change. Nothing, it seemed, really lasted forever, and Aaron knew this. *Man, I care for you so much! Now I know what it's like to be in love.*

"Aaron?" Stefan broke his reverie. "The plan; what is it?"

"Actually, it's rather simple...give up."

"What?" Catrina defensively interjected. "Give up?"

Stefan said nothing. He waited for Aaron's reasoning. If anybody knew about the Nightworld, it was Aaron. Aaron had been in that dark place for over three decades. He had felt the fiery warmth of that hell, been subjected to tortures inconceivable, and had coexisted as a monster with the others who had come to be his brothers and sisters in a family of madness.

"Well," Aaron hesitated a moment, "we can't run from them, that's true. And even if we could, where would we go? This whole town is under some spell; nothing's working and nobody can help us. We're all alone in this. I say if they want Stefan then Stefan should go to them."

"Then what?" Catrina was befuddled by Aaron's theory. It disturbed her how this man claimed to care so much for Stefan and, yet, was just as eager to give him up to the Nightworld.

"Once they have Stefan, the Order will make the attempt to sacrifice him."

"Right!" Catrina snapped. "And if they do that, then we're all fucked!" Catrina's head ached and she took a deep breath. She spoke calmly now, trying to compose herself with a rational understanding reiterated to Aaron. "We're trying to prevent the Nightworld from killing Stefan, Aaron. If they succeed in doing that, to my understanding of what you all keep telling me, this world will be tainted by every bit of evil that lingers on the other side of that doorway."

"That's if they make the sacrifice."

"I don't understand," Stefan voiced his confusion. He still couldn't fathom that they were speaking of his own possible death. Yet, none of it seemed real and Stefan was waiting for the moment of the nightmare, probably the last frame when it came time for the blade to go into him, to awaken in a bed flooded with sweat.

"If we can stop them before making their sacrifice, if we can throw the process off kilter, then the Nightworld will be purged from this world."

"But how do you plan on doing that?" It seemed Catrina was filled with doubt. There was no chance in taking the risk. No, she wouldn't risk her best friend for a plan that had no salability whatsoever. Then again, she couldn't help but wonder if she had much of a choice. Where was her strength when she needed it most?

"Well…first of all, you have me. Remember, I *am* more than human, Catrina. There's you and Lucien, of course."

"Where is Lucien?" Stefan inquired.

-3-

Lucien remained where he had been when Aaron left his side to converse his plans with Stefan and Catrina. The young kid, a pale figure against the black night, was mesmerized by the heavens. *The purple dome. So beautiful. Power. So much power in that picturesque twilight sky. Taste. Tasting the power as each flicker of lightning reflects and refracts off that purple iridescence. Reflecting, yes, like the blade of a knife capturing a beam of light.*

Lucien recalled holding the knife with which he'd butchered his mother. That was power—each bloody pummel of the weapon into beautiful soft flesh. And she had no say about it! It was *he* who held the power in his hands, the power to destroy anything that was in his way. Surely, his mother was in the way. A sinister smile etched his face for but a moment. *I removed her*, he reminded himself.

Yes, you did, an alien voice in his mind reassured him.

I would have killed that cop too.

No need to do that, the voice replied. *The cop is already dead. But had he lived, you would have surely removed him.*

Yes, I think so.

Stop second-guessing yourself, Lucien. You would have. Just like you removed that monster that almost killed you.

Lucien rolled his eyes into his head to remember the demon Lillian. *But I didn't kill her.*

No, but it was because of you that the creature was slain. Had you not been there to distract that monster, Catrina would have never been able to defeat it. You're the one who has the power Lucien.

Power. The mental image of his wielding the sword at the demon boosted his ego. *Sword. Shiny and beautiful like...the knife I used to kill mother. Like the sky. Look at the beautiful sky!*

You won't let anybody stand in the way of what you want, will you Lucien?

There's nobody else in my way.

What about Aaron? Did you see the way he kissed Stefan? Did you see how they look into each other's eyes? You like Stefan, don't you?

*I like Stefan and...*Lucien's mind hesitated...*I guess I don't mind Aaron. Catrina said that Aaron cares a lot about Stefan. I like Catrina.*

Maybe she's getting in the way too...

Lucien jolted and his heart skipped a beat when he felt the hand grab his shoulder. It was Aaron. Lucien quickly dismissed the mental conversation from his head as if a sin he would have to atone for.

"Lucien? What's going on, man?" Aaron noticed that the young man looked a shade whiter than he naturally did. Lucien's entire body trembled.

Lucien returned his gaze to the sky. "It's beautiful, isn't it Aaron."

Aaron targeted his glance skyward, taking observation of the purple atmosphere and the lightning that flashed beyond its perimeter. "Yes," Aaron agreed. He grabbed Lucien's chin and made the young man face him. "But it's the *Nightworld*, Lucien. This happened because they are coming through the doorway to end this all."

Lucien's eyes darted back and forth as if not wanting to believe that the bedazzling miracle in the sky was from a source considered so evil. "I don't understand," the young man said as he ran his fingers through his hair that was as black as the night itself. "Why are the cars all stopped? Why are the people unable to move?"

Stefan and Catrina's ears perked when hearing Lucien's question. It seemed that they all awaited a rational explanation from Aaron.

"It's the Nightworld," said Aaron as he looked back to Catrina and Stefan. "They have isolated Spook Valley from the rest of the Earth realm. It's a spell that is cast as the Order enters this world upon making the sacrifice that will bring the two worlds together. It's difficult to explain, but we're in our own separate dimension. The people in Spook Valley are really moving around as we speak. They're in a separate time and space."

"Then why are we able to move about here?" This was Lucien again with his constant questions.

"Because we are *aware* of the Nightworld. We are all part of the process in one way or another. We have all either seen or been victim to the Nightworld. Therefore, we are here, under its spell."

"Then the spell has to be broken," Catrina muttered. *God and Goddess guide me through this night; help me in protecting Stefan from this awful evil.* Empty. There was no confirmation of Catrina's call to the God and Goddess. And why was that? Surely, she realized she was weak and it was much more difficult to stay in tune with her inner power, her *Chi.* But what she felt when she called out to her deity was nothing more than purposelessness. Could it be that the spell cast by the Nightworld was so strong that it isolated her from the God and Goddess? Could a spell be that powerful as to cut off one's belief and religion? She had to center herself. *But I have no energy,* Catrina gave credence to self-doubt.

Lucien studied Catrina. She appeared so weak. She had to stop this! After all, she was a powerful witch. Why was she not doing anything? She looked so tired, and Lucien felt all hope was lost. If Catrina couldn't save them, who could? What hope was left? *I don't want to be here. I don't want to be in this place! I want out!*

The voice within Lucien's head called to his fears. *You don't have to be here, Lucien. The only reason you're here is because of them. If you'd never met them, your life would be different; you'd be somewhere else doing the things that young men do.*

What else would I do?

There's a whole world waiting for you Lucien. You don't need any of these people. They're only going to get you hurt. They're standing in the way of your life!

Standing...

...In the way, yes.

But I don't want to leave Stefan! I love him!

There are others like Stefan. Other men who don't have the weight of the world on their shoulders. Others, just as beautiful, that you could be making love to. Stefan doesn't even give a damn about you, Lucien. He has only put you in the middle of this entire mess. He would assume you dead rather than touch you the way you want him to.

I'm just here because I was in the wrong place at the wrong time. None of them really care about me, do they? They think I'm just a kid, don't they?

Yes. You know that Catrina would help the others before she would ever think about helping you.

No, Lucien struggled with his brimming insanity.

Yes. Deep down you know it. None of them cares if you live or die. You are only in their way.

No, they are in MY way.

Yes.

I want a knife...

A fear choked Catrina as she shivered from the sinister look etching Lucien's face. He stared at her with dead eyes as if he were not here in the same place as she and the others. If looks could kill, she'd be exhaling her last breath. "Why are you staring at me like that, Lucien?" There was a tremble in her voice.

Stefan and Aaron beamed their attention toward Lucien.

"What?" Lucien blinked his eyes a few times. "I'm sorry, I was just thinking."

No, something's not right, Catrina noted.

"Can you stop this, Catrina?" Lucien asked her as he approached.

Catrina took a cautious step backward. Something was amiss in Lucien's demeanor. One minute, he was scared as a child and, now, he walked with his head high in a confidence unexpected.

"I'm…not…sure," she spoke slowly, making a queer glance to Stefan and Aaron.

Aaron and Stefan bridged the gap between Lucien and Catrina. Aaron couldn't pinpoint what was going on, but Lucien's eccentric behavior had him on alert. Aaron watched Lucien come to a halt before him.

"Who can stop this?" Lucien asked. "How will it be stopped?" His voice consisted of a monotone as if he had lost all emotion.

Aaron looked at all three of them. "A sacrifice has to be made, but I think I can stop the Pact from being completed."

"But I'm the one who has to initiate it all," Stefan acknowledged.

"I'm afraid so," Aaron confirmed.

"And there's no other way?" Catrina couldn't believe that the only way to stop the Pact was to give in to the Nightworld's longing for Stefan to be sacrificed.

"Catrina," Aaron attempted to make her understand, "Stefan and the doorway are connected. He opened the doorway and this will not end until the doorway is closed. Stefan's like a honing device. We can't run from the Order. They're going to get Stefan either way, whether he volunteers himself or they use force to get him. Nevertheless, Stefan will have to go to them."

This will not end until the doorway is closed, thought Stefan as he recalled those same words said by Breckin. *Breckin, where are you now? My first love gone from vampire to ghost of this world. Are you seeing any of this?*

"And your plan to stop the Order?" Catrina waited for an answer.

"Plain and simple. We go in for the attack. If we can all band together and fight off the Order, perhaps it will prevent the sacrifice from having to be made. I need you to focus on your powers as a witch, Catrina. And, Lucien," Aaron redirected, "you have to be strong as you are now and be prepared to battle."

"That's easier said than done," Catrina remarked. "My powers are not 'up to par' right now, so to speak."

"We have to do what we can. I'm going to transform into my lycanthropic state and attack the Order. Once the battle begins, there is no stopping."

"I'm ready," Lucien called out to the other three with an unexplained and sudden confidence.

You see how he's giving orders? The voice within Lucien made him notice.

He replied, *I see how he gets in the way of everything...*

-4-

It was the final move of the Nightworld, the one magical moment that would bring two worlds colliding and merging into one another. They had set the stage so brilliantly, with an ancient wisdom as deceptive as any ever known. The Thirteenth had crossed and, now, each of the Order of Perennial Darkness appeared to float from the monolithic doorway that bridged their world and the Earth realm.

The sky was purple—a commanding spell cast to isolate Spook Valley from the rest of the world—and an eerie silence made its way through the darkness of the night. Beyond the purple dome, the skies were flickering. A storm hovered over Spook Valley and refused to move on. However, its hammering rains were unable to break through the force field that surrounded the town.

All six of the Order of Perennial Darkness—Sainte Dante, Saint Cassius, Saint Batiste, Saint Collin, Saint Trace, and Saint Israel—stood in horseshoe formation with their backs to the hissing doorway of the Nightworld. The open end of the circle welcomed their sacrifice, Stefan Powell. Saint Dante stood in the back center of the formation, pointing the dagger outward toward all that was in the desert beyond, as if the weapon were a honing device that sought their sacrificial chosen one. Surely, Stefan was there, hiding in the shrubbery along with the witch Catrina. But, as *Damia* had assured them, she would be no match for them or their plan. *Damia* also pledged that he would be waiting, just beyond the doorway, for the sacrifice to be made so that he could enter the Earth realm.

The Order of Perennial Darkness stood in silence, surveying the area of the dark desert before them. So this would be their new kingdom—this setting of cactus and desert that stretched on for miles until it gave way to steel towers. The atmosphere felt far less than the scorching heat of the Nightworld, but these deserts were said to be hottest during the season of summer. The Order tried not to observe too much of their surroundings, for they would have an eternity to study the deserts and towers and mountains and hills. This would be their new kingdom, an extension of the Nightworld governed by *Damia.*

Although the hoods of their robes concealed their faces of rotted flesh and decayed bone, their eyes seared blood red as they each unrolled their respective scrolls. The crackling of the parchments, as they were being undone, was the only sound within the immediate area. They were ready to begin, prepared to succeed in their last battle with the one known as Stefan Powell. It was time for the Nightworld and the Earth realm to fuse.

A voice broke out from among the six of the Order, the voice of Saint Dante. He pointed the blade of the fated dagger toward the heavens. "Stefan Powell. I call you. Stefan Powell. Come to me. You cannot resist my call. It is time for your destiny to be fulfilled."

-5-

They walked slowly through the desert, past all of the plants that gave life to the land—the saguaros, the yuccas, the brittle tumbleweeds that miraculously remained still—trying to bide time with each measured step that would bring them to the clearing where the doorway to the Nightworld had remained for the past months. Stefan and Aaron walked side by side in front of the group. Catrina walked alone with Lucien following directly behind. There were no words exchanged between any of them at this point. There was only a hesitation brought on by the haunting fear of what may come when they faced the Order of Perennial Darkness.

Catrina took in steady breaths, trying to reach the best meditative state while maintaining her weakening pace. *God and Goddess, I need you now. Stefan needs you. Aaron needs you.* She made another attempt at focusing herself, willing her mind to contact that sacred and mystical place where she would find hope and strength. However, the pain in her back aborted the attempt. The pain was beginning again. Why? Why couldn't her agony cease? Yet, this pain, this sharp feeling in her back was unlike the flaring sensation she'd experienced earlier. The flaring didn't crawl; rather, it poked into her back. As if on cue, Catrina craned her neck to see Lucien following behind. His eyes stared beyond her. As she turned her back to him once again, she couldn't help but shiver from some alien instinct.

She's not going to save you, Lucien. She's worthless to you now. Just like Stefan and Aaron are worthless. You know, they're going to die anyway. Slow and horrible deaths...all of them!

Lucien gave off a muted snicker. *I don't care anymore. I'm going to remove anything in my way. I'm leaving Spook Valley.*

Silence in Lucien's mind.

Did you hear me, voice? I'm leaving this place and I'm never coming back.

You can't. You're trapped.

Maybe now.

If Stefan weren't around, you wouldn't be trapped.

I know.

If Aaron weren't around, you wouldn't have to feel that cringing sadness in your heart.

I know.

If the witch Catrina weren't around, there would be no more monsters in your life.

I...know. I don't need you telling me. I don't need anybody. I don't need you, voice! Go away. I need the knife.

Stefan walked along with Aaron, their footfall in sync with each other. He couldn't believe that, after all these months of fighting the Nightworld, he was going to give in to them. There was a terrifying sensation that raped his mind and sped throughout his body. *If they don't stop the Order, I'm going to die. If I die, then everything will crumble into ruin. All of this would have been for nothing. Breckin, how I miss you! And, Aaron, I will never see Aaron again if they don't stop the Nightworld.*

"Stefan Powell…" the voice was low and sinister in its annunciation, and it wrapped around his body, swirling from his mind into his limbs. His heart began beating into frenzy. "…I call you Stefan Powell…Come to me…" And he recognized that apprehensive voice, for it had bid him farewell from the Nightworld. It was one of the Order. "…You cannot resist my call…It is time for your destiny to be fulfilled." The adrenaline that coursed through Stefan's veins was racing his heart to impossible speeds. Sweat began to form upon his forehead and along the small of his back.

No, he wasn't going to do this! He couldn't give up to the Nightworld. No! His mind was set. Still, something was pulling him as if he didn't have to go to it of his own free will. Stefan thought if he halted, this stringlike force would drag him along the desert floor until he was face to face with the Order of Perennial Darkness. *It's time to wake up now*, he told himself. And then, in his mind, he hollered, *Wake up! It's the end of the nightmare! Wake up dammit!* Stefan's face cringed as the tears began to flow from his eyes. He ceased walking any further toward his "destiny."

Aaron immediately stopped along with him, viewed the tears running down those smooth, high cheeks. Aaron was aware of how tough this would be on Stefan. Everything thus far was composed of death that existed on a veritable dreamscape of apprehension. Yet, this moment was Stefan's and Stefan's all alone. "Hey," Aaron addressed him, "you're going to be all right."

Stefan wildly shook his head, catching a glimpse of Catrina and Lucien behind them. "No. No I'm not. I can't do this, Aaron! We can't stop this! The Nightworld has won."

"No," Aaron opposed, "the Nightworld hasn't won. You have to do this, Stefan. There's no other way."

"I'm not going through with it. I can't!" Stefan's cheeks were flushed.

"You have to believe that we can defeat this."

"The Nightworld's too powerful. I *can't* believe that we can stop this, Aaron. Catrina can hardly stand and you can't take them on your own!" His sobs were echoing throughout the desert. God, the Order probably heard his cries of despair. Now he really wanted to end it all. Leave, do something; get the hell out of this place.

Aaron drew in a breath. "Stefan, you *have* to believe that the Nightworld can be stopped. You believe in me, don't you? You believe in all the monsters that have come from that place."

Stefan nodded.

"So why's it so hard to believe that such a force can have a weakness. There is always a way to stop evil, Stefan. Sometimes we have to look between the lines. Sometimes, we have to dedicate our time so that we can discover that weakness. And it always doesn't turn out good, man. Sometimes…we have to make our own sacrifices to stop the impossible. And those sacrifices never go unnoticed." Aaron gazed deep into Stefan's eyes. "I'm telling you…you are going to make it."

Stefan was speechless. He felt so comforted by Aaron's words. Oh yes, he loved this man and he knew Aaron's words were authentic and spoken from the heart. "I love you," the words spilled over his quavering lips.

"I love you too." With that, Aaron placed his mouth over Stefan's. It felt as if the world had stopped. Their tongues tangled in a dance of affection, a kiss of desire, of ageless love, of love unconquered.

Stefan held onto Aaron, embracing him tightly with his trembling arms. *I could stay in this moment forever.* He refused to let go. His tongue explored Aaron's mouth, his eyes remained open (just like Aaron's), and the giddiness of lust probed at his insides. In those eyes, those brilliant emerald eyes, Stefan could see a promising future along with Aaron's past. This moment was still, and yet it moved; just as time had stopped in Spook Valley, yet, continued in the rest of the world. Their kiss gave birth to paradoxes within a paradox.

Catrina managed an enervated smile. It was great to witness love flourish in the midst of horror.

It doesn't matter to me. Have each other. I don't care. Lucien's mind composed its own contradiction in terms. He was calm and, at the same time, he was enraged. "I said I was ready," he yelled to the lovers ahead of him. "Let's go!"

Catrina pivoted from the picturesque scene. "Lucien!" she scorned.

Get out of my way! All of you! Lucien rushed on past Catrina without giving her a second glance.

Catrina remained speechless and befuddled by Lucien's actions. It came down to jealousy, plain and simple. That's what she told herself. Young love and being scared. It must be tough for Lucien to cope in a world where the guilt of his mother's death and the horrors of the Nightworld existed. Catrina was quite surprised that Lucien hadn't cracked already. However, seeing him on edge made her think twice about how long it would be before he exploded and…did what? What would Lucien do if his temper finally boiled over? Catrina refused to think of the mental picture of Lucien trying to harm any of them.

Catrina made a lazy run ahead to catch up with Stefan and Aaron. She put her arm around Stefan and pecked his cheek with her lips. "Hey, things are going to get better." She managed a smile although she had her own skepticism to what she'd just said.

"Both of you need to be careful. And watch Lucien, he seems on edge."

"That would have to do with that little kiss the two of you shared," Catrina informed Stefan.

"Oh man." Stefan had forgotten how Lucien had clung to him during their very first meeting. Of course! Lucien liked him. Stefan emptied his mind of the potential thoughts of drama that would result from Lucien's jealousy. There were other important things. *Like the possibility of your death*, a voice in his head insidiously whispered.

Lucien had left the three of them behind. Aaron, Stefan, and Catrina started walking toward the center of the desert again, toward the clearing where Lucien, hopefully, would be waiting.

"Stefan Powell," a loud voice erupted into the night. The voice was deep and echoed past the three. Catrina jumped from the sudden voice.

Stefan cringed at hearing his name; his heartbeat sped up again.

"What the hell was that?" Catrina asked.

"That was one of the Order," Aaron answered, not turning to look at Catrina.

-6-

With each step that Stefan took, the will to hesitate the situation was reflected by his slower pace. His mind raced with images of his death and bleaker images of the Earth realm being taken over by *Damia* and his minions. He thought of a dagger plummeting into his heart, thought of a life without Aaron, and then he thought of death again. The fear had gripped his body so tightly, it reverted the decision in his mind of not giving up to the Order of Perennial Darkness. No, he was going to fight! There was no way he was going to give them his life that easily. But if Stefan were to truly make that his final claim, now would be the time to act upon it.

The three of them came to a halt just outside of the clearing. They remained hidden behind the shrubbery and cacti.

Lucien was on the other side of a large plant, watching the six men who stood stock-still in front of the doorway to the Nightworld. The cloaked man that stood in front of the others was directing the blade of a knife to the sky. Lucien peered up at the purple sky once again, studied the beautiful dance the reflections of lightning made, and observed the dagger that gave off a similar gleam. *Knife...beauty...I'm going to leave...remove them all.* The random inner talking of Lucien's mind incessantly spoke. There was no more quiet stage to think something out. There were only words, many words that continuously looped in his mind, not allowing silence to eclipse them. They became the ghostly whispers of insanity, the venomous tongue of madness.

Beauty...sadness...leaving...mother...knife...Catrina...mother...in my way...sword...Stefan... love...leaving...Aaron...remove...knife...werewolf...witch...monsters...death...

The words would not cease; they repeated in a different order each time like a hundred random thoughts attacking Lucien's mind all at once. He targeted the dagger of the Nightworld with his wide-open eyes.

"What's he doing?" Catrina asked Aaron.

"He's just standing over there watching the Order."

Aaron looked to Stefan. "Are you ready to do this?"

Stefan glimpsed at the Order. The hooded men stood motionless. And the dagger; that was the dagger they would use to thrust into his heart. Concealed beneath their hoods, Stefan imagined that they were staring right in his direction, simply waiting for him to do what they all knew he must. "I'm not going,' Stefan announced. " Fuck this. They can come for me if they want, but I'm not giving myself up."

"They're not going to let you escape Stefan," Aaron attempted to rationalize with him. "And it is better that we face them here then wait for an unexpected visit which we will be unprepared for."

"Unprepared?" Stefan mocked. "We're not prepared at all. Not for—" His words were cut off by another voice. "*Stefan. Help me.*"

"Who is that?" Stefan questioned.

"Who's what?" Catrina asked.

Aaron glanced at Catrina who, in turn, gave him a puzzled look.

"*Help me*," the voice called again. Stefan couldn't believe it. He knew that voice well, had missed it for some time now. Yes, he knew the pain in the voice, that same voice that spoke to him in their midst of passionate lovemaking.

"Breckin?" Stefan called.

"Breckin?" Catrina stated, perplexed.

"*Stefan, help me escape.*"

Although the voice resounded throughout the desert, easily audible from all sides, Stefan knew from whence it came. Sure enough, when he positioned himself toward where the doorway to the Nightworld stood, Stefan's assumption had been confirmed.

The Order was completely gone from view. The monolithic stature of the black doorway gave off a whirring sound as the border around it pulsed with blood red colors. Then, the baritone cries of Breckin and the rhythmic sound of a booming *thump-thump* obscured all other sounds. Stefan viewed an arm jutting from the giant black rectangle that was the entrance into the Nightworld. *Thump-Thump.* Breckin! Breckin was trying to escape. He must have done something to the Order to stop them and now he needed Stefan's help. The thumps continued like a thunderous drum, mesmerizing Stefan as he came out of hiding and approached the doorway to save Breckin. "Breckin," he called as if in a trance.

"What are you doing?" Catrina whispered. "What's he doing, Aaron?"

"I don't know. It's like he doesn't even see the Order standing there. Get yourself ready for anything!"

She nodded a confirmation to Aaron whose eyes had begun to glow red. The two watched the spectacle from where they stood, remaining quiet but prepared to battle the Order of Perennial Darkness.

Each step that Stefan took was in cadence to the blaring *thumps* that continued to hypnotize his mind. He had emerged from the shrubbery and made his way across the clearing and to the doorway. "I'm coming, Breckin," he called out. The rhythm continued to lure Stefan toward the doorway where he saw Breckin's muscular forearm and hand that grasped at the air, inviting another hand to pull him from the Nightworld. "I won't let them kill you this time."

"*Help me,*" Breckin's voice screamed.

But in between the clamorous beats that slowed in pace Stefan heard another voice. This, too, was the voice of Breckin. *But Stefan...*

Thump.......thump......

...I'm already...

Stefan reached to grab the hand from the Nightworld.

...dead.

Stefan had expected the icy flesh of Breckin's arm when, without warning, an instantaneous pain plagued his hand. He briskly pulled his hand back to find that it had been sliced across the palm. Blood anxiously spilled from the wound and, as Stefan brought his attention to what lay before him, he found that there was no doorway at all. Instead, one of the Order had stood before him, wielding a dagger that donned a red-stained tip.

Stefan's body exploded into panic. *Oh god no! It was a trick!* And with his mind racing, Stefan realized that the voice he heard, the one before he grasped for the imaginary arm jutting form the doorway, was in fact the voice of Breckin's ghost trying to warn him. Did he truly think that Breckin was alive and trying to escape that dark world again? And…oh, the pain! The burning sensation of his wound crawled along his arm and within his veins. Stefan's hand began to grow numb and the numbness crept along his arm and into his shoulders that fell in a slouch. He gasped for air as he turned to run from the Order of Perennial Darkness who stood amused by the spectacle. However, as he pivoted, Stefan's legs gave out beneath him, paralyzed by the same deadened feeling that had made his arms go limp with motionlessness. What was happening? He fell to the ground and was immediately turned over by one of the cloaked men. The other five of the Order formed a circle around Stefan's immobilized, prone body. There was no feeling left in Stefan's body whatsoever. Yet, he could blink his eyelids and watch as the Order of Perennial Darkness loomed over him with their scrolls unraveled.

"Stefan Powell," Saint Dante spoke, "Your time has come."

Far above him, Stefan witnessed the glittery display of the lightning above Spook Valley and beyond the purple atmosphere.

Catrina cringed when she beheld the dagger slicing into Stefan's hand. She gasped and practically leapt to his rescue. Aaron held her back from doing so. "We have to save him, Aaron!"

"Timing is crucial," Aaron explained. "Stefan is a state of paralysis right now. They still have to read the scrolls before making the sacrifice."

"What are you trying to tell me?" Catrina anticipated, eyes darting back and forth from the appalling scene of Stefan lying frozen before the Order.

"We can't afford to mess this up, Catrina. I know the precise time to interfere with the Pact."

"And until then?"

"Until then, we wait; and you focus on contacting the powers within you."

Catrina had noticed how the hairs on Aaron's arms began multiplying and covering any bare portion of cinnamon flesh upon his hands. Aaron was transforming before her very eyes. However, she had witnessed Aaron's transformation into a werewolf many times and the process never took this long. There was a piece of instinct, perhaps the only instinct that made itself present at the time, that Aaron's prolonged morphing and her inability to contact the God & Goddess were somehow connected. Not to mention, Lucien's odd behavior. When did it begin? Catrina gazed up at the sky above her.

Lucien didn't notice Stefan's capture or how the Order had encircled Stefan's body. His full attention was on the sheen of the dagger Saint Dante held. *Knife...remove...mother.* He surfaced from behind the overgrown ocotillo plant that had concealed his pale form. Each step he took had gone unnoticed by any of the Order. There was no fear eating away at his insides, no trepidation of the unknown creatures before him. There was simply nothing in his mind. For it was void of all emotion and of all things, save for the dagger that hypnotized his every thought.

Attempting to rationalize the weakening of her magical abilities, Catrina Taylor's attention was diverted by a rustling close by. When she targeted the sound, she observed Lucien making an approach toward the Order of Perennial Darkness. "Lucien," she yelled in a whisper. "Lucien! Not yet!"

From the corner of her eye, a new phenomenon materialized. The blood red border of the doorway had begun to spider-web across the black entrance. It looked as if the entrance into the Nightworld was nothing more than a piece of cracked tinted glass. In the same instant, the ruby hue had spread all over the entrance, completely eclipsing the blackness altogether. The colors swirled with one another and appeared as spinning vortexes of blood. "Aaron, something's starting to happen and Lucien…"

He was nowhere to be seen. Aaron had vanished from sight. From behind her, Catrina heard a steady growl that caused her to freeze. The feeling of abandonment embraced her—Stefan was useless in his current state, Aaron had evidently shapeshifted into his werewolf alter ego, and Lucien was making his way toward the Order. Dammit! She had half the mind to run out into the clearing and snatch Lucien, but it was too late. She watched the scene unfold before her eyes as she continued to pray to her God and Goddess.

Lucien abruptly stopped behind the cloaked man known as Saint Dante. The hoods of the other Order members gestured toward Lucien as Saint Dante turned to face him.

...knife...

"What have we here," Saint Dante spoke in a deep voice of amusement.

Lucien stared into the darkness that was Saint Dante's face, into the hollow hood that concealed every bit of the monstrous visage. "I want the knife."

"You want…?"

"The knife," Lucien repeated himself. His voice was etched with determination and carved with authority. "I want that knife…now."

Saint Dante hoarsely guffawed to the heavens, waiting for the young boy to leave. However, Lucien remained before him with eyes staring at the dagger as if it a precious jewel. "Foolish mortal child," he raised his voice, "what would you do with the dagger? Do you want to be the one to sacrifice Stefan?"

"Yes," Lucien boldly answered. "I'll kill him, I'll kill all of you, and then I will kill the others. Now, I demand you to give me that knife."

Others? Saint Dante thought. Who did this child think he was? He would stab the boy with the dagger now if it weren't for the fact that it would ruin the sacrifice of Stefan Powell.

Stefan lay on the ground. Although he was unable to move any part of his body, he observed Lucien from the corner of his eye and could hear every word being said. Fear gripped at his heart. Was this part of their "plan?" What exactly did Lucien mean by saying he would kill the others? *He's lost it, and I am powerless to save Catrina from this combination of evil and madness!*

Saint Dante turned back toward the matter at hand. Lucien made a brisk and fierce attempt at grabbing the dagger. But, before his hand came close to touching the infectious blade, a force from within the swirling doorway shook the foundation of the desert. From beyond the maze of curlicues that obscured the black of the entrance to the Nightworld, a dynamic and high-pitched roar like that of a jaguar emitted. Saint Dante immediately revealed the source as that of God *Damia.* God *Damia* had promised no interference from the mortals of the Earth realm during the sacrifice. Just like any God faithful to his followers, *Damia* did not fail the Order of Perennial Darkness.

A long cylindrical mass that pulsed in ruby color, shot forth from the doorway and made contact with Lucien's stomach. The foreign mass was so powerful that it launched Lucien some twenty feet away as he went airborne. Lucien's landing was broken by a large century plant that cradled him to the ground.

Damia's voice exploded into the Earth realm. Within the doorway of swirls, two black orbs stared outward to Saint Dante. "Make the sacrifice," *Damia* roared.

Saint Cassius began, as he read from the parchment he held close to his hood. His voice was raspy and the words that discharged from his throat were completely unintelligible. It was an alien language altogether, perhaps one created by the Nightworld. Yet, the words rolled over his half-decayed lips in foreign expertise.

Catrina was shocked. All her hopes of stopping the Order from sacrificing Stefan to the Nightworld had been lost, especially after viewing Lucien's failed attempt at extracting the dagger from the hand of one of the Order members. "Lucien," she called out in a soft voice. "Lucien, are you all right?"

Catrina turned toward the area where Lucien had landed but couldn't see a thing. With the atmosphere purple, the shadows of the desert were darker than ever. She had to find Aaron and tell him her theory. The dimensional environment was causing her loss of focus on her gift. Catrina gave credence that this was also the source of Aaron's prolonged transformation and Lucien's ignorant bravery. She pushed her way past ocotillos and devil's claw bushes in an effort to seek out Aaron, her last hope.

-7-

Lucien ignored the soreness in his back, as a result from the fall, and stood to his feet like an undying cyborg that couldn't register sensation. There was no pain to feel; there was no emotion to give way to tears. There was only the knife. His determined mind dictated that he would walk back toward the Order of Perennial Darkness and try to get a hold of the weapon once again

Before he reached the clearing, where he could hear a raspy chant of one of the cloaked fiends, a glimmer caught his eye. At first, he thought it nothing more than the reflection of the sky hitting the remnants of a puddle of mud created from the earlier rains. However, once he targeted the source of the gleaming more closely, he found it to be that of a blade. It was that of the sword he had handled once tonight already. The sword he'd tried to use on the demon that knocked him into the air the same way that phantasmal object had ejected from the doorway.

Lucien knelt to extract the sword hilt that was partially embedded in the mud. The power he felt as he held the claymore in his hands was amazing! It sent a shivering impression down his spine and a charge to his brain.

Nothing...can...stop...me.

-8-

Catrina continued to call Aaron's name in a desperate whisper. Her feeling of abandonment was ever increasing. Alone in this haunted place. Stefan, useless in his state to fight off the Order of Perennial Darkness. Lucien, unable to be found. And the same applied to Aaron. Although, she knew he wouldn't call her name back, for he had transformed into his wolf form, she thought that he would have at least made an effort to snarl, growl, or give any sign that he was around and hadn't fallen captive to some unseen force of the Nightworld.

Catrina could still hear the first of the Order of Perennial Darkness reading from his scroll. What did the words mean? What horrifying incantation was he speaking to initiate such a sinister crime on humanity? Only five more left to read their pieces of the pact and then all hope would be lost forever. *God and Goddess*, she attempted the call. Nothing. Weak. She felt so weak and could no longer stand. She was alone in this place.

Catrina's legs went limp as she fell to her knees. The pain had returned. The searing of her flesh, the mysterious pain in her back that made her feel like a blade was being jabbed into her, and the exhaustion—all of it hit her at once and she could think of nothing more to do than clasp her hands over her face and cry uncontrollably.

-9-

Through fierce eyes that seared red, the werewolf observed the defeat in Catrina Taylor. It showed in her slumped shoulders that bobbed up and down as she cried.

What the werewolf saw next was inconceivable.

-10-

Lucien weaved in and out of the desert shrubs, taking slow and cautious steps. He was like a phantom against the night, his movement both flowing and graceful.

Sword...remove...mother...monsters...werewolf...

Her back was turned to him.

...witch...

Her weeping kept her from noticing him.

...remove...

Lucien pulled the claymore back in a horizontal motion, preparing to thrust it forward with all his strength.

...I'm leaving this place...

-11-

Catrina Taylor sniffled as she wiped at her swollen eyes. She realized her sobbing was childish and was in no way helping in the rescue of Stefan. No, she had to pull herself together; she must get through this…the final battle between the Nightworld and the Earth realm. If it came down to it, she would attack the Order of Perennial Darkness on her own, with every ounce of strength left in her. If Aaron and Lucien had fled, she would do it on her own. It didn't make a difference if she died trying because life would be synonymous with a slow death if she couldn't save Stefan.

She closed her eyes, putting as much focus into her prayer as she could. She called the God and Goddess once again. The barrier that kept her and her faith separated had to be broken. Beyond her silent calling, a noise like that of a snap infiltrated her mind. Catrina fluttered her eyelids open as a roiling fear caused a lump to form in her throat.

The sound emitted from directly behind. She didn't want to turn and see what awaited her. No, the horror was too much for her heart that already jolted into a high-paced spasm. Yet, she could not fear; she had to face whatever stood behind her. As she craned her neck to the right and the remainder of her body followed suit to the movement, she gave off a shriek that sliced through the silence of the immediate area.

Lucien stood before her, head bowed and eyes staring maniacally through her. He appeared a madman with no look that etched his features. He was straight-faced, his pale luminescence brighter than that of any ghost or vampire she had ever imagined. He held the claymore in his hand, pulled back, and was prepared to thrust it into her.

Catrina briskly recoiled from the frightening young man and scurried to her feet. She backed away and could feel that she was backing into a large ocotillo plant longing to embrace her. Attempting to rationalize with him, she spoke. "Lucien," her lips quavered, "no. No, don't do this."

Lucien's voice held no emotion to it. It revealed a monotone quality that glamorized the effect of his insanity. "Remove. Remove. Remove."

"Lucien!" Catrina hollered his name, her back against the brunt of the desert plant that kept her from escape. "This isn't you! It's this strange dimensional spell the Nightworld has cast. It's not allowing us to focus on our strengths! Be strong, Lucien! Don't do this!" She hadn't time to release her inner power, especially since it was more difficult to do so while under the atmospheric spell of the Nightworld.

"You did this to me." Saliva spilt over his lips. "All of you trapped me here. I'm going to remove you all one by one. Remove." Lucien pulled the sword back a few more inches and began pushing it forward.

"No!" Catrina's piercing scream engulfed the night. She winced as Lucien drove the sword onward.

Lunging out of the darkness, the werewolf landed hard against Lucien's side, throwing the young man down to the muddy desert floor. A loud thud made the sound of Lucien's skull hitting the ground.

Catrina gasped for a breath as she went to grab the claymore in front of her. Before she had a chance to pick it up, the werewolf grasped at it with its clawed hand and hurled it. It whistled as it spun into the night, glimmering like drifting stardust as it disappeared into the bowels of the desert.

The werewolf leapt atop of Lucien who was not moving at all and had been knocked unconscious by the fall. The werewolf howled into the night as it bared its jagged teeth at the purple skies. Its mouth shot downward toward Lucien's neck, ready to rip out the young man's jugular.

"No, Aaron!" Catrina halted the werewolf's horrid attack.

The werewolf turned to her, its eyes burning into her soul.

"Don't kill him! It's not his fault. It's the Nightworld."

The werewolf growled as it turned its head toward Lucien again. It sniffed about the boy's neck and face.

Catrina knelt beside the werewolf, bravely grabbing its snout and turning its ruby eyes to meet with hers. "We're fighting the wrong people, Aaron. This is what the Nightworld wants. We have to rescue Stefan. They're reading the incantations now. We have to stop this, Aaron. Leave Lucien here. He's not going to hurt anybody while he's knocked out." However, there was still a part of her that refused to believe Lucien was harmless.

The werewolf forced its gaze back toward Lucien as Catrina got to her feet. The werewolf appeared to have been walking away from Lucien's prone, unconscious body. However, the werewolf briskly turned again and made one fleeting claw at Lucien's chest. Catrina let off a peep, as if a preamble to a terrifying scream, before she realized that the claws of the werewolf had barely broken the skin of Lucien's chest. Just enough to warn him that, if there were a next time, Aaron would rip the young man into shreds.

-12-

Catrina and the werewolf peered at the Order of Perennial Darkness from behind the desert shrubbery. Catrina wondered why it was that they only gazed at the spectacle and why they weren't setting Aaron's alleged plan into action. She wished she could get an answer from him. But she knew that to be impossible in his lycanthropic state. She could only watch in terror as the Order surrounded Stefan and wondered what could be going through her best friend's mind. Did he feel that his friends had abandoned him? That all hope was lost? Catrina continuously glanced back and forth from the Order to Aaron. She kept twirling a lock of her auburn hair in her fingers, frustrated that all she could do was witness the horrific scene becoming.

A silence permeated the area as Saint Dante finished reading his scroll. Within the pause between the readings of the incantations, Saint Dante knelt and swiped the blade of the dagger across Stefan's chest in one swift, flowing motion.

From the concealed darkness, Catrina winced as she viewed the streak of blood that appeared from Stefan's wounded torso. She realized that they were preparing his body for the sacrifice, separating the flesh around his heart with a single slice of the knife after each of the Order read his portion of the pact. And after the sixth scroll was read, Catrina knew that the final strike of the knife would be right into the heart of Stefan Powell; thus, bringing the Nightworld and the Earth realm crashing into each others' realities.

What did it feel like to Stefan—unable to move, gazing at the horror looming over him, hearing the cryptically spoken words of dread that they all abhorred? What fears consumed and ate at Stefan from the inside out, as he lay powerless against the fateful dagger that cut into his flesh? Surely, he'd felt forsaken by his friends who were nowhere to be seen. The reality of it all must have been so apprehensive to Stefan, like a dream one knows he is dreaming but unable to force his body to awaken.

Catrina was brimming with pity for her best friend. She couldn't watch this, no! She couldn't observe the Order of Perennial Darkness frighten him mentally, emotionally, and physically. And Aaron, Aaron was simply gazing from behind the shrubbery and not making a move.

The second member of the Order had been reading his scroll for sometime now. There would be another designated slice upon Stefan's chest. And then another, until all that was left was one final plummet of the dagger into his heart. Catrina refused to standby and watch any longer. Although Aaron had told her that there had been a precise time to interfere with the Pact, her emotions took over all rational thinking. She surfaced from beyond her hiding place, ready to battle the Order of Perennial Darkness from sealing their pact to merge the world. Whether she had contact with the God and Goddess or not, she still had her own strength. Although it was depleting with each minute that passed, she refused to give up.

"Stop it," she yelled at the sextet of hooded humanoids.

Saint Israel's reading of the parchment ceased and Saint Dante immediately turned. "Leave, child! Or we will destroy you along with him." Saint Dante gestured toward Stefan with the gleaming dagger.

Catrina reached within her inner self once again. Still, no contact with the God and Goddess; yet, she focused more on her own strength. "If you don't leave him alone, I will take that dagger and mutilate each and every one of you bastards."

The cloaked heads of the Order of Perennial Darkness turned in her direction. "Witch," Saint Dante realized. "So, you are the witch who destroyed Lillian."

The werewolf emerged, galloping on all fours and halting at Catrina's side like a loyal pet.

"And, of course, Aaron. Aaron, the subject of beast and man. We've missed you, Aaron. God *Damia* is going to swallow your soul."

The werewolf growled with contempt.

Saint Dante turned his back toward both. "Neither of you are any match for God *Damia*, and we have his protection. I tire of these interruptions. Continue reading Saint Israel."

Catrina and the werewolf took no more than a step before the vicious cry like that of an attacking cougar shot out from beyond the doorway of the Nightworld. Just as with Lucien, two cylindrical spears of blood red erupted from the doorway. However, instead of striking Catrina and the werewolf, the rods had encircled their bodies, bending and swirling around them like a bloody transparent whirlpool of plasma.

Their bodies were gracefully lifted from the ground and came to a halt just feet above the desert floor. Catrina and the werewolf were unable to move a muscle or voice their horror. Their bodies silently hovered beside one another and faced the ritual as if they were the captivated audience to a brilliant and terrifying play.

No, Catrina resisted in her mind. She was just as immobile as Stefan's body that lay at the feet of the Order of Perennial Darkness. Surely, there was nothing more she could do. This was it. Now she and Aaron could only be witness to two worlds merging. *But this can't be it! We can't fail at this!* Suddenly, all of her thoughts of the past days came flooding into her mind—the battle with Zander, the near death she'd almost fallen pray to at the hands of the demon Lillian, and the consoling of Lucien who looked to up to her like a mother figure with all the answers. And where were those answers? She had to break through the barrier of the Nightworld's spell, touch her spiritual center with all the vigor of her mind. For there was no other way. Her body would not be able to break free of the paralyzing force that wrapped around her and created a red tint for her to view the world through.

Saint Israel finished the reading of his scroll. Catrina watched, for that was all she could do, as Saint Dante made another horizontal swipe of the dagger against Stefan's bare chest. A thin streak of blood pooled to the surface. As much as Catrina wanted to scream for Stefan, she was unable to do so.

Time was running out as the third of the Order immediately began to read from his own scroll.

From the corner of her vision, Catrina made eye contact with the werewolf. The eyes of the beast appeared invisible against the red force field that surrounded them. Still, Catrina thought that she caught the image of a tear near the ruby eyes of the werewolf.

Without warning, an ethereal form appeared directly before her. Had she the power of movement, she would have flinched from the immediate appearance of the phantom. She instantly recognized the ghost before her—his dark hair, ivory skin, and emerald eyes that appeared sienna through the red film that veiled her vision. She anticipated calling his name, as if he the savior to her nightmare. *Breckin!*

"There's no need to use you voice to speak, Catrina. We can speak to each other in our minds," the voice in her head said, smooth and deep as she remembered from the séance she'd recently performed.

"Breckin," she desperately called, *"you have to save us!"*

"I am unable to do so, Catrina. I am powerless to do anything physical in this world. I am a ghost, remember? My clinging to the love of Stefan has summoned me here to the place where he will meet his demise. Time is fast approaching, Catrina. If the Pact isn't stopped and the Order of Perennial Darkness sacrifices Stefan, this world will be nothing more than eternal damnation with chaos and monsters running wild. I would suffer just as you would. I must be set free, Catrina. You must stop this."

"But how? Aaron had a plan to interfere with the Pact, but now that chance has been ruined."

"Look deep within you, Catrina. Focus yourself beyond all of this and reach into yourself as you always have. Tap into that magical world of yours. I know you are powerful enough to do so."

"But..."

There was no need to argue with Breckin's ghost; it had drifted from view. Helplessness crept about Catrina's stock-still body as she witnessed the third of follower of *Damia* reach the end of his reading and Saint Dante making another ritualistic slice of the dagger against Stefan's flesh.

Beyond the Order of Perennial Darkness and Stefan, the doorway swirled in hypnotizing curlicues. Catrina gazed into it, beyond the sacrificial scene and into the red on red colors, until her entire vision was eclipsed by obsidian.

-13-

Stefan had heard Catrina's voice after the first attack of the knife sliced through his flesh. The pain upon his chest seared, itched, and crawled over his body in a freaky cadence that he would never be able to describe. As the icy blade of the dagger pierced his skin, Stefan wanted nothing more that to shrink back into the earth upon which he lay. Fall into the moist and embracing foliage of the desert, yes! Yet, he was unable to do so. He was unable to recoil from the attack of his body, unable to scream in agony, unable to fight back or call for help to his friends. To Aaron. Would he ever see him again?

Catrina's voice had called to the Order, pausing the reading of the Pact. And then Stefan heard the growl of a wolf and knew it to be Aaron. How he wanted to turn and gaze into those ruby eyes that loved him back, even in Aaron's most bestial form. The cougar scream of *Damia* infiltrated the night, just as it had done when Lucien's voice had attempted to halt the Order of Perennial Darkness. From below the looming disciples of the Nightworld, Stefan witnessed two bolts of red pass over his body in the direction of his friends. What had happened? Were they killed?

Stefan's mind raced with so many haunting thoughts that his head had become like that of a classic, dilapidated mansion filled with dark memories and ghostly specters. His heart burst into frenzy and the horrific heavy beats had become his resting rate. He was defenseless against his adversaries. He could only lay there and watch as each read his scroll, optimistic that, somewhere beyond this makeshift altar, hope would find him a savior.

The scene was altogether eerie, a mesh of animated colors and dreadful chants. The words that echoed over Stefan's immobilized body were spoken in a cryptic tongue with no emphasis on any of the text being read, and even pauses between each and every word that would surely haunt him if he made it out of this alive. Stefan would focus on the above purple skies, hesitating to feel the blade of the dagger run over his flesh after each reading. The assault of the blade that divided the skin on his chest was never predictable. The first had caught Stefan off guard. He'd expected the second and tried to prepare his mind for it, but that didn't stop the jolt of terror from shooting through his prone body. Now, the third assault of the dagger tore at his flesh and Stefan felt he would vomit from the horror of it all. Soon, another would follow in this pattern leading to the final plummet of the dagger into his rushing heart that would bring it to a shrieking halt.

As much as he wanted to close his eyes, he couldn't. Stefan was forced to watch and witness what he was beginning to accept as his fate. If there was any shred of hope left in his mind, it came in the prayer of having a quick death.

-14-

Although her eyes were wide open, a serene darkness concealed all sights and sounds of the horror that took place before the levitating body of Catrina Taylor. The obscurity was warm, comforting, and cradled her like a Mother embracing her child. If death was oblivion, this is what it would be like—a silence without echoes and screams, a state of mind that saw naught, a void that dawned before the creation of anything. This was Nothingness. This was *Ain.* That is what Catrina's belief had deemed the place before birth from whence everything came. This was the home from which she'd emerged and to which she would return. This was the feast before Life and the celebration of Ascension. There was no other place safer than this darkness of organized energy and balanced harmony.

Giddiness stabbed her body's center, below the sternum and above her stomach. Warmth. There were so many rushing feelings of love and heat that invaded her body and soul. It was the same sensation of floating as she had experienced before when in her coma. Though, she had never reached *Ain* before. No, never this setting that was close to legend of the Wiccan belief and Jewish mysticism. Her focus must have been so powerful at the one point of complete vulnerability that she catapulted her state of consciousness to this wondrous place.

God and Goddess, her mind overflowed with the euphonious call that amplified in her mind. Deep into the darkness, Catrina saw a pinprick of white light. The tiny white fleck grew larger to that of the size of a dime. It seemed as if she were gracefully flying toward it as she began thinking that she was in a tunnel. The white sphere grew to monolithic proportions, until it had completely obscured the darkness of her world. Catrina reached out her hand to the light, anticipating the touch of the miraculous wonder.

All of a sudden, the horrific face of something more wretched than a demon and of monstrous size pushed through the light. It screeched into the world with the ferocious cry like that of a cougar or jaguar on the attack.

Damia.

The darkened state of mind that had become Catrina's surrounding world slowly filled in all around her, as if a graphic artist were penciling it in. Around the face of the beast, the doorway of the Nightworld appeared, framing the creature's ungodly visage. Above her, the purple skies washed over the atmosphere. Once again, Catrina felt her body go into a state of paralysis as the red orb appeared around her once again, cradling her in a bloody colored womb. The desert floor beneath her feet reappeared, and the scene of the Order of Perennial Darkness encroaching Stefan and chanting their incantations, once again, made itself visible.

Back to reality, she thought. However, Catrina was fully aware that she had made some type of contact with the God and Goddess. She was propelled into the consciousness of *Ain*, of Nothingness, and tapped into that part of her inner self that had been previously barricaded by the forces of the Nightworld. Now, if only to harness that inner power to escape these force fields that trapped her and Aaron.

The oversized head of *Damia*, the godlike beast of the Nightworld, poked through the doorway. Surely, he would emerge upon the sacrifice of Stefan. For now, the creature wailed banshee cries into the twilight and would witness the last three of the Order initiating the dreaded Pact that would open the doorway wide enough for *Damia* to enter the Earth realm.

If Catrina had control over her body, she would have stared forward with her mouth agape, gawking at the monstrosity in the doorway that lingered between two worlds. The beast known as *Damia* had long black talons for claws that clung to either side of the doorway. The head and neck of the creature were colored a deep maroon shade and the sharp edges of its face appeared etched to jagged points all about its façade. *Damia*'s eyes were black opals that pierced the shadowy world of the night. Two large horns arced high above, like antennae to the Heavens, and curlicued near the razor sharp tips. And when the God of the Nightworld shrieked, his open mouth presented three rows of jagged and pointed teeth that encircled a forked tongue like that of an enormous serpent.

This was the beginning of the end and Catrina didn't have to second-guess it. There was no more time left. The entire scene played out just as it had in her mind haunted by this possible ending. From the corner of her eye, she saw Aaron still immobilized, just as helpless as she was. *Aaron is the key*, the voice of Breckin revisited her mind. *And Aaron had a plan*, she reminded herself. It was at that point that Catrina realized, even if she could escape the uncanny force field of the *Nightworld*, she would need Aaron to stop the sacrifice. However, it was not as important for her to escape as it was to free Aaron from his own state of paralysis.

The giddy sensation above Catrina's stomach returned—her inner self. Now, if only to harness the energy there. In front of her, *Damia* roared from the doorway of the Nightworld, the Order of Perennial Darkness continued their readings of the Pact, and Stefan was one step closer to his death. In the throes of anticipation, Catrina was able to connect with her magical powers.

With her mind unhampered, a rush of nausea passed over Catrina Taylor's body.

-15-

Another carve of the icy dagger across his chest, and Stefan experienced the warm blood that emitted from the wound and spilled over to his side.

The fifth member of the Order began to speak.

The timbering roar of some unnatural beast brought on heated breaths that skimmed over Stefan's body. He recognized that haunting inflection as that of *Damia*. He recalled it from his visit to the Nightworld. The creature must have been only feet away from him, ready to leap from the netherworld upon his sacrifice. Stefan's horrified mind cringed at the thought of the beast devouring his body.

He made an attempt at moving his hand but it was to no avail. Stefan anxiously willed his mind. *Movement! Oh God, let me move!* There was nothing comparable to the horror that stormed his mind. To know that he was on the brink of death and that, with his sacrifice, the rest of the world would be damned and helpless from the Nightworld and all its monstrous minions.

Where was Catrina? Where was Aaron? And Lucien for that matter? Were they destroyed? All the hope that Stefan had left abandoned him. The images of everything he had done in his young life had flashed through his mind. So many things he would have done differently, so many things he had taken for granted. Had he known that this would have been the end of his life, in this moment and in this time, things would have been different. He would have given more to love surely. He would have cherished each and every day of his life. He would have been less selfish in the time he spent with Catrina. He would have heard her out more, listened more to her problems instead of dumping his on her each time they came together for a visit. He would have held more onto love. Breckin and Aaron—just fleeting images of porcelain faces that he would never touch again or never profess his undivided love to.

Stefan's thoughts were broken by the searing sensation of the dagger slicing at his flesh and his world was propelled into a slow-motion shock. Every sound he heard and every sensation that crawled over his body decelerated. The cryptic language that spilled over the final hooded man's lips, the one who wielded the sacrificial dagger, was low and muffled. The whipping snarl of *Damia* seemed to last forever. He could feel every particle of his being amplified by pain and numbness. Stefan was succumbing to the distress of the final reading of the incantations. The realization of just how close he was from being sacrificed to a chaotic underworld infiltrated his unmoving body. He wanted to scream. He wanted to wake up. But this was no dream and any hope he harbored had been completely purged.

-16-

The giddy phenomenon that fueled Catrina's connection with her power slowly traveled through each of her limbs as if it were replacing the lifeblood within her. Ignoring the scene being played out before her, she mentally sang her own chant.

Powers That Be, God and Goddess,
Release Aaron from the hold of Evil,
Sun and Moon, Power of the Four Elements,
Earth, Air, Fire, Water,
Bring life to the werewolf,
So it is, and so shall it be!

The chant ran incessantly through her mind, repeating over with more enthusiasm. As she ended her prayer each time, the sensation of her powers coming to be charged her body more.

Powers That Be, God and Goddess,...

-17-

One final slice divided the skin upon Stefan's chest. The last incantation had been read.

...Release Aaron from the hold of Evil,...

Saint Dante's form loomed over Stefan and Stefan's heart felt as if it were going to cease from the horror of the hooded blackness that stood over him. *Damia*'s boisterous roar of victory infiltrated the night.

... Sun and Moon, Power of the Four Elements,...

Saint Dante spoke, his voice echoing to the Order of Perennial Darkness. "With this sacrifice, a new world will bring with it new life, new souls and new flesh to feast upon. With this sacrifice, we open a doorway eternal from the Old World into the New World."

... Earth, Air, Fire, Water,...

Damia's talons gripped tighter to either side of the doorway. The god-beast of the Nightworld began pulling himself through the doorway, now that he could step foot into the Earth realm. The sacrifice allowed him to do this without consequences. Now that the sacrifice was about to be made, *Damia's* monstrous flesh was given strength to cross into the new world that would tremble and bow before the god. Electrical sparks exploded behind *Damia*; the Nightworld and the Earth realm began to fuse. The foundation of Spook Valley rumbled as *Damia*'s goat-hoofed foot made contact with the desert floor.

... Bring life to the werewolf,...

Saint Dante bellowed to his lord. "I offer this sacrifice to you God *Damia*, ruler of the Nightworld and new God of the Earth Realm!"

Damia arched his back and roared to the new heavens that awaited him. His boisterous cries traveled for miles on the still night airs of Spook Valley. *Damia* continued snarling to the overhead skies, ready for the sacrifice of Stefan Powell to be made.

Saint Dante began to raise the dagger over Stefan's heart.

Stefan observed the purple light from the skies reflect off the gleaming silver blade. He wanted to move now more than ever. Stefan yearned for his eyes to close. He was forced to bear witness to his last moments on Earth. Spasms jolted his stomach as he followed the tip of the dagger that would come to a pause high above him before being plummeted into his heart.

...SO IT IS, AND SO SHALL IT BE!

A force unlike any other she had felt in her life ignited every fiber of Catrina's being. It felt as if lightning erupted from within her body and exploded all around her. The red force field that held her captive shattered and splintered off into the twilight. Catrina abruptly fell to the floor of the desert, landing hard on one knee. She quickly looked up toward the Order of Perennial Darkness and fell backward from the sight off the monstrous form of *Damia* who howled to the stars above. Her fearing eyes targeted the dagger that was paused at its highest point above Stefan. Scurrying to her feet, she craned her neck toward the werewolf that had been freed of its own prison as well. "Aaron," she called. But the werewolf was already on the move.

The werewolf shot forth on all fours like a bat out of Hell, leaving a trail of mud flecks behind its powerful gait. The werewolf was upon the Order in no time and powerfully leapt, launching from the desert floor.

Catrina stood frozen to the becoming scene.

The knife came down and Stefan began vomiting. Various lights danced off the luminous silver dagger as it thrust downward. In an instant flash, an animal filled the narrow gap between the dagger and Stefan.

An earsplitting yelp emitted into the night.

Catrina screamed with all her energy.

A thunderous boom divided the night skies.

The dagger had been thrust into the werewolf and the animal fell hard atop of Stefan's body.

Damia began screeching as the doorway directly behind him whistled and created a vortex that defied the gravity of the Earth realm. The blood reds swirled faster and gave way to pitch black hues. The creature held tightly to either side of the doorway as the eddy behind him began sucking him back into the Nightworld. *Damia* continued shrieking at impossible tones that broke the speed of sound as he twisted and writhed in attempt to escape the doorway's pull.

The Order of Perennial Darkness held their hands to their ears. One by one, the siren screams of their god ignited their bodies and caused them to burst into fire and orange dust. Each of the Order disintegrated from the outside in, spontaneously combusting into everlasting nothing.

The purple dome over Spook Valley spider-webbed and cracked away, revealing storm clouds that brought a drizzling rain to the desert.

Catrina wanted to run to where Aaron and Stefan lay motionless. However, the beast of the Nightworld was near the two, trying to defy being pulled back into its own world.

Damia clawed at Stefan and Aaron, attempting to grasp onto one of them in a last ditch effort to create havoc in the Earth realm. The creature's unending cries resounded throughout the desert. Its heavy footfall caused little quakes that made the ground tremble. Finally, the vortex that became the doorway to the Nightworld swirled faster, producing a powerful force that inhaled *Damia* into its gaping mouth. *Damia*'s shrieks echoed away into nothing. The doorway folded into itself and created a loud thud, as if a chamber door were shutting and forever sealing the secrets of a tainted world.

-18-

Catrina let out a combination of a scream and a tearful cry as she ran to where Stefan and Aaron's bodies lay.

The furry exterior of Aaron's werewolf form had vanished, disappearing into the follicles from whence they grew.

Stefan felt the weight of the naked body upon him, reached up with his hand to adjust the head of the body by turning the chin, and looked into Aaron's eyes that appeared dull and without color. Stefan stared into Aaron's eyes, a faded emerald losing its value, and whispered. "No, Aaron. Don't leave me." Stefan's eyes filled with a flood of tears.

Catrina rolled Aaron's body off Stefan's and onto its back. Catrina wept at the sight of the dagger that was embedded deep into Aaron's heart. Stefan pulled himself to his side and held onto Aaron's hand.

Aaron's lips tried to mouth something but no sound emerged. Instead, a gurgle brought with it a fount of blood that crept over his lips.

"Don't try to speak, Aaron," Stefan cried. "I'm going to pull this dagger from you, OK. Just hold on, baby." He wiped the tears from his face and cautiously brought his hand to the hilt of the dagger.

Catrina disrupted the process. "Stefan," she said, face flushed and silently weeping. "It's no use. The blade is silver."

"No," he bawled. "He's not going to die. I won't let him die!" Stefan pulled at the hilt of the dagger and a wincing pain washed over Aaron's face. Stefan halted. "Please, Aaron. Please! Don't do this! You have to live, Aaron. We stopped them. You stopped them! You can't die now! It's not supposed to be this way. I love you," Stefan's words trailed off into another sob.

Aaron gripped Stefan's hand with his last bit of strength and used the other hand to reach up and touch his face. "I love…" the words were faint, barely audible, "you too, Stefan." Stefan's name was the final faint whisper that emitted from Aaron's voice.

Aaron's irises were clouded over by a shade of white and his flesh lost all color. In a single instantaneous moment, Aaron's entire body fell like ash upon the muddy desert floor and melted into the puddles leftover from the ending rain.

"No," Stefan denied as he beat the foundation of the desert with his fists.

Catrina closed her eyes and said a prayer for Aaron to the God and Goddess. She embraced Stefan and cried with him.

Moments later, they could feel a hand on each of their shoulders. Upon looking up, they witnessed Breckin in his ghostly form. A smile etched upon his face, Breckin's translucent body slowly launched from the ground. Stefan and Catrina gazed at the spectacle as Breckin spiraled away into the pre-dawn skies high over Spook Valley. His soul was finally at rest.

Stefan and Catrina continued holding each other as the beginnings of a new day brought a peeking sun over the mountains.

-19-

Lucien's eyes fluttered open. His head ached horribly, but it didn't stop him from immediately noticing that the purple skies were no longer visible. Instead, they were replaced by brilliant pink and orange hues, the color of dawn awakening the desert.

He didn't remember much of the night previous. In fact, the last thing he recalled was the beautiful color of the sky that encapsulated Spook Valley. Reminded of the Order of Perennial Darkness and the threat to Stefan, Lucien jumped to his feet.

He raced through the desert, toward the clearing where the doorway once was. But there was no doorway to be found. Instead, he saw Stefan and Catrina embracing and cradling one another in solace.

Lucien walked up to the two. He placed his hand on Catrina's shoulder and she recoiled from his presence. Catrina observed the look of confusion on Lucien's face—the way it made his eyes squint and his brow arch in wonder. *It was a spell of the Nightworld*, she told herself. *He probably doesn't remember a thing.*

Lucien scanned the area and directed his gaze to Stefan. He noticed the cuts upon his bare chest. The blood there was crusting. "Are you all right, Stefan?"

Stefan would not speak.

"He's fine," Catrina spoke for him.

"I don't remember anything," Lucien admitted. "Where's the doorway?"

"We stopped it," Catrina sighed. "It's over."

"Where's Aaron?" When neither Stefan nor Catrina answered, Lucien realized that Aaron must have not made it.

Catrina stood up and almost immediately fell over. Lucien caught her. "Thank you," she said. "Stefan, come on."

"I'm not leaving," Stefan said defiantly.

"There's nothing more we can do here. Come on, Stefan. Let's get out of this place." She extended her arm to him. He gripped onto it as Lucien helped Stefan to his feet.

Stefan knelt down and picked up the dagger. Besides the memory, the weapon would be the only piece of Aaron he had to show for.

-20-

They emerged from the desert victorious, holding onto one another as survivors only could—arms around each other's waists, carrying the weight of one another away from an exhausting war.

A few cars passed along Firehouse Road. Spook Valley was back to normal once again.

The impressions of fear still carved unique lines onto the faces of Stefan, Catrina, and Lucien. After all, the horror of what had happened would stay with them forever. The hideous monsters of the Nightworld would enter their dreams for a long time to come. The loss of the ones they'd loved the most would innocently haunt their waking lives in the coming years. They would never forget the trials and tribulations they had suffered through or the ultimate battle of good versus evil that consumed their lives.

Sometimes, the memory is all we have as we go forward into the future. And, sometimes, to let go of that memory means forgetting about all we have done to get to where we are.

Stefan, Catrina, and Lucien stood beside Catrina's car parked off Firehouse Road. They gazed at the sky of a new day. Behind them, the desert grew alive with jackrabbits, snakes, and prairie dogs; creating, once again, its own ecosystem no longer in danger of being vanquished by a netherworld of evil.

EPILOGUE

New York City

-1-

Catrina Taylor hated the way her footsteps echoed on the subway platform. She didn't mind taking the subway in the morning, or even in the afternoon, when she came back from work, an occult shop called The Third Eye. During her morning and afternoon commutes, there were always hundreds, if not thousands, of people surrounding her. There was always safety in numbers.

She had never ridden along a rail train in the evening hours. The passengers appeared the opposite of the men and women dressed in suits and power skirts with whom she was used to traveling. The people who rode the subway in the evening appeared as human monsters, what with their multiple body piercings, colorfully spiked hair, and tattoos that covered all their exposed flesh. However, it never bothered her—their weirdness or the way they looked at her as if they were going to rob or rape her. Catrina knew she was protected.

From beyond the darkened corridor, Catrina heard the sound of a raspy voice coughing. It was probably some transient who dwelled beneath the city. Catrina was shocked to find that a stifling percentage of the city's population dwelled underground. Of course, she had heard such stories before, back when she lived in Phoenix and Spook Valley, but she validated what she thought was an urban legend when she arrived three months previous.

Three months. It was difficult for Catrina to believe that she had been in New York for three months now, impossible to think that the last time she'd seen Stefan was that long ago. In the time after her arrival, between getting a job and settling into her studio loft, Catrina had neglected to call Stefan. She had been so busy trying to get her life together, attempting at putting all the horrors of Spook Valley behind her and setting out on her quest to find answers. Catrina continuously reminded herself that she didn't runaway from the small town or the nightmarish memories of it. She had to come to New York. She sought certain answers and was on a mission. She longed to fill a certain void in her life, seeking closure to a chapter long left unread.

Catrina targeted the sign that read 91st Avenue, with an arrow pointing in the direction of a tiled staircase, and began walking toward it. Her footfall resounded throughout the empty platform. It was joined by another set of echoing steps. Catrina took a quick glance over her shoulder and observed a man in ragged jeans and a torn t-shirt. His hair was sandy blonde, long, and greasy. He looked like he hadn't shaved in days. The man's eyes gazed back, squinting at her and appearing menacing. Catrina picked up her pace, knowing that the stranger was preparing to attack her. Her instinct was keener than ever; her powers, had reached their apex.

Before she arrived at the steps that led up to the city streets, she came to a halt and turned toward the threatening stranger.

-2-

He'd known that she had seen him. The fact made itself obvious when the young woman had quickened her pace. He lingered behind a tiled column and emerged. The stranger loved the way she looked, reveled in the strange brew that was her scent, and enraptured by her lengthy auburn hair that fell in long waves down her back. Oh, how he wanted her. She wouldn't be able to refuse him; for she was so petite—thin arms and legs. But he had to make his move and do it quickly. She was approaching the stairs that would lead her topside into the city. He would have to get her before she reached the stairs, muffle her screams with his oversized hand, and drag her into one of the subway tunnels in order to have her. But that didn't present a problem to the stranger. After all, he had succeeded every time before. His mind briskly recounted the faces of his victims, the terror that etched their trembling lips as he entered them and thrust away. He felt his organ grow instantly hard.

He made his move.

He followed her trail, his heart racing from the knowledge of her own performing the same action. As her pace got quicker, his steps were made with longer strides. A ten-foot gap bridged the distance between the two, when the young woman turned toward him. He stopped dead in his tracks, surprised by the confrontation.

The young beauty said not a word. But she stared at him. When she did this, the stranger's mouth fell agape. Her eyes were swirls of blue, green, and black. He could feel them touching his soul, tingling the edges of gray matter near the front of his brain. Suddenly, from all around the young woman's body, electric blue waves of light surrounded her. The lines and curves of the phenomena formed into the shape of hands that briskly snapped and recoiled like attacking snakes. She didn't speak. But in the man's mind, he heard what could only be her singsong voice. *Leave now*, it warned.

Without hesitation, the stranger pivoted and ran back into the shadows. He leapt down, near the rails of the subway, and bolted down one of the adjoining tunnels. He ran far enough, until he felt safe. For the first time in his life, the man was scared and began to cry. There was something wrong with that woman.

-3-

Catrina reached topside of the city. Lights flecked the night all around her. The buildings this far west weren't as tall as the ones downtown, near Central Park and Times Square. That was an area where steel and stucco skyscrapers that endlessly reached toward the heavens eclipsed the sky. It was certainly nothing like Spook Valley and not even close to the frenzy of downtown Phoenix.

The memory of Spook Valley ignited her thoughts of Stefan again. She curiously wondered if he and Lucien had received the postcard she'd sent over a week and a half ago. She still couldn't predict how long it would take to receive mail internationally.

She walked along 91st Avenue, paying close attention to the red-brick buildings that began to thin out.

-4-

It had taken Catrina a lot of convincing to her mother that she knew her brother had lived longer than her family had led on. Her religious parents were simply in denial and didn't approve. Just like when they didn't approve when she had left for Spook Valley. Mother and Father's religious tactics had pushed all their children away. And then they would forget about them, thinking that they were in league with the Devil and that a visit from them would taint and undermine Mother and Father's religious upbringing.

Shortly after her trials in Spook Valley, when Stefan announced his departure with Lucien, Catrina paid a visit to her Mother. Mother was so anxious to see her and had immediately assumed that she had seen the error of her ways with practicing such "Satanic" rituals. Mother thought Wicca and Satanism were one in the same. That was how bad her religion had misinformed her. However, when Catrina had told her the reason for her visit, Mother immediately began preaching verses from the Bible. Catrina voiced her blame of Mother and Father for Zander running away as a teenager. She made it clear to Mother that had it not been for their upbringing, Zander would still be in Catrina's life. Her mother viciously shook her head in denial and told Catrina to leave the house immediately.

As Catrina walked out the door, her mother expressed, "You won't find him. But if you do, the two of you must come back to Jesus."

"I'll find what I need," Catrina said, as she walked out of the house and drove to the Greyhound Bus Station.

Catrina knew her destination was to be New York. She recalled Zander back in Spook Valley; at least, the dead version of him, the Nightworld version. Still, there was a truth to Zander's words when he spoke to her upon awakening from her coma. There was a love for her that he conveyed and, perhaps, a yearning he secretly desired to be released from that hellish world. Catrina knew he hadn't made up the story about being in New York City.

-5-

Catrina ambled through the Maple View Cemetery, past the array of uneven tombstones that appeared to grow wildly as if an unkempt garden of marble. She walked toward the structure that appeared a small house within the necropolis. The tingling sensation in the pit of her stomach grew. It was a feeling of excitement, a sentiment comparable to that of a child who anticipates the opening of gifts. It felt right. Catrina knew that this was the place.

The wrought iron gate creaked when Catrina pushed it open. The clank it made, as it hit the cement wall behind it, echoed throughout the tomb. Catrina stepped into the mausoleum and an overwhelming rush came over her, tickling her entire body and causing her to laugh.

She glanced toward the corner of the mausoleum. For a moment, she saw a ghostly impression of a young man. It was Zander! He was huddled in the corner, trembling. His head came up and his eyes met with hers. A slight smile appeared upon his face before his form dissolved into the chilly air.

In that moment, a moment she would cherish forever, Catrina Taylor felt whole, as if everything she had fought for in her life and every road she had traveled thus far had been worth all the tears and sacrifices she had made.

-6-

Calgary, Alberta Canada

Snow blanketed the city in a white veil that stretched from the rolling hills of the Canadian Rockies, south to Stampede Park. The Bow River, along Macleod Trail, proved an unmoving outlet of water, frozen and iced over for the remainder of the winter months. From Centre Street, the observation deck of the Calgary Tower, the city's fourth largest structure, disappeared into the low cloud cover as heavy flakes floated to the ground beneath it on 9th Avenue SW. Just north of the Calgary Tower, near Edmonton Trail, a place where the summer tourists can walk along pathways that will lead them to the base of the Rocky Mountains, Stefan Powell peered in wonder at the winter's first snow.

Stefan was infatuated by the weather phenomenon; for he had never seen such a storm back in the hot deserts of Arizona. Back in Spook Valley, there were only heavy rains from the monsoon during the summer season. This was entirely new to him, just as Canada was.

He had decided to leave Spook Valley three months previous, after the battle with the Nightworld had ended. Stefan couldn't live in that place, not with those horrible memories that would haunt him every time he drove down Firehouse Road. Not to mention, Lucien was a wanted felon and reluctant to turn himself in. The best thing for the both of them was to leave Spook Valley, leave Arizona altogether. Better yet, leave the country entirely and get as far away from that place as possible. Though the memories remained in forms of nightmares. There would never be a way to escape those remembrances.

Stefan had offered for Catrina to come along with them. However, Catrina had some soul searching to do of her own. She had told him that she needed to find out what had really happened to her brother, Zander. She was to head to Phoenix and visit her mother before leaving for New York.

The morning after their battle with the Nightworld, when the three of them had returned to Stefan's apartment, Stefan had discovered a folded letter partially tucked beneath the mattress of his bed. The letter was from Aaron. Aaron, the lover lost forever to the Nightworld by his valiant action to save Stefan from being sacrificed by the Order of Perennial Darkness. The letter was written a day earlier. Aaron knew he was going to have to sacrifice himself to save Stefan. That had been his plan all along. Aaron didn't plan on living; he didn't plan to see Stefan ever again. In the same letter, Aaron had written: *There is no other way. As long as I am around, a piece of the Nightworld will be around you, Stefan. And I can't put you in harm's way ever again. I love you and will always remember the time we shared across the decades.* Stefan had wept the entire day until his body gave way to much needed sleep.

Recalling the letter's contents, Stefan wiped a tear from his eye. The gelid air stung his ears. He stood on the balcony of his apartment, staring at the towers of downtown Calgary, watching the snow blanket the city. It had such a calming effect on him, the way the snow covered the asphalt in its purity of white flakes. It gave Stefan a sense of freedom, a signification of starting over again.

He turned and made his way into the apartment. Taking a seat at his desk, he retrieved his journal from the top drawer and began writing.

From the Journal of Stefan Powell

Well, it feels like forever since I've last made an entry in this journal. Perhaps that's a way to let me know that I need to take more time out of my life to concentrate on such things if I ever plan to be a published poet. Then again, the past six months have not exactly been a typical life. What with battling an evil dimension hellbent on taking over the Earth and losing two lovers whom I will never see again.

It's time to start fresh and forget everything I have experienced. I have burnt my manuscript entitled Dark Hearts. After all, it was my infatuation with the subject matter within the manuscript, demonology, which allowed the doorway to the Nightworld to open in the first place. I plan to start a new poetry collection, this time, based on love and love lost. I can't help but feel that if the power of my convictions for the Dark Hearts manuscript allowed such an evil creation to enter my world, perhaps this new collection of poems will bring love back into my life. Today would be a great day to start it; it is the season's first snow and everything is beautiful!

I haven't heard from Catrina lately. I hope she is doing well and has found some of the answers she is seeking. The move away from each other has taken a toll on our friendship, but we both had to do what was meant for us. She moved to New York to find the much-needed answers regarding her long lost brother. And I moved to Calgary, Alberta to get as far away from Spook Valley as possible.

I brought along Lucien, a young man that I met during my ordeals in Spook Valley. I've grown to understand him, have helped him in dealing with his past, and am trying to give him direction for his future. He's told me many times that he is "in love with me." I'm trying to make him understand that I'm not the one for him. I don't share the same feelings for him that he has for me. Still, I love him as a friend and I feel as a sort of "protector" of him. He's just learning life, becoming a man, and I think that he'll find his path soon.

Love. I miss Aaron so much! I wish he were here with me. Sometimes, I think about the two of us living a normal life that we never had a chance to live. Things like going to the top of the Calgary Tower, going out to dinner at one of the nice establishments downtown, or even taking a walk along the Bow River. If he were here now, we could light a fire in the fireplace and hold each other. I still wish he never died, but what choice did he have? It was either his death or mine. And my death would have brought with it, horror for the future of the Earth (realm). If you can hear me Aaron, I love you and will always love you with all my heart. Your memory will never be forgotten.

"What are you writing?" The voice was that of Lucien. Stefan gently placed his pen beside the open journal.

"I'm making a journal entry."

"Get any writing done?"

"No, I'm thinking about starting on a new project after I'm done with this. I'm hoping to get into the habit of writing regularly. This," Stefan gestured toward his journal, "is the start of it."

Lucien smiled. It was hard to think that this same young man committed the heinous crime of murder several months previous. His face was innocent, untainted by any cruel society in the world. His smile was rather charming and produced dimples Stefan had never noticed before. "Well, I'll let you get back to work." He turned and approached the kitchen.

"Wait," Stefan called to him. "What's that in your hand?"

"Oh, I can't believe I forgot! That's why I came in here in the first place. We got a postcard from Catrina." Lucien handed Stefan the glossy, colored postcard that boasted the downtown lights of New York City.

Stefan flipped the card over. It read: *I miss you both! Hope everything is going great. My Nancy Drew antics have gotten me a step closer to finding out more about Zander. Of course, you'll be the first to know! Write me and let me know how you're doing. I was hoping to visit for Christmas. Can you believe winters in the North?!? Love Always, Catrina.*

Stefan smiled and handed the postcard to Lucien. "Can you put that on the mantle?"

"Sure thing. Oh, by the way, dinner's at 7:30."

Stefan raised his eyebrows in curiosity. "Dinner?"

"Yeah, I'm cooking. I met a guy named Matt. I hope you don't mind. I invited him to dinner."

Stefan was shocked from what Lucien had just said. Met a guy? Dinner? "This guy…Matt…you like him?"

"That's why I invited him to dinner," Lucien remarked in playful sarcasm.

There was a silence between the two men as a smile embellished Stefan's lips.

"Oh, what?" Lucien teased. "Did you think I was going to wait for you forever?"

Stefan nodded, understanding. "So, if I said *I* was going to invite *you* out to dinner tonight…"

Lucien chuckled. "Stop leading me on like that."

"No, I'm glad you finally found somebody to care for, Lucien. It would be an honor to meet him. Now let me finish!"

"OK, OK, go be creative; I'll get out of your hair."

As Lucien exited, Stefan added, "And try not to burn down the place."

"I'll try," Lucien laughed as he called back.

In closing, I want to make this my final mention of the Nightworld. There's no need to remember that place, and I fear having to do so.

I suppose I'll never know the origin of the Nightworld or how long it has existed. I'll never know if there are others in the Nightworld just as innocent as Aaron and Breckin. I have fought my battle and, luckily, have won. Still, I can't help but wonder if all it will take for the doorway to open again is another believer. After all, the Nightworld thrives on believers of the occult, people harboring the same convictions of certain monsters just as I had. If that is the case, I presume that the doorway is simply in limbo, just waiting to be opened by another such believer. And all I can hope is that, if that time comes, that person will have the same strength we had to defeat such a dark place. Not only for their sake, but the sake of all humanity.

Stefan gently shut the cover of his journal and placed it back into the top drawer of his desk. He gave one more glance at the falling snow outside the bay window. The day gave way to dusk as he powered up his computer.

www.ingramcontent.com/pod-product-compliance
Lightning Source LLC
Chambersburg PA
CBHW030820310726
48980CB00006B/570/J

* 9 7 8 0 6 1 5 2 4 3 6 9 6 *